NIGHT WILL FIND YOU

ALSO BY JULIA HEABERLIN

We Are All the Same in the Dark

Paper Ghosts

Black-Eyed Susans

Lie Still

Playing Dead

NIGHT WILL FIND YOU

JULIA HEABERLIN

FLATIRON
BOOKS
NEW YORK

NIGHT WILL FIND YOU. Copyright © 2023 by Julia Heaberlin. All rights reserved. Printed in the United States of America. For information, address Flatiron Books, 120 Broadway, New York, NY 10271.

www.flatironbooks.com

Designed by Jen Edwards

Library of Congress Cataloging-in-Publication Data

Names: Heaberlin, Julia, author.
Title: Night will find you / Julia Heaberlin.
Description: First edition. | New York : Flatiron Books, 2023.
Identifiers: LCCN 2022054092 | ISBN 9781250877079
    (hardcover) | ISBN 9781250877086 (ebook)
Classification: LCC PS3608.E224 N54 2023 | DDC 813/.6—dc23
LC record available at https://lccn.loc.gov/2022054092

Our books may be purchased in bulk for promotional, educational, or business use. Please contact your local bookseller or the Macmillan Corporate and Premium Sales Department at 1-800-221-7945, extension 5442, or by email at MacmillanSpecialMarkets@macmillan.com.

First Edition: 2023

10 9 8 7 6 5 4 3 2 1

For Rhonda Roby, supernova

NIGHT WILL FIND YOU

———————

Perfect as the wing of a bird may be, it will never enable the bird to fly if unsupported by the air. Facts are the air of science.

—Ivan Pavlov, Nobel Prize–winning physicist

———————

Virtually every major move and decision the Reagans made during my time as White House chief of staff was cleared in advance with a woman in San Francisco who drew up horoscopes to make certain that the planets were in favorable alignment for the enterprise.

—Donald Regan, in his memoir, *For the Record*

———————

PROLOGUE

The steps to the basement were steep for a little girl hugging the wall on the way down.

There was no banister to hold, just a sheer drop-off into the dark, a concrete floor below that would break me.

I understood that my only business down here was to grab a load out of the cranky washing machine at the bottom of those steps and claw the wall right back up.

Under no circumstances was I to explore its intimate and creepy chaos or a particular little black book, about eight by ten and two inches thick, that was held together by a snap. The click echoed off the moldy walls when I opened it.

I wasn't a particularly brave little girl. I was afraid of roller coasters, backflips, horror movies, even the wall beside my bed. At night, after my mother turned off the light, I'd bang my fist on the wall to be sure it was solid. Because my sister complained, my mother limited me to fifty thumps—not so many as it sounds and never enough. I was certain I would slip through the wall where I slept, and no one would know where I'd gone tumbling.

And yet, a few times, when the house was empty and the washing machine silent, I opened the little door off the kitchen and risked tumbling.

I'd pick up the flashlight that sat on the top step. My chest throbbed. The smell of earth and decay filled my lungs. And I'd creep into an underworld carved into the side of a Virginia mountain. I was sure it sat right on top of the hell adults liked to talk about. The lightning crack in the filthy concrete floor was proof of desperate souls banging to get out.

I'd make my way to the center of the basement, carefully stepping over the crack. I'd stand on my tiptoes and wave my hand in the air until I felt the tickle of kite string that dripped out of the ceiling.

When I pulled it, and the bare lightbulb scattered the shadows, it was as if I'd entered my mother's brain. Here is where she painted portraits and abstract blobs of color on wooden easels, where she cleaned camera lenses and her gun, where people on paper emerged like ghosts from stinky solutions, where she hung old tools with big teeth.

Here, in an old trunk, is where she stored a grim book of photographs.

It was a book of horror. A book of sorrow. A book of death. Of dead *people*. And it was my mother who was on the other side, looking through the lens.

As a single mother, she tore through countless ways to pay our bills. Waitress, hairstylist, lumberyard lady, lunch lady. Maid, secretary, forklift operator, plumber's assistant, car show model.

She was the beautiful, blue-eyed Cinderella who didn't get to work on time, whose pretty feet blistered in shoes too cheap to fit quite right, who read palms at lunchtime. Her employers fell out of love with her as fast as they fell in.

My tenth year, the year things went wrong, was marked by her acceptance of a job as county morgue photographer. This meant my mother photographed people from the scene of their death to the table where a coroner dug around their organs. The first time I saw a close-up shot of a Y stitched in a hairy white chest, I wondered if it stood for Yonder. As in Up Yonder, like in the hymn.

During her first month as a crime photographer, she came home with red eyes and blue fingers. The job had been open seven months when she signed on. It covered a sprawling rural county in the middle of a Blue Ridge Mountains winter.

Nobody wanted a phone screaming to get your coat on in the middle of the night when it was five below. Nobody wanted the holiday suicide shifts—to crawl up dark, icy roads to a cabin with a cheerful light and a bloody floor. December through February in the mountains were prime time for cabin fever crazy.

For training, my mother was handed a camera, a pack of blue booties, and a laminated card with her picture on it. She was told to shoot wide, then as close up as she could "take it." Meaning, don't throw up and disturb the crime scene.

My mother was good at it, the pictures of the dead. I'd sit cross-legged on the basement floor and turn the pages, the cold and wet seeping through to my thin underwear.

I'd lay my small palm over each shot.

A dead man on an autopsy table.

Heart attack, I thought.

A live dog by a body of water.

That dog loved a sad somebody who went in and didn't come out.

A young woman with creamy skin, limbs sprawled at right angles on kitchen tile. High heels. Her blood, pooled and black, because it was a black-and-white photograph.

Her husband got away with it.

I felt the closest to my mother while I sat with that book of dead people. She was hard to know even with so much to love about her.

She could put together a thousand-piece jigsaw puzzle in a frenzied afternoon. She sang a twangy "Amazing Grace," fostered feral kittens, told dirty jokes, smoked cigars every New Year's Eve, wrote stories in perfect calligraphy, could do math in her head faster than anyone I knew, sketched charcoal portraits of me and my big sister when we weren't looking and left them on our pillows.

And yet she was also capable of shooting a picture of a dead woman with a cold and calculating eye.

The day my mother caught me, my bottom froze to the floor, the book like a brick in my lap. I counted each of the twenty-one clicks of her heels down the basement steps. She'd gotten home early from a job interview.

It was two weeks before we had to run.

She didn't yell. She knelt beside me on the floor. I could feel the concrete chill running through her black tights as if it were my knee, my bone.

I whispered: *How could you take these pictures?*

She whispered back: *Why did you open the book?*

And then she pressed her lips to my ear: *Because you are like me.*

My mother's finger still plays a scale down my spine when I remember.

She *knew*.

She knew that a dead woman trailed after me when I climbed up the stairs and fell back into the warmth and light.

She knew why I was compelled down into the basement again and again—the feeling that I was supposed to *do something*.

Because the dead lady on the kitchen floor wasn't contained by the snap on my mother's book. She didn't just follow me. She slipped off her bloodstained heels and followed my mother, too.

EIGHTEEN YEARS LATER

PART ONE

PART ONE

1
—————

I lay my palm flat on the picture. It covers a pile of bones.

I think her name starts with *A* or *E*.

Definitely a vowel.

She is embedded in the earth like a forgotten shipwreck on the ocean floor.

The voices of two men drift under the closed door—a childhood best friend who believes I brush shoulders with ghosts and a stranger who thinks I'm a joke. Both are cops. Both are agitated. I wish they'd burst in, get it over with, tell me to continue or not with this dead girl lying under my chewed pink fingernails.

The walls in this police interview room make me ache from the inside out. I've been here often enough lately that I've memorized every scar in this room. The ominous black marks on the walls, the handcuff scratches on the metal table, the tile floor with the big chip and brown stain.

I stare at a pale crescent line drawn between my thumb and forefinger, one of nine scars on my own body. It seems like a lot for a twenty-eight-year-old who still wouldn't call herself brave.

My friend Mike feels differently about my fearlessness. He has enticed me to this interview room five times in the last couple of months, late at night, an open secret in the police station. I overheard my nicknames from two cops gossiping at the sink while I sat in a bathroom stall.

Mike's Medium.

The Poltergasm.

The rumor is, after I look in my crystal ball of the dead, Mike throws me on this table and cheats on his wife.

All I've ever seen in a crystal ball is nothing. Mike would never cheat, not with me. He'd arrange this table the same way every time—with two chilled cans of Coke and a pile of unresolved case files—and then he'd leave.

No more than ten files, only photographs, that was our agreement. That's all of the dead I could take in one sitting. At my request, no details of the crimes.

I'd examine each of Mike's files carefully, sticking a Post-it on the outside after I closed it. Many times, the word I wrote was *Nothing*. Mike didn't care. He said cops were thrilled with forty percent accuracy on psychic tips and that I was averaging forty-two.

Mike left an occasional surprise. A plastic bag with a little girl's bloodstained pink bow. A man's watch with the hands stuck at 3:46. A bone the size of a small fingernail that looked like part of a bird but was really the tiniest, most fragile bone in the human face. The lacrimal bone. Part of the tear duct. It helped the girl it belonged to cry while she was being tied up with torn pieces of her T-shirt.

It took about three hours in this room to trigger a headache that would stab my head for days.

I'd leave things in a neat pile afterward, including the plain brown envelope with cash inside, probably from Mike's own pocket.

The outside of the envelope was always marked VIVVY ROSE, in the same block letters written on the get-well cards Mike brought to the hospital when I was eleven. Those cards stood like protective cardboard soldiers on my windowsill: a pig tucked under a quilt, a dog with a stethoscope, an alligator with a bandaged tail.

Today, Mike has graduated me to late morning, a public and busy one. I'm getting an official introduction to this skeptical cop I'm about to meet. I'm examining the photographs of a single important case, not ten.

The crescent scar has begun to ping. My hand is still flayed out on the dead girl. *Anna? Eleanor?*

The edge in Mike's voice is rising, like right before he punched a high school jock who asked if I could predict his tongue down my throat.

I don't want to be here almost as much as I never want to let Mike down.

I flip to the photograph of the girl's skull, held by small anonymous hands in purple gloves. It looks as polished and cleaned as a marble bust in a museum.

I ruffle the stack of photographs like cards, halting randomly on the mourners at her second and final grave, the one where she wasn't buried by a killer like a stray dog. Pull out my phone to switch on my magnifying glass app.

Outside the door, sudden silence.

My head jerks up when it opens. A uniformed young female cop with a bottle of water in her hand stands awkwardly in the doorway. DIY dye and nail job, a face with a sharp kind of Texas pretty that lasts only so long before the sun takes its toll.

"Hi. I'm Piper Sikes. Mike thought you might want a drink."

I quickly flip over the stack of photographs before she moves closer.

"Thanks." I unscrew the top, expecting her to leave.

Instead, she scrapes out a chair for herself, positioning it intimately in front of me. She pulls a small tube out of her pocket and begins to draw on pink lips with a steady hand. Bobbi Brown's Hippy Shake, a color my sister wears sometimes, even though her hips are as flat as this girl's. Seems like very odd behavior. But I can be odd, too.

"Hydrogenated polyisobutene, isodecyl isononanoate, oxycoccus palustris," I murmur.

"Is that some kind of incantation?" Piper's voice is slightly above a whisper.

"Sure." I take a swig of water. Piper has no idea how many chemicals she applies to her lips, her cheeks, her eyes, her hair, all in pursuit of beauty. My sister knows because I've been reciting them to her off labels since I was eight. She just doesn't care.

"You're the psychic, right?" she presses. "I just wanted to give you a heads-up before Mike brings in Jesse Sharp. He is the *last* detective to believe in somebody like you. I had him for class three years ago. The first line and last line of every lecture was, 'Feelings manipulate facts, so don't have any.' And psychics are all about feelings, right?" She taps on the stack of photographs. "You should know—this case right here, it's not the one Mike . . . they . . . want you for. It's a *test*."

With the last three words, her eyebrows hike into pointy mountains. I never let a single quirk of my face telegraph anything. I hide my own eyebrows with bangs.

Piper lays a translucent white arm on the table, palm up, like I'm going to draw her blood. Now I understand. She wants me to pull her future from the lines on her hand. She wants reciprocation for the things she just told me and shouldn't have. It's the act of a desperate woman, not a good cop.

"Do you mind a quick reading?" she asks tremulously. "I'm not sure I should marry Waylon, the guy I'm living with. My mom and sister don't think I should, anyway. Should I not have said his name? Is that bad? How does it work?" *Not like this. Not with me.*

But her face. It's so puckered with worry. I draw my finger along the Life Line on her palm, which ends way too short if you go by those sorts of things. I lightly trace all the lines on her palm until chill bumps pop on her skin. The Marriage Line. The Heart Line. The Fate Line.

I act like I don't see the ugly, dark blue fingerprints painted in the soft crook of her other elbow or the makeup that almost succeeds in hiding a faint pink line on her right temple. I know an expert job of covering a scar because I've done it. I don't think female cops hide a scar they're proud of getting on the job.

I gently remove her engagement ring, a diamond the size of a sunflower seed. I press the ring into the inside of her wrist until it makes a small red circle.

"Metal," I say, "is excellent at conducting two things. The truth. And evil."

I shut my eyes. I ask Piper to close hers.

I tell her that if the imprint of the ring's circle stays more than ten seconds, Waylon will kill her if she doesn't leave.

All of this is bullshit. But so is the idea of Waylon as a decent man.

I've counted to nine when my eyes flip open and I realize that the soft breeze on my face at count five was not the air-conditioning bumping on.

A man is leaning against the open door, arms crossed.

I don't need a red circle on my wrist to know he is trouble.

☽ ✧ ☾

Piper leaps up, her eyes glued to the indentation on her skin.

I'm on my feet too, certain that this is Mike's detective friend, Jesse Sharp, wondering how much of my bullshit he heard. Whether Piper was a setup. If Piper was the real test, and, in fact, the better actress.

Photographs are scattered all over the floor. I'm fuzzy on whether it was Piper or me who accidentally swept them off when we jerked out of our chairs; all I know is that my phone flew too, painfully smacking the floor.

Only three steps in and Jesse Sharp feels on top of me. Body, dense. Ego, denser. The gun at his waist, inconsequential, a prop he doesn't need.

Mike is right behind him, an apology on his face. He'd told me that Sharp was tough, persistent to the edge of reason, as black and white as Escher. But he said nothing about this kind of domination. There's much less of everything while he's in the room. Less air, less space, less me.

My phone. I don't see it anywhere near my feet, setting off a little panic. It must have slid under the table. I'd temporarily disabled the password this morning, so I didn't have to repeat punching it in, a bad habit of mine. I refuse to enable face recognition.

I don't want either of them traveling through the photos I've snapped of strange objects, scrambled notes dictated by whispers, an internet search history that has Google analytics in a tailspin about whether to target me with ads for the antipsychotic Latuda or Jordan Peele horror movies.

I drop to the floor, crawling all the way under the table until my fingers find my phone's slick surface.

The screen jumps to life, revealing a new hairline crack, like a bad luck mirror. The tips of Sharp's boots are a foot from my face, pointy black omens so close he could kick the phone out of my hand. The sadistic Brothers Grimm taught me early to ignore warning signs like this at my own peril. Fairy tales are where "special" girls like me are hacked to pieces. Magic and foresight are a curse that could chop off my hands, paralyze my voice, impale me in the gut with a steel-toed boot.

I snatch up the photographs under the table and scramble out, all knees and feet and butt. I smell a whiff of dung on his boots. I don't like this perspective, him hovering, me at the bottom of the tree.

Sharp is holding the photograph of the crime scene shot from the air, peering at the dump site, a rectangle of fresh brown in a lush bush of green, the one where three blurry white figures in CSI jumpsuits around the grave look like angels have touched down.

"I startled you," he says. A fact, not an apology. He's offering a hand up. Calloused fingertips, short nails. I see a brief flash of that hand in urgent motion, clutching the hair of someone in the water, going under.

I ignore the hand and the image, pull myself to my feet.

"Thank you." I snatch the photograph, tucking it with the others.

The door is shut. Piper, a lucky escapee. Mike has braced himself against the opposite wall, holding a few more pictures from the floor. Silent. Ceding control, even of introductions.

"Tivvy, right?" Sharp is asking. I flip my head back to him. "Or should I call you Vivian? Vivian Rose Bouchet. Pretty name for a psychic. Imaginative. Something I expect you've had to live up to. Like Sharp."

"It's Vivvy. With a *V*." I'm immediately sorry I responded. He's not a man who makes mistakes like that unless it's on purpose. The only *t* in my name is the silent *whoosh* in Bouchet. French genes, my mother claims. *She made it up for our birth certificates*, says my sister.

"Vivvy doesn't call herself a psychic," Mike interjects. The *I've told you* is unspoken.

"It has a bad connotation," I stutter. "Like how the word *Christian* is sadly devolving. Not all psychics speak the truth. Even when they truly believe they are."

"Are you a Christian?" he asks pointedly. "Is that why your eyes were closed when we came in? Were you and Officer Sikes praying? Do you prefer for people not to know you're a . . . Christian? Is it something you don't want to admit?"

Jesse slides out a chair and props a boot on it. "I've interviewed a lot of people who play with the truth. Pathological liars. Oscar-worthy actors. Christians, Jews, Muslims. Eighty-six of them now in prison. Seven on death row. Two executed. Thirteen still free."

"Let's get this moving," Mike interjects impatiently. I'd almost forgotten he was there. "Vivvy, Sharp wants to get your take on these photographs. He has asked that I leave the room. He thinks you'll make more progress." Sarcasm, like syrup. "Is that OK with you?"

None of this is OK with me, Mike. My mother died only ten days ago, and now you're dragging me into this.

"Of course," I say. The battle in the hall, Mike lost.

"I'll call you later." Mike hands me the rest of the photographs, tosses off a salute, and shuts the door.

I picture my face right now, bright angry spots burned high on each cheekbone. *Red roses*, my sister has called them since she first held me as a baby and my wails practically blew out her eardrums.

I turn away from Sharp and begin to lay the pictures in neat, perfect rows.

"You keep track of those thirteen liars?" I ask under my breath. "The ones who got away?"

"Until they are marks on my bedpost," Sharp drawls. "Until I'm buried myself."

All this bravado makes him hard to read. Especially when I sense he's about to poke a knife in my belly to test how tender I am.

I summon up the little girl from the Blue Ridge Mountains who turned out to be brave when she needed to be.

We'll see. Some people are better at twisting a knife in me than others.

☽ ✧ ☾

I've finished setting up the board for Sharp. The photos shiver in place as he slides into the chair on the opposite side of the table. He gestures for me to do the same.

I am now in my sweet spot, where even the most cynical are holding their breath for me to speak. Everybody believes a *little* in something they can't see.

I travel his face boldly. His eyes, a murky sea. My sister has eyes like these, scary little changelings, cold then warm, gray then green. True, then false. She doesn't pretend to be psychic, but she is the best of us at lying. Her big lie, the one between us, is a jagged crack I step over because it seems too deep to fill.

"Mike told me the story of how you and he met," Sharp begins.

The first prick of the knife.

I shift slightly in my chair. Finger the fuzzed edge of one of the pictures.

He stretches his lean body, long arms yawning over his head. His knuckles graze the wall behind him. The tip of his boot pokes my bare ankle under the table, two inches from a long rake of scar. His phone buzzes on the table, which he ignores as his body retreats.

"Stop me if I get any of this wrong," he begins. "You were only eleven, a new girl in town. He was fourteen. Mike didn't say so, but

I'm guessing you had a crush on him. He walked home every day, passing right in front of your living room window. Earbuds in, music on high, decompressing from a day at middle school. No reason to suspect that a little girl with red hair and crooked glasses was going to burst out of her front door, yank out his earbuds, and scream that he was going to die. You told him urgently about your recurring dream. A blue horse. A horse that was going to kill him. You were very insistent about that. He told you to *get your redheaded butt away from me*. Mike has a real unique way with wordplay.

"The next time, you were waiting on your front porch. The time after that, cross-legged on the sidewalk, blocking his path. That's when he switched his route."

He starts up a slow, rhythmic tap of fingernail on steel table. *Click, pause, click, pause, click, pause, click, pause.* Did Mike tell him sound is a trigger for me? I slip my hand into the pocket of my jeans, to reassure myself it's there. Press my finger into the sharp point but not enough to make it bleed.

He's watching my hand in my pocket, wondering. But it doesn't stop him. "You figured out his new routes. You followed him. More often than not, there you were, a twenty-yard dash behind him. He called you Bad Red Penny to his friends when they laughed about his baby stalker. It prompted his own dream—well, more of a nightmare—that a red-haired girl in a blue coat stabbed him to death. How am I doing? Mike tells the story better. Especially after a couple of Shiners."

I don't think anyone has ever told this story better. Maybe it's because Sharp's voice dips so low in parts, like he swallowed coals. Maybe it's because I've never heard these details. The story is a long space between Mike and me that we mostly leave alone. I feel wrong listening, guilty even.

"It's Texas," I say. "Big on horses. Not on coats." I gesture to the table. "The pictures? Can we please get to it?"

Jesse's phone jumps again. Not even a flinch from him. Like it isn't there. Like my question *isn't there*.

Click, pause, click, pause, click, pause, click, pause.

His tapping is driving nails into my brain, turning it to pocked coral.

In one quick movement, I pull my hand out of my pocket, lean over, and clutch his finger in my fist. Touching him is nothing like touching Piper. It is the shock of electricity that I knew it would be. And, I can tell, not just for me.

I drop his finger.

"You can finish the story, or I can," he says evenly.

I nod, barely. "You can end your game, or I can."

He deliberately folds his hands in front of him. "Just a minute more. I'm near done." He clears his throat. "It was tough for Mike, just getting in his boy muscles. The start of macho. He didn't want to admit that a little girl was scaring him to death. But his mother threatened to ground him because he was now late all the time for his Thursday piano lesson, his Tuesday tutor. His new routes to avoid you took twenty minutes longer, sometimes thirty. So . . . then his mother knocked on *your* door. Yelled at *your* mother. Do you remember?"

Your child needs serious psychological help, can't you see that?

Yes. I remember.

"At his mother's insistence to be brave and on time, Mike returned to his usual route that took him in front of your house. *Brave. On Time.* Words to live by, eh? About a block before he got to your yard, he would turn the music even higher. Still, he couldn't resist. He'd glance up at the porch, where your mother ordered you to stay. She probably told you not to say a word. That your silence was safer. More powerful. The porch gave you a long, clear view."

Click. Pause. One deliberate tap.

"I read the police report," he says. "Teenage driver in a blue Mustang hops the curb on the sidewalk right in front of your lawn. Seventy-five-pound girl pushes middle-school lineman out of the way. But you weren't quite fast enough. And Mike, he blames himself. He thinks that if he'd listened, he would have still been dodging you, taking a different route home. And you wouldn't have that limp when you're tired."

Now it's Sharp who leans forward.

"Some people would call this story a confirmation of your other-worldly powers," he says quietly. "You know what I call it? I call it the seeds of a dysfunctional relationship."

I wait, but the question doesn't come. The one about whether I think that blue Mustang was a coincidence or my divine insight. I might finally, after all these years, tell the truth.

Sharp gestures to the pictures. "Let's see what you've got, Bad Red."

VIVVY'S DIARY, AGE TEN

Goal 1: Stop knocking on my bedroom wall at night.

Goal 2: Stop chewing my nails.

Brig says she could take care of both problems if she tied my hands behind my back. She painted No Bite on my nails today. It tastes horrible. I told her that it has denatonium benzoate in it, the most bitter compound on Earth. They use it in toilet bowl cleaner. She said that it won't kill me but that she might kill me if I keep reading her all the chemicals on labels and knocking on the wall every night.

I don't want to have a Y cut in me like the man in Mom's dead people book in the basement.

I only chewed on my thumb tonight.

But I still knocked fifty times.

2

've lost track of how long Jesse Sharp has been waiting for me to declare my spiritual revelation about this case.

I've slid the photographs up and down and sideways on the table, finally narrowing them to the five that speak most—mourners spilling out of a funeral tent, a silver charm bracelet lying among brittle leaves and black berries, an Instagram selfie, the skull lovingly held by purple gloves, the drone shot of the crime scene spying down into the forest that explains why for so long only God and her killer knew where she was.

I separate the photo of the charm bracelet from the other four. It vibrates with terror but doesn't feel like it belongs.

The girl is practically prowling out of her selfie, six inches of bared belly above camouflage leggings, insulin pump at her waist. So vulnerable and young and sexy, it hurts to look. I separate the pictures of her blue eyes and her empty black skull eyes, bookending them on either end of the row. It doesn't help. Both still accuse me of being a fraud.

Sharp strums through his texts while I think, his boots propped on the table inches from her face. Like the kind of cowboys that tourists believe are pulled up to every bar in Texas but who prefer the lonely wayback of their properties. His boots are soft-polished on top, well-scuffed on the sole. Kangaroo skin, so he's not sentimental about animals, or at least not ones that punch. Handmade, $2,000 plus, so not broke.

Boots this custom-crafted are more comfortable than running shoes—the boot maker so exact he probably knew where Sharp's second metatarsal hits the ground. Sharp works his ass off in them, I'm certain of it.

I'm an encyclopedia of what feet and hands can tell you. My mother fed my morbid scientific curiosity very early on with odd details she learned at crime scenes.

I can guess a lot by shoes, but footprints—boot prints—give facts. Height, weight. Whether you're standing in place or running in terror. Unabomber Theodore Kaczynski attached smaller soles to his shoes to fool the FBI, which he did for twenty-six years.

Sharp's boots leave a deep, don't-forget-me mark in the soil. I know that, too.

I want to shove them off the table—tell him it's disrespectful to me and this murdered girl. I want to say that a lot of the time I'm wrong when I go at it this way—that it works better if whatever comes to me is uninvited, not because I'm told to think about it. Not because a disturbing selection of photographs is laid in front of me.

Like that flash when I saw Sharp's hand for the first time. I don't know if Sharp's saving someone or drowning them, if I'm glimpsing the future or being jerked into his past. Either way, I know it's fated. Done.

"Her name starts with a vowel." I interrupt the silence, going for the easy points.

He slides his boots off the table, eyes still glued to the phone. "About a fifty percent chance of getting that right."

"It starts with an *A* or an *E*."

His eyes lift. Flicker confirmation.

"Go ahead and tell me her name," I say. "I'd like to say it out loud. It will . . . encourage me." *Encourage her.*

"Audrey. Also her grandmother's name. She was ninet—"

I hold up my hand to stop him before I know whether Audrey was nineteen or her grandmother was ninety.

"Are we *playing* or not?" I ask, irritated. "If so, it's by my rules. When I ask you for information, *give me only that information*." I tap the photograph from the cemetery. "I think whoever killed Audrey was at the funeral. She knew him. Her family knew him. He hugged her mother. *Smelled her perfume and sneezed*. But he isn't in this shot."

I roll my eyes, so I don't have to watch him do it. "I know," I say. "You're thinking, *big deal*. More than half of all female victims are killed by someone they know."

"Ninety," he states. "Ninety percent. I'm making a mental note to ask who sneezed at the funeral."

"I don't think Audrey was killed or buried in Texas." I'm determined to beat all that certainty out of him. "I don't think she's *from* Texas. Which makes me think it's not your case." I hold up my hand. "Don't say anything yet. The killer was younger. Or older and in incredibly good shape." I hesitate. "And there's something about a green-striped sheet. Don't bother to look; it's not in the pictures."

"He was young or old. Got it. Did he carry her all the way up there or did she walk up on her own?"

"She . . . was carried or dragged."

"Why?"

I hesitate. "She was diabetic. A teenager who blew off her disease. Maybe bulimic. It would have been a tough hike even if he didn't incapacitate her in some way."

"This is what you *feel* from the great beyond or this is what you *see* when you look at these photographs?"

"She's all bones in her selfie," I say flatly. "An empty bag of red Doritos and Oreos in the trash behind her. I *see* that."

But I also *feel* the fingernail in her throat like a fishhook. *Taste* the raw sewage in her throat. *See* the soggy orange chips floating in the toilet bowl. *Artificial color Yellow 6, Yellow 5, Red 40.*

"You can understand my problem with you, right?" he asks.

"Not as much as my problem with you," I shoot back. "I'm doing this as a favor. Mike told me you needed help finding a missing girl. But this particular girl has been found, hasn't she? You're showing me a closed case. Using it as a test. Of me. My abilities. My character. Just tell me what happened to her."

He taps his forefingers together like a church steeple until I feel like screaming.

"Audrey Jenkins," he begins. "Almost twenty. Killed ten years ago by her step-uncle, Jeb Waverly. He dragged her up a hill on a sled and buried her on state park land in Oregon. He confessed eight years later—not to me, by the way—when Audrey wouldn't stop screaming in his ear while he slept. He'd slid her senior portrait between the mattress and the box spring. It was a picture he'd stolen from one of her mother's frames at the wake. Bold, I'd say. I use this case in one of my criminology courses. On the observational score, you passed with flying colors."

"Is this what you call an apology?"

"I'd apologize if the sheet had green stripes," Jesse says.

"Do you know for certain that he never used one?"

"Look, Mike was upset that I wanted a pilot run on a closed case—that I wouldn't just take his word about your . . . skills. But I needed my own baseline for your crazy, pardon the word, before I used you on a case about which the mayor is quietly breathing like fire down the chief's neck."

I'm certain he wants me to ask, *What case?*

"I don't like being used," I say instead.

"Not as much as I don't like the idea of using you. You're a PR nightmare. Mike thinks he still walks the earth because you're on it. That's a conflict. If you said you were the reincarnation of Princess Diana, Mike would find you a crown."

"I was alive when Princess Di died. So that would not be possible."

He crosses one boot over the other. "My aunt Eddie believes MI6 bumped her off because she was pregnant with Dodi Fayed's baby."

I shrug. "There's an emotional engine to conspiracy theories. No one wants to believe someone as special as Diana could die an ordinary, random death."

"No one wants to accept that *anyone* can die an ordinary, random death. Vivvy, I can't be the first person on Earth who has wanted proof that you are what you say you are."

Vivvy. Too intimate. The first time I've felt like someone who uttered my name should ask permission.

"I've never claimed to be anything," I say tautly. "I never *asked* Mike to pull me into any of his cases. I'm only back in town on a temporary leave of sorts because my mother was dying. I returned to take care of her for part of the summer. I usually work and live in the Chihuahuan Desert full-time, but right now I've been going back and forth. As a professional stargazer in Big Bend country, I do not focus on communing with dead people or very many live ones, for that matter." I never introduce myself as an astrophysicist. Too showy. That's what my mother told me the day I received my doctorate—to put it in a drawer.

I'm certain Sharp knows all about me anyway—that, like a good sham psychic would, he's already drained Mike of answers and looked up every available written word on me since I was born.

"Condolences," he says softly. "Mike told me you were a wunderkind—that at twenty-five years old, you recorded some funky light way out there in the universe that might indicate we are not alone. Got a big-ass grant to try to confirm it. Sounds like appropriate work for someone like you."

"I caught a glimpse of artificial light coming from a planet far beyond our own system," I say stiffly. "Light that is unexplained."

"Well, let's see what light you glean from this." He's drifting closer, pulling another photo out of his pocket, small, maybe four by six. I can smell the salt on his skin, the peppermint on his tongue, the dirt on his boots, the faintest odor of a sexual encounter.

His scent is about to drown me.

"Take a look." He lays the photo on the table. "She's the case.

The mayor thinks that finally finding her missing body after eleven years is his ticket to ride."

I glance down at a child of three or four. Perky pink bow on her head. Behind her, the blurred bars of a jungle gym, the blackish green of a tree urging me into its shade. This picture was taken before instant filters turned our worlds to hyperreal, when dead spirits could still comfortably hang out in photographs as shadows and glare.

The girl in the photo is silently repeating the same thing to me over and over, just like she did two weeks ago when Mike left that same pink bow in an evidence bag.

Except, the bow was flat and spattered in blood.

It was wrong, so wrong, but I broke the rules that night and slipped it out of the bag. Rubbed its sharp clip against my cheek. Let one of my own tears stain its fabric before I even realized I was crying.

I remember exactly the single word I wrote on the Post-it. I now realize that scribble is probably why I'm sitting here—why Mike thinks I'm the one to help bring closure to this case. Mike's power over me—my desire to please him, to save him—is something I've wrestled with my whole life.

"Are you all right?" Sharp asks.

I abruptly step away from the table.

"I can't pardon the word."

"What?"

"I can't pardon the word *crazy*."

"I haven't gotten this far in my job handing out a lot of respect."

"Which reflects your lack of imagination." I haul my backpack from the floor, flip it over my shoulder. "You never intended to *use* me no matter what I said. You just wanted me to be the one to say no. So, good job. I say no."

Sharp appears unmoved. But I'm not quite done.

"Something about your test case, the one that's closed, bugs me." I reach across the table, take one finger, and deliberately drag the photo of the bracelet in front of his face. "This charm bracelet did not belong to Audrey Jenkins. Whoever it belongs to is still missing. It's in your case study by mistake. Sloppy of you. We wouldn't want to confuse your students, would we? Or me?"

The beat he takes is longer than it should be.

His fist, drawn into a ball. *Now* he's moved.

This picture hit a nerve, more than all the others.

"Interesting," he says tightly. "I show you a closed case and you want me to open a new one."

☽ ✧ ☾

I sprint to my Jeep, parked in the far corner of the police station lot, but it doesn't matter how fast I run. The girl in the pink bow is right behind me, feet tripping on my heels, her pudgy little legs growing long and tanned and lean with each stride.

I hop in and slam the door behind me. Wait for a second. Blessed silence. The girl has evaporated, which is how it works sometimes. I switch on the ignition and lift my face, willingly blinded by the July glare pouring through the open roof. The sun is as hot as the door-knob to hell. It's also heaven after the bitter chill of two hours in an air-conditioned box.

"Vivvy." At the window. Jesse Sharp. Unbelievable. There are at least fifty cars in this lot, and my Jeep is hidden by a white wide-body pickup with fat, obnoxious fenders. My sister calls them side boobs.

How did he even see me? Sharp is pushing a thick file folder strapped with three rubber bands through the open window.

"Read the case on the missing kid. Tomorrow. By three."

"Are you not listening? I said *no*. And I'm sure Mike told you that's not how I work anyway." I shove the file back at him. He makes no move to take it.

"Maybe you need to rethink how you work." His mouth is a tight line. "This girl's grandmother is throwing her fourteenth birth-day party today at an empty grave in the cemetery while her only daughter sits in prison instead of right beside her, an arm around her shoulder. She deserves to know if what you wrote on that Post-it to Mike is true. And how you know it."

He stalks around the front of the white pickup. I hear the chirp of a remote, and in less than a minute he has roared out of the lot. He misses scraping my Jeep by an inch.

VIVVY'S DIARY, AGE TEN

Mom said she burned her book of dead people. She told Brig and me that we are not allowed to go in the basement anymore. She thinks we don't know that she has started taking strangers down there when we're in bed.

Last night, it was an old lady and the night before that a man with a blue tie and a small notebook.

When I asked Brig, she told me it was none of my business, that my business is to unload the dishwasher and to clean my room, which she says stinks like something died.

I knocked sixty-two times tonight while Mom was in the basement. Brig saved her money and bought herself new earphones to sleep in. I worry she won't hear me if I scream.

3
---

live is what I wrote on that Post-it. The little girl in the pink bow is alive. She's somewhere out there in the world, turning fourteen today, whether she knows it's her birthday or not.

I've parked in the cemetery by an old oak that offers leafy cover for my Jeep. Camouflage wasn't my first choice of Jeep colors, but I bought it for a sweet price off a Texas hunter who had just married a very pretty Vermont vegan.

Usually, I sweep these powerful binoculars up to the sky, not past ancient gravestones so worn and nubby they look like black rocks dropped from the sky.

It's not hard to spy the balloons several hundred feet past them.

They're pink, like her bow. I count three men and five women gripping hands in a circle around a gravestone, heads bowed, the balloons handcuffed to their wrists. Our death rituals haven't changed that much since time began. I'm too far away to hear anything, but three television cameras confirm I'll be able to watch it all with dripping commentary on the evening news.

The little girl's story is scattered across my passenger seat. When I broke the rubber bands on the file in the car, I told myself, *Just one page*, but one page turned into two and three and then I stopped counting. The deeper I traveled into the file, the more it tickled a vague memory of my mother mentioning the disappearance of a Fort Worth girl while I was a college freshman in Boston. Her house, not that far from ours.

I was distracted that year, developing the new me in a place where no one knew the old one. The national media was distracted, too. The horror of the Sandy Hook massacre, the shooting of Trayvon Martin, a Princess Kate pregnancy, the *Fifty Shades* mommy porn revolution.

This case barely puffed a smoke signal outside of Texas in the beginning, even though it was built of perfect tinder.

A lovely, well-off couple, both respectable Texas lawyers, who met at the University of Southern California.

A pretty three-year-old daughter named Lizzie with a heart-shaped freckle on her shoulder.

A crumbling Victorian gingerbread mansion with so many nooks and crannies and hiding places, it would take Sherlockian effort to find them all.

Nicolette and Marcus Solomon were renovating the Victorian back to glory when little Lizzie went missing. She was last seen standing in her kitchen in a blue sundress with daisy shoulder buttons, and then never again.

Her mother swore she was out of the kitchen only ten minutes to take a phone call. Her husband was two hundred miles away at his dying mother's side. All the doors had dead bolts Lizzie couldn't reach, one of their very first orders of business before moving in.

Nicolette made a frantic 911 call, assuming that Lizzie had gotten stuck somewhere in the five-thousand-square-foot house, playing a new hide-and-seek game she'd made up for her teddy bear. She'd called Lizzie's name for fifteen minutes until she became terrified that her little girl was smothering somewhere, trapped.

Firemen arrived. After that, the police. Then the dogs.

Nicolette Solomon never changed her story in nine grueling interviews—four with the initial Fort Worth detectives on the case, three more with the Texas Rangers, another two with the FBI. Her husband, a family law attorney, sat in on every one of them.

From the community, equal outpourings of sympathy and incredulity. How and why would a child disappear from her kitchen at ten in the morning?

Wasn't it tragic, unbelievable, *weird*? More than a hundred volunteers, directed by cops, hunted through hotel parking lots for a lurking car that a neighbor described as a gray or blue sedan with an *L* and an *8* in the license plate.

Nine days later, a full-blown conspiracy theory began to smolder.

The husband reluctantly and temporarily left the search efforts for an emergency run to East Texas to bury his mother. For almost two days, Nicolette was alone. Deep into both nights, neighbors on either side of the mansion heard loud banging coming from inside the house.

Was Nicolette Solomon entombing Lizzie in the walls? Did she kill her daughter by accident? On purpose?

Texas Rangers arrived with their own sledgehammers and dogs with better sniffers.

They found the pink bow under the toddler bed with Lizzie's blood on it, which Nicolette—but no doctor—said was from Lizzie knocking her head while climbing on a nearby park's jungle gym.

Bags of lime powder, explained by the couple as their solution for covering odor in a crawl space that had been used by feral cats while the house stood empty for twenty years.

Proof that Nicolette's phone call that morning was outgoing, not incoming, and to a twenty-four-year-old rodeo star client of hers with a two-thousand-acre ranch, an endless burial ground.

Texts indicating the two were having an affair.

Nicolette Solomon was convicted a year later. No body. Circumstantial evidence that included a piece of Lizzie's preschool art that could have been a bloody fight between her parents or a plate of spaghetti. Testimony from two friends who said that Nicolette, over two bottles of wine, had told them the week before Lizzie disappeared that she regretted marrying so early and having the burden of a toddler.

On the second anniversary of their daughter's disappearance, Nicolette's husband entered the mansion he'd abandoned and tried to hang himself from a banister that broke and saved his life.

It's too much to know.

I tighten the focus on the binoculars. The balloons are taking off for the clouds, the crowd mostly dispersing. A man is sliding himself between a hunched older woman in a pink-flowered dress and a reporter sticking a microphone in her face.

The man's body language is saying, *Knock it off.* Maybe a protective son. Maybe an obsequious mayor, the one latching on to the still missing Lizzie for his own political reasons. Then the man's head turns. His eyes are bullets shooting straight through me, even though I know that's not possible at this distance. I drop the binoculars.

Not her son. Not the mayor. Jesse Sharp, the cop who doesn't believe in feelings. I would have picked up on his presence faster, but he'd traded his cowboy persona for that of a stockbroker and looked remarkably natural in the transformation. Beige pants, collared blue shirt, classy green-and-blue-striped tie. Only the boots stayed put.

I cautiously lift the binoculars. His hand is pressing the small of the old woman's back as he escorts her back to a candy apple Buick sitting a few hundred feet away. He helps her into the driver's side before disappearing on the other side of the trees, where I'm guessing he's parked.

I don't pick my way across the cemetery until the only human beings I've seen for twenty minutes are two diggers at work in a far corner.

Elizabeth Rae Solomon's gravestone is surprisingly stark.

No engraved angel or Bible verses.

No dates, not even one of her birth.

Just her name.

And four words.

Not here but everywhere.

I kneel, the backpack sliding off my shoulder and clunking to the ground. I search through its inside pockets for the best digging tool I can find, which turns out to be a screwdriver.

I pry up a small patch of turf at the base of the stone before unclasping the silver clip that holds my hair in a long tight ponytail. The clip is shaped like a silver crescent moon, with *Vivvy* engraved in delicate script. My mother gave it to me. She'd decided the crescent was my symbol ever since the day I picked up a timber rattlesnake going after Brig, sunning herself in a pink-and-blue-striped bikini, and threw it across the yard. The snake bit a deep curve. I was fourteen, but it never faded.

A hot wind shivers the grass. Shivers *me*. Mom is here. Her grave, still a mound of red dirt, only a thousand yards away. I almost didn't come when I saw in the file that Lizzie was memorialized in the same cemetery where I stood a little over a week ago with my sister, Mike's black suit outlined against blue sky.

I drop the moon in the hole. A long red strand from my head is still attached. There's profound power in hair, so I leave it. Women used to bury a lock of their hair with dead lovers. My mother liked to say she could see a future in a shred of hair long before DNA could find a killer through the beehive of an ancestry site.

I tamp the sod back in place until it looks undisturbed.

This is more of a trade than a gift, a full confession of sorts to Lizzie for stealing her hair clip out of the evidence bag at the police station and tucking it in my pocket. I'd carefully separated the metal clip from the bow and tucked the pink fabric back inside the bag, hoping Mike would never notice. *The DNA from the bloodstains*, I'd reasoned, *still there*.

I've used Lizzie's hair clip for a prick of pain like other people snap rubber bands on their wrists. To focus. Crowd out the demons. Her clip replaced an arrowhead, which replaced a copper cross, which replaced an earring post, which replaced an infinite number of things with points and edges that I had kept in my right pocket since I was ten, until I either lost them or they lost power over me.

I stole Lizzie's hair clip because it was sharp and small, not because I heard her say *Alive*. That's what I told myself.

Happy birthday, Lizzie, I whisper. *Let's get this party started.*

I know with every nerve in my body that I'm being watched as I walk away.

Maybe Jesse Sharp.

Maybe a tiny part of Lizzie that still remembers where she's supposed to be.

VIVVY'S DIARY, AGE TEN

I read today that when you're cremated, you don't get the whole body back like I thought.

It's just the bones pulverized to sand by a machine. The tissue evaporates in the oven. Brig told me that no one wants to hear my science facts while they're eating.

She and Mom had another big fight. Brig wants to know who our father is, and Mom told her we don't have the same one. She told Brig to stop complaining about everything, especially the smell in my room.

Brig slammed her bedroom door.

Mom told me to leave her alone.

She said there is something wrong with this house.

She told me not to knock tonight.

I did, but very soft.

4

_____

From the litter of shot glasses on the bar, Mike's way ahead of me. It's strange, out of character, for him to invite me to a dive bar at the witching hour, when the sun and moon are changing places. When wives and husbands are beginning to wonder why their spouses aren't home yet.

I'm guessing from Mike's cryptic text that he wants the scoop on my morning with Sharp and thinks liquor will smooth away any bumps.

Mike's back is to the sparse crowd, figures scattered in the shadows behind him like one of our abandoned chess games when we were kids.

I check out the room like Mike trained me to when I enter someplace unfamiliar. On the dance floor, king has met queen, the only other woman in the bar. In the corner, two rooks in baseball caps eye her curves, convinced she's still up for grabs. Four pawns, less macho types, cluster in a booth, power in numbers.

And Mike—he's the gutsy knight, the surprise killer with the horse thighs, who can take any of them with simple strategy and a limited move.

I walk over and wave my phone in his face instead of saying hello. "You asked me to meet you at _this_ address. At a place called T. J.'s. The neon out front says Steve's Toboggan."

"Sorry about that. Force of habit. The owner decided to change the name about a year ago. It hasn't caught on with us regulars."

I wave at the man behind the bar with a shamrock tattoo on his forearm unboxing an assortment of bourbons. "Are you Steve?"

He looks up. "Everybody's Steve. What can I get you?"

"Topo Chico over ice with lime, Tito's, and a cherry. Sugar on the rim, please. And something with grease and jalapeños."

I swivel my stool toward Mike. "Here's the short version. Fixing me up with Jesse Sharp—not going to work."

"I'm not asking you to kiss him."

"He doesn't believe me," I say forcefully. "I can't work with that. And let's be realistic: I haven't been leaning into my . . . special skills for years. I'll make errors; he'll be waiting to pounce on them. Also, I'm compromised. I've read half the file."

The part about me not leaning into my special skills is a little blue lie—what I call all lies to Mike since I saved him. My special skills are on duty 24/7, daytime and dreamtime, like I'm the fille de joie of a very demanding pimp.

He didn't know it, but Mike was right about one thing when he sat me in front of the department's coldest files. It has always been the missing and the murdered who like me best. Usually, I can flap them away. But I've dropped a few anonymous tips in the mail. Made a call from a burner to somebody's mother. I'm like an ER doc with the adrenaline to stitch the wound, or pump CPR, or diagnose a slow death, and then the ability to let the patient go forever, to never see them again. That's what I tell myself. That I let them go.

". . . you need to understand Sharp," Mike is saying. "He's got enough guts to hang on a fence. Underneath the swagger, there's more swagger, and underneath that, a pretty diabolical brain. He's *the* go-to guy with convicted serial killers, eating Domino's pizza and talking baseball with them at picnic benches, so they'll confess to where they buried a dozen more daughters. If you didn't know him and sat down, you wouldn't be able to tell which one was the killer. He's crawled so deep in their DNA, you wonder if he can crawl out.

My point is, he is whatever he needs to be to win. If a little Method acting and pizza won't do it, he'll pull out another tool."

"He seems to be using more of a sledgehammer with me."

Mike sets his shot glass firmly on the bar, a sign the lesson on Sharp is over. "Susan Jacobson, fourteen, Staten Island. Ashley Howley, twenty, Columbus, Ohio. Holly Wells and Jessica Chapman, ten, Soham, England . . ."

I hold up my hand. "I get it, I get it. Missing person cases reportedly solved by psychics."

"Richard Kelly, seventeen, Limerick, Ireland," he continues. "Melanie Uribe, thirty-one, Pacoima, California. Mary Cousett, twenty-seven, Alton, Illinois. Edith Kiecorius, four, Brooklyn . . ."

"Is this part of your strategy to convince Sharp? He will find the holes in those cases. There are always holes."

"Etta Smith was not even technically a psychic when she led police to Melanie Uribe's body in a canyon," Mike continues. "She was a shipping clerk who heard about her on the radio. She had a vision of Melanie's body and took her family to the San Fernando Valley to find her. To the *spot*."

"And the cops still didn't believe in Etta Smith's psychic abilities even when they identified the body," I counter. "In fact, they arrested her for the murder. She spent four days in jail."

"Until the men who actually raped and killed Melanie confessed. Why are you being difficult? These are your people."

Your people. "You know how I feel about this, Mike. For every good psychic, there are thousands of con artists who rip people's hearts out. What about the psychic who told the mother of Amanda Berry on national television that she was dead when in fact she was being held captive in a basement in Cleveland for a decade with two other girls? The mother died a year later from heart failure, thinking her daughter was gone. What about that anonymous psychic who called the Liberty County Sheriff's Department to summon the full barrel of Texas law for a futile search for a mass grave in East Texas?"

"Was that the case that turned out to be rotting meat?" Mike shrugs. "So what? You might make a few mistakes. Show me a cop who doesn't."

We both go silent while Steve plops my dinner in front of me: a bottle of Topo, a sugar-rimmed glass with four cherries and two fingers of vodka chilling on ice, and a paper container with yellow cheese oozing over a logo that says: *T.J.'s Bar and Grill. We'll Never Change.*

"One adult Shirley Temple and one large nachos for the lady," Steve announces. "Extra peppers and cherries for being the bar's fantasy girl of the day. My tips have tripled since you walked in."

Mike shifts his body, shoulders forward like a linebacker. Steve gets the message.

I wait until Steve's back to stocking bourbon, taut muscles quirking under a white T-shirt. Prison time seeps out of every pore.

"Did you see the Aryan shamrock on Steve's forearm?" I breathe out. "The letters on his knuckles?"

"Yep. That's not Steve, by the way. That's an ex-con who hasn't lasered off his tattoos yet in case he goes back to Huntsville. We've had a few chats."

"*A. C. A. B.* Does it still mean 'All Cops Are Bastards'?"

"I thought it meant 'All Cops Are Beautiful.'" He starts lining up his empty shot glasses, not meeting my eyes. "How are you doing? You know, with your mom?"

"Really? You're asking me how my *grieving* is going?"

"I know. The timing on involving you with a high-profile cold case . . . isn't great."

"It technically isn't cold, is it? Lizzie's mother sits in prison, convicted."

"There's still an intense amount of public interest about Lizzie. Too many questions without a body, Vivvy. And they feed a small but growing campaign about her mother's innocence."

"And the mayor?"

"The mayor has decided *I Found the Girl Fort Worth Couldn't Forget* has a nice ring to it. He sees Lizzie as a zip line to his upcoming bid for governor."

"There's some other reason you are dragging me into this." I'm suddenly sure of this. "It isn't just the bow."

Mike's eyes, intent on mine, confirm it. "Do you ever remember any cops stopping by your house when you were a kid?" he asks.

"I lived with my mother, so yes. She had a love-hate relationship with cops. Cops arrested her. Cops slept with her. I remember one *was* a bastard."

"Do you specifically remember a cop talking to her about the Lizzie Solomon case?"

"What? No. Not that she'd tell me anyway. And I was in college when this happened." The scar on my leg is pinging, out of order. For some reason I can't explain, I don't want to tell him my mother had mentioned a kidnapped girl at least once to me on the phone. "She was like a priest with her psychic readings. You know that. What are you getting at? You think that my mother had something to do with Lizzie Solomon?"

"Lizzie's mother, Nicolette Solomon, is suing the city. She filed an FOIA from prison and got the case files, all 2,301 pages."

Mike tips his glass and takes the last watery swallow.

"I'm still not following, Mike."

"Ms. Solomon found a short statement from your mother in there from about a year ago. It's vague. Like she came in to make a statement and got cold feet. References the car a neighbor of the Solomons said that she saw in front of the house the day Lizzie disappeared. Your mother said it was definitely gray, not blue. A Chevy, not a Buick. The cops weren't polite when she said she was a psychic, and I think it went downhill from there. But Nicolette—she wants to know more."

"Kind of a problem since Mom's now flying on another spiritual plane," I say flatly. "And you already knew all of this when you handed me the pink bow." A statement, not a question.

"It might have been serendipitous." He licks a yellow glob off his finger. "Did you know 'nacho cheese sauce' isn't regulated by the FDA? I don't like when you look at me like that. It takes me back to the first day we met, when I was a middle-school ass."

"My mother made stuff up sometimes to get attention. Take it from someone who knows."

"Nicolette Solomon doesn't think that. She thinks you're the next best thing to your mother. The key to her freedom."

"And Detective Sharp?"

"You aren't wrong. He thinks you're a grenade."

☽ ✧ ☾

A half hour ago, after "Steve" slid over a sample shot, I switched from Tito's to Katy Trail Oro Blanco Grapefruit Flavored Vodka. Steve knows his Dallas distilleries.

He is alternately calling me Pippi and Lucy, and I'm thinking he had a lot of time to kill in prison reading kids' books and listening to canned laughter.

I've determined the spot under his left eye is not a suspicious mole, but an open teardrop tattoo waiting to be colored in.

It means he's still going to kill someone—it's just not finished. I don't want to be responsible. The cloying, sweet tone of vanilla overwhelms me whenever he walks within a foot. That's how fear has always smelled to me, like baking sugar cookies. In this case, the fear is not Steve's or mine, but the person in his line of fire trying to creep into my head.

I told Mike I needed a breather about the same time I downed the second shot. I was angry. At him. My mother. Now everything is pleasantly numb, especially my nose.

Mike has started up the game we played in the hospital, when my eleven-year-old foot was hiked in the air like a crane. *The best sixteen days of my life*, I think sometimes. Mike showed up every afternoon after football, always bringing something. Butterfinger bars, trivia books, his mother's chocolate chip cookies, Superwoman comics, a chessboard.

And this game. *Our* game. He made it up just for us. Called it Truth or Conspiracy. We would play for hours, a perfect distraction from physical pain, unrequited prepubescent feelings, my obsession about knocking fifty times on the hospital wall behind the bed, which ticked off an old lady with gangrene on the other side.

"Truth or Conspiracy," Mike says. "Bluetooth was named for a tenth-century king named Harald Bluetooth."

"Conspiracy," I respond instantly. "Ridiculous."

"Truth. Harald Bluetooth Gormsson worked a miracle bringing Denmark and Norway together in medieval times like wireless links computers and cell phones. The inventors of Bluetooth also considered 'Flirt'—you know, connecting but no touching. Bluetooth was originally just the placeholder, but it stuck."

I picture Harald. Gold crown on his head, dead blue tooth in his mouth. With my finger, I make a river through the cheese left on the bottom of the empty nacho container.

"Truth or Conspiracy," I say. "Tyromancy is the practice of predicting the future with cheese. Women write the names of their prospective lovers on pieces of cheese. The first cheese to mold is their true love."

"Spell it."

"T-y-r-o-m-a-n-c-y."

"The 'romancy' part is a little spot-on. You're eating a cheese substance. I'm going to say conspiracy."

"Truth. *Tyros* means cheese in Greek. *Ancy* means 'divining by means of.'"

"The things you learned at your fancy college, Dr. Bouchet."

"I learned it from one of my mother's bedtime stories. OK, last one. Truth or Conspiracy. As of 1998, half of Iceland still believed in elves."

"Why 1998?"

"Because I assume elf surveys aren't done that often."

"Well, I certainly hope it's true." He has suddenly hooked his finger under my chin, pulling it toward him. He hasn't touched me this way since I was seventeen. The shiver runs to all the places it shouldn't. He'd just said it himself—a touch moves it beyond a flirt. It attaches a cumbersome, dangerous wire.

"I've missed you, Vivvy," he says softly.

I jerk my chin away with effort. "She doesn't know we're here, does she?" Ten feet away, the bartender reacts to my rising voice, turning his head in the casual way perfected by ex-cons.

"Your *wife* doesn't know any of it, does she?" I hiss. "Not about your asking me to help with cases since I've been back. That you and I have had private contact of any kind."

"Wait, Viv. Please. I'm sorry. I've drunk too much."

"Find someone else, Mike."

I'm not going to tell him that I'm carrying Lizzie's stolen hair clip in my pocket, or that the dirt of her grave is still on my fingers. That I won't be letting go of Lizzie, even if I'm on my own. If she's like every other determined ghost I've known, she won't let me.

Behind us on the tiny square of dance floor, one of the rooks in a baseball cap is making an unwanted move on the queen.

Mike is torn about which of us to go after as I slam out the door.

I know it won't be me.

VIVVY'S DIARY, AGE TEN

Tonight, Mom was the mom I like best. She told me one of her bedtime stories. I've missed her stories since she's been so busy in the basement.

They are always about something interesting. Like how the ancient pyramids line up with Orion's Belt in the sky, or the Jiffy Effect, where tons of people are positively sure they remember something that happened in history different than the way it is now.

Like how Jiffy peanut butter supposedly never existed, it was always Jif, and how the BerenSTEIN Bears are really the BerenSTAIN Bears, and how the witch in *Snow White* never said "Mirror mirror on the wall" although everyone is sure she did. Mom says this is not a memory issue, but more proof of alternate universes and how we bounce around in them. She said if I grow up to be a scientist like I want, I can prove that.

Her story tonight was a fairy tale about a beautiful princess named Mary with hair like gold and skin like whipped cream who was the lover of both a king and a prince. The weird thing is, they were brothers.

The princess became a problem because she knew all their secrets and threatened to tell the kingdom. The king and the prince made a plan. The prince secretly snuck into her castle and drugged her with a poison drink. A lady-in-waiting found her dead in her chambers.

The prince fled to the nearby ocean where a giant bird landed on the beach to carry him away so no one would ever know he was there.

Except the sand on the beach was magic, and when the bird took off, the sand swirled all their secrets into the air for everyone to hear for all time.

The sand and secrets swirled up and up, all the way to Venus, the goddess of love. It made her angry.

She turned her hands to fire and molded the sand into a sword of copper.

She threw it to Earth and killed the king while he rode in a carriage with his beautiful raven-haired queen, who wore a crown of pink diamonds.

When Venus saw how sad she made the queen, she tried to swallow her anger. Every day, she gathered up the queen's tears as penance. But when the prince decided he wanted to be king too, her anger returned. She froze her hands and rolled the tears into a crystal ball. She held it up to the sun so a sword of light would strike through the ice into the prince's heart.

Afterward, she threw the crystal ball into the sky and called it the moon.

My sister was listening through the vent. She said she thinks the stink is actually inside the wall between our rooms. She said Mom's fairy tale is a conspiracy theory about an old movie star named Marilyn Monroe. Brig said that we need to stick together, and we need to stick to facts. She said she loved me, which she hardly ever does.

5

It's been three hours since I left Mike in the bar. I swore afterward, furious, that I wouldn't come tonight. But here I am, kneeling in a driveway across the street from his house, a shadow, jogger, *stalker* tying her shoe.

I was in place last night, and the night before, and the night before that.

Above me, a clear, unpolluted universe, like in my dreams.

The moon, a clipped yellow toenail.

Mars and Venus, tiny diamonds in precise positions.

A summer sky like this is the only map I've been given to the timing of Mike's death other than the number twelve and the incessant thumping hooves of the Blue Horse. I meant to tell Mike right after the accident, as soon as they stopped pushing morphine in the hospital, that the Blue Horse was still out there, coming for him. The blue Mustang, just a bump of the fender.

Over the years, the dreams would pause for a few months, then start up again. Since I've been back in town, they've pounded harder and fiercer than ever before, like Mike's time is almost up.

Like my mother died on purpose so I could return to finish the job of saving Mike—the kind of irrational thought it's easier to erase when his finger isn't hooked under my chin.

Mike's house is modern and low-slung, with large bare picture windows that are warm rectangles of light. No curtains. Interior designers call it the undressed window, sexy and clean. The Mike I used to know would not live like this. Like a target.

Even from a hundred feet away, his life is in high-def. Crystal shimmers in the dining room cabinet. The blue-and-white abstract above the orange couch floats like a sail in the ocean or a cloud in the sky. A blue horse in the wind.

The holster is jabbing my thigh. I adjust it slightly. It holds my mother's gun, which she cleaned regularly. I found it hanging on a pink plastic hanger in her closet. The holster, with her belts. It feels cool and familiar in my hand. Mom taught Brig and me to shoot in the backyard of our house in the Blue Ridge Mountains, where gunshots were a daily echo up and down the road that snaked between hills.

Headlights curve around the corner. I quickly slide behind a sagging branch. Mike is just now pulling his old Beemer into the driveway, the door to the detached garage rising like a noisy drawbridge.

Mike's homecoming routine is the same every time. He strides across the breezeway from the garage to the house, checking the lock on the side door, some sort of fancy Schlage. From there, he strolls into the middle of the front yard.

His head swivels in every direction, soaking in the silent street, the porch lights that look like tiny diamonds to Mars and Venus.

A suburban Friday night. Reassuring. It shouldn't be.

The guilt about not telling Mike the truth eats at me all the time. But everybody was so *happy* back then. It became harder and harder to bring it up. He was alive. *I* was alive. From that moment on, everything was better.

Mike's family covered my medical expenses, including three surgeries on my foot. An "anonymous" donor paid off our house, a rental—which we would have surely been kicked out of before I finished middle school—and opened a college trust fund for my sister and me.

More than that, Mike's family made us feel like a normal family, when Brig and I were pretty sure we had different fathers and a made-up last name.

Every Christmas Eve was celebrated at Mike's family mansion on Elizabeth Boulevard, a live wreath with a red bow in every window, white lights twinkling on every tree instead of just the old colored string Brig and I hung in two big dips across the porch. Inside, at a hot chocolate bar, Mike snuck Kahlúa in our Santa-face cups. We ate leg of lamb with orange peel and mint. Watched *It's a Wonderful Life*.

At midnight, Mike's mother always asked my mom to read everyone's palm even though I know Mike was the only true convert. Even though I knew that his mother thought that Jesus was the one who put me in his path and believed Jesus rising from the dead wasn't supernatural at all.

My family became entirely less weird in a neighborhood that had judged us since the first stick of ugly furniture was carried in the door. A neighborhood that gossiped about the pink streak in my mother's hair; the thirteen silver rings on her fingers; the hand-lettered sign in our window that advertised psychic readings; me and Brig, a red-haired elf and a blond Rapunzel, so suspiciously smart we jumped a grade. Most of all, they wondered about why we had to bring our heebie-jeebies from the Blue Ridge Mountains to their normal street on a pretty iron-flat piece of Texas.

There were no royal babies being born, no Osama bin Ladens being buried at sea on the day we left the Blue Ridge Mountains. Just my mom, my sister, and me blinking at the local television cameras while the cops were still searching the basement and the walls of that little house cuddled up against a steep hill of pines. I've buried the memory deep like a bad therapist told me to, but Lizzie and all her hidey-holes are making it itch.

Almost straight-up twelve on my watch.

Twelve-oh-one. Twelve-oh-two.

Mike's inside now.

Through the glass, he sweeps my little nephew, Will, into his arms.

I watch my sister plant a kiss on his cheek.

VIVVY'S DIARY, AGE TEN

Brig was right. I looked up Marilyn Monroe and the Kennedys. Marilyn was the princess and the Kennedy brothers were the king and prince. The queen in the pink diamond crown was Jackie Kennedy in her pink pillbox hat.

The big bird landing on the sand was a helicopter. A movie actor named Peter Lawford helped Robert Kennedy escape in one from the beach behind his house on the same night Marilyn Monroe died. The neighbors reported that it got sand in their pools when it took off.

Except that's not the official story. The coroner says Marilyn Monroe killed herself in bed with fifty pills. There was an empty bottle next to her.

I think there's lots to be suspicious about. Robert Kennedy says he was never there, even though a witness saw him near her house. There was no glass of water in her room for her to swallow the pills.

I don't think she would kill herself naked. I wouldn't.

Also, the housekeeper didn't call the ambulance for an hour, and she stole the sheets and washed them right away.

Brig says Marilyn was just a sad person with a crazy mother and a bad childhood.

I don't know. I think Marilyn was murdered. I hope she doesn't visit me.

My mom has another visitor tonight. I can hear her crying all the way up here.

153 knocks.

6

A cloud has sifted over the moon by the time I slide the Jeep into the driveway of the one-story cottage where I grew up after we moved to Texas. Mike, alive. The joy of reprieve. The despair that I'm chasing a horse on a carousel that will leap off any second.

My mother's house is a brooding silhouette, a chunk of limestone forever altered by her death. It wants me to go. It knows I won't bring peace.

Brigid made it clear at the funeral that she is leaving the task of sorting through our mother's mayhem to me. *It's your turn.* The prodigal daughter. While I stared at stars and drew accolades, Brig stayed here and coped with my mother's growing, unbalanced tirades. Brig was the one called to the house by a neighbor in the middle of the night when Mom stood screaming in the street, dressed in a man's white T-shirt that hit her at the knees and nothing else. Brig was the one who dragged her to the neurosurgeon for a brain tumor diagnosis that defied my mother's intuition and mine but not Brig's common sense.

I think often how hard it was for Brig to grow up being the only normal person in our house, the one who didn't knock on walls or spread tarot cards for money on the dining room table, who believed in black and brown horses, not blue ones. She was both a pain in the ass and my single-minded protector, keeping me grounded, mentally stable, so I wouldn't lift off like a balloon and pop on the first branch.

I dangled dream catchers and pressed glow-in-the-dark stars to my bedroom ceiling, planted a fairy garden with a toothpick draw-bridge and a tiny round mirror lake, buried secret love poems to Mike under a moonstone crystal. Brigid hung a poster of the Venice canals and the Harry Potter castles of Cornell University and locked herself in her room, studying her way to valedictorian. And yet, look how it turned out.

I'm the scientist. The astronomer who already has a PhD at twenty-eight.

She's Mike's wife. The owner of a prelaw degree she never ignited.

Do we always have to sacrifice, regret one thing for another? Could Brig not be a saint without also being a martyr? Could I not chase a dream in space without also being the selfish one?

I may have saved Mike, but Brig saved me. Not one without the other.

I've drifted onto the lawn, where the spell of the past is acute. I stand at a tiny hole, invisible in the grass, a marker. Here is where I saved Mike. My mother poked a small plastic cross into that hole every day, and every night the cross was stolen, part of her karmic outreach.

I keep finding bags of those toothpick crosses jammed in drawers with toothbrushes and socks and batteries, ready for duty.

I broke a nail yesterday trying to scratch off a cloudy piece of cel-lophane tape in the living room window that the Texas sun had spent years ironing on. It marks the former spot of the poster board sign that Brig and I were instructed to make a week after we moved in.

Asteria the Psychic, Walk-ins Welcome.

"Print our phone number big enough that passing cars can read it," my mother, the newly branded Asteria, insisted. We knew then that Mom was unlocking all the doors for whatever angels and de-mons lived in her head.

Brig got out of bed at two a.m. one night and used a marker on the sign to turn one of the 3s in our phone number to an 8. That fooled Mom only until the phone stopped ringing. After that, it rang all the time, at any hour. Whatever the percentage success rate of my mom's predictions, her ability to provide hope for $50 an hour was off the charts.

I twist my key in the lock, pull the door as tight as I can, jiggle the key a few more times, ease the door back and forth until it opens. Neighbors bought expensive security systems; ours was a warped and difficult door, an ancient keyhole.

Every shadow inside is a lonely cat missing my mother. *Where is she?*

I want so much to fall into my old bed, stare at a ceiling pocked with the outlines of the glow stars that fell off years ago. Instead, I'm pulled to the room at the end of the hall. I haven't touched this doorknob since my mother was removed on a stretcher in a black body bag.

I shove open the door to see if she's there.

☽ ✧ ☾

Mom called it the waiting room.

My eyes play in the dark, where she and death hustled each other at checkers. A bed neatly made, dirty sheets disposed of, by a kind hospice worker. The sting of bleach. Empty walls, because at the end, Mom said it hurt her brain to stare at anything but a blank canvas.

The only sign of urgent life—the blinking red light of the answering machine on her bedside table. She returned calls to clients until two weeks before she died. I promised her I would do the same after she was gone, until it stopped blinking. She told me not to lie to her.

It's still hard to believe that not long ago, she was propped up in bed, a blue-and-gold scarf wrapped around her head. That scarf is still on her head in the grave, an image that keeps sneaking up on me. My mother refused chemo yet insisted on shaving her scalp.

She died three days after she predicted she would. In her last hour, she whispered that I would find a sign from her in the sky on my birthday.

I will watch for those signs every January fourth until I die. And three days after, on January seventh. Whenever I look into the sky, which is often. "Being off by a day, a month, a year doesn't mean we are *wrong*," my mother told me. "As long as it *happens*."

I've always been under my mother's unrelenting spell, in the gray area between intuition and insanity. Whatever was wrong with her brain is wrong with mine. I try but fail to bury myself in stars that are hydrogen and helium, not archers and bulls, passageways and premonitions.

Thirty messages, the voice mailbox at its limit. The psychic business has boomed since the psychological mayhem of Covid and Trump, with no signs of retreating. I punch the play button, breaking free a river of dread.

A woman panicked that her stillborn, unbaptized baby hasn't crossed over. Another terrified her plane will crash on the way to England, asking if she should take American Airlines Flight 1602 or British Airways 1210.

A young girl dreaming over and over that her little brother will fall down the stairs and break his neck, but her mother won't let her stack pillows on the bottom landing. An old man begging to know if his wife, who has dementia, is in a realm where she can see everything, including him sleeping with a neighbor she'd always hated. Lonely, worried people hoping for a scrap of light and love. Lots of regulars who can never find it.

I hit stop. Rewind. Lay the gun on the bedside table. Hang the holster over the back of a chair.

For almost an hour, I sit on the edge of the bed, a secretary scribbling down names and phone numbers, terror and worry.

I hit the last message, left at 4:06 p.m.

"This is Nickie Solomon trying to reach the daughter of Asteria Bouchet. Sorry for your loss." She butchers the snooty "French" and pronounces it *Boo-chette* like a typecast Texan, even though the case file Sharp gave me says she speaks three European languages.

"I got a letter from your mother today," she continues. "It's dated two months ago. The prison guards hold our mail as punishment. I need you to use your special powers to figure out what got blacked out by the censors, and by the censors I mean a guard named Brando." The words *special* and *the censors*, soaked in derision. "I'm tired of filing motions in this place. I'm *innocent* and not as in *not guilty*. As in *inn-o-cent*. Your mother and I had some business, so now you and I have some business. You're on my visitor list for Sunday afternoon. *Show. Up.*"

Nicolette Andrea Solomon, inmate at the Mountain View Unit in Gatesville where Texas stores its bad women. Big, smart doe eyes that a jury didn't believe. Owner of a Victorian mansion that once hosted a party attended by Louise Brooks and Charles Lindbergh. A husband named Marcus who tried to hang himself there like a chandelier.

What in the hell did my mother have to do with this?

At least this woman isn't playing a passive-aggressive game of manipulation like Mike and Sharp. She's full-bore aggressor. She's *ordering*.

The crescent scar in the crook of my thumb is beginning to ping.

It's usually the first of my nine scars to go active. Soon, they'll be in unison, one scar calling another.

One, two, three, four. Five, six, seven, eight. At nine, I can barely breathe.

My mother, whose birth certificate and headstone read Janet Bukowski, not Asteria Bouchet, told me this pinging was a sign of the gift. Every scar, an entry point for spirits. Brigid, named for the goddess of serenity, said it was the start of a panic attack. I think maybe it's both.

I lie back on the bedspread, careful not to touch the side my mother used. I jam my hand into my pocket, fingering the sharp silver teeth of Lizzie's hair clip.

I lie there in my mother's bed, weighted by invisible anchors. If I tried to lift my arm or a leg right now, I couldn't.

I expect Lizzie and her pink bow to burst through the door at any second.

But it's not Lizzie who comes, or my mother. A young woman is faceup beside me, blue eyes wide and unblinking, her head on my mother's pillow. She has slung her arm over and is jangling a bracelet in my face, the charms brushing my cheeks like tiny dull knives.

I open my own eyes and jerk up. The bed is empty. No girl. No pillow.

I had recognized several of the charms. A unicorn, a butterfly, a heart engraved with an *A*. The charms belong on the same bracelet I saw lying in the leaves in a photograph on the table at the police station, mixed up with the others. The picture that seemed to antagonize Sharp when I said it didn't belong.

The one I thought he included by mistake.

Except I don't think Jesse Sharp makes mistakes.

VIVVY'S DIARY, AGE TEN

Mom hired a man to put a fancy new lock on the basement door. I didn't like the way he looked at Brig. It's the way lots of men look at Brig. But this one knows where we live and how to get in.

202 knocks.

7

'm startled awake by three impatient question marks, a text flipped from my boss. She wants me back. She's likely sitting in her observatory office, under an aching desert sky, crossing off her to-do list. She's a bow-and-arrow kind of woman, generally direct, which works great unless she's unhappy. I roll into a sitting position, still in my mother's bed and wearing my stalking outfit from the night before.

I stare at an icicle slash of morning sun on the floor, struggling with how to respond. I understand my boss's frustration because I share it. Time is almost up on my hefty three-year grant—a mission to confirm tantalizing glimpses of sodium-based artificial light from an exoplanet that is light-years away. The glimmer I saw almost three years ago was so distant that, if it's truly from another civilization, it could be one that died before the light reached my eyes.

I have only twenty-eight days before my uplink/downlink/command codes to the satellite will expire. If I continue to find nothing, it will be harder to convince someone to pour more money into my search for a lightbulb in a universe awash in naturally occurring electromagnetic frequencies, a chaotic camouflage for what I'm seeking.

There will be only a few rare nights left to aim the telescope when the star and planet and satellite are aligned and the weather up there is cooperating, when I can experiment with the right combination of thirty-nine filters, mechanically moving over the lens of the satellite's telescope like a giant Viewfinder.

I text back and tell her I'll be there full-time, fully focused, in two weeks, when the planet and star of my obsession will be obediently back in position. In the meantime, I remind her, other scientists are using the satellite for their own passion projects.

I don't tell her that I'm torn about where I belong. That I'm teetering on the edge of the black hole on Earth that almost swallowed me as a child. Hallucinations and knocking. Voices and pleas. Mike, and this obsessive need to protect and please him. Things I'm better at shutting down in the desert.

There was only one reason I agreed to play amateur criminal psychic for Mike, something he had hinted at for years. I thought I might bump into the Blue Horse in one of his cases. It sounds as ridiculous as it is.

My mother would say that the Blue Horse in my dream could be out of sequence. The horse might have killed Mike in a previous life or might show up in his next one. Time, not linear.

If my mother gave me a grip on any truth, it's that we are limited in our perceptions. Even hard science says the universe itself does not behave as if we are all in one moment of *now*. Theoretical physics equations can work backward and forward, and how *is* that?

Humans on the political left and right can agree on little but that the sun rises and sets every day. Except it is the Earth, not the sun, that is moving.

As an astrophysicist, I feel oddly grounded when my eyes travel the sky. It's like walking down the beach of a giant deserted island trying to find a footprint, a discarded Coke can—something never intended to be a message, yet it is.

It's not as simple with lost girls who haunt me with their pink bows and unicorn charms. I'm swimming alone in an ocean, not even knowing where their island lies, hoping I don't drown.

☽ ✧ ☾

My boss doesn't respond.

A cold shower and four cups of coffee later, I have stuffed twelve trash bags. The dining room table is stacked with an assortment of crystal balls, Ouija boards with planchettes, glass jars of loose-leaf tea that smell like dead grass, charts of the moon cycles that my mother used to paste every month on the refrigerator like other mothers displayed their children's drawings of spoked suns.

I stretch a pendulum back. Let go. Brig and I used to play silly games with it. My mother used it to determine the future.

The candle closet in the corner now hangs open, perfuming the air, dozens of every color and size, unburned and half-burned. All of them, going out to the curb. I unsuccessfully tried to convince my mother that chemical fragrance from a candle is toxic, maybe as dangerous as secondhand smoke.

But my mother believed in ceromancy, the reading of melted and hardened candle wax. Gastromancy, the interpretation of stomach noises as voices of the dead.

There was, in fact, nothing my mother considered outside her realm of psychic expertise. In an old file cabinet, I had found an unsolicited astrological chart on Ted Cruz that says he will be in big trouble in 2032.

My phone chirps from the kitchen counter. I hope it's a response from my boss about my return date. Instead, it's my sister, who hasn't texted or called me since the funeral. My mother's passing clipped the fragile thread that held our constellation together.

I've worried all morning that she'd had her virgin psychic flash, and that it was watching Mike touch my face in a dark bar last night.

**Bubba Guns is streaming live on
YouTube. Watch NOW.**

I've never seen Brigid uppercase a word in a text, or mention Bubba Guns. I know who she's talking about. Unfortunately, anybody would. Bubba Guns has declared that chemicals in the water are turning catfish gay and that the government operates "weather weapons" to turn on earthquakes and tornadoes when the people get too rowdy or need distracting.

His podcast and *The Bubba Guns Show* on Sirius radio hang in the top ten. His Twitter feed is incendiary and busy. He operates on multiple platforms, streaming live at random when he's in a foul mood. I know all of this, and that his real name is Bob Smith, because the UT astronomy intern who sits in the office next to mine is obsessed enough to make weekly memes with Bubba Guns's pudgy face on an asteroid aimed at Earth.

It's because Bubba Guns has a thing for outer space that I listened to him once, for exactly one minute and thirty-two seconds.

I plug in my AirPods. Fiddle with my phone. See more of a snarl than a face. Hit unmute. His grating voice seeks out the corners of the room.

". . . Bouchet is not your garden-variety psychic, even though by all accounts her mother was. Bouchet has a doctorate in astronomy from Harvard and works at an observatory near Big Bend National Park. The rumor is, she's out there contacting aliens. Her boss hasn't returned my calls. Bouchet's own voice mail says she's 'on leave.' But the question is: Why have the Fort Worth police decided after all this time that she's the answer to the disappearance of Lizzie Solomon? And why are they keeping it a secret? It's JonBenét, Texas-style, folks. We'll get to more on the interesting past of Ms. Bouchet after a quick commercial break. In the meantime, let's get some chatter going. Tweet me @therealbubbaguns and hashtag this one #the gingerbreadgirl. You'll know why if you've ever driven by that Victorian monstrosity where little Lizzie is supposed to still be plastered in the walls. Back in three."

VIVVY'S DIARY, AGE TEN

I got a 105 today on a paper I wrote about the moon.

Mom read it but she didn't put it on the refrigerator like she usually does. She said that the moon could be a giant projection in the sky put up by China every night and that there's no proof astronauts landed there.

Brig told me not to worry, my paper was great, that Mom forgot to take her pills.

But I can tell Brig is worried. She's obsessed with the smell in the vent between our rooms. All I smell lately is vanilla and No Bite.

She made me swear not to tell Mom that she found the key to the new basement lock in her jewelry box. She is going to sneak down there to get a screwdriver so she can open the vent.

I knocked so many times tonight I didn't count.

Something bad is about to happen.

PART TWO

If you don't embrace the methods, tools, and discoveries of science, your next obvious step is to dispose of your cell phone.

—Astrophysicist Neil deGrasse Tyson

I'm telling you folks—nerds are one of the most dangerous groups in the country because they end up running things. But they still hate everybody because they weren't the jocks in high school. So they play dirty little games on everybody. They use their brains to hurt people.

—Texas conspiracy theorist Alex Jones

8

Will Bubba Guns tell the truth about me? One of his out-rageous lies? Which would be better?

He's off on a wild ramble: Elizabeth Smart, stolen from her bed; JonBenét Ramsey, found in her basement; Lizzie Borden's house, now a bed-and-breakfast. He hasn't yet circled back to Lizzie Solomon, plastered in the wall.

A story that could be told in five minutes is going to stretch to take thirty or forty, like on a thousand other shows and at every wedding where you are seated next to a stranger.

He's leading into the commercial break with a tease. *In sixty seconds*, he says, *I'll tell you the dark secrets of Vivvy Bouchet, so-called astrophysicist and psychic child hunter.*

I'm numb, no longer watching, just turning myself over to the sound. Phone in hand, I stumble my way to a chair in the living room, shoving a stack of my mother's bills off the seat.

A woman with a sexy throttle is advertising a special self-defense weapon, a gun built "*by* a woman *for* a woman, to accommodate the delicate bone structure of the female hand."

If I'm one of the first fifty to register on the gun seller's site, I receive a free box of bullets. If one is spray-painted gold, I will be the lucky winner of a guest spot on *The Bubba Guns Show*.

"We're back." I physically jump, not ready for his abrasive purr.

"Vivvy Bouchet. I love letting that name roll off my tongue. It's like a Friday night sip of Garrison Brothers whiskey, and I'm not getting paid for saying that. Well, maybe I am. But I'm damn proud that Garrison Brothers is made right here in Texas, land of fact and freedom. Now let's get to some fact about Vivvy Bouchet."

In his mouth, *fact* sounds like a dirty word.

Except, right now, fact is what Bubba Guns is providing.

I *did* save the life of the cop now involved in Lizzie's case. My sister *did* marry him. I *did* turn down a job at NASA to work in the desert, even though I still do one-offs for them. My mother's name *was* in *People* magazine once upon a time. She *was* arrested at least twelve times for fraud and never charged because, as Bubba Guns joked, "I guess it's hard to convict a fortune-teller when it turns out true love is not around the corner."

Bubba Guns is a hypnotic charmer, tying snake tail to snake tail. Like Rachel Maddow if Rachel Maddow were on mushrooms. He's only there to sell bullets, but nobody cares.

When Bubba Guns finally clears his throat with serious intention, it's like he's doing it in my stomach. I know in that second, I haven't escaped. I know what his regular fans already do—that he's not a big tease with no payoff. There's a tweet and a TikTok and a meme and a Facebook post on the way, and hundreds of thousands of hands itch to get to it.

"My producer has got her hurry-up finger going like a lasso," Bubba Guns is saying. "She wants me to get to the point, the one that y'all have been waiting for. I don't know if this was one of Vivvy Bouchet's psychic deals or not. But when she was a kid, she found something all right."

☽ ✧ ☾

I'm ten years old. Blue Ridge Mountains. Sitting perfectly still in the dark on the fourth basement step from the top, Brig's thigh pressed against mine.

Two books on a shelf.

Scared. Afraid to move. Eavesdropping.

Behind us, the door to the kitchen is cracked an inch because I silently begged Brig not to close it all the way. She wouldn't even let me turn on the kitchen light. She found the keyhole by touch. A chill has run up the basement staircase, tickling its way under the hem of my thin nightgown.

The tiniest glow has crawled up the dark stairs with it. It allows me to make out the blue ducks with yellow bills on my fuzzy sleep socks.

Brig's feet are bare, the pink polish on her toes chipped like she stepped out in a hailstorm. There is no polish at all on her left pinky toe. Three toes over from that, a tight silver toe ring, and underneath that, a red blister that will be infected in two days. I will stare at the Band-Aid, her chipped pink toenail polish, and yellow polka-dot flip-flops from the view of my airplane seat when we decide to run.

Brig is gripping my hand harder. The air is thick with mold and microscopic flecks of coal that float around down here like a fine black salt. I always brushed off a sandy layer of it when I opened Mom's book of dead people.

Brig brings me abruptly back by clamping her wet lips on my ear. She whispers for me to breathe through my nose. When she pulls away, she leaves cold spit in my ear, tickling a nasty shiver. I give her a sideways shove, but I do what she says. It makes my breathing quieter, and my heart drum harder. I wish, *wish* Brig had not dragged me out of bed to listen.

Brig is wedged so tight against me that the metal tip of the screwdriver in her pocket is digging into my side. She'd found it under the bottom step in a toolbox left by Mr. Dooley, our landlord. In Brig's other pocket is the key to the basement.

The bottoms of Brig's feet and my socks are coated in black. So is the back of my nightgown and the seat of Brig's sweatpants. Later, when we scrub them in the bathroom sink so Mom won't know, Brig will say Basement Black should be a paint chip color.

I need to pee.

Voices are floating up the stairs. My mother. Someone else. A woman. The wall in the stairwell doesn't open up until four steps past our feet. They can't see us. We can't see them.

My mother's tone is soft. Soothing. Like when I came home crying last week. I'd warned a teacher that she was going to have an accident, and just like I predicted, she rear-ended the deputy principal's truck. She insinuated I might have fiddled with her brakes.

"Your son liked the color blue, didn't he?" my mother is asking.

"It was the color of Layton's favorite baseball team in fifth grade. The Eagles. They won every game." The woman's voice is thin and shaky.

"Layton wants you to think of the color blue when you're missing him. Look up at the sky. Go to the lake. If you see an eagle, Layton says to know it is him. That he can't come often, but that he *will* come."

"Oh my God, I saw an eagle a few weeks ago. Out on Gatlinburg Trail."

"Layton says you came to ask me a specific question."

A silence stretches. I'm afraid they've heard me breathing.

"They didn't find his truck in that gorge for a couple of days." The woman, finally. Her voice has new steel in it. "I want to know if the morgue was lying to me out of kindness when they said he died right away. If he had a lot of pain. I keep dreaming that he called out for me."

"He died immediately." My mother's answer is absolute. "He hit the first tree, and even before he rolled, it was straight to heaven."

This isn't true. I can hear him moaning through the trees.

The woman's sobs explode with relief. I feel her guilt whooshing by us, swirling up, out the basement door crack, through the open kitchen window, up to the eagles and past the clouds.

There's the squeak of a chair being pushed back. Brig is gripping my arm, tugging at me to go. I know Mom is holding her, the woman I can't see.

This lie might have been the moment I loved my mother the most.

Brig is yanking me up. She's pulling me through the kitchen door while I stumble on a thousand needles, my foot asleep.

"Mom's working another scam." Brig, angry. She's already tugging me down the hall. "Social Services is going to come and take us away."

I know that Brig wants me to be horrified that Mom is using the basement to hide a little psychic business. But when Brig shook me awake, I thought we were going to find a whole lot worse. What, I don't know. But worse.

Something is wrong with this house. Those are the words, from Mom's own lips the other night, that have been keeping me awake. And now Brig's bomb: *Social Services is going to come and take us away.*

Brig insists we strip and wash out everything in the bathroom, then hang it all in her closet. Back in my room, she fakes like she's tucking me in. She's really trying to rub flat every wrinkle in the sheet, a compulsive game that the sheet wins every time. For each one she flattens out, three more pop up. Her sheet-smoothing is my wall knocking.

"Mom helped that lady feel better," I say quietly.

"Come on. 'The color blue'? The whole Earth is *blue.*"

I watch her bite pink polish off a thumbnail like a chipmunk.

"Only seventy-one percent," I say, unable to help myself.

"What?"

"Only seventy-one percent of Earth is water. And the ocean— and the sky—aren't blue at all. They just appear blue because the air and water disrupt the yellow and red light frequencies. What we're actually seeing is the sun's blue light."

"I don't know who drives me crazier." Her voice is quiet fury.

"We don't know that Mom is . . . taking money," I protest. "Then it really wouldn't be illegal."

"Viv. Come *on.*"

A wet drop splashes on my arm. I want Brig to be too tough to cry.

"Maybe nobody knows these people come here," I suggest

practically. "Maybe they want to keep it secret between Mom and their dead person." I reach up in the dark to hug her, a rare thing lately.

"It takes one unhappy person to send Mom to jail," she says, prying my hands off her neck. "And then where are we again?"

Outside, the woman's car in the driveway chugs to life. Two headlights streak across my wall, briefly flashing on Brig's face, mascara streaked like her tears came out black.

I'm desperate to help Brig feel better, to tell her that Mom was being kind.

But Brig would just ask how *I* knew that the woman's son lived for a long time after his truck bounced off pine trees and slammed into the forest floor.

Long enough for Layton to be sorry about the fight he had with his mother before he left the house. Long enough to call out for her.

Long enough.

"Tomorrow, we're going to find out what's in the vent stinking up our rooms," Brig tells me abruptly. "I don't care if I have to rip out the wall."

☽ ✧ ☾

Predawn. This is Brig's show. I feel numb, and sleepy. We are lying flat on our stomachs staring at the vent. I'd retrieved olive oil from the kitchen and Brig is busy wiping it on the screws because they weren't budging.

I'm holding the flashlight with one hand and pinching my nose with the other. The vent is emitting its sick, sweet odor. The carpet smells like the bacteria of every renter before us.

It's the cheapest our landlord could install, a quarter-inch thick and rough as rope. The skin on my bony elbows is already crisscrossed with white scratches from their contact with the floor. I've skinned my knee bloody twice on this carpet and not once on the driveway.

It's 6:14 by the clock on Brig's bedside table. I managed three hours of sleep after our trip to the basement. I have only two hours before the parent-student conference with Mrs. Allen, the science teacher who called Mom to complain about the brakes. This meeting seems much more important than the vent.

I'm torn whether to tell Mrs. Allen that it was her husband who messed with her car. She's a bad teacher who goes strictly by a thirteen-year-old science textbook. If she ever stared up into the sky, it was only to look for rain or the Rapture. But I don't want her to die.

"Why can't we do this tonight?" I whine as Brig inserts the screwdriver again. "I heard Mom say to spray air freshener in there."

"Don't you think I tried that? She says old houses smell, the vent is rusted in place, and I'll crack the plaster taking it off. She said to sleep on the screened-in porch if it bothered me so much." Brig's voice sounds frayed and higher the more she speaks, like a singer with laryngitis who can't make it up the scale. "She didn't want me to leave any property damage. She said . . . we might not be in this house long. Like always." The last part, almost a whisper.

I can't think about this right now—moving again, or why. "Her alarm goes off in fifteen minutes," I remind Brig.

"The screws are moving."

"Vivvy to the rescue," I say, snapping the cap on the olive oil.

Brig tugs the vent. It pops out of the wall in a cloud of dirt and plaster. I see a few roaches belly-up. I can make out the glow of my blue star night-light through the slats.

Brig has rotated her face so it's inches from mine. I know that look by heart. *Stick your little hand up the vending machine. Untangle my necklace with your tiny fingers. Reach your chicken bone arm behind the couch for the pen I just dropped.*

"I'm not feeling around in there," I say firmly.

"Your hand is so much smaller. You've got no nails."

"Not. Doing. It."

"You're such a baby. Give me the flashlight." She grabs a

basketball sock off the floor and slips it on her hand like a puppet. She darts the flashlight into the wall.

"I see something." She reaches in past her wrist. Past her elbow.

There's not a single instinct telling me what's in there. Brig's mouth collapses like she just got shot. When she yanks out her arm, she holds tissue and bones. It's barely recognizable as a rat.

Brig is bent over, gagging.

She's battled a rat phobia ever since she went nose to nose with one in her bed at our last rental. Mom had reminded Brig that she was born at midnight, during the Hour of the Rat in Chinese astrology. That it was a lucky meeting.

I pick up the carcass with the nearest piece of Brig's clothing and race to the kitchen, dropping all of it in the trash can on top of last night's spaghetti scraps.

I think, as things go, a rat isn't so bad. But when I glance down to close the bag, I realize I'd used Brig's favorite T-shirt. It's now bleeding with rat guts and mushroom-laced pasta sauce, one barely distinguishable from the other. I hesitate for just a second before I finish tying the knot on the bag and sling it out the back door as far as I can.

I'm desperate to wash my hands, but Mom is already flushing the toilet down the hall.

I tiptoe back to warn Brig—to make sure she has recovered enough to put everything back the way it was, or if she can at least throw a towel over the opening. I wonder how she will get back at me for using her T-shirt, if it will be a little hot sauce in my milky-pink Froot Loops or toothpaste in my Oreos or red food coloring on my toothbrush or glue in my shampoo bottle.

The vent is still gaping open. Brig had gone into the hole again and pulled out something else.

Her hand is deep into a small, dirty red purse with a fake ruby on the clasp. She's turning the fabric lining inside out to make sure she's got everything.

On the floor is a tarnished lipstick tube, a ten-dollar bill, a chewed-up candy bar wrapper, a small pile of change, a set of house keys, and a driver's license.

I wonder why I didn't feel this in advance, what I'm feeling right now.

I don't have to read the driver's license to know that Brigid has found what is wrong with this house.

9

_____

see a clear snapshot of Brig, me, and Mom. We're standing on the front lawn of that ugly rental house, staring in disbelief, like a family watching its home burn to the ground.

Except there weren't hoses and firefighters. There were troopers and yellow tape.

The cheap red satin evening bag that Brig dug out of the wall belonged to a woman named Lisa Marie, in honor of Lisa Marie Presley. Her own last name was spelled P-r-e-s-s-l-y on the driver's license, a name she'd kept against all holy tradition when she got married, because she thought it was the one thing that made her special.

Several years earlier, the night she disappeared, Lisa Marie had been officially divorced for a month. She ran out of the Christ Has Mercy Church dance after watching her ex-husband snake his hand down the back of the barely legal youth director during a slow dance.

The town's money had been on her having jumped drunk off a mountaintop close to the scenic overlook where her old station wagon was found, and her body wasn't.

Brig's money was on Mr. Dooley because she'd caught him peeking in the bathroom window at her on one of his weekly lawn-mowing visits.

My mind had hummed along, unusually blank, no thoughts what-soever, like there was not a bone in my body or a voice in my head that could predict things.

We took the purse to Mom immediately, and she called one of her former morgue friends.

Mom told us that the four crusty black stains fit the pattern of fin-gerprints she'd photographed on clothes at crime scenes—bloody ones.

Within hours, two state troopers and a couple of bar buddies of theirs were slamming pickaxes into the crack in the basement floor because Mom told them she had a "feeling" about it.

Every bird dog and German shepherd in a mile radius was put to work in the backyard. It wasn't by the book, and it was a lot of conclusions jumped to at once, but it was efficient.

There wasn't a thing under the basement crack. The four men hit what had to be virgin, dawn-of-time dirt before giving up.

A border collie named Bertie found Lisa Marie right at twilight. She was buried under the pretty pink mountain laurel in the far corner of the backyard, the one Mom told us to avoid because every bit of it was poison to touch or eat—so aggressive that its flower stamens popped up and slapped bees when they landed.

Mom always seemed fully aware of what could hurt or kill us.

That turned out *not* to be Mr. Dooley, who successfully pointed his finger right away at the renter two renters before us, an itinerant coal miner who owed him more than a thousand dollars and was locked up three counties over for a rape.

We didn't know that then, while we stood on the lawn watching a black body bag slip into the back of a hearse and our future turn south.

But Bubba Guns knows a lot about it now, in the present. He's spitting his final fury into my mother's living room.

"It's a little creepy, isn't it? I mean, a psychic who found a body in a wall as a child is being called in to work on a crime *where there could be a child in a wall?*"

The first outright lie.

Lisa Marie was not found in a wall. I had nothing to do with solving her case. The case wouldn't *exist* if not for a dead rat and my sister's un-psychic diligence. Lisa Marie would still be food for a greedy, poisonous tree.

"Is Vivvy Bouchet truly clairvoyant or did she just build her reputation out of a horror show from her childhood?" he continues. "Is she damaged? A pretend scientist who believes more in voodoo? A rip-off artist in it for the attention? And isn't the body-in-the-wall thing too, I don't know—convenient?"

I furiously rip the AirPods out of my ears.

Damaged. Pretend scientist. Rip-off artist. This suddenly doesn't feel like the work of a lunatic podcaster running low on material about Joe Biden's weather weapons or Bill Gates's eugenics plot or Prince Charles's life as a vampire. It feels orchestrated. Personal. Like there's purpose and commitment to breaking a chunk of ice off the high-profile Lizzie Solomon case and using me as the hatchet.

His rapid-fire paranoia feeds mine. Is Bubba Guns coordinating with the police? The mayor? Jesse Sharp? *Mike?*

I have a career at stake. Secrets I'd like to keep to myself to maintain the career I've worked so hard to create. Science is fickle about who it loves. The loudest, most determined voice is the one that is believed, that attracts the money, even in the heady world of research and PhDs. I still don't read published papers without the initial assumption that there could either be bias or data twisted to suit a theory. Guilty until proven brilliant. Because someone always has a stake.

I try to tell myself that much of what Bubba Guns is hyping could be dug out of the archives of *People* magazine or Virginia newspapers or the memories of the nosy people in our neighborhood who gossiped about us after we moved in like refugees from a carnival show.

It doesn't really matter. What matters is that most people had *forgotten*. And that he is threading in lies.

Three-fourths of the houses on the block in Fort Worth where I grew up had turned over in the last eighteen years. The handmade sign in our living room window long gone, unnecessary as Mom's clientele quietly grew.

I was no longer pointed out as the strange little girl with red hair and big glasses who saved a wealthy Fort Worth family's kid from a swerving car, or as one of the daughters of a fortune-teller who'd solved a murder back in Virginia, or as anything but a woman who likes to be left alone in the desert, studying alien moons shaped like potatoes.

And my colleagues—as far as I knew—they'd never had a clue about my past. Not until Bubba Guns decided to dissect me on the air without anesthesia, one more body in his cadaver lab where he leaves people flayed raw who will never be sewn back up.

It's a self-defeating thought. And isn't it the opposite of what I tell the budding middle school scientists who visit the observatory? Don't I tell them to never let the bully win? To fight when they're picked on? To be their brilliant odd little selves? To repudiate the world of social media?

That all is not lost? That we have two billion years to turn around a celebrity-driven, warmongering, big-foot culture before the sun inevitably burns the Earth into a piece of charcoal?

To be skeptical of everything but the kind of science that has knocked out plagues, flown helicopters on Mars, allowed them to stream soccer games from across the ocean and text their grandma in Italy?

I reluctantly wriggle an AirPod back in my ear, as if just one will somehow make this more tolerable. Bubba Guns's voice is dipping to saccharine levels of sentimentality.

". . . Lisa Marie Pressly's tombstone in the Blue Ridge Mountains is etched with the words: *No sadness No sorrow No trouble*. Her parents picked out those words, lyrics from an old Elvis gospel tune, 'Peace in the Valley.' I'm gonna give it a try right here on the air. I ask that wherever you are right now, even if I get a little pitchy, keep your head bowed for every missing son and daughter on this Earth."

His rich bass rolls like liquid coal. It's a very decent voice. Deep.

Able to travel to tender places. Not pitchy at all. It would more than ground a small-town church choir.

An echo pulses, as if it's a chorus of Bubba Guns, like every house in the neighborhood has turned up their speakers. Like my colleagues at the observatory are booming it into interstellar space to see if aliens like it better than what we're spinning out there right now—Chuck Berry rocking "Johnny B. Goode."

Bubba Guns's ability to spout hate and then cozy up to the Lord is insidious. It's well known that Bubba Guns has declared Sandy Hook a fraud, recommended the death penalty for women who have abortions, read the names of men who died of AIDS while playing Queen's "Another One Bites the Dust"—and then prayed.

I can't do it. I can't stand another second of it. I hit mute. Except I'm still hearing Bubba Guns croon, every word, even though I don't know the words. I power down my phone. He's *still singing*.

An auditory hallucination? My mother was best friends with those. I walk into the living room. The song is louder here, floating through the gap at the bottom of a living room window that will never close all the way.

I fling open the front door.

Black boots, a little red cemetery dirt on the right toe. Glock holstered like a body part. An expression that Jesse Sharp must save for me.

He has thrust out his phone so I can see Bubba Guns on the screen holding a finger gun to his temple—the still for his podcast, his Sirius show, his latest bestseller, and an electronic billboard that hovers over every Dallas Cowboys game.

There's no longer video. This image is the one that he and his producer want as ingrained as the American flag. He continues to wail his very best Elvis from the phone speaker. I think I see his thin lips moving, even though I know that's impossible. It's his *picture*. He's crooning about the Lord calling him home. He's intoning about gentle bears, tame lions, night as black as the sea.

About peace in the valley.

Jesse's face on my front porch, black as the sea.

10

It isn't a good time right now.

My mother's words to most people who showed up at our door unannounced—a moonstruck teenage couple hoping for a quick reading, young men in cheap ties ready to monkey-climb our roof and spot hail damage, cops relaying a neighbor's complaint about my mother attracting vagrants.

Sometimes she sent me to say it.

That line doesn't work on Jesse Sharp, not today, probably never. He shuts off Bubba Guns with a finger and shoves past me. I smell a whiff of last night's tequila. More sex. It intrigues me, all this sex he's having.

Sharp takes several seconds off from being angry to observe the manic state of my packing up the house—the storm of bubble wrap, tissue paper, boxes, and plastic containers that create an obstacle course across the long rectangle that makes up both the living and dining rooms. A hippie-style orange bead curtain that used to divide the space is piled in the corner. I was sick of getting tangled in it, of it tickling me like my mother's hand in the middle of the night.

His eyes travel over a living room that hasn't changed since I was twelve—a TV set in front of the window that blocks the sun and prying eyes; two blue velvet armchairs from an estate sale; a print of the

Magritte with a train chugging out of a fireplace; a battered, sunken green couch whose comfort will never be matched.

The other half of the rectangle was always in constant metamorphosis—one minute, a place to do homework or eat Thanksgiving dinner on flowered china; the next, a dark psychic den. My mother had reimagined her business from the chilly, atmospheric basement in the Blue Ridge Mountains to a dining room in a Texas neighborhood where the sun fell like fire on the roof. Hell could easily enter either one.

My mother had the transformation of this space down to a science—yanking blackout curtains across the dining room's bay window, opening the armoire to showcase its array of vials, firing up candles, slinging a red scarf with a gold moon over the table, arranging a crystal ball in the center like it was a Ming vase. *People expect it.*

Now Sharp's eyes are traveling *me*. Black sports bra, black yoga pants, black Asics, last night's black mascara bruised under my eyes. *Sexual*, I think. Maybe an unsanctioned tactic to make me feel vulnerable. It's working.

"My ninja look," I say coolly. "What are you doing here?"

Sharp's presence is consuming the room like back at the police station, replacing Bubba Guns, who is still blessedly silenced. Only it's *my* room. I understand the law of physics that prevents me from leveraging Sharp's body out the door. I don't understand the law that he thinks allows him to be standing here.

Better if he's sitting. If *I'm* sitting. I gesture to the blue velvet seat in the living room clear of debris and prop myself on the arm of the couch, slightly higher. I'm happy to see his long legs have nowhere easy to go. He finally stretches all the way out, boots crossed under the coffee table.

"So, Bad Red." A sharp undertone. "How long have you known Bubba Guns?"

"How can you think I had anything to do with his insanity?" I work to keep a tremor out of my voice. "My career is on the line. Astrophysics is a tight bunch with an exclusive hierarchy. It's like years of being fiftieth in line to the throne *if* you behave yourself. My colleagues believe aliens exist because no intelligent ego could rule that out; they do not believe that aliens make regular trips to the UK to scribble crop circles. They believe in algorithms that will predict you are going to buy a pistachio KitchenAid mixer this week; they do not believe some short-story writer in 1898 predicted the sinking of the *Titanic*. My boss has a sticker on her door that says: *Science—like magic, but real.* You *understand*, right? *I cannot be magic.*"

"Quite a speech. Take a breath. Your skin is very . . . white right now. Look, I'd like to think you weren't seeking attention, but I can't quite get there. You had to know this whole situation could leak at a police station. It would only take one frustrated desk cop who thinks all the glory should go to him and God, one who could use a little extra cash."

"You were just insinuating it was me," I spit out.

"Keeping my options open."

"Maybe stop knocking God and take a closer look at your stone-cold atheists. Most of my mother's clients believed in God."

"And the rest?"

"The rest hoped she could prove to them God exists."

He's staring intently. I have the oddest feeling he wants to lick his finger and wipe away the mascara under my eyes. Instead, he leans farther back, threads his fingers in a steeple. "Ten minutes into this Bubba Guns 'exposé' on Lizzie Solomon, we had reports of someone climbing the fence in Fairmount at the house where she went missing. That mansion was already a fire hazard, a magnet for bored teenagers, now it's going to be overrun again by curiosity seekers. And no damn alarm system. People are going to chip at the house all over again like it's the Berlin Wall. We'll have to station a car there. Set up yet another tip line. Our social media team will be chasing thousands of dead ends on Twitter."

"Wait," I interject. "I read online that house sold to a developer who wanted to knock it down."

"A historic preservation group stepped in. There have been plenty of offers. Lizzie Solomon's father is refusing to sell or live in it. He pulled off favors from a city councilman and a court judge to leave it empty indefinitely. I doubt any of them really believe Lizzie might reappear in the kitchen someday, but they are humoring him."

He's gripping the arms of the chair, the muscles in his forearms pulsing. "Are you getting the big picture here? In the last fifty minutes, my job just got fifty times harder."

"I'm glad we've established that this is about you."

"It's about *you*, honey. *You* are the reason I'm here. *You're* the reason finding Lizzie is going to be just a little more impossible than it already was."

I push myself off the couch arm and head back to the front door, where I'd dropped my backpack. I'm trying to contain my fury about the razor edge of his judgment and the slick syrup of *honey*. I rifle through the pockets of the backpack a little longer than I need to, finally pulling out Lizzie's case file.

I cross over to the chair, holding it out to him. "Done. *Out*. Go."

Yet again, he doesn't take it. I slap his shoulder with the file. Nothing. I drop it on his lap, papers spilling out across his legs. He sweeps them onto the floor in one movement.

"I want a baseline to better handle the media." It sounds like an order. "Not about Lizzie Solomon. About Vivvy Bouchet. Let's start with what you had to do with a murdered woman in the Blue Ridge Mountains."

"Will it get rid of you?"

He doesn't answer. I weigh this, letting the silence grow a little uneasy. This could be good for me. I want my response to Bubba Guns's lies documented. I pull the phone out of my pocket and hit record. Prop myself back on the couch.

"That won't hold up in court," he says easily.

"It might hold up with your boss, whoever that is." I glance at my favorite possession, the wristwatch set to alert me to planet rise times and International Space Station flyovers.

"You get fifteen minutes," I say. "There was nothing psychic about finding that poor woman, if that's what you're asking. My sister pulled her purse out of the vent between our rooms in the rental house where we were living. But—and it's a *big* but—Mom told the police and reporters she discovered the purse herself through her clairvoyant powers. She explained to us privately that she lied to distract attention from us, but it was really because she thought it would add a little cachet to the fortune-teller biz she was starting up in the creepy basement of the rental house. That's why she told the cops to dig there first. She fessed up to that too, but only to us, and much later."

"And yet?" he prods.

"And yet, it didn't matter. Within twenty-four hours our lives were screwed. Everyone in town, every reporter from *out* of town, figured out the FBI had temporarily stashed us in Room 24C of the local motel while our house was being excavated as a crime scene. *C* stood for *courtyard*, by the way, which meant we had a back window overlooking an alley with weeds sticking out of the cracks, and two lawn chairs. One of those lawn chairs usually held a long-term motel guest *smoking* weed. We ended up sneaking out that way. He was nice. The man smoking weed. Might have saved our lives." I pause to take a breath. "I need a drink. Watch where you step."

I'm up so quickly he has no choice but to follow me to the kitchen. He drags out one of the cheap spindle-back chairs kissing up to the table. It squeaks dangerously when his weight lands.

Two hundred pounds? Two twenty? Are his lovers tiny and squishable or fully up to the challenge? I reach into the pantry for the whiskey bottle hiding behind the olive oil and red wine vinegar. From the cabinet over the sink, I pull out two small, shot-sized jelly glasses with faded cartoon prints.

"It's twelve twenty-two," he points out, "p.m."

"Thanks for helping keep track of our short time together."

"I'm talking about the whiskey."

"Bubba Guns would approve, no?"

I set a glass in front of him, pouring up to the zigzag line on Charlie Brown's shirt. I fill my own glass closer to the rim.

"Looks like apple juice to me." I hold up the whiskey in salute. "Here's to Lizzie. And Lisa Marie." I take a deep swig. I hate whiskey, but I love the way it makes me feel. The figure etched on the side of my glass has been worn to red and blue fragments, the shape unrecognizable. Too many runs through the dishwasher. Too many sisters fighting over who got to drink out of Wonder Woman's superpowers.

Charlie Brown remains on the table, untouched. Sharp's eyes are focused only on mine, uncomfortably so.

"You were at the motel," he reminds me.

"News vans," I say tightly. "Reporters at the vending machine buying me Snickers bars. Lots of cars. Party atmosphere. Occasional shots being fired in the air. Around midnight, things seemed to have settled down. We were all tucked in. I remember putting the pillow over my head to shut out the squeals and heavy breathing from the room next to ours. I didn't hear at first when one of Mom's clients came banging on the door. She was a widow who had visited Mom earlier, in our basement, to apologize to her dead husband. She'd had a secret affair with his brother while he was still alive and wanted to be sure ahead of time all would be kosher when they reunited at the pearly gates. At the motel, she'd threatened to sue Mom for running a psychic business with a corpse in the backyard and causing so much mental anguish it brought her cancer back. The cops finally took her away."

"That's a lot of detail for a little girl to remember," Sharp says.

"I wouldn't interrupt. Clock's ticking." I tap my watch. "In the morning, Mom was heading to the lobby to get her free cup of coffee. She almost stepped on a dead squirrel dropped on our motel room doorstep, one shot to his little head. There was a note pinned to his chest with a dart. My mother told us many, many things she shouldn't have told little girls. But she would never reveal what was written in that note, so that tells you how terrible it was. I had to learn in *People* magazine that the squirrel was a present from some Appalachian gang. Lisa Marie's killer had hanged himself in his jail cell. He was the gang's primary heroin source. They were pissed off that we had

any part of ratting him out. They shot our landlord's cat for his part."
I let another sip of whiskey burn down my throat. "I'm almost finished. With the whiskey. And this little interview."

Sharp nods, shifting awkwardly, one of the chair legs wobbling
like an old man. I wonder if he lives in a house filled with giant furniture, if his girlfriend is swallowed by his bed, the comforter wrapping
her like a down burrito. I almost ask it out loud. But I stay on track.

"We stayed in the motel room all day. Cops delivered us heat-lamp
pizza and powdered sugar donuts from the gas station. That night,
a man with a baseball cap brought Mom a Nike duffel filled with
cash. She told us it was escape money from the FBI, that we were
going into the kind of witness protection where we didn't have to
change our names, as if such a thing even exists. But Brig said that
she'd overheard Mom call one of her old lovers, the owner of a car
dealership. She threatened to expose him to his wife if he didn't get
us out of there. *That's* the story I believe."

Sharp leans forward, acting as if he's intrigued beyond a sense
of duty.

"The local paper ran a front-page piece." This part, not something I expected to say. Pure emotion is driving me now. "It said . . .
that my mother was fired from her morgue job for trying to raise a
body from the dead at a crime scene. In the same story, my sister was
described as 'unnaturally beautiful' and I was 'an unsettling child.' The
town was ready to throw all of us in the lake to see if we'd float like
witches. Maybe now you can understand why I would never partner
with Bubba Guns. Why I would never want to go through that again."

I had nightmares about being dragged from my motel bed and
tossed in Midnight Hole Falls, even though it was three hours away.
The top of my head bobbing in black water, the waterfall a dull roar
in my ears. People cheering on the shore as I sank to the bottom, like
they do outside courthouses when a death penalty verdict is read.
One of the first things I asked for when we moved to Texas, even
before a telescope, was swim lessons. If I needed to, I wanted to be
able to swim for two hours to save myself.

Right now, I need to take a breath. Shut up entirely. It strikes me that his sledgehammer works pretty well on me. He's getting exactly what he wants. I reach over for his glass, a hint for him to go, planning to dump his whiskey in the sink.

His hand grips mine before I can pull the glass away. Pain shoots up my palm, in the crease of my Life Line. I see the flash of water again, like when we touched at the police station—and this enormous hand, *his* hand, reaching toward hair spread like frantic snakes in the water. An image slams into that one—the almost charmless charm bracelet, lying in dirt, leaves, and berries in that photograph at the police station. I smell the pungent recipe of earth and pine.

"Brigid Bouchet, so beautiful, it's like a fairy mated in the afterlife with John Kennedy Junior." Sharp, interrupting my trance. "I always liked that line."

His words are a slow burn up my chest. Not because of the whiskey. He'd just repeated a reporter's description of my sister from a UK tabloid, circa 2005.

"You knew all of this," I say angrily.

"How could I know all of it? Like I said, I'm getting your baseline. Consider it a polygraph."

Sharp loosens his grip. I snatch my hand out from under his.

He tosses back the whiskey, then sets the glass so softly on the table I know my recording won't pick it up. *Like he's not a rule bender. Like it was never swallowed.*

"Is this your way of insulting me?" He's grinning. "Giving me the Charlie Brown glass?"

I'm standing, thinking I don't care about the laws of physics anymore. I have the strong urge to land a punch.

I step closer, fingers curling. "Charlie Brown was a good guy," I say. "A lovable loser. I think of you more as a hate-able winner."

"Well, which team would you rather be on? Huh, Bad Red? The winner's or the loser's?"

I can tell by his expression that he's seen my fist. He's up and moving, already unlatching the screen door that leads to the two ruts of the alley driveway. He's not at all interested today in twisting my arm behind my back.

"Meet me at the Solomon house at ten thirty tonight," he says. "I'll text the address. I'd like to get . . . your take."

It slides out of his mouth like an invitation to dinner. Like my fist isn't still curled in a ball. Like it isn't strange of him to choose a night tour of an old crime scene over one in broad daylight.

I shake my head slowly.

"You'll be there," he says, so sure of himself. "We both know this isn't about me. Or you. It's about finding Lizzie."

11

'm right where Sharp said I'd be tonight, an hour and a half early.

I test my foot on the first metal rung that runs along the decrepit back fence of the Solomon house, getting just a little sway. I don't weigh that much. Even in the dark, this will be an easy climb.

No alarm, Sharp had said. No lights, either, except for a dim streetlamp and the glimmer behind the curtains of a second-story window next door.

An oak spread like a circus tent is doing an excellent job of hiding me. I'd passed two street signs declaring that a neighborhood watch program protected this block seven days a week.

I'm less worried about that, or the cops out front, than being observed by a neighbor or two or three venturing out to check the sky, scheduled to turn vicious later. Texans are obsessive about their night tornadoes, which flick away sleeping houses like they are pieces on a Monopoly board.

The storm is a shifting red target on my watch's weather radar. I've set a timer to vibrate on my wrist in forty-five minutes, planning to be long gone by the time it or Sharp arrives.

I'm already straddling the top of the fence, getting my bearings. The moon has not given up yet. I can make out the sharp tips of three of the gables through the thicket of leaves, and the tenor but not the words of the raised voices in front of the house. They belong to two cops and four teens denying the smell of pot—part of my drive-by surveillance before parking a few houses down.

A relatively quiet night so far for the Solomon house, but the night is long. I was raised to believe that three in the morning is the devil's hour, when evil is busiest and insomniacs jolt awake not really knowing why, until Brig told me that was a ridiculous myth straight out of *The Exorcism of Emily Rose*.

I shut my eyes briefly, listening, because I love the other sound up here, the one the wind is kicking up. *Mysterious voices.* That's what Mom called trees rustling before a storm. *Psithurism*, if you're a scientist.

As always, too much chattering in my head.

Forty-three minutes left on my watch timer.

I lean over and grab the thick arm of the oak draped over the fence. Most of the trees I've climbed at night were a ladder to see the stars. It's an easy decision to climb down this elephant oak versus dropping twelve feet from the fence top and landing on an ankle that still tingles two decades after the accident.

I stretch out, half sliding, half crawling down the limb, until I am greeted by a wide view of the house—a tiered pale pink wedding cake that appears gray and gloomy in the shadows. I swing myself into a sitting position, hanging tight to the branch above my head.

The intricate scrollwork that inspired Bubba Guns to hashtag Lizzie "the gingerbread girl" is barely visible in this light. I now count five gables in silhouette. I can make out the first-story wraparound porch. The iron railing of the widow's walk on the third. A turret on the east side, like a paper tube that a wedding cake designer would ice for show.

I'm curious if this turret is just for show, too—an architect's empty, hollow space. The turret is the background for half the national media photos I've come across, inspiring headline writers from Austin to New York. *Who Took the Texas Rapunzel? Cold Case Cinderella.*

Those weren't the only photographs I studied. The file Sharp gave me contained several historical portraits of the Solomon house: a formal black-and-white Hasselblad portrait from 1918, snapped by its English architect; a shot of the house with a fresh coat of yellow for a 1962 real estate flyer; and the 2012 digital snaps from the crime scene photographer, when the crumbling state of the house was a crime itself, and the only yellow was the ribbon of crime scene tape calling Lizzie home. Only three owners, but thirty-two of its ninety-four years were unoccupied.

Almost a century of human history is pressing against my brain, stacking up like waves.

The only thing I know for sure about this house is that Lizzie Solomon was only a few pages in a very long book.

☽ ✧ ☾

It isn't until I'm halfway across the backyard that I remember the light switch on my baseball cap. I've never worn this cap before—my haul from a $10-limit Secret Santa exchange at the observatory Christmas party—but it seemed like a good idea to be hands-free tonight.

I pinch a spot on the brim firmly to turn on two tiny LED lights. I'd practiced this in my living room. Pressing firmly was the only way the cheap device operated. Its intense brightness in the gray ink of the backyard is sudden and startling. I immediately try to turn it back off. Multiple times.

No go. I'm lit. *Neighbors.*

I swivel my head quickly, the light casting a fifty-foot trail. To my left is an overgrown garden, to my right is a newer, stand-alone garage—a 1950s-era add-on, the no-frills groom's cake.

In front of me, en route to the back porch, stretches an obstacle course of two-by-fours, plywood, and white plastic bags giving off the rotting stench of wet soil. Renovation materials never used. In less than twenty seconds, I'm on the porch, out of sight.

Earlier, I'd plugged the words *how to sneak inside Lizzie Solomon's house* into a search. I instantly found a Reddit thread mentioning an oversized doggy door for the Solomons' German shepherd that had been built into one of the back doors. The comment said it was *a perfect fit for small women or men without too much butt*—a dodgy piece of advice from @SkinnyMinnie22, who tried it herself or just made it up and, either way, is probably still living with a parent.

It turns out the doggy door *is* there—a tempting hole with torn plastic flaps that the wind is slapping against the frame, the magnets that held them in place long gone. It looks size 4-ish to me.

I wonder why the Solomons' German shepherd didn't protect Lizzie when she was in trouble.

I wonder why this doggy door isn't boarded up.

I wonder if I should turn around and not break into a house with too many unknowns.

I get stuck about halfway.

☽ ✧ ☾

Sharp has just finished tugging me out. I'm flat on my belly on the porch. I can still feel where his thumbs pressed into the top of my hips, his fingers wrapping around bare skin at my waist where my shirt slid up.

"There was a much easier way for you to manage this, Red. Watch me." The first real amusement I've heard in his voice. More chinks off my dignity.

I know exactly what he is going to demonstrate because I'd considered it before diving in headfirst. He kneels on the porch and reaches his arm up through the dog door to the inside doorknob, locking and unlocking the knob. "You don't need the wingspan of Manute Bol to do it. Or you could have waited for me and entered legally with a judge's order."

"Are you going to arrest me?"

"I haven't decided. You're lucky I'm early and alone."

I push myself up, trying not to wince at the scrape on my belly from being wrenched out of a rusted metal frame or worry too much about when I had my last tetanus shot. "It . . . felt less like breaking and entering to me if any animal could do it," I mutter.

"You are blinding me with this thing." He grabs the cap off my head, turns it off with one press of the button, and hangs it on top of an old porch lantern jerry-rigged to a post. "Another prowler tip: Don't wear the star of Bethlehem on your head. I personally question whether the wise men actually saw a star, but *you're the astrophysicist.*" I didn't know Sharp could enjoy himself this much.

"You indicated cops weren't watching the whole property," I say defensively. "Just a car out front."

"I said, there are no alarms. And that doesn't sound like an apology to an officer of the law."

I pause, deciding how to answer. "I'd personally commit to, yes, there was a celestial event around the time of the birth of Jesus. A supernova, a comet, an unusual alignment of the planets. *Magi* literally translates to *astrologist* or *astronomer*, so those men definitely had their eyes on the sky. Magi were polished into 'wise men' and 'kings' for the permanent record because astrologers didn't exactly fit with Christian ideals."

"More proof that blurring the truth started as far back as Jesus." *Further back than that*, I think. He drawls this out while dragging me by the arm through the back door. I stumble along behind him, not feeling much choice.

He flicks at a wall switch, illuminating a very small, narrow room with shelves and cabinets that line both walls. A flat marble work space runs below one set of cupboards. There are three more human doors, one straight in front of me, two ahead on either side, so four ways out, five if you count the dog door, which I no longer do.

We're in what used to be a high-traffic butler's pantry, where servants dressed plates into art that was appreciated for just seconds instead of immortalized on Instagram. The only hints we're not in 1918 are the plastic coat hooks stuck on the wall by the door above an IKEA-like organizer with four cubbyholes. *Lizzie, Mom, Dad,* and *Pepper* are still scrawled in black marker over each one. Only

Pepper's still holds anything—a red leash, a can of WD-40, and a hammer.

"This way." Sharp is still pulling me along. I've let the power shift become official. He quickly sweeps left, depositing me in the middle of another room. He fumbles for a switch that lights a dim ceiling bulb, which, after the grimness of outside, is like removing a pair of sunglasses too soon.

It takes several blinks to realize the room is completely gutted. Violent gashes in the wall expose a wood skeleton. Bare pipe and electrical wires snake every direction. No stove, no refrigerator, no cabinets, no table and chairs. This disemboweled mess is the kitchen where Lizzie disappeared.

"What happened . . . here?" I ask softly.

"A combination of police diligence and looters. This was one of the few rooms the Solomons had completely renovated. They left everything in place, waiting for Lizzie to return, even after the police did their thing. When a thief started selling the mugs from the cabinets for $100 apiece on Craigslist, the Solomons agreed to remove the rest of the kitchen to discourage activity. Nicolette Solomon was already in prison. She asked her brother, a contractor, for help. He went overboard."

"And the rest of the house?"

"Her brother stripped much of it, but there were plenty of wood curlicues and stained glass left to take as souvenirs." He crosses his arms, impatient. "You're here. What are you feeling?"

"Burning humiliation," I reply. "A wish that we'd never met."

"What do you feel *about Lizzie*? Can you tell me where she was standing the last time her mother saw her?"

"Two feet to your left. By the light gray patch where the refrigerator was. It was marked with a red X in a diagram in your file, which I told you not to show me. I *feel* like you're just going through the motions here. For your boss. But to answer your question, the kitchen isn't doing anything for me."

"Would you like to lead the way instead?"

"Seriously?"

"Wherever the energy pulls you."

"I guess I prefer that to being physically dragged. I hope you know where the light switches are."

"Most of the lights beyond this room have been smashed. You'll have to watch for glass. And squirrel shit." He waves a flashlight I hadn't seen before.

"Remind me why we are doing this at night?"

"To avoid the trolls of Bubba Guns, who will snap your picture like they're shooting a gun."

Or shoot a gun like they're snapping my picture.

"Are you recording this?" I ask.

"Yep. Body cam." He touches a small device on his shoulder that I originally thought was a small flashlight. "For both our sakes. Where to?"

"Lizzie's . . . room. Obvious, I know." I don't hold back on sarcasm.

He reaches into his back pocket, pulling out a folded paper. "The schematic. I haven't been in this house for two and a half years. I can't remember exactly where her room is."

"Upstairs. I'd like to go alone."

"Oh, Red. For so many, many reasons . . . no."

I wasn't expecting a yes. I've already stepped into a narrow hall that leads toward the front of the house. Sharp and his light stalk close behind, our shadows rippling along wallpaper whose long-feathered birds are ripped to shreds, like the birds themselves went to war.

We've reached a large, circular foyer. The red and blue lights of the police car out front are staining the opaque ovals of glass on either side of the grand entrance door. The yellow glow of Sharp's flashlight travels up a double staircase with rails that make me think of the strings of a fine piano. The once elaborate chandelier above our heads is shattered, hanging like broken teeth.

"Imperial," I say softly.

"What?"

"When a staircase is divided into two parts like this—separate sets of steps leading to one landing—it's called an imperial staircase."

"And this is important how?"

"Wait. Be quiet." I stand perfectly still, falling into the past. A young woman, black hair cut in a flapper bob, descends the staircase to kiss the cheek of a man she shouldn't. Two old friends say their very last goodbye without knowing it. A boy in red cleats is sneaking out past curfew. A grieving father is crashing to the parquet floor after trying to hang himself from a rotting post.

And Lizzie. I feel Lizzie.

"There's the spot her father tried to hang himself." Sharp points his light fifteen feet up to the only part of the stair railing that has been reinforced with a large piece of plywood backing.

"Lizzie used to put her hand here." I caress the elaborate ornament carved into the top of the newel post, a mermaid with a long rope of twisting hair. I trace the rough scales of her tail with my finger, thinking of the man who chiseled them one by one, who lived and died across the ocean and spoke a delicate language that is a flute in my ears.

"Lizzie could only reach high enough to touch the bottom of the mermaid's tail," I continue. "She would have to stand on the third step—here—and lean over to touch her hair." I find myself on the third step. "She fell from this spot more than once. Her mother told her, *In a year, you'll be tall . . . enough.*" My voice catches on the last several words.

"I can't tell on this schematic which room up there is Lizzie's," Sharp interjects, as if I haven't said a word. "We'll have to just keep hitting rooms until we find it."

"It doesn't matter," I say. "I'll know."

On the twelfth step, my watch vibrates against the skin of my wrist, a silent alarm. The storm, moving our way.

12

Lizzie's room is as empty as the kitchen. Emptier. Sad, swept, airless. It reeks of fresh paint. The walls are a faint blue or gray color under the beam of a flashlight. Gash-free but with visible, raised patchwork under the paint. Brushstrokes that remind me of careless wind patterns in the sand. Brig always painted her childhood room blue, but it was more of a womb than a tomb.

Where are you, Lizzie? Why can't I feel your pulse in here?

This loud, blue stillness—it's how I imagine it would be standing inside Edward Hopper's austere portrait of an abandoned old mansion that is metaphorically and physically cut off from the world by a railroad track. A house with only the whistle of a train for company.

I purse my lips and blow silently, a thin stream of invisible smoke. Sharp is pacing, wearing a boot path in the dust. He's clearly waiting for me to say something. Silence bothers him when he's not the one using it.

"Marcus Solomon paints over the graffiti in his daughter's room at least four times a year." Sharp, unable to give me time, to let the moment stretch. "He shows up even more just to hang out. He brings a two-foot-tall portrait of Lizzie that a friend painted for him, a cooler of beer, and a card table chair."

Sharp taps his finger near a nail in the far wall. "He hangs the picture here. He places the chair six feet in front of her painting and sits for hours, staring at an ugly, amateur rendering of his daughter with only the slightest likeness, and reads a Bible. I know this because one of my cop friends has pounded a few with him and crawled pretty deep inside his head. Calls him pathetic. Or pitiable. One of those *p*'s. A guy born in a Cormac McCarthy novel with no way out."

Well, you're right there in the pages with him. Did I just say that out loud? I don't think I did. Sharp's face hasn't changed. When my head feels this way, wavy and unstable, sifting images, I never know. My sister was the keeper of my mouth growing up—jabbing me in the ribs, whispering, *Shut up.*

"But he ignores the rest of the house? And won't sign on with a security company? It makes no sense."

Sharp shrugs. "If I'm being fair, he can probably barely afford the taxes on this place. He's living in a mobile home park in South Fort Worth. Marcus Solomon's career never recovered. I mean, he was a suicidal family law attorney with a wife in prison for his daughter's murder and a lot of clients who thought he helped hide her body."

"Does he visit his wife?"

"Every Tuesday."

"You think he's guilty?"

"You tell me," he says evenly. "You're the one who insists Lizzie is alive."

I'm opening the closet, coffin-sized, with a wooden rod at eye level and two bare plastic hangers. The fresh paint extends in here but it's an even sloppier coat. When Sharp swerves the flashlight, I can make out the words *Yo estuve aqui* underneath a thin lick of blue.

Yo estuve aqui. I was here.

Lizzie doesn't feel very alive to me right now, but I'm not telling Sharp that. I deliberately face him. "It's going to be a lost cause if you insist on me contacting Lizzie while you're present. It's why I climbed a fence to do this alone. Even then, I had serious reservations about anything happening."

It doesn't work like this. Lizzie would be more likely to give me serious hints if I was standing in the shower shaving my legs.

He fiddles with the camera on his shoulder, aiming it lower, at my face. "I doubt that," he says. "Mermaid tails and all. What's next?"

I walk over to a tight bay of three windows that create a nook. Her twin bed used to be here, tucked right up to the glass, so she could lie down and see out either side. It's not Lizzie talking to me, it's the house. Sharp would not understand the distinction, so I keep it to myself. All three windows in the bay are painted shut. The hardware, original. The old glass, rippled but without a crack. No one who tucked her in this bed wanted Lizzie to fall out. *So why would they kill her?*

"How about the turret?" My tone is brisk, professional, like a real estate agent determining a price point.

"Too dangerous to climb without natural light." His answer is immediate and firm. "Better when the sun's streaming through the upper windows. Even the widow's walk is a safer bet at night than the turret."

"Even the widow's walk before a storm?"

He glances at his phone. "We have a few minutes. I'm game."

I don't have a flash of insight, just a terrible thought.

It would be a cruel hoax if her skeleton is still lying up there on the roof.

☽ ✧ ☾

I've always been a fan of looking up and not of looking down, which Sharp picks up on as soon as we scale the ladder.

A handsy old professor once told me while we peered through a telescope that it was unlikely for an astrophysicist "worth her plutonium" to have a fear of heights. But that's me.

My nerves are perfectly settled when I'm up in a tree with something to grip. But the widow's walk that crowns the Solomon house—it's like a fenced grave on a mountaintop worthy of a quick and nervous prayer, then retreat.

Sharp had gone up first. He extended a hand down from a trapdoor in the third-floor ceiling of what was basically a glorified closet with a broken padlock. He yanked me onto a square patch of copper sheeting and under a giant, still troubled sky. The moist air is like the hug I didn't want from that handsy old professor. A weathervane arrow is twirling on one of the peaks like a Ouija board confused about which way to point itself.

I quickly assess the sky. Hard to tell exactly where the storm stands. Ominous clouds are skittering like whispers over stars. A warning breeze is flicking at my hair.

Mars and Venus are still holding position, taunting me. I check my watch, thinking of Mike. Wondering where he is. Worried about him even if it's still more than an hour away from midnight, even if the sky is not clear enough, even if the crescent moon is now slightly too thick to be the one in my dream with the pounding hooves.

The deck up here is big enough to maybe hold a party of five on a hot summer night. As proof it still hosts parties, an empty red wine bottle is propped against the front railing—low, tumbling over territory.

It takes a second to figure out what Sharp is doing—flashing Morse code to the cops in the cruiser. I'm guessing it's to let them know it's him on the roof, a colleague, and not a trespasser who slipped by them. At least I think it's Morse code. I always meant to learn it but was far more drawn to the zeros and ones of binary computer language than dots and dashes. Sharp gets one quick blast of headlights in return.

Sharp jiggles the railing to test its sturdiness. I wonder if I'd be brave enough to reach out for him if he went over. I'm still constantly wondering how brave I am, a worry I'd hoped to lose somewhere along the way. Right now, my feet are still planted firmly in the center of a copper deck aged to the color of algae.

"I've always wanted to check it out up here," Sharp is saying. "A guy we hired to run a drone said this widow's walk was in surprisingly good shape. There's still an intricate working drainage system from the 1900s. You don't want water gathering on a widow's walk." He leans over the railing a little, gesturing to something under the eaves of the house.

"I'll take your word for it." *Please move away from the railing.*

"You realize that Lizzie would never have made it up here on her own," he says.

"The second you had to pull over an eight-foot ladder to reach a trapdoor in a ceiling," I reply. The ladder was its own test of anxiety, with old round dowels for rungs that spun under my feet as I climbed. I was surprised the ladder hadn't been stolen. There must be an etiquette of some kind among Solomon house intruders.

I reluctantly step forward for a wider, if dizzying, view of Sharp's light roving the rooftop. Broken shingles, steep pitches, sharp peaks, blind bends. A window set into the curve of the turret is an inhuman leap away.

"The city scoured this roof for Lizzie regardless," he says. "In my opinion, a suicide mission. They even pulled in an architect from the UK who specialized in old Victorians and castle structures, to instruct firefighters on harnesses and strategy. A firefighter slipped and broke a leg anyway. The city took a long pause, figuring if a firefighter with twenty years of experience couldn't manage it, neither could a three-year-old girl or a thirty-year-old mom carrying a three-year-old dead girl on her back. In the last few years, authorized and unauthorized drones have tried to see into some of the darker crevices. Most of them crashed and burned." Sharp's flashlight is suddenly beamed more closely on my face. "What, you doubt that?" he asks.

"Your file said that the Solomons were big hikers. In great shape. That they climbed Emory Peak in Big Bend for their honeymoon and Anthony's Nose out near El Paso for their fifth anniversary. I saw the picture of them on top of Anthony's Nose *with* camping backpacks. That's Herculean." And not on my bucket list.

"Tell me something I don't know," he says dryly.

I consider him for a few seconds before turning north to the darkest part of the sky, still untouched by clouds. "OK, I will. Follow my finger. That bright star right there, at the tip of the Big Dipper's handle? It's called Alkaid. The light we see right now started its journey to us a little after World War I. Alkaid is also part of the tail of the Great Bear constellation. Homer mentions this Bear in the sky in *The Iliad*. It's also referenced in the book of Job."

"I've never found a need to read either."

"North is a very unlucky direction in Chinese fortune-telling," I continue, ignoring him. "Northwest, where Alkaid sits—that's the absolute worst. If my mother read your fortune, she would have told you to never, ever point your gun in the direction of that star."

"I was with you right up until you told a Texas cop which way to shoot his gun."

"Plenty of hunters and soldiers used to follow that piece of advice—to absolutely never point their weapons toward Alkaid. It was one of the most powerful astrological stars in medieval times. My mother thought it was . . . magic."

"You expect me to believe any of this?"

"I expect you to consider something besides the obvious. There is a fine line between myth and truth, Detective Sharp. Between coincidence and design. On that, Bubba Guns and I can relate. You want to know me a little better? Really *know* me? My whole life, I've struggled with my belief in science versus this *thing* my mother called a gift. But I don't always accept the truth—that these two forces inside my head thrive on each other. We are given imagination to expand our worlds, and science to confirm it. They are not mutually exclusive."

As always, I sound more articulate, more passionate out loud than in my head. Maybe I've gone too far with Sharp, but with every word, the ground feels sturdier. I want to find a lost girl, and if it takes baring a little bit of my underbelly to make that happen, so be it.

I want badly to reach him. "I know you are a man who must have seen terrible things. Made ungodly decisions. I *understand* this. I've tried to find peace with how predatory and vicious the universe is, both up there and down here. Dying stars exploded violently to create the miracle matter that made humanity. Birth is violent—a woman splits herself in two shoving a child out of her body. Greedy black holes eat stars that get in their way, which is also exactly why, on Earth, Princess Diana and Marilyn Monroe died—and myths were born. I'm certain that constellations we can't see yet will be named after them someday, and our ancestors will wonder about *our* grasp on reality."

"That's depressing . . . or a little beautiful," he mutters.

"It's whatever we want it to be, isn't it?" I say eagerly. "Whatever we choose to see? Kids look up at the sky and are told the Big Dipper is a cup to hold water. But ancient Arabs believed the Big Dipper was a funeral procession, and that the stars that outline the cup actually make a coffin. Alkaid, Mizar, and Alioth—the stars that form the handle—are the mourners. The daughters of the *bier*, to be precise."

"Drunk daughters?"

"In Arabic, *bier* means sarcophagus. Casket. Coffin."

"You're ruining the Big Dipper for me. Which version would you have told little Lizzie?"

"Children deserve to be innocent as long as possible." My tone holds longing. For Will. "I would have told Lizzie to drink from the golden cup. That she is protected under the star of Alkaid. But that would have been a lie."

"You seem like you're changing your mind, Red," he says. "Hedging your bets on whether Lizzie is still with us."

"I don't know." My voice sounds so lost up here. "I thought I did. Know, that is."

"The whole bit with the mermaid tail on the staircase?" His rigid doubt is sliding a wall between us again.

I'm ten years old again, back in the mountains, imagining crowds cheering from the shore of Midnight Hole Falls. *Witch, witch, witch.* A shadow behind me is shoving my head under.

"I don't know what to make of you," he says. "I thought it would just take a little tour of this house for you to wave the white flag."

A surprise gust of wind bends me over, closer to the edge.

Sharp lurches like I have him on a leash. His breath shivers my ear as he steadies me. He doesn't let go, not for several seconds longer than he needs to. His face, only inches away, is unreadable. I hope mine is, too. Every single time he touches me, I feel something I don't want to. Fear. Dark, inexplicable attraction.

I slide a step back. "There's somebody else standing on top of this house with us," I say quietly. "A personal ghost of yours."

"I think we've done enough of this for the night, Red."

The sky is spitting at us. I gaze up. Mars and Venus have vanished. "I'm not talking about Lizzie," I persist, as a big wet drop lands on my cheek. "I'm talking about the other missing girl. The one who belongs to that charm bracelet in the leaves, the picture that got 'mixed up' in the photos you laid out at the police station like a game of bloody solitaire." I wait for a response. There isn't one.

"Don't worry." I lather on the sarcasm. "I'm not saying she is an actual ghost shimmering on this rooftop. And I do think you want to solve Lizzie's case. But it is this other girl who is in your head. All the time."

"You are extrapolating a lot from the sloppy work on the part of the detective who handed me the photographs." Scarily calm.

"I think you keep that picture of the charm bracelet in the lineup just in case you run across someone, anyone who knows something. I didn't need to have a special gift to observe your reaction when I picked out that photo. You've laid that picture down hundreds of times, haven't you, mixing it here and there? In front of suspects accused of other crimes. Your students. Fellow cops. But I'm the first to notice. And *this* is why we are standing on this roof testing my theories on Lizzie even though intellectually you find me utterly implausible."

It's impossible to stop myself. "You could easily tell your boss I'm nuts. A charlatan bringing terrible publicity to the force. You could convince Mike to let go of me this once, especially with Bubba Guns screeching. You could deny, deny, deny me. But your mystery girl has you wondering if I know something. You aren't sure." This rush of words—it's a risk. Because I'm not sure, either.

Sharp has shut off the flashlight. Only inches separate our two silhouettes. My hair is beginning to slap my face. The raindrops, more insistent. The trees below are tossing and talking.

"We need to get off the roof," Sharp orders.

"I know how badly you want to think I'm crazy," I say softly, "but there's a part of you that isn't sure. That is *afraid* of me. Because God forbid if God exists, and I can see through a tiny pinhole."

A sound startles both of us. Musical. Discordant. We turn our heads at almost the same time.

The wind chimes on a neighbor's porch floating up. That's what my sister would say.

A string of fairies tap-dancing on an iron railing. That would be my mother.

What do I say? I *say* nothing. But when I close my eyes, a girl without a face is furiously jangling a charm bracelet.

Sharp is bending down, tugging up the trapdoor, fighting the wind. I hope for a piece of moonlight to slice open his face, to expose him, but both the moon and Sharp have disappeared.

☽ ✧ ☾

I'm back in the butler's pantry, on my knees. Hail is clicking against windows already cracked. The bones of the house are whining.

Sharp hadn't spoken as he'd braced the ladder for me to descend from the roof. I'd marched ahead of him this time, down three halls and two staircases, in prisoner mode. When we reached the kitchen, he'd announced that it was time for community service.

Now Sharp has a nail in his teeth. I have a dozen in my hand.

He is neatly arranging a piece of scrap plywood over the inside of the dog door. I'd scoured the kitchen floor for nails, which were plentiful, while he'd grabbed the wood from the backyard and the hammer from the cubbyhole.

"Let the Solomons fucking sue me for property damage," he'd said grimly. "I'm shutting this dog door down. Lizzie can break a window to get in. She won't be the first."

I've been handing over nails one by one, a dutiful nurse. With every whack of his hammer, my insides jerk.

There is nothing delicate about those hands, nothing cautious about his movement, nothing uncertain. Sharp builds things and tears them down, *that* is certain. I want to see the little boy he was, but I can't summon him. Did he begin by curiously observing the complex behavior of ants? With stomping their piles to watch them swarm? Or with a carelessly dropped match to light them on fire?

Was this thrum of danger in the DNA of him when his mother rocked him to sleep? Or was it acquired and nurtured with every notch he carved into his mythic bedpost?

I've seen the four-week-old embryo inside a stranger on the street whose shoulder brushed mine—but I can't see through Jesse Sharp.

All I know for sure is that he can make a person feel safe, or terrified, whatever he chooses, and ever since we dropped down from the roof, I've been a little closer to terrified.

The storm is moving fast on my watch, but we're in the thick of it. A leak from the ceiling is forming a peninsula down the back of Sharp's shirt.

I'm exhausted—eager for this night to be over, for Sharp to say, *See you, chick,* or *So long, Red,* or whatever mildly sexist taunt he wants as long as he lets me go home.

I briefly consider leaping over him, racing into the rain, climbing the thick trunk of the oak that would surely be too clumsy an effort for a man his size.

He's lying on the floor, faceup, grimacing, to get a better view of his project. He must trust me, or not think much of my chances against him. His Adam's apple, which looks permanently sunburned, is right there for me to jab with a nail.

Does he know that almost every woman past sixteen thinks like this without thinking? That when I walked in this pantry an hour and a half ago, I immediately considered that the WD-40 in the dog's cubbyhole could be as good as mace? That situational awareness is an itchy second skin? That if women like me acted on every defensive thought in our heads, there would be a lot fewer bad men left?

My eyes flicker over the four doors in the butler's pantry. All of them, except for the door to the kitchen, shut. I consider the one with the padlock and face the facts: I don't have the stamina left to run anywhere, inside or out.

"Where do these other doors go?" I babble, just to break the silence. "One must lead to the dining room, easy access for the servants to lay the table. But what about the door with the glass knob? And the one with the padlock? Does it lead to the turret? It's like that old game show, *Let's Make a Deal*. My sister and I used to watch reruns when we were in between rental houses, stuck in a motel room. One contestant, three closed doors. Depending on which door you chose, you might get two goats, or five bushels of beans, or a brand-new car."

I can't tell if Sharp's listening. I wouldn't be. His arms are over his head, pulling at either side of the plywood to test its stability. The effort lifts his shirt, baring a taut belly and his gun.

"The show has terrible probabilities for contestants to get what they want." I can't seem to stop. "My sister and I always wanted the goats or the donkey. There's an actual statistical problem named in honor of the host. The Monty Hall problem. But Monty Hall said it couldn't be solved statistically because he was the one who manipulated the game, that he played off the psychology of each contestant. He said the outcome was always uncertain except maybe to him. Math, not a factor."

Monty Hall thought just like you, Sharp.

Sharp's whack at the last nail is the exclamation point that shuts me up. He slides his body into a sitting position, arms casually dangling around his knees. I don't know what he's done with the hammer.

"Here's a probability problem," he drawls. "You, Red, are trapped by a serial killer. Let's say, in the middle of a Texas storm. If this is the conversation you choose to make yourself more human to him, you'll be dead."

In one swift move, he pulls me up. I have nowhere to go. His body is a wall in front of me. The leftover nails in my hand clatter to the floor.

Seven inches above mine, his eyes are bloodshot and tired, but the sense he isn't done with me is unrelenting.

"Why don't you ask Lizzie's mother tomorrow?" he asks. "About the probabilities of the doors? About what's behind numbers two, three, and four? Of the chances she's innocent of killing her daughter?"

I struggle to keep my face blank. My stomach is back to a panicking roll.

"That's right, Vivvy. I know about your little meeting at the Mountain View prison unit tomorrow afternoon. Heads up. The fence there is razor wire."

When he steps back, the storm is over. The house, exhausted from holding fort. Sharp's breath is coming faster, more jagged than when he was swinging a hammer.

It's the first time I know.

He sees danger in me, too.

13

I t's past midnight when I stumble to my mother's room, her answering machine blinking with a fresh set of problems. The responsibility overwhelms me. But that's not why I'm back in here. I pick up the phone receiver and begin examining it.

My stomach is still bleeding from the encounter with the doggy door and from navigating back up that tree, the trunk digging into my skin like the spikes of a pineapple. My hair, still wet from the soaked leaves. I can barely remember my parting with Sharp at the Solomon house, just that he abruptly told me to slip out of the yard the way I came in.

I hated Sharp a little more when I stumbled on the last rung of the fence, a glancing blow to my ankle.

But now, this old phone. No scratch marks or evidence of tampering with the receiver. I pull out the table and search the phone cable. No uninvited adapter, no little white box that doesn't belong. So far, no evidence at all of a bug, a tap, a DNR, a Title III, a Richard Nixon, whatever the police are calling it these days. Mike always makes jokes about cop slang, like he's a refugee from *The Wire*.

Even in its depleted state tonight, my mind is running toward full paranoia. There could be a sound frequency pickup anywhere in the room.

I examine the beaded lampshade by the bed. Nothing but a mouthful of dust.

I dismantle a picture on the dresser of Brig and me at my high school graduation. I think about running a flashlight behind the untamed bushes that crawl up the side of the house and are stuttering like a bad typist on the window.

I consider barging across the street to knock on the trampy beige RV that my mother's misdemeanor-prone neighbor has claimed he's parking in front of his house for the days his wife kicks him out. I've never seen him ignite the motor even though his wife has loudly told every nearby planter of petunias that she has a gun ready to fire at him. Curtains hang over every bit of glass, and a sunshade of the Confederate flag blocks the windshield. Five neighbors say they've called the city for its removal.

The cops could have set up a concave antenna in there, translating the vibrations from my window into audible recordings. Sometimes, I wish I didn't know so *much* science.

I tug my cell out of my pocket, press the number 3, hit send. It rings twice before he answers.

"What the hell?" It's a hot whisper on the other end. "We're . . . sleeping."

"Have the cops been bugging my mother's phone?" I demand to know. "How long? Exactly how much do you think she knew about Lizzie Solomon? Tell me. *Now.*"

"It's OK." Muffled. Mike, his hand over the speaker, is reassuring my sister, not me. "It's just work," he tells her. "I've got this. Go back to sleep. I'll check on Will before I come back to bed."

"Hang on." Mike is back in my ear. "I'm moving to the kitchen."

I can see him, on cop alert in seconds, slipping out of bed in white boxers while he white lies to his wife. Tanned, bare chest that is etched in my mind from all the waterskiing weekends on his father's agile and expensive boat since I was a child. On one of those weekends—just one—102-degree sun, a six-pack of Coronas, and the loose ties of my first and last red bikini came very close to changing the course of things between us. At least that's what I will always wonder.

I know all about Mike's devotion to white boxers, 700-thread-count white sheets, a white-hot sex life. My sister shared these intimate details about Mike's bedroom habits one night after several glasses of wine, as if I were a random best friend and not a sister who loved her husband, too. As if we've all moved on. Because drunk or not, she hoped it.

I'm just as guilty of pretending.

On nights of free babysitting, I've folded Mike's white boxers on their couch side by side with my nephew Will's diapers, hot from the dryer. My sister's thongs are so barely there, I link them like rubber bands. Sometimes, I see her legs entwined with Mike's, the business side of creating little Will, who I'm certain should be on this Earth just as he is. Sometimes, it's like their four legs are wrapped around my neck, choking me.

"I just got back from the Solomon house," I say angrily. "Your friend Sharp insisted that I meet him there. We ended up on the widow's walk."

"What? Are you all right? You get panic attacks on a Ferris wheel."

He seems genuinely surprised. *Unless.* Unless he told Sharp himself that a roof would be a very good place to shake me up a little.

"If you aren't bugging me, how else did Sharp find out that I'm going to prison to see Nicolette Solomon today? Unless, you know, he's psychic, too." I swallow a breath. "Don't you cops need a court order to invade a person's *life*?"

"Today?" Mike, confused.

"*Today.* After the sun pops up."

"At Mountain View? Not a good idea, Viv. Every female criminal celeb in Texas calls that place home. Darlie Routier, Amber Guyger, Yolanda Saldivar. National journalists and documentarians constantly clamor for interviews. You—popping over to visit—that's a pretty high-profile thing to do with a famous podcaster tweeting a warpath right now. Brig has tried to call you all night. It's been a shit day over here, too. She's concerned the Bubba Guns stuff is going to leak—"

"Into her pretty, pretty life?" I interrupt. "You mean, she's worried her mommy group will be talking more about her psycho sister than deciding whether they should read *Untamed* or *How to Be an Antiracist* first?" I instantly wish I could take it back. I hate myself when I sound this bitter.

Mike takes an audible breath. "Jesus—and I'm praying *directly* to Jesus with every ounce of my Catholic blood—I wish you two would work out your issues for good. Your mother did a number on both of you."

"I guess we could blame it on my mother," I say dryly. *I guess we could pretend that when you touched my chin in the bar, you were doing it without intent.*

"Vivvy . . . I . . ."

"Stop," I interrupt. "Explain, or don't."

"There's no hidden agenda on my part." Defensive. "Lizzie Solomon deserves justice. *All* of those cases I asked you to look at deserve justice."

"I find it hard to believe your ambition and Sharp's play no role in this."

"Can we talk about this in the morning?"

"Mike. *Have the police tapped my mother's phone?*"

Silence.

"No. I mean, as far as I know, *no.*"

"Well, Nicolette Solomon wasn't using the official prison line when she dialed up my mother's answering machine. There was no chatter up top about how I was receiving a call from an inmate. She left a simple and not very friendly message, like she was right next door. She had to be using a burner."

"Right."

"They still sneak those in, don't they?"

I could back a truck into his silence.

"Mike, you owe me some kind of answer." Tears are pricking my eyes.

"OK, Viv." A weighty sigh. "We've been listening on and off to Nicolette Solomon for years. It's part of a routine effort to find Lizzie's body. And for the last two months, we've had a snitch sleeping in a bunk close enough to hear her teeth grinding at night." I make out the squeak of the patio door sliding shut. He's moved to the backyard. "I can sneak you into the prison with the cruiser tomorrow to avoid any Bubba vultures. I'll even sit in. I'll tell Brig to go on out with Will to the lake to meet my parents. I'll tell her I have to work."

Mike, asking me to play. But only by his rules. I've never trusted him less.

"Go to the lake, Mike. Stop lying to your wife. It just reminds me that you lie to me, too."

☽ ✧ ☾

I hang up and walk blindly to my bedroom. I fall back on the sheets, staring at the one faint glow-in-the-dark star still hanging like a dying wish since I pressed it in place sixteen years ago.

I fight the impulse to close my fingers into a fist.

I can't.

I knock.

Softer, then louder.

Fifty times.

☽ ✧ ☾

Hooves, trampling my chest. Brig, screaming. Mike, holding her back with an expression that assures me I'm the one who's dying.

My heart is the only noise in the bedroom when I thrust myself up, plunging deep into my lungs for air. Not terrible for a Blue Horse dream. Mike survived.

I count twenty slats across the floor made by the morning sun. I take in as many breaths. I know the routine.

I fight the urge to call Brig to make sure she's OK, or to strum through Bubba Guns's Twitter feed, or to nervously troll the local Sunday morning online headlines. I don't even ease my guilt by reading through my sister's pile of texts. I know what they say. *Call me.*

My finger does what it always has to calm me, what it should have done from memory last night. It reaches up the wall to trace the nine stars of Andromeda, the Chained Lady, one of the eighty-eight constellations sketched on the glow-in-the-dark poster plastered beside my bed. The beautiful Andromeda is worthy of 722 square degrees of sky after being chained naked to a cliff by her father as a sacrifice to a sea monster.

When we moved to Texas, my mother tucked me in this back bedroom far from hers and Brig's so I could knock on the wall to my heart's content. It was Brig who couldn't stand the thought of me alone in a compulsive spiral.

She bought the poster at a garage sale for seventy-five cents, tacked it up, and sat with me every night until I was more interested in trailing my fingers along the shape of a centaur and eagle, a lion, and a queen than knocking my knuckles raw.

Brigid assured me over and over that Andromeda was saved by the hero Perseus just in time. But she said that didn't matter because Andromeda was made up. Greek myth. I would ask, a refrain for the rest of my life: *How do we know for sure she was saved?*

I throw on a thin robe of my mother's and pad barefoot to the living room window. I pull the curtain. The street is Sunday morning quiet. Still. Everyone at church, or inside eating breakfast tacos and grapefruit. No cop cars. No Mike. No Jesse Sharp. Not even my neighbor's ugly RV with *It's Drive-o-Clock Somewhere* painted on the side.

The quiet doesn't erase the ache left from the Blue Horse stomping my chest. The skinned mark on one of my knuckles from last night's knocking. The dizzying feeling that I'm clinging to a cliff

like Andromeda, the ending uncertain except to anyone reading
my story.

⟩ ✧ ⟨

I rip off the foil of an outdated blueberry yogurt and settle in at the
kitchen table with my laptop to review the two-and-a-half-hour route
to the prison. I read through the unwieldy list of rules at the Mountain View Unit, where there is no mountain and no view.

Do not bring smartphones, pill bottles, seemingly innocent objects
like pens or glitter nail polish in glass bottles that could be weaponized.

Do not wear a skirt more than three inches above the knee and
make sure all cleavage is tucked in its rabbit hole unless I want to be
provided a courtesy paper gown.

I try three different looks in front of my mother's foggy full-length
mirror before settling on a slightly wrinkled yellow cotton dress out of
Brig's old closet that hits just above the knee, a light cream summer
sweater to combat air-conditioning, and pink flip-flops with yellow
stars printed on the inside of the soles like a happy surprise. Flip-flops
are on the approved list, although I'm thinking they could get a few
good slaps in.

Most of what's in my backpack—and the backpack itself—is un-
acceptable contraband, so I keep it simple. I write Nicolette Marie
Solomon's inmate number, which I'd found online, on a small piece of
paper. I tuck it inside a clear Ziploc bag with my driver's license. I
weight it with $10 in change scrounged from my mother's dresser to
use in the vending machines, allowed, in case I'm feeling generous
enough to buy a convicted felon some potato chips and a Snickers
bar. I don't think I will be.

I throw my hair into an exceptionally messy bun without the help
of lethal hair pins or rubber bands. I darken the roots by brushing
black mascara at the sides and top for a little tough-chick drama before running the same brush through my lashes.

I go heavy on the eyeliner, rare for me. I dig through my mother's bathroom drawer for the least congealed foundation and decide against it. My desert brown is fading, but not that much. Our mother's pore-less skin is the one genetic bonus that Brig and I both accept without complaint.

In case Mike is right about media trolls, I want to look as little as possible like the five pictures of me that pop up when *Vivian Bouchet* is typed in a search bar.

The employee photo for the observatory is a pale, no-smile affair snapped during a period of heavy research duty. If fluorescent white is a skin color, I had it.

Second, the official school photo of me at age ten with a vivid poof of red hair and startled eyes behind wiry glasses. It ran in the local paper after I saved Mike's life.

Third, fourth, and fifth are media shots snapped outside that rental house in the Blue Ridge Mountains before the cops tumbled us into a van for the motel.

In those pictures, I am mostly a blurry afterthought. In two of them, I'm not even named. The cameras' eyes were stuck on Brigid's beauty. I've never been jealous, not of that. Because it comes with more chains than Andromeda's.

It wasn't until a few years ago that I saw a print of Rembrandt's interpretation of Andromeda. He hung her by her wrists from the cliff, breasts bare. He painted her terror, not her beauty.

Andromeda is shown raw and imperfect, the way I think Brig would like to be seen if she could ever throw off her and everyone else's expectations.

Andromeda was a sacrifice to the sea because of her mother's bragging, the way I'm certain Brig feels about our mother every day of her life.

I start up the Jeep around twelve thirty. When I tilt the rearview mirror, I make out the hood of Sharp's white pickup a block down, marking time.

14

I wait for Nicolette Marie Solomon, inmate #1992210, in a cafeteria-like space vibrating with prisoners, families, and forced hope. The amount of love and regret in this room is clobbering me. The smell of dead lilies. *Despair.* And vanilla. *Fear.*

I might not last long.

My eyes are glued to the door where I was told my prisoner would be emerging, but so far, nothing. I'm worried she's changed her mind, then relieved that maybe she did.

If I wasn't sure my little yellow dress marked me as a first timer, I'm getting enough smirks from other tables to confirm it. I feel like a piece of gossip at a dysfunctional family reunion where only half the people got the message to wear the orange shirt made up for the occasion. My attire did pass prison-rule muster, except for my beloved smart watch, which I'd stupidly forgotten to take off.

A headache is drifting behind my eyes. It hung on for the whole car ride, while I counseled one of my mother's clients on speakerphone and watched Jesse Sharp work a careless tail.

Sharp waved the first time he passed. The second time, he hung beside me for several seconds, pointing down, like he saw my mouth moving and knew I was talking on the phone. I lifted my fingers from the wheel. Hands-free, Detective Sharp. I'm allowed.

I was already edgy about helping the woman I picked for the first callback, whose voice had wavered from her hello. First, I had to deliver the news that her favorite otherworldly contact was now in the other world. I didn't need Sharp driving around me like a drunk fly.

It'll be easy, I'd tried to reassure myself before tapping in her number. *It's rocket science. Right up my alley.* Her flight was tomorrow at nine twenty a.m. Her name was Taylor. She was not going to go to her brother's wedding if she didn't get a call back assuring her the plane positively wouldn't crash.

I'd wanted to offer the pure scientific truth—that statistically, there is a 99.999985 percent probability she'd survive a plane ride, even if something broke. There is a .000015 percent probability of crashing every hour she's on a plane. If she flew, on average, an hour every single day, it would be more than 18,264 years before she died in a plane crash.

And a truth just as big: I didn't have a single psychic vibe on her destiny.

But I knew she didn't call my mother for truth.

For her, reality was the shriek of headlines. *What about Malaysia Flight 370? The Twin Towers? The couple walking on a beach in Miami who got wiped out by a Cessna, engine out, that they couldn't even hear coming?*

Taylor called for comfort. An imaginary spell.

So I told Taylor that it would be perfectly OK to sit in 13A on a flight to England because thirteen is lucky for Taylors.

I told her that Taylor Swift used to draw the number 13 on her hand before she took the stage for every concert and that she should do the same thing in purple ink on her palm thirteen minutes before she walked onto the plane.

Taylor sobbed her gratefulness when I told her that my session with her was free, a goodbye gift from my mother. When we hung up, she was off to crumple her bridesmaid dress into a suitcase and buy a purple pen.

Now that I'm sitting in a room where bad luck feels statistically out of control, I'm panicked that I've delivered her death sentence. My mother would have told her not to fly.

One of the two guards circling the room bumps against my shoulder. I don't know if it's on purpose or an accident, but I immediately sit like a nun has put a yardstick at my back.

A little girl of about six at the next table has already been ordered twice by the same grim-looking guard to stay in her seat or on her mother's lap. Her mother, an inmate, is a white woman who barely scratches eighteen. Bruises run like a path of gray stone up her arm. That her child can sit in her lap is a kindness I didn't expect from the Texas prison system.

Adults can't even peck each other on the cheek in here. But this little girl can soak the heat off her mother's skin. Carry that memory like a bedtime story when she closes her eyes tonight.

The girl is staring at either my dress or my bag of quarters with hard longing. What the hell. I grab a large handful of quarters out of the bag, make deliberate eye contact with the guard who appears more amenable, slide off my chair, and walk six feet to lay the change on the little girl's table.

The mother, head down, mouths a thank-you. The girl hops off her lap and wraps her arms around my waist.

The guard is already on top of me, leaning into my ear. "If you get up again, I won't take you out of here, I'll take Shawna's little girl and the aunt who brought her. I'll take them off the visitors' list for a month. You understand? Not your punishment, but it's still your punishment?"

The guard's badge reads Misha Westwood. Misha confiscates the quarters. She returns to her circling only after my yellow dress is firmly planted again.

I go back to staring at the door.

When Nicolette first emerges, I don't recognize her.

I think she's destined for a visitor in the back until she plops opposite me, swinging her legs under the table. Even then, I open my mouth to say it's a mistake.

"Hey, Bouchet." She pronounces it perfectly. "Welcome to my mountain."

☽ ✧ ☾

Lizzie's mother is no longer the chill-aired Texas blonde with the pinched waist from her wedding photo in the file, or the gaunt woman drawn by a cruel and clumsy hand in courtroom sketches.

There's a dull sheen and a slight frizz to her brown hair, a muscled thickness to her waist and arms, and a grin so stiff, it's like a scary tattoo.

Her eyes travel the feminine pearl buttons on Brig's old cardigan.

"Are you going to say anything, Bouchet?"

"I'd say *Nice to meet you, Nicolette*, but your invitation wasn't very polite."

"I'm Nickie in here. Anything with 'ette' is like a pussy call inside a prison of horny female felons. What's up?"

"What's *up*? Well, *Nickie*, the cops are listening to you. There's a snitch practically sleeping with you." Not what I planned to say first.

"The snitch would be Elaine. She's on the other side of my brick cubicle. We pleasure each other occasionally."

"You know?"

She shrugs. "I'm a lawyer. My father was a Louisiana district attorney and not an honest one. I learned at his whipping knee, and he liked a switch he made me pick out myself and cut off a backyard tree. I know every trick. I also know how to—"

"They might be listening right now. With a laser beam surveillance device that detects sound vibrations. Or maybe there is something sewn in the hem of your pants. Or stuck under this table." I start to run my hand underneath. She reaches over to grab my shoulder.

"Don't," she says insistently.

"Strike two." Misha the guard is directly behind her, knocking Nickie's hand off me.

"What was strike one?" Nickie asks innocently.

"Ask *Sunshine* here."

Nickie shrugs as Misha crosses the room to break up a hug two tables down. "We can only hold hands," Nickie says. "We'll get to that in a bit. Are you feeling all right? You're very paranoid."

"You think?"

"Is it that Jesse Sharp who has you going? I hear he's back on my case. He has paid me a visit a few times since I've been in here. Thinks he'll get me to confess to murdering my baby if he sticks his tongue in my ear, which he has done a few times. Metaphorically, of course. He's the type I fuck. He *knows* he's the type I fuck—the type that always seems an inch away from killing something. One of the girls in here that he helped convict said she thought he was in love with her until he put the cuffs on. Even then, she wasn't quite sure."

She leans in. "I've heard he's been suspended before. Messed with a crime scene. Girl, still missing. But I don't need to tell you. You're the fucking psychic." The last part, so low I had to read her lips.

"I'd prefer not to be called a *fucking psychic*," I snap back.

Nickie glances around, overdramatically drawing a finger to her lips. The huggers are being escorted out, both guards distracted for the moment. "Cussing, not allowed. If they'd heard, it would be strike three. You're not what I expected. Self-control, OK? We have a limited time for our business. You sound *angry*."

"I *am* angry. You threatened me. I just drove two and a half hours to this purgatory of terrible decisions with Jesse Sharp on my tail."

She throws her arms wide, embracing the room. "You have something against people who made a mistake? Do you think you are *better* than us?"

"Is that what it was?" I say coolly. "A mistake? To kill your daughter?"

I'm ripping out Nickie's guts under the wary safety of Misha's eyes. I need to feel this part of Nickie for myself. To be sure she's innocent. That Lizzie's not a figment that would run to the shadows if I swallowed two little pills.

"I'd invite any inmate in this room to my Thanksgiving table before I'd have those country club bitches who abandoned me," Nickie hisses.

"You can't be saying this place is full of new best friends," I say evenly.

She leans in just short of halfway across the table, about an inch from the rules. "I'm not saying that at all. Half of them think I'm the slightly kinder version of Darlie Routier for killing just one child, not two. They think I should be on death row here with the other child killers and the assassin of the beloved Selena and the woman who stabbed an eighty-year-old man with a paring *knife*, a butcher *knife*, and a *fork*, and then shoved a foot-long *lamp pole* five inches down his throat. Let me tell you, I'd still rather sit down to a nice bloody steak with any of them than my next-door neighbor who told everyone she heard me board up my dead child in a wall."

I'm caught up in the bitter, cartoonish twist on her face. The words she emphasizes. Her rage. I don't believe this woman was ever able to control her emotions. The jury saw it too, and it almost swept her onto death row. She was one wishy-washy libertarian juror away from taking her last breath as one of the few women that gentlemanly Texas has been willing to kill.

"We have a name for the women here on death row," she spits at me. "We call them The Bonnies, for Bonnie of Bonnie and Clyde. I am *not* a Bonnie. *I am innocent.*"

I'm thinking, *Who's angry now?* A random, unexpected image wavers behind my eyes. I close them, even knowing it won't erase anything, that it will only fill in the edges of the picture.

"She was only twenty-three," I say dully.

"Bonnie Parker? That sounds about right. She was barely an adult when she got shot up. A kid—eighteen, nineteen—when she met and fell for Clyde Barrow. It's one of the few violent movies they'll show in here. You know, as a lesson to us."

"I'm talking about the girl who killed the old man. The one on death row."

"Brittany Holberg? Not a girl anymore. Fifty. Do your research."

"I don't know her name. I didn't do any research. I do know she didn't just use a *fork*, a butcher *knife*, a paring *knife*, and a *lamp pole*," I say. "She also stabbed him with a *grapefruit knife*. I'm pretty sure the old man had used it that week as a letter opener." I can almost make out the return address on an envelope.

"She was a stripper. He wanted sex." I slam my eyes shut again.

"Bouchet, come on back. Come on, *come on*. Jesus. Open your eyes. Stop swaying. I'm not up for a scam of useless information you found on the dark web about a case I don't give a crap about."

I let the envelope in my mind slide away, making room for another image. Only then do I raise my eyes to hers.

"You jammed your thumb in someone's eye over blue Jell-O." Not accusing. Just a statement.

"Yeah? Big deal. Everybody in here knows that."

"While you did it, you were singing 'Blue Christmas' in your head."

A few seconds go by.

"Not exactly," she says rigidly, "but you have my attention. Are you here to help me or not? We've got five minutes left. Maybe ten."

"Tell me what the letter from my mother said. The part that wasn't censored."

Nickie shifts in her chair, considering me. "Well, you are both hung up on blue. *Dear Nicolette*, she wrote. *Blue is an unlucky color for you*. Kind of a problem since I can't change the color of my own goddamn eyes. She told me nine was my unlucky number. There are three nines in the address at our house where Lizzie disappeared and two in my inmate ID number. I was born on June ninth. All of this, public information. Then she pulled out the big tease. She said that she knew who took Lizzie and where she was. The rest was blacked out, almost a third of the page, except for her signature. That's what made me a believer. That someone in here thought what she said was worth hiding. Because *they know I was set up*."

"Are you sure my mother wrote it?"

"I just gave you three goddamn paragraphs of proof."

"Is GD not a cuss word? Proof needs to be definitive. Was it typed?"

"Not typed. Handwritten. Are you suggesting it wasn't her writing?"

If we're being recorded, how much do I want them to know?

The fact is, I'd overheard my mother begin a hundred readings exactly the way she started Nickie's letter—with colors and numbers. A way to ease in with a new client. Establish some easy stuff, before she got to the hard stuff. Unlike Nickie, they were always ready and willing to add cement to whatever my mother said.

"Was there a tiny X drawn in each corner of the letter?" I ask.

"Yeah. I thought that was odd. You know, maybe a little kissy face added by a guard who has a thing for me. Is that some kind of proof it was her?"

I nod slowly. Probably. Yes. "My mother never wrote on a piece of paper without adding those four X's in the corners. She didn't even skip them for a grocery list or a permission slip for a school field trip where she only had to sign her name."

Nickie presses her temples like a migraine is crushing her.

"She used X as the variable," I continue. "The unknown. My mother thought X was mystic." Even as it applied to science.

"I can't get a good bead on you," Nickie fumes. "You're all over the place. Grapefruit knives and blue Jell-O and laser beams and algebra lessons. I know you're smart. You know what I am? Forty-one years old and determined to get out of here before I'm forty-five. Which means we need to focus."

She leans back across the table. "That *blue* Jell-O was lucky. It's the only reason I'm alive. You know what they called me after that incident? Not Nickie. *NicU.* Like the intensive care unit for babies. Because I'm the preemie prisoner in here you don't want to mess with. Because I'll *nick you.*"

That's just what you want to think, Nickie. What you want to hear from your groupies. What they really believe is that you are the worst of the worst. A baby killer.

A fresh image is blinding me. Blood drying brown on a 130-thread-count pillowcase.

A frizzy chunk of Nickie's brown hair spilling onto the sheet, unattached.

Gaping blue eyes with a dark green rim, just like the ones facing me across the table.

The tunnel in my head, wide open.

"I didn't come here because of your threats." I speak as calmly as possible. "I came here to tell you that I'm giving this two weeks. That's it. I'll set up another visit when and if I have anything new. I want to be absolutely clear: I'm not here for you. I'm here for Lizzie." An echo of Sharp.

"So you *are* going to help me. Sweet." A relieved smile emerges. It reveals a shadow of someone else. "Let's make up. Hold hands." Her arm reaches across the table, palm down.

"What?"

"Just do it. Hold my hand. I hardly get a kind touch in here."

I reach across hesitantly. She grips my fingers. I feel the edge of the small piece of paper instantly.

"We're going to be friends," she says softly. "Maybe more than friends."

"I don't think so."

I snatch my hand back, the paper in the nest of my fist. I slide it up the cream sleeve of my sister's cardigan. Basic sleight of hand. I am my mother's daughter.

There's a nod of approval in her eyes. Maybe even admiration.

"Nickie, someone in here is gunning for you." A whisper, barely there. "I just . . . saw it."

She lets out a coarse laugh. "You don't think I know that? If they can gut a big fish like Jeffrey Epstein, I'm just a guppy in a bowl." The bluster leaks out of her. "I'll take your two weeks."

She didn't ask whether I think Lizzie's alive. I didn't ask what her husband says when he visits every Tuesday or about their secrets. Each of these questions, a pebble skimming the surface. As soon as we ask them, there will be little we can do to stop the ripple. It will have to run its course. That's science. If I've learned anything from science, it's that everything we do, every kiss on the cheek, every flipped finger, every rocket ship to Mars creates undulating waves.

I need to be careful. I need to know more before I let Nicolette Solomon dig around my soul.

A shriek from the front of the room effectively ends all conversation. Every head at every table angled in one direction.

A guard who isn't Misha has a light hold on an elderly woman, sobbing, maybe struggling to say goodbye for the first time. Or for the three hundredth?

The prisoner she's visiting isn't so young herself. She's still seated, face just as tormented. *Sisters*, I think. One who was lucky, one who wasn't.

Misha the guard is nowhere in sight.

And then I spot her. She's ushering the little girl back from the vending machines, their arms full of candy. It makes me feel a notch better about humanity.

I stand up to leave. "I'll be in touch."

"Take my advice," she says. "Keep Sharp off your tail. And his tongue out of your ear."

15

Outside the door, I slip into the women's bathroom and lock a toilet stall, hoping a sharp-eyed camera operator didn't catch our exchange. Hoping no one rushes in to yank me off the toilet and confiscate this piece of paper.

I open it up. At first glance, perfectly blank. I run my finger over the top. A series of raised bumps.

A six-bit binary language. Braille, I'm betting.

Tiny, compact constellations that I will need to decode somewhere besides a prison bathroom stall with graffiti that says, "Warning: Suspicious tampons will be removed."

I pass through the metal detector holding my breath. No one stops me for a pat down. The guards are barking and distracted, irritated that the woman lugging a cake in pink Tupperware and another dressed like she dropped by after a porn shoot did not read the master list of rules. The line to pass through to visit felonious loved ones is five times as long as it was when I arrived.

"Vivian Bouchet?"

I flip my head abruptly. I don't recognize the man who uttered my name, third up to pass through the metal detector. It probably took him a good half hour to progress that far.

His face is unforgettable, like a famous character actor's whose name you can never place. His cheeks and chin sag with the weight of every year he's ever lived, which I'm guessing is about forty. Or fifty. The intelligence in his eyes is the only bit of light left.

A prison pastor, maybe? If so, he looks like one who has shouldered so much despair he no longer believes God exists, but still feels a duty to play along.

His eyes aren't budging from me. He steps out of line, his coveted spot swallowed immediately. Half of his expression is hidden in the folds of his basset hound cheeks.

"Do I know you?" I ask politely.

He sticks out his right hand. I take it. No flashes. His left one wears a platinum band. I glance longingly toward the exit.

All I want is to reach my Jeep without incident. The piece of paper Nickie slipped into my palm is riding in my panties like an itchy tag. I'd just passed a sign at a vending machine that read, "We do not accept money pulled out of undergarments," so activity with undergarments does appear to be on the watch list.

I return my mind to the man in front of me, still talking. "I'm sorry," he says. "I'm being rude. I'm Marcus Solomon. Lawyer. Husband of Nickie Solomon."

That wasn't even on my guess list. The pictures of Marcus Solomon in the file were of a slim, attractive man fully capable of a leading role.

"I'm her second guest of the day," he explains. "The prison is making an exception to the one-a-day visitor policy because I'm acting as an attorney this afternoon. Between you and me, a half lie." He half smiles, or at least I think he does.

"More to the point," he continues, "Nickie told me you were visiting today, and, frankly, I googled the hell out of your accomplishments and those flying saucer eyes."

I give him the slight quirk of a smile he so clearly wants.

"I listened to Bubba Guns trying to dissect you on the air," he continues blithely. "I wouldn't want to be in his crosshairs."

He waits another beat for me to fill in the blanks. Defend myself. I don't.

"Did it go well with Nickie?" he prods.

"That's for her to tell."

"A psychic with ethics. Discreet. I like it. Look, I'm sure you gathered that Nickie has this fantasy that Lizzie is still alive. Hell, maybe that fantasy is *keeping* Nickie alive. She says a mother *knows*. But a lawyer like me knows, too. If Lizzie were out there to be found, my private investigators would have found her. The truth is that our story, Nickie's and mine, is statistically guaranteed to have your typical tragic ending. A hiker is going to stumble onto Lizzie's bones one day, or someone will finally spit out a deathbed confession. I can't decide if I want that moment to happen before we die. Knowing has its own price. You know?"

I do.

He studies my face carefully before he lays a hand on my shoulder. "Your mother's letter has lit a crazed spark in Nickie," he says quietly. "I'm asking you to be careful. She might have a shot at an appeal. It won't help if she appears mentally unbalanced. Seeking clues on other planes, if you know what I mean."

I shift my body toward the door, hoping he will take the hint.

"You probably wonder why I believe her. Everybody does. If only the jurors had understood about the banging, I think they would have, too."

"The banging?" I ask vaguely. I'm thinking about last night, when my fist connected with the wall.

"The banging the neighbor heard coming from the house. Nickie did that sometimes, hauled off at walls with a sledgehammer, not just because our walls needed gutting, but because it was a release. Her version of a punching bag. I suggested it when we bought the house, and her therapist approved it. Nickie had a tough break. She was raped by three boys at a frat party when she was a freshman. According to her therapist, it likely played a big part in what led to her sex addiction. Other stuff. Her issues challenged my love for her but never erased it." He shrugs. "I have the feeling you would have been a juror who understood."

I instinctively slip my right hand, the one with the Band-Aid on the knuckle, behind my back. Knocking. Banging. He's right. I might have been the holdout.

"I don't remember reading any of that being introduced at trial," I say.

"It wasn't. The defense lawyer I hired thought that if she had enough rage to ram a sledgehammer into a wall, jurors might decide she'd let that same fury loose on a child. Can you understand?"

It's like he stood at my bedroom window and watched my battle with the wall last night. I like to think that Brig and Mom are the only people in the universe who ever knew about it. But that's just a pretend game I play with myself. Secrets are passed on like Kleenex, until people twenty times removed are wiping their noses with them.

Like this moment—I'm betting Nickie Solomon would rather her husband not stand in the middle of a crowded room and tell me she had been raped by three men. *Men, not boys*, Marcus.

The question is, why did he expose that terrible wound? So I'd sympathize with her? Understand her behavior better?

Or is it to help justify a terrible lie they are telling about what she did with Lizzie?

16

In the parking lot, Sharp is waiting for me behind mirrored aviators, arms and boots crossed, slouched against the door of my Jeep. I'd hoped we were going to avoid talking at all. The ear licking, suddenly and graphically top of mind.

When we'd arrived at Mountain View, Sharp surprised me and swung his truck into a parking space at least a dozen down from mine. His head was still a dark spot in the truck window when I'd glanced back before passing through the door to the building.

Now here he is, unable to resist a confrontation. Because what else would it be? I walk stiffly toward him, head down, strapping on my recently confiscated watch, making sure that the face is set exactly the way I left it, all my apps in order.

I preempt him as soon as he's close enough to hear. "It would be illegal for anyone in there to strip stuff off the Cloud using my watch while they had it in their possession."

"I'm not standing on 160-degree asphalt for a tête-à-tête about your paranoid delusions about law enforcement. I'm here to give you a heads-up. Bubba Guns made a bonus podcast for the weekend. It dropped while we were on the way down here. It's about you."

"That's why you were pointing," I say, almost to myself. "When you passed me."

"I was a few minutes in and realized you shouldn't listen to it while driving if you got alerted to it by a text from a well-meaning friend or colleague." *Or sister.* "Trust me. Turn off your phone. Just listen to some Dixie Chicks or whatever a chick like you listens to. Wait until you get home to your Charlie Brown whiskey glass to deal with Bubba Guns."

"Chicks."

"What?"

"They're just The Chicks now. No 'Dixie.'"

I play along with this meaningless banter while a sick dread is settling in my gut. I tap the text icon on my watch. Three from my boss. Eight from my sister. Two from Mike.

"Very considerate of you." The ashes of my headache are back in business, merging into a single flame behind my right eye. "Did anyone follow me here? Besides you, of course."

"I've been tracking plates in this lot for the last hour. All on the visitors' list. No media. You're safe."

"I ran into Marcus Solomon in there. He's safe?"

"Define what you consider safe."

"Funny. Are you even going to give me a hint at what Bubba Guns said on the podcast?"

"Nothing people are going to believe. Sane people, anyway. It isn't about the Solomon case." The last sentence, almost an after-thought.

"The Solomon case is the only reason I should be on his radar."

"He talked about your research, Vivian. In the desert. Your *top secret* research."

I try to push off a rush of nausea, steady a tremor in my legs. This lying media clown will get me fired if he successfully makes me an object of national ridicule.

I reach for the Jeep door and climb in, forcing Sharp to sidestep. *Is Lizzie worth all of this? The missing girl with the charm bracelet? Mike?*

"Waco and Fort Worth traffic are going to be heavy," Sharp says. "You want to follow me?"

"What do you think?" My tires, a little low on air, shriek out of the lot.

☽ ✧ ☾

The slitty-eyed windows of Mountain View's bunkers are watching as I whip away. The souls of Nickie and six-hundred-plus angry women are screaming *Help*, clinging to the fenders, trying to ride me to escape, insisting they don't belong on this ninety-acre plot of misery.

At the exit, I yank the wheel right on Farm to Market Road 215 instead of left toward Waco, sweep another left turn, and then a right, and then a left and right.

The best way to feel the muscles of Texas, to ride its natural curves and bends, is by traveling the Farm to Market roads. That's just what I'm doing. Feeling the roads. Feeling fury.

I drive until I've lost the voices. I pull over in a dirt rut, staring into a picture of harsh beauty that hasn't changed much for a hundred years. Barbed wire fence, big sky, blackbirds, and silence like glass waiting to be broken.

Get the farmers out of the mud. That's the lobbying slogan that took off after Texas opened its first Farm to Market road in 1941.

Well, I'm in the mud now.

Bubba Guns's podcast is queued up on my phone. All I need to do is press the arrow. For a few more minutes, I watch for oncoming dust in the rearview. I don't think Sharp was fast enough. Maybe he didn't want to be.

A crow lands lightly on the telephone line that stretches ahead of me. Every human emotion carried on that fragile string, on the invisible electrical impulses that fly past crows at the speed of light. What we can't see or hear is everywhere. It's faith. It's science.

Two caws rip the quiet. Two caws is good luck, according to Mom. Five caws, something's dead or dying.

Six more crows noiselessly drop in place. Twenty. I count an audience of fifty-two before setting Bubba Guns loose in the chilled prison of the Jeep.

☽ ✧ ☾

"Friends, Texans, aliens," Bubba Guns begins. "Welcome to our special bonus weekend podcast that digs into the psyche, so to speak, of the Texas woman we've been hearing a lot about lately, Vivian Bouchet. Is she part of a genetic legacy of psychics, legitimately hired by the Fort Worth cops to find Lizzie Solomon, our long-lost baby girl? Or is she a West Texas astrophysicist with her eyes on alien skies?

"Well, folks, aliens may be the bigger story. In the coming week, we're going to take a hard look at Vivian Bouchet, an enigma worth unwrapping. We're going to start with her possibly covert job as an astrophysicist. Our sources have told us she did a little bit of work getting us to Mars, where we're digging for alien worms. Our *better* sources say she and Elon Musk are cooking up a plan to meet intelligent alien life in the Chihuahuan Desert. You heard that right, Big Benders. Consider the facts. Elon Muskrat is on a mission. He has moved into the Lone Star State, setting up a little rocket launch site called Starbase near the Mexican border in South Texas and a rocket testing facility in McGregor. Tesla headquarters has made the jump to Austin. I've got a prayer in to Almighty God that Mr. Musk doesn't end up as my next-door neighbor running his for-shit solar-powered lawn mower and bragging about turning Austin into "a mini-California" like it's a damn *compliment*. Like all the California home-seekers-slash-earthquake-wildfire-escapees have a right to outbid native Texans on a right to live here. Do y'all know the joke: *What's the difference between a Yankee and a damn Yankee? A Yankee goes home.* Well, it applies to Suckramento and SmellA, too. If I sound a little extra pissed, I'm on my third Shiner. My producer is on her fourth and wanted me to share a little tidbit that Shiner was invented in Shiner, Texas, in 1909, by a Bavarian immigrant man named—what else, folks—*Kosmos*. Now who says Texas doesn't support immigration?

"Back with more on the *cosmic* Vivian Bouchet in a few."

The crows swoop off the line in one fluid motion. No caw. Just a silent warning.

I text my sister.

    I don't know Elon Musk.

I text my boss.

    I will call you tomorrow at 7 A.M.

I tweet at Bubba Guns with fury, ignoring every bit of my intuition.

    I'd love to be on your show.

17

Halfway back to Fort Worth, I yank the Jeep into a gas station packed with white pickups, as common in Texas as the handguns stored in their center consoles. Not a Tesla in sight.

Yet another white truck has swerved in from the service drive and negotiates around the stack of vehicles lined up at the pumps. It disappears on the side of the convenience store, out of view before I can tell if it's Sharp.

It doesn't really matter. Pee or die. I need a bathroom, icy caffeine, and to slip Nickie's note out of my underwear before my butt presses every braille dot flat and unreadable.

I'm inside the store for approximately eight minutes. When I emerge, my teeth deep into a glazed donut, Sharp is handcuffing a red-faced middle-aged woman whose shoulder is planted against the giant spare on the back of my Jeep. I'm just in time to catch her spit a glob of mucus on his cheek. I drop the donut.

The woman's fingertips are the color of Cheetos. Her shorts are riding up her crotch. Her T-shirt says *It Ain't a Vaccine.*

Littering the ground—two cans of spray paint with missing lids and a large hunting knife that's slashed at least two of my tires. Looped in traffic-cone orange across my windshield is the word

Bitch with the *B* crossed out in black and a *W* inserted in its place. *Witch*.

"My . . . Jeep," I stutter out.

"Another ace criminal in action," Sharp says with irritation. "I don't recommend you partner up." He gently tips up the woman's chin and points for her benefit to a camera above the store's glass double door. "That was a thousand-dollar spitball."

His words trail off into the air-horn blast of a siren as a local patrol car stops short behind my Jeep. Sharp flips around, holding out his badge for the new officers before they even emerge. He's on their territory.

I wordlessly dip my finger into a splotch of paint on the hood. The next time I'm aware of Sharp, he's reaching out to still my right hand, which is swirling the orange and black paint on my windshield into a foggy mess with a wad of fast-food napkins.

"It's going to take a professional." Sharp snatches the napkins from my fingers and tosses them into a lidless trash can by the door.

I half fall to a sitting position on the curb.

Sharp hovers, a hulking shadow against the blare of sun, not saying a word while I try to pull myself together.

I think about eclipses. The ones in the sky, beautiful and blinding. The ones on Earth that shroud lost girls so we can't find them, maybe ever.

Boots and running shoes and flip-flops step around me like someone crying on the curb in front of this gas station is a daily occurrence.

Like these feet belong to people who wouldn't bother with a little girl in a bow whose frantic face is pressed to a window.

Like they would step on a lost charm bracelet, pick it up, ask no questions, wipe the links shiny with polish, and latch it on their own wrists.

One man taps a cigarette ash while he brushes by me. It singes my bare arm before landing on the skirt of my sunny yellow dress, a black snowflake.

Sharp kneels, flicking off the ash like a piece of bad luck. It's the instinctual act of a brother, a lover, a tricky cop.

"You want a ride?" he asks.

☽ ✧ ☾

The inside of Sharp's pickup smells like a bitter dark roast coffee or gunpowder, I can't decide.

Black earth lies in clumps all over the industrial floor mats. A camouflage Bison cooler, cold enough to chill a heart, swallows most of the back seat. A lasso is tossed on the floor behind Sharp, a brown stain I don't want to think about on a noose that is stiff as a wire.

I observe all of this before climbing in. I feel oddly compelled to accept his offer, like someone has finally bullied me onto a roller coaster. I clutch the giant, wide-open paper map of Texas taking up the passenger seat and set my backpack at my feet. Nickie's note is hidden in an inside pocket, waiting to be translated.

While Sharp presses the ignition, I negotiate with the map, collapsing it perfectly in seconds, an act that calms me far more than the deep breaths I've been sucking. It's like the wooden Mensa puzzles my mother used to stick in our Christmas stockings. Solvable, if you become one with it.

"That hasn't been folded for ten years," Sharp says. "Go ahead. Make fun of it. Everybody does."

"I love paper maps," I say automatically. "Of the Earth. Of the sky. They help you acquire deep knowledge versus surface knowledge. Google Maps can tell you out loud how to get from point A to point B. But it's shallow information. It doesn't embed. You get perspective from a map, a more geographical sense of the surroundings. Touching your finger to the paper and tracing a route, even if it is just a hike—it's a more sensual, sensory experience. You log it in your brain, sometimes forever."

"I'll try that explanation next time on my eleven-year-old niece."

That sets me back for a second. I don't want to think of Sharp as an uncle—as an object of fondness. Not with a bloody lasso in his back seat.

"Who was she?" I bluntly change the subject. "The woman who attacked my Jeep."

"Barbara Jean McClean of McKinney, Texas, according to her driver's license. Barbie to her friends."

"That's seriously her name? Being cursed with that might explain everything. Is Bubba Guns one of her friends?"

Sharp shrugs as he swings the truck onto the highway. "One of the few who are the many. We'll find out more when she's booked. The patrol cops said they'd be in touch. I put them off, but they'll be in touch with you, too."

"You told me I wasn't followed." Accusatory.

He shrugs. "She claims it was coincidence. She recognized your Jeep. The color. License plate. Your nose. Who knows? It's a game to these people who find their prey through social media. Gives them purpose. A sense of community, like a church. They've got spotters everywhere. A texting system so they can tag-team a vehicle. I've encountered drug runners with less sophisticated communication."

"And you being here? A coincidence?"

"What do you people call it? Predestination?"

"If you're a Presbyterian, maybe."

Sharp half smiles, then grimaces. *"I'd love to be on your show."*

It's like scissors cutting paper. My tweet in his mouth is a surprise, although it shouldn't be. He had been waiting an hour to say it.

"Seriously, Vivian?" he asks. "You're lighting the flammable hair of a thousand more Barbies. A hundred thousand."

I stare out of the dark tint of the passenger window. "I don't want to talk about this. Or my conversation with Nickie Solomon, if that's on top of your bucket list right now. But you need to know that I will not let a media freak take down my career. Or turn my sister's private life into a circus so she's too scared to let my nephew play in his own front yard or always feels the need to defend herself—defend *me*—to reporters and neighbors and her goddamn book club."

My anger has nowhere to go in the vacuum of the truck.

"Vivvy, I get it," Sharp says. "But you need to focus on the short-term goal here—the very noble act of bringing closure to the case of a missing girl named Lizzie. Not meeting Martians in a desert. Let Bubba Guns burn himself out. He'll get tired of you."

"Oh, Jesus, *there are no Martians*. We shouldn't even be on Mars, in my opinion. It's like Death Valley. We're digging on Mars because it has clear air, an atmosphere that allows the human eye to see the landscape. Because human survival there is more likely. *Because we recognize it*. Venus is a far more interesting soup. Hot, nasty clouds. The powers that be think *too* hot. But deep-sea creatures in our oceans live in thermal vents without air. They absorb iron from the ocean to build hard skin. Aliens will *adapt*." I'm not sure where this rant sprang from because I don't share it often. I just know I don't want to talk about Lizzie.

"What I'm hearing is, scientists can be as divisive as cops."

"If by *divisive*, you mean collect ratty data and a lot of egos and then form completely divergent opinions—then yes. We don't even know what dark matter is, but scientists will claim it makes up 85 percent of the universe. Really, tap any scientist and you have a theory. Which, ultimately, is very good for humanity."

Sharp places a large hand on the console. The narrow space between us, intensely intimate. "Dark matter," he says softly. "That about covers all of it for cops. One hundred percent. Vivian, I need to say that you are not at all what I thought."

I shift uncomfortably in the seat. "That's the second time I've heard that today." Everything in me is saying not to let down my guard. That he's pulling out his most delicate scalpel. That I won't even feel it on my skin until it is touching bone.

"For the record," I say coolly, "I'm not chasing aliens with Elon Musk. I'm hoping for just the tiniest spark of light. The universe is expanding at such a rate, the space between us so infinite, that I don't think we'll ever touch fingers with other intelligent life."

"Well, that's a very big letdown. Come on, though. Believer to skeptic. How does Vivian Bouchet imagine intelligent alien life?"

"Imperfect," I reply instantly. "I don't know why we tend to think aliens will have it any more together than humans."

☽ ✧ ☾

Sharp breaks the silence five miles short of home to say he'd like a bathroom break and to pick up a six-pack of Modelo.

Unexpectedly long Sunday, and all that. His home fridge, beer-less.

I'm not sure why Sharp thinks a regular white lie will fool me—I'm sitting a foot from his phone. It's been vibrating in his pocket impatiently for the last hour and a half.

I say no problem—I'll wait in the truck while he runs into the gas station. I'm guessing he's checking in with "the office," assuring them he has whipped me and my tweeting under control, asking when he'll get a transcription of my conversation with Nickie at the prison.

I find it telling that he hasn't asked a single word about Nickie or mentioned their cozy prison chats.

Sharp's been gone less than a minute when I lean down and let my hand roam under my seat. In the pocket beside my seat. Nothing.

I flip down the passenger side visor and find a messy version of myself in the mirror. I push some wild hair behind my ears with fingers painted orange and yellow, like Halloween worms.

I pop the glove compartment. A larger collection of maps. Oklahoma. Colorado. New Mexico. A nice one of Big Bend that I'd like to swipe. I open the Big Bend map halfway and place the black pad of a finger on a band of empty terrain, the approximate location of my favorite spot on Earth. I leave a smudge.

Latex gloves. A pack of antibacterial wipes. A compass. A mini Maglite. A heavy-duty portable phone charger with four tiny blue lights on full power. Two granola bars with twenty whopping grams of protein. A ballpoint pen. A Swiss Army knife that looks like it could have been his grandfather's. Two black nylon face masks stamped with *Police* in big white type. A small bottle of Benadryl tablets. Truck registration and insurance. It's a very roomy, well-stocked glove box.

I envision the contents of mine, bouncing along with the tow truck driver hauling my Jeep back. Three packets of electrolyte solution. A bottle of Nyquil. Pens and pencils. Some backup binoculars. A well-fingered, disintegrating map of West Texas not nearly as nice as his. An old snakebite kit with a tiny blade that was in the Jeep when I bought it.

I keep the snakebite kit as a reminder that *cut at the fang mark and suck* used to be considered good scientific advice not that many years ago when, in fact, putting your germy mouth on the open wound of a snake bite is about the stupidest thing you can do. To be a good researcher, I must reassess. Seek more proof. Always. Which I'm doing right now.

My hand continues to wander the truck. I pull up on the latch of the truck's center console. It doesn't give. I tug again. Run my fingers around the edges looking for a latch I've missed. Instead, I find the slick metal surface of a custom lock.

The light outside is failing. The Texas sun, when it decides to finally go down, wastes no time in its last sixty seconds. Through the lit windows of the gas station, I can make out the shoulder of Sharp's pale blue shirt.

He's second in line behind a woman who's plopping her toddler on the counter along with a full plastic shopping basket.

I tell myself I've got at least two minutes.

I scramble over the console, jabbing the ripped skin on my stomach into the steering wheel. It's karmic payback, a sign I should stop what I'm doing. I bend over anyway, wincing, and run my hand under his seat. Discover a set of flares. Zip ties. A hammer.

One final invasion of his privacy before giving up. I pry down the driver's-side visor. A confetti of paper sprays my face. A dozen receipts. More.

I try to catch one floating into the back seat, and another now on the floor of the passenger side. Receipts for gas. Food. Rope. Garbage bags. A motel. This is clearly where he stashes the stuff he wants to expense.

When I glance up, Sharp's already at the front of the line, head down. Probably running his credit card.

He can't find me like this. It will destroy the fragile bit of tolerance we have for each other and that seems very important if I'm going to find Lizzie.

Gathering up the receipts turns into a full-blown game of Twister.

One is still lying behind me, under the seat, its white edge just out of reach. The large console, too much of an obstacle. I'll have to leave it. I stack the receipts neatly, align their top corners, decide they're too tidy, mess them up a little.

It's not until I start to stuff them back up that I notice another piece of paper firmly clipped to the edge of the visor. About three by five. Not the thin tissue of a receipt.

Blank. Something on the flip side, I know it.

I don't have time.

Sharp is still in the store, but barely—he's standing with the woman and her toddler a foot from the glass door. Animated. Pointing. Giving directions.

The woman is what my mother would call a "Grand Interventionist." A stranger sent to help me. To distract.

I place the receipts in a niche on the dash. I unclip the paper from the visor, careful not to tear it.

I turn it over in my palm. I can't make out much in the curling dark of the cab. It's definitely a photo. A muddy silhouette. A waterfall of unruly hair spilling down. Someone leaning against a tree? A truck?

I pull the photo closer to my face. Try to angle it so the icy lights by the gas station pumps behind me can help. When I blink, I make out a tiny, tiny detail. I blink a second and a third time, and I'm not sure if I'm just imagining it. It comes, it goes.

I whip up my head again.

Sharp's not inside anymore. *Where?*

My pulse, in my ears.

There he is. A tall shadow two cars down, bending into the back seat of a car. Maybe strapping the toddler into her booster seat? Helpful? Genuine?

Is he that kind of man? Or another kind?

I glance back to the picture in my hand, desperate to see all of it.

Oh, what the hell. There is an intervention going on.

I punch on one of the overhead lights.

I don't want to be right, but I am.

18

'm frozen to the seat. My brain is yelling, *Move.*

It chills me, this picture clipped to the visor of Sharp's truck. I caught a cute, fresh face I won't forget in that two-second, on-off flash of overhead light. A charm bracelet clipped to her wrist.

Her terror is shrieking under my skin. My blood feels like her blood. She's telling me she is dead as much as Lizzie has been proclaiming she's alive.

I work to compose myself. What does this say about Sharp? Hiding this photo in his truck, where his skin sweats and breathes, is the male version of a picture in a locket. Only worse—because *she is gone.* It's the sign of a man who can't stop loving something that doesn't exist anymore. Or that he feels guilty about. Or that he's obsessed with. Maybe all three.

Every other object in the truck suddenly feels as ominous as it does practical. The zip ties. The paper map that would allow him to turn off his GPS. The hammer. The latex gloves. The lasso, sized for a neck.

I'm certain the charm bracelet on this woman's arm is the same one lying in the leaves in the photograph at the police station. The photograph Sharp placed on the table with the ones from another crime scene. Why? Why is he hiding her face in his truck and sneaking a crime scene photograph into the open? Why will he talk to me about Lizzie Solomon but say nothing about this girl he wears like an iron shroud?

The charm bracelet in the leaves had only a few charms. The one on the woman's wrist in the visor photograph is loaded, an intense, packed record of a young life. A clatter of sound that would have announced her arrival every time.

I search my memory of that picture at the police station. Black berries. Dead leaves. A silver unicorn. A butterfly. A heart with the initial *A*.

I want to compare both bracelets with a magnifying glass. I feel a pressing need to draw the shapes of those brittle leaves as if they will tell me a story.

My body is still motionless. In Sharp's seat.

Move.

My fingers aren't cooperating very well as I force myself to clip the photo back in place. I add the receipts, shove up the visor, tumble out of the door.

☽ ✧ ☾

I have arranged myself against the large black custom grille on the front of the truck. I didn't have time to run around to the other side and pretend I never moved. I'm breathing hard, more from panic he'll figure out what I did than exertion.

The wire mesh, still hot from a day of sun and a running engine, burns through my thin dress. Sharp left the motor on so I could stay cool. Because he was the kind of man who helped tuck a child in a car seat, right?

I close my eyes and see my mother.

A handcuff of memories.

That's what my mother called charm bracelets when Brig and I begged for them one Christmas. She'd shaken her head. A crystal, not a charm, tumbled out of the little velvet bags she put under the tree for us.

The past only weighs you down.

I hear Sharp open a door to the truck behind me. I don't think he sees me in front of the hood. He'd switched off the headlights before going into the store.

He's taking his time with something. Maybe he's noticing I've messed with his receipts, or he can smell my scent perfuming his leather seat.

Maybe he thinks I ran from him. Maybe he thinks I see things about him he doesn't want me to when, in fact, his mind is a rock I can't drill.

Sharp could pretend he didn't notice me over his monster hood. Press the gas. *Psychic Couldn't See Her Own Death Coming.* That would be Bubba Guns's show tease.

I stumble to the passenger's side on rubbery legs. Yank open the door. Sharp's not in the front seat. He's leaning into the rear door on the driver's side, messing with the cooler.

"What are you doing?" he asks, annoyed.

"What are *you* doing?" I ask back, nonsensically. "I wanted some fresh air."

"It's a fresh ninety-five degrees," he mutters.

The words, the tone, normal for Sharp.

He dumps a roar of ice into the cooler before methodically beginning to dig deep vertical holes for his beer. One hole. Two holes. Three holes. Four. Five. Six. He pushes the bottles in until only the flat of the metal cap is showing, like the crown of a head in the water, about to disappear. *His hand, reaching out. Hair, floating like snakes.*

Is it me? Is he drowning *me*?

Chink, chink, chink from the back seat. Ice against glass.

It's setting off a terrible tambourine.

The same as when the charm girl stormed my house and shook her bracelet in my face.

The same as when my mother agitated the ice in her metal travel coffee cup full of whiskey, trying to drown the voices.

The same as when I heard the clank of Nickie's handcuffs.

"Are you getting in?" Sharp asks.

☽ ✧ ☾

Sharp pulls the visor down just enough to tuck in a receipt, and my breath catches.

I have no idea if it's the one that drifted under his back seat or if it's brand-new, from the store.

He doesn't say a word. I feel glued to the seat as his foot lays on the gas. I wonder if he planted that picture just for me.

☽ ✧ ☾

It isn't until Sharp swings the truck in front of my mother's house ten minutes later that I realize I didn't tell him how to get here. He took the shortest, best route. He knew the way like his finger had traced me on paper. Like I was a rutted road.

My head turns toward the house, dark and as unwelcoming as ever. Its expiration date has come and gone like a rotting piece of fruit. It even smells like it when I step out of the truck and get a hit of garbage cans waiting on the curb for pickup. Everything composting in the hot summer night. Banana peels, used condoms, decaying meat.

"I'll walk around." Sharp shifts the truck into park. "Do a quick check of the yard."

"Are you saying I should be worried about another lunatic lying in wait?"

"Aren't you?"

"This house is listed under my mother's birth name, which does not begin with Asteria and does not end in Bouchet." I work to steady my voice. "I think they'd have a hard time finding me."

I have no idea why I said that since it's not true. This house, where I lived from ages ten to eighteen, is the first address that will pop up if someone gives my name a try. Just a few clicks and a $10 fee away.

The only place I've ever truly felt anonymous, safe, is in the desert with the javelinas and the snakes.

While Sharp travels the yard with a high beam, I flip on every light in the house. Check the closets, under the beds. Feel unsure even when I'm done.

I open the front door just as Sharp's boot hits the top step on the porch.

"Do you know there is an empty pup tent in your backyard?" he asks.

"Yes. It's for the little girl next door."

Emme. She used to run away to the streetlight in front of our house. She'd stand there with a tiny suitcase with her doll in it. No clothes, just Molly the Dolly. Mom talked to Emme's mom before setting up the little tent in the backyard for her to run to instead.

That's where Mom brought her banana bread with melting butter that sank into its pores. Told her the legends about the stars. Declared that being autistic was a gift. That Emme saw what others couldn't.

"Emme and my mom . . . they became . . . great friends," I murmur. "Emme sang a song she wrote for her at the funeral. The lyrics were beautiful." *Andromeda now holds you in her arms.*

"Tell *Emme* to stay out of your yard until the Bubba Guns stuff resolves itself. Maybe I'll drop by and talk to her mother myself. I can't guarantee his followers draw the line at children, especially if they mistake her for yours." Sharp is already off the porch, pressing the remote on his truck. Ready to yank a beer out of the ice and call it a day.

I jump four porch steps to catch up with him. As his engine starts a low-roll thunder, I'm banging on the passenger window with my fist. The window slides down, the blue light of the dash bathing Sharp's face. I'm not sure why I'm doing this, just that I have to.

"Nickie Solomon told me that you tainted a crime scene once, maybe more. She implied that you shine your badge with blood."

"I doubt Nickie Solomon was ever that poetic," he says dryly.

"I'm paraphrasing." I hesitate. "I saw a vision of a charm bracelet in my head when she said that." It's a lie rewarded with silence.

I start again. "When I picked the charm bracelet from your photo lineup, it made you believe in me for a second. You want my trust? This is the way. By telling me everything you know about these two lost girls. The girl with the charm bracelet. And Lizzie. As long as they keep asking me for answers, I won't give up on either of them. Do you understand? *You cannot hide anything from me.*"

The snake has crawled out of my mouth, the one I work so hard to keep hibernating. The one my sister says to never, ever let out. The threat that has venom but no teeth.

Sharp switches the truck in gear.

"I never said I wanted your trust, Vivvy."

☽ ✧ ☾

I slap shut every curtain and blind in the house. I check the backyard for Emme's shadow, the front yard for midnight wannabe Bubbas, my mother's bed for ghosts.

I rip off my sister's old yellow sundress, tearing one of the straps, mourning its death after spotting a large streak of orange paint near the hem. I'm hoping Brig doesn't have a sentimental attachment to this piece of clothing she abandoned here.

The dress reeks of the prison. And not just the dress. My hair. My skin. Like I'm sweating out a bad flu.

I wonder if this terrible smell is specific *to me*, to my experience. If every other visitor in that room today thinks they walked out of there smelling the same as when they went in.

I toss the dress and my underwear into the washer and slam it shut. I run the water as hot as I think I can stand it. My bathroom is a swirl of fog before I step in the shower.

The water is a relentless, welcome drill on my face. My eyes sting from the mascara and eyeliner now running a thin black river down the drain. By the time I've finished scrubbing my body red, I can't tell where today's surprise sunburn lines end or begin.

I towel off my hair and throw on a pair of shortie pajamas from late high school that make me look and feel like a child. I packed for two weeks, not months, when I first showed up to help with mom. On my few rushed trips back to the telescope, my mind was on the sky, not on grabbing up wardrobe supplements.

My feet pad wet prints across the wood floor. I pick up my backpack, still lying in the foyer. I retrieve two things from it: my phone, turned off since I floated a tweet at Bubba Guns, and Nickie's note, which has been nagging me for the last three hours. On the kitchen table, with careful fingers, I unfold and flatten out the creases in the small piece of paper. I leave the phone in its coma.

After grabbing one of the crystal glasses from the dining room cabinet, I pour a whiskey like an adult. I sit in "my place" at the table—my back always to the stove, toasty in winter, a sweat-fest in summer when the coils of the air conditioner would freeze up from exhaustion. My fingers run over the rough bumps on Nickie's note. I take another sip. And another, until the hot shower and the whiskey are best friends, and my laptop is blinking to life.

I wonder if Nickie knows there's an eccentric asteroid named Braille.

9969 Braille, to be exact, the 9,969th asteroid to be discovered.

It's elongated. A rare Mars-crosser. A slow rotator. Noted by NASA's *Deep Space 1* as it flew by like an elderly injured eagle on its way to the more spectacular comet Borrelly. Named for Louis Braille, who was jabbed in the eye by an awl, living in agony as a child, before he went on at fifteen to transform the silent night writing invented by the French army into a literary code that blew open the world for the blind.

I stare at the spray of dots on my small piece of paper.

Translating books into braille textbooks is one of the most coveted jobs offered to prisoners at the Mountain View Unit. I doubt Nickie is that well behaved or lucky. But she's likely made some friends who know the alphabet.

When I was a kid, I ran my fingers on the raised dots on ATMs and bathroom door signs that distinguished men's from women's. I cast my eyes over a braille alphabet on the back of Helen Keller's

The Story of My Life. That's about the extent of my proficiency with braille. I do know that braille takes up a lot of space. The first Harry Potter is five volumes in braille. The Bible, maybe forty.

It turns out, Nickie has given me only six specific letters.

It takes about two minutes to translate from a braille cheat sheet online, then another fifteen to double-check with four different websites. It's a strange word.

L O O P E R

I have no idea what it means. I rack my brain for any symbiotic connection to the case file. I don't remember a road, a person, a business, a town—nothing with the name Looper.

I consider the letters in all combinations. With spaces. With capital letters. Without.

L Ooper. Lo Oper. I add letters Nickie might have missed. *Loop her.* Backward, if she is being slightly tricky: *Repool.*

I power up my phone. The opening screen lights up with a train of notifications.

As expected, @therealbubbaguns is one of them, already holstered on Twitter.

Welcome to MY space @stargirl2001

I type out an angry response, poised to let it fly.

It wasn't easy growing up as a weird girl who talks to ghosts and is as pale as one. It wasn't easy letting lies stand.

I've silently walked away from dozens of word bullies who've left marks more permanent than stones.

There is no doubt. *They won.*

Not this time.

I hear Sharp in my head. My sister. The cursor blinks at me for five more minutes before I slowly erase each letter one by one. It's like forcing bullets back up a barrel.

19

He picks up after the fourth ring, breathing in ragged gasps.

"Are you already having sex?" I demand. "You have an inordinate amount of sex."

"Vivvy. What the hell."

"I have a question."

"Can it wait? I'm running."

"At midnight? I'm sure you are running. I want to know what the word 'Looper' means to you. If it means anything. That's it. All I need."

A muffled exclamation, like he has jerked the phone away.

"Say that again." He's back on the line. Clear.

"Looper. L-O-O-P . . ."

"I know how to spell, dammit. Where'd you get that?" He allows about two seconds of silence.

"I'm coming over. I'm not that far."

He hangs up before I can say no.

☽ ✧ ☾

I don't know why, but I thought Sharp would be pearly white underneath the jeans and the boots. That the brick-red farmer's tan would break off right below the neck.

A sheen of sweat under the porch light has turned his legs and arms to copper. His hair is wetter than mine right now. I'm staring at white running shoes. Shorts that reveal sinewy muscle. A faded gray tank that hangs loose under the arms that look like they work horses and cattle, not a machine in a gym.

I'd never imagined him out of those black boots. Or running. I figured he was a man with a very quick draw, who only moved if he met someone with a faster one. It doesn't matter if what's underneath is better than I expected. What's going on *between* us is what scientist types like me call a repulsive force.

He's eyeing my mother's daisy-print robe, the one I threw on over my pajamas, never intending to let him in. The robe is from an era before her era. My mother loved daisies. She called them the *day's eye*, because they woke up at dawn, full of hope and magical herbal properties. I considered daisies to be just one more thing that was watching me, sometimes from the vase on the dining room table. Most recently, from the spray on my mother's grave.

Sharp brushes by me like a wet dog. I stare out the door into the empty street. No truck.

Why is he running this close to my house? Or was he dropped off?

"Don't you live in an apartment on the other side of town?" I ask, trailing him. Mike had mentioned that.

"Can I have a towel?"

He's tossing that remark behind him, already on his way to the kitchen. He sneaks a quick, surgical glance around the room. I was ready. The only thing left on the table is my laptop, screen dark.

I start rooting through the hand towels in a drawer by the sink. "I figured you always carried a gun."

"What makes you think I'm not?"

I try to figure out where it is while I toss him a terry-cloth dish towel from better days, one that's been washed until soft, considered clean, but still smells faintly like old grease if you bring it up to your nose. He rubs it across his face, along his neck, over his hair, doesn't complain. Lays it neatly over a chair before he sits in it.

I set a cold bottle of water in front of him. I think his gun must be holstered at his back, under his T-shirt.

"Looper," he says conversationally, as if reminding me.

"Right." I remain standing. "Looper. I have no context for this. I promise. It just seemed important." Almost completely true.

"Looper is a nickname for Casey Gibbs, mostly what his mother and fellow ropers called him. Looper was the rodeo circuit kid that Nickie was fooling around with at the time Lizzie disappeared. The person Nickie was talking to on the phone while her daughter, Lizzie, vanished from the kitchen. I'm assuming that's still Nickie's story? That she told you nothing different?" I'm surprised at his instant willingness to share information.

He holds up a hand.

"Answer, don't answer. You want a theory? My theory is Casey 'Looper' Gibbs was involved. Always a better suspect than Marcus Solomon, Lizzie's father. Looper inherited two thousand acres of ranch land in a trust from his grandfather. We ran dogs over the quarter of it accessible by dirt roads, looking for Lizzie's body. Somebody would have had to use a four-wheeler to get over most of the terrain, a difficult prospect when hauling a body. We've done drone searches over the most likely areas through the years. A big zero."

"So then why do you think . . . Looper had something to do with it?"

"My gut. *Because* there was nothing. It takes a lot of grit and determination and callous to bury a child in a hidey-hole so deep it's as if she was never born. I watched Looper rope. Saw the grit. Saw the determination. Saw the callous." He takes a swig of water. "You've got to consider what it takes to dig a grave in Texas clay. Most people will do a half-ass job as soon as they begin to sweat. Lizzie's father would have. He was half-ass all the way when it came to physical labor. Lawyer hands that would have blistered and bled and been instantly noticed by the cops. Look at the way he put in that trim in the dog door. If he'd done it right, which would take about ten more minutes than he gave it, you wouldn't have that scratch." I involuntarily place my hand on my stomach, as if he can see through my robe. "His paint job on the walls of Lizzie's room looks like he was slapping a raw chicken."

"Nice imagery," I say.

"When you talk to Nickie," he continues, "why don't you ask about *her* sex life. About how she could sleep with a man who always yanked a calf's neck with his rope a little harder than he needed to."

"Do you really believe that . . . Looper and Nickie worked together? That one of them killed Lizzie and helped the other cover it up?"

"Now, that would be heinous, wouldn't it? That's why I'm here—to get the breaking news from your crystal ball."

I don't take the bait. I do what used to drive Brig crazy. I distract with science.

"Did you know a guy once slapped a raw chicken until he cooked it?" I ask. "Converted thermal energy to kinetic energy. It took eight hours. 135,000 slaps. For years, physicists said it was possible, but no one could ever do it. It took a college student willing to work on a lot of contraptions and a lot of failed theories that didn't pan out. He got there because he didn't give up."

"Are you offering this up as some kind of life lesson?"

"I'm just saying that dismissing me will be your mistake. That even with the help of my 'crystal ball,' I always slog ahead on a practical path using the other part of my brain. You want to know what my brain is telling me? It's telling me to talk to Looper even if you already have. You don't have to be on board, but don't get in my way."

Sharp releases a hoarse laugh. "I hope you have better contacts than I do. Because the courts have declared Casey 'Looper' Gibbs dead."

☽ ✧ ☾

I try but can't sleep after Sharp leaves. I drag an old quilt to the backyard like Brig and I used to when we were kids and stare into the light-polluted night that surrounds Fort Worth.

I can only make out Venus and Alioth, a star so bright even ancient Babylonians babbled about it.

I'm missing my mother, not knowing if she's here. Missing the stars, even knowing they are there, behind a curtain of corrupted sky. I long to be lying in West Texas, one of the darkest places on Earth, where the quilt is above me, spilling with milk and sequins, reminding me I am lucky to be alive in this incomprehensible miracle.

Instead, I'm thinking about a dead man named Looper. About nineteen braille dots on a piece of paper.

Sharp's details were short and brutal.

Nickie's rodeo star lover of four months drowned in Lake Texoma eight years ago at age twenty-seven. Looper's fishing spot that day was a tall, slick rock dubbed the Alamo by the renegade boaters who use it as a marker on a lonely, restricted part of the lake known for a ruthless undertow that can suck people under.

A lake patrol found Looper's belongings at sunset. No boat. Just a pyramid of twelve Shiner beer cans, nine empty; his wallet, stuffed with four hundred-dollar bills; a cooler with two striped bass struggling to breathe in shallow water; and a wooden cross, which he'd carved himself, on a silver chain. His mother recognized it immediately. She said her son wore it when he roped, all glory to God, but he always, *always* took it off before he jumped in the lake.

"The story is that he dove off that rock drunk, and a three-hundred-pound catfish ate him." Sharp had been staring at me across the kitchen table with a straight face. "I can see you don't believe that. My uncle Owen was a diver in that lake. Twice, he saw a catfish in Texoma bigger than he was. There's a lot we don't know about what's going on in those waters. It's a ninety-three-thousand-acre stretch. Might as well be your sky."

"I don't disbelieve anything. It's just interesting that *you* believe a fish story." *That you believe in a myth that swims in a man-made lake.* "No one was with . . . Looper?"

"No one claims to be."

"And?"

He'd shrugged. "The lake never gave the body back. But it's that way sometimes. Official cause of death is accidental drowning. Because there was intent to swim. He took his cross off." His face, still straight.

"What if he ran? Has been in hiding?"

"He'd be a lot smarter than I thought he was."

"What about suicide?" A way to wrap this up more karmically even if it means I'm wrong about Lizzie being alive.

"He wasn't the type."

"I don't think there is a type when it comes to suicide."

"Trust me. There's a type who'd kill anybody but himself."

His eyes started playing a memory, a film just for him. Eyes, usually so perfectly controlled, revealed someone who has seen too much. Done too much. An hour later, I'm still bothered by them.

☽ ✧ ☾

Fifty yards in front of me, the shadows of branches flicker across the top of Emme's tent, like skeletons at a ritual dance. It's hypnotic. When I was a kid, I found peace sitting in this exact spot, thinking about the world in motion. The flutter of leaves in the wind, the explosion and rippling of a puddle after I chunked a rock in it, the friction of my butt on a hot slide, the chaos of Coke bubbles in a glass.

Tonight, the spin and sway of the branches bring no peace. It doesn't matter that I know nothing alive is in that tent because I checked it and the gate lock before spreading out the quilt on a patch of bumpy lawn.

The lasso in Sharp's truck is bothering me. A new idea won't stop beating. Did Sharp enact his own justice for Lizzie Solomon? Did he follow Looper to the lake, steal the rope out of his truck, tighten it around his neck like a ring of fire, and haul him back to his two-thousand-acre abyss of Texas clay where he will never be found? Or was it a fierce dance of water and muscle, up close and personal, until Looper's bobbing head gave up and sank below the surface?

Am I seeing the end of Looper in those flashes of water I'm getting? Was that the silent film playing in Sharp's eyes?

I tighten my fingers on the handle of my mother's gun, resting on a cotton patch of pink polka dots. I haven't let go of it since I lay down. I am comforted mostly by knowing the plain physics of it—maximum destructive energy delivered with the most minimum energy returned to the shooter.

It will be useless to me if Bubba Guns's followers are setting up their own armed camp out front. I know that for most of them, carrying a gun is like carrying a wallet. Texas gun culture is tied up in history and survival and myth, ever since Apaches, in a stunning prairie ballet, could pelt the invaders of their territory with as many as twenty arrows before a single-shot pistol could be reloaded. Ever since survival depended on how well you swung a lasso like the one in Sharp's truck.

I want to believe that the lasso is Sharp's, not Looper's, and that he uses it to tug a feisty calf or to rope fence posts over and over in some sort of cowboy meditation at sunset. I want to believe that humans are progressing in the right direction, slowly thinning out the violence in our DNA. That we are like the lasso, a more humane and less bloody cowboy tool than its predecessor, the hocking knife, a crescent-shaped blade on the end of a pole, which cut the ligaments in cows' back legs so they couldn't run.

But I know that we came from stars that are not laughing above me, like in *The Little Prince*. They are not twinkling, an illusion created by our atmosphere. Tonight, like every night, the stars I'm staring at are either already dead or trying to survive in their own pool of violence—storms raining iron, galaxies eating one another, black holes ripping apart whatever drifts too close.

I've drifted too close to Sharp. I know that.

This is when things get hard.

When I don't know whether it's my imagination in control, or something else.

☽ ✧ ☾

I jerk straight up on the living room couch around four a.m., disoriented, heart pounding. The TV is talking about a strange weather pattern in the Gulf.

Ten feet away, a sound is rustling outside the front door. It's still dark, about two hours before sunrise.

One of Bubba Guns's spray can acolytes? The return of Sharp? Emme's cat?

I slide to a particular place by the window and lift the edge of the curtain, where I've checked out night visitors since I was ten.

No one is there.

I flip a switch in the foyer and crack open the door. Light floods the chipped wood slats of the porch but not much past it.

An engine revs a few doors down, turning over like a shovel of gravel in my stomach. I wrap my mother's robe around me and step onto the porch, surveying the windows and the door while keeping one eye on the yard, where the light ends and the dark is gathering like a mob behind an invisible rope.

No orange paint is debasing my mother's house. No furious words.

When I glance down, the relief is a cool rush.

It *was* Miss Georgia, Emme's cat. There, on the mat, the kitty lost her tag.

I reach down.

Flip it over.

Not a tag.

A charm.

Engraved.

Vivian.

20

The charm is lying flat on the kitchen table just behind my third cup of coffee. I can see one of its five points, like the tip of a knife. The charm is sterling, delivered without a scratch or a fingerprint. Shiny. New. Made just for me.

I'm trying to push down my queasiness and focus on the paper-tissue voice of my boss, Dr. Catherine Estrella, who just called at 7:02 a.m. for the call I promised to make to her at 7:00.

Dr. Estrella's claim to fame—besides bearing a name that means *star*—is writing a bestselling book titled *I'm as Real as You Are* that frankly addressed whether we live in a universe that is a computer simulation.

The book was a solid toe dip into the conspiracy theory arena, so it's not a big surprise that Dr. Estrella opens our conversation somewhat empathetically on the Bubba Guns front. Dr. Estrella and her sotto voice hit the fury of the talk-show circuit and the Twitterverse for a solid three weeks.

Except we both know the difference: She did it on purpose, with the full backing of our top bosses, and waist-deep in real math.

Her answer to the question she posed in her book was an emphatic *no*—we're not artificial rain trickling through a green code like in *The Matrix*. It doesn't matter that Elon Musk might believe it and Neil deGrasse Tyson has given it a fifty-fifty shot.

I swallow another sip of cold and bitter coffee. Dr. Estrella has assumed the floor this time. She is assuring me that Bubba Guns is an *uneducated toad, a salesman, a narcissist, an embarrassment to conspiracy theorists*, while I am *a brilliant researcher, the future of astrophysics*.

As for my psychic *tendencies*, she is *no doubter* in other *kinds* of "science"—a *kooky* aunt of hers had predicted that her third child, Rune, was hiding behind her "twins" long before an ultrasound found it. That said, I need to be *careful* that the observatory doesn't get dragged into something *too otherworldly*, if I know what she means.

"We believe you are a researcher par excellence, solidly wedded to science," she assures me. "If you can help use any . . . *brand* of science to help find the body of that poor girl *quietly*—Libby, is it?—do so with our blessing. Give her a happy ending. Just keep ghosts and aliens out of it."

The disturbing things she has found out about me are now resting on a new bottom clef in her voice. My sparkling-clean résumé had stopped far short of the Blue Ridge Mountains.

Dr. Estrella is walking the edge with me—pissed that I didn't keep her in the loop about my psychic-to-the-cops gig but also not wanting to piss *me* off. Not yet. After all, she hitched her wagon to my star. And I'm far from being the first crazy scientist she's nurtured.

She clears her throat in the squeaky way she always does when she's about to get to her point.

"Our project," she says. "Where exactly does it stand? I know you've made appropriate treks back from Fort Worth to the telescope when the planet has transited to the ideal occultation in front of the star. Has it resulted in anything at all that I can share with the foundation?"

"Not since we last spoke." I breathe out. "Nothing publication worthy. I'm looking for the glint of a needle to reappear in a chaotic, pulsing sea. You know that."

"With all this . . . publicity . . . there is concern that you are . . . unfocused. There is so little time left on your grant. The university is concerned that our chance of being first in this field is clearly declining with the launch of the James Webb Space Telescope and other scientists developing similar projects. Finding artificial light is going to be a very competitive field, another big shot at identifying intelligent life. As you well know, it could rival listening for radio waves."

And we've listened for decades, and all we've picked up are a bunch of pulsars and crap. I'm pretty sure that all scientists should be rooting for one another, and that her last sentence was directly quoted from my grant application. She sounds rehearsed. I'm wondering if someone important just sat down in the chair across from her desk. Or if I've been on speakerphone in a crowded boardroom the whole time.

"You know that it takes time and a stroke of luck," I say quietly. "I missed one night of good observation." The day my mother died. "Otherwise, I feel I've been living up to the faith the foundation put in me."

"Vivvy. Dear. You know I trust you. When it was suggested you were too young for such a hefty grant, I reminded them Einstein was rocking the world in his twenties. It's just unfortunate that Bubba Guns is sensationalizing your . . . gifts, which by extension, tarnishes the school and the foundation."

Dr. Estrella has dribbled up to her main point.

"I'm counting on you, Vivvy," she purrs. "Two weeks, like you promised, and we're back to normal, OK? I can only hold off the dogs for so long. Tell me you get it?" I hear both the plea and the warning. She wants the university's name stamped in the corner of a PowerPoint presentation that will travel the world with me and create an earthquake in the field of astrophysics.

"I get it," I say hoarsely.

My boss won't protect me if this goes bad.

The wilderness trail to my past—any secrets I hoped to keep—is now littered with footprints. Dr. Estrella's. Sharp's. Mike's. Bubba

Guns's. His internet hikers are crashing even deeper into the brush, and there's nothing I can do to stop them.

☽ ✧ ☾

I'm sliding the charm onto one of the silver chains from my mother's jewelry box when I hear the footsteps.

The foyer. Now the living room. One set? Two? Me, in my mother's bedroom. The gun, on the kitchen table, no use to me.

Whoever it is, brazen, because the nine a.m. sun is streaming through my mother's bedroom curtains. I know I locked the front door.

I grab the closest thing, which is my mother's cane.

I nearly take out my sister's eye when she steps around the corner and over the threshold.

"Jesus, Viv." Brig grabs the cane out of my shaking hand, automatically propping it back into the corner where Mom always kept it. "I have the only other key, don't I? Who did you think it was? I thought you were sleeping. What am I supposed to do if you won't answer my texts?"

I drop onto the bed, sucking in deep breaths.

She slides beside me onto the mattress, like I didn't almost accidentally maim her, which I have almost accidentally done at least three other times since I was born. She's eyeing the open jewelry box on the dresser as she sets her purse between us, a vintage red Coach bag that was a present from Mike's mother.

"I'm not taking anything," I say defensively, as if that is the most important concern right now. "I'm just borrowing . . . a chain. We will split all the valuable . . . sentimental . . . stuff when I've finished with the house. You dumped this job on me, you know."

My eyes are frantically searching the floor. I'd dropped the charm in my panic. The chain is curled on the rug an inch in front of Brig's flip-flops and perfectly pedicured blue toenails. The charm, a gleaming little star, has slid off, landing a few inches past that. Brig reaches down and scoops up both.

"How many times do I have to tell you, I don't want any of Mom's things?" Brig is examining the charm but doesn't hand it back. "Pretty. I don't remember this."

She glances up. "What are you staring at?" She brushes at her cheek. "Do I have something on my face?"

You. You are what's on your face. I still find myself glued to her beauty in the oddest moments, staring like the rude man on the bus.

She has a single dimple, an imbalance that somehow makes her face more perfect. It suddenly disappears. "Did Mike give this charm to you?"

"What? Brig, *no.* My . . . coworkers at the observatory . . . sent it as a gift. I just want to make sure I don't lose it." At least the last sentence, true. I do plan to hide the charm and chain somewhere in the chaos of Mom's jewelry box. But I don't want to explain to Brig that the charm was dropped like a cold kiss on the welcome mat. I know what she'll say. *Go home.* I know what she'll do. Tell Mike. Who will tell Sharp, who has a history with a certain charm bracelet, a coincidence that is eating at me.

Brig is slipping the charm back onto the necklace, negotiating with the delicate clasp. "There," she says, satisfied. She sets it on the opposite side of the bed from me and reaches for the fat yellow envelope sticking out of her purse.

"What's that?" I ask.

"I want you to go after him. Bubba Guns. Take him down permanently. Before he ruins our lives. This will help." She lays the envelope in my lap.

It's such an abrupt shift and not what I'm expecting—for Brig to be my sudden ally. I never expected Brig to be my ally again, not for a very long time. Not after we scratched each other's souls like feral cats while picking out our mother's coffin.

"Don't open it now," she insists. "Later. After I leave. There's a lot of good stuff in there that the general public doesn't know. Don't look so surprised. I volunteer on some pro bono cases for one of Mike's lawyer friends. I've learned a few tactics, especially during domestic abuse cases where the husbands try to destroy their wives on social media. I decided I was wrong. You should fight back. But *armed*."

I finger the top of the flap. "Did you do anything illegal to get this?"

She shrugs. "Maybe slightly unethical. I used some of the law office's software without asking."

"Does Mike know?"

She shakes her head. "Mike thinks we should leave it alone. Ignore Bubba Guns. Wait for him to drift off to another shiny object. He thinks it won't fester. People will forget. And he says that if it triggers a good tip on Lizzie Solomon, all the better. But you and I both know people don't ever forget."

She clears her throat roughly. "Which leads me to part two. Of why I'm here. I was wrong to accuse you . . . especially while the coffin guy was selling us on cherrywood or particleboard. I don't really believe you ever slept with Mike and lied to me."

She begins to smooth a wrinkle in the sheet that isn't there. "We both know that I'm the one who slept with Mike and lied to *you*. I knew you loved him when I did it. I lied about that, too. Even to myself."

We've danced around this for years. She's never gone this far. I've never known if she felt a second of guilt. Now that she has stepped a foot in the water, I want to scream at her not to wake the snakes.

"The first kiss with him was accidental. Two weeks after you left for college."

Only two weeks. A dull pound begins in my head. *How could any man deny her beauty?* Even right now at her most candid—skin pale, hair messy, eyes and lips and cheeks not emphasized by liners and paint.

"We were both missing you, feeling a little abandoned." Brig, not stopping. "I don't know who kissed the other first. I told myself that you would never have gone so far away to college if you really wanted him. If he was your priority. That I deserved his stability. A cop with a gun and a family with money. Someone to take care of *me.* I honestly don't know if I really loved him then or loved what he represented. But, to be clear, I love him now. More than anything."

"He never wanted me," I say stiffly. "He told me at the engagement party that I was like the sister he never had." He'd dismissed whatever had simmered between us with a cliché.

"You would have been like jumping off the moon for him. Thrilling but uncertain. His mother . . . disapproved. And you left him, Vivvy. *You left.*"

She lays a hand on my shoulder. "But why doesn't matter. You two are unfinished. Mom said it twice—the day after my engagement and the last time I saw her in this bed with that hideous scarf around her head. She told me there would be a moment I could repair us, but I might not like what it required. That if I didn't do it, every single thing I loved could be destroyed. It's why I was so angry at her at the end. At you."

My mother, manipulating Brig to her last breath.

"I think you should sleep with Mike." Brig's voice is firm. Loud.

I can't have heard her right.

"What . . . are you . . . saying?"

"I'm giving you permission. This is the only way you and I will ever know for sure."

"Brig . . ."

"I just ask that I never know the details."

She grabs her bag, slides it into the crook of her elbow, and lets out the breath she's been holding. I smell the faintest whiff of breakfast Chardonnay. Her eyes are not their usual opaque pools. There's a disturbance in the water. Maybe I'm finally meeting the creature who sleeps on the bottom.

Just like our mother, Brig is even more beautiful and magnetic in pain, when tears are close to falling. It makes me ache for her and seethe at the same time. Because Brig's permission is a noose, not a key out of prison.

The chain is dangling from her hand. Before I can stop her, she slips it over my head.

"Take it from someone who is always afraid of losing things—this is the best way to keep it safe. Close to you. Around your neck. Do us all a favor. Take off that daisy robe of Mom's and throw it away, will you? It's creepy."

I'm barely listening. The chain, shivering against my skin. The Blue Horse, thumping. Is that a whinny or a scream?

can see straight down the plump cleavage of the twentysomething girl adjusting the mic in front of my mouth. The V of her sunburn leads right to either a mole or a small crumb of chocolate.

She's told me her name is *Joie, the French spelling,* and settled me in my chair with a chilled, sweaty bottle of water and a high-end set of cushioned headphones. Across from me, the slick surface of Bubba Guns's desk reminds me of luxury car wood-grain paneling.

The surface of the desk is empty, just like his chair. The "guest" side and his side are divided by a crystal-clear acrylic partition that rises three-quarters of the way to the ceiling—I don't know if it's to prevent guests from spraying him with bullets or vice versa. Behind the desk, a small bookshelf holds a row of framed shots of him shaking hands Forrest Gump–style through history. A family portrait hangs on the edge.

We'll be streaming live and also recording it for his podcast. I try to breathe deeply and can't. *This was a very bad idea, Brig.* I feel like I'm suffocating—like the black acoustic tiles that line every square inch of the walls are preventing every bit of air from getting in.

"Bubba has us turn off the air conditioner in this room on purpose," Joie says as I catch a trail of sweat running down the side of my forehead. "He thinks it encourages more intense and passionate conversation. Sorry he's late. He usually is. It's a characteristic he hates in other people. He docked my pay two weeks ago, even though I was in traffic sitting behind a wrecked eighteen-wheeler. It would help his staff if he didn't insist on renting out a floor in a downtown Dallas skyscraper. He could do the show from anywhere. But he likes the cachet of the Fountain Place address. And the sound quality of this studio is stunning." She shrugs. "He's not a terrible guy. OK, sometimes he is. But he could dock my pay twice a month, and I'd still be making obscene money for an English lit major."

Joie arranges a piece of my hair drifting toward the mic. "You know, if you don't mind me saying, you're pretty for a scientist. I mean, *you're pretty*. Unqualified pretty. Your employee headshot doesn't do you justice." She hesitates. "Sometimes that helps with Bubba. If you're pretty."

"Any other tips?" I ask brusquely. "Can I count on him to stick to the conditions he agreed to in our emails?"

"Tips? With Bubba? The obvious. Don't tick him off. Don't get personal. He'll eat your lunch on that. Any agreement you have going in will fly out the window. Maybe compliment him once or twice if you can. Play to his ego. Although that can backfire."

"Did you help do his research on me?" I ask bluntly. "Make up some of the lies?"

She's busying herself across from me, adjusting the height of Bubba Guns's mic. "How many are actually lies?"

"Do you feel good about it?" I persist. "Now that you've met me? See that I'm a human being?"

"I'm going to tell you what I tell every person who sits in that chair. Bubba will not introduce himself to you. There will be no small talk. He will press that red button over there and dive right in like a German bomber. I've worked with him for half a year and I'm still not sure that he ever knows what he's going to say before he says it. Like I said, it's not personal."

☽ ✧ ☾

Bubba Guns arrives ten minutes later, slugging down a bottle of green kombucha, dressed in a tucked-out *Fire Up with Bubba Guns* T-shirt and faded jeans. He's skinnier than I expected and deeply tanned, with toes bared in Teva sandals, like he just stepped off an island. I watch him flip on the one fan in the room, aimed at him. It's less than a minute before five-thirty p.m., the scheduled start.

He doesn't acknowledge my existence before he settles back in the chair and pushes the red button, suddenly electrified. His face, transformed into his bulldog snarl. I feel in my pocket for my usual reassurance, for something sharp to poke in my finger, even knowing nothing is there. I'd left Lizzie's hair clip that I stole from the police station on the bathroom counter. I told myself that I didn't need a crutch.

"Hi, folks," Bubba Guns begins. "I'm drawling like a cattle rancher with heat stroke, it's so damn hot out there. And it's about to be hot in here. We're live today with a *very* special guest, Vivian Rose Bouchet, the astrophysicist-psychic *hot* on the case of the missing child Lizzie Solomon, who disappeared more than a decade ago in her house of horrors in the Fairmount neighborhood of Fort Worth. Miz—pardon me—*Dr.* Bouchet is limiting me to three questions on the actual case—per her agreement with law enforcement, she tells us—which I'm saving until the end of the show. But we will have no trouble killing time. This is the first show where we've had a Harvard-educated psychic-astrophysicist-alien-chaser sitting in our studio—hell, she might be the only one on Earth. We're going to start with one of my favorite topics, the conspiracies of outer space. Tell the people: Do you believe in them, Dr. Bouchet?"

"Aliens?" I stutter out. "Or conspiracies of outer space?"

"I think we can agree they overlap, Dr. Bouchet. Let's start with something basic. Do you think we landed on the moon?"

"I *know* we landed on the moon."

"Do you think NASA is incapable of lying to the American people?"

My heart is already beating out of my chest, my silk shirt flutter-ing like a red butterfly. What's with this NASA line of questioning? And what's the best example? Should I give it? The observatory has a running contract with them. Somewhere out there, my boss is turn-ing up the volume.

"I can tell you're struggling with this one, Bouchet."

I lean into the mic. "We know now that the first shuttle that shot into space had a fifty-fifty shot of catastrophic failure. The likeli-hood was that its two astronauts—heroes John Young and Robert Crippen—would die. However, NASA didn't really have hard figures at the time. Regardless, they announced to Congress and the world that their chances of dying were closer to one in a million. If NASA had told the world they were unsure of their chances, the shuttle might never have left Earth." It falls out in a monotone, like I'm re-citing at a physics conference. I'm not sure if that's good or bad for my cause.

"So you think there are justifications for the government to lie to us on a regular basis." Flat. A statement.

"I didn't say that. I'm simply answering your question with an accurate example."

"Is heaven above us like Sister Mary Seraphine told me in second grade?"

"What? I'm not sure what you're asking. Are you asking if angels with wings are sitting on the clouds?" I don't try to keep the disbelief out of my voice. "The celestial cloud cities of the Renaissance paint-ings are illusion, of course. So is Van Gogh's peaceful starry night. Outer space is a cranky, hungry, dark, *dark* place."

"So you don't believe in God. Just a big, fat black nothing. Like most scientists."

"It's a complete misconception that most scientists don't believe in God," I snap. "Many scientists I know *do*. The question we ask every day is, How Did God Build This Thing? I simply said heaven is not like walking through a Renaissance painting."

"Your idea of heaven and hell, Doctor?"

I swallow a breath, wondering how honest to be. "Heaven, if I'm wishing, would be getting to choose our own wisdom. Maybe darting among the stars one day, and the next, riding up the atoms of water molecules through osmotic filaments to an orchid petal."

"And hell?"

"Would be absence of intelligence. Being an amoeba with no brain."

"All righty, then. If you don't mind, let's pivot just a tad from Renaissance angels and setting up house in an orchid. The rumors are that you're chasing alien life in the dark skies of South and West Texas and using your God-given telepathy to do it."

He's making me sound like a lunatic. "*You* said that, *Bob*. No one else." With those four, hot words—not monotone—the audience knows I despise their commander. That he's under my skin. *Not* good.

Facts, Vivvy. Facts.

I clear my throat roughly, which probably sounds like a chain saw through the mic. "We have only one data point—our own existence—to believe there is something like us in our observable universe. The Drake equation and the Fermi paradox both mathematically address why we haven't met aliens, but they can *only* rely on assumptions based on the existence of human life on Earth. One assumption is, we might not be important or interesting enough to visit. It is also possible we are a gorgeous sapphire spinning alone. And fucking it up."

"The good doctor said *fuck*. She's admitted to having an existential crisis. I think we're getting somewhere. Come on now, Doctor. Even Congress is formally investigating alien visitations. And you can't deny that two of the world's richest men are on the hunt, using Texas as a base. Why did Elon Musk choose to buy up the tiny middle-of-nowhere border town of Boca Chica, Texas, for his big SpaceX goings-on and his monster Starship enterprise? And why did Jeff Bezos settle his rocket launch site out near Van Horn? I'll tell you why: They're lonely places where no one can goddamn see what they're doing in a state that believes you goddamn got a right to your own business. Are those two working together on behalf of the government? Hell, are they working to colonize Texas with an alien species? Are they using you to give it credence, a space-junkie psychic with a hotshot degree?"

"Elon Musk sees the future of civilization on other planets," I say stiffly. "Jeff Bezos wants to send manufacturing to outer space so we don't destroy this planet."

I've ripped the piece of paper I'm clutching, right in the middle of my list of talking points. I haven't gotten to any of them. I'm not the subject of this interview yet, just the conduit for his crazy. He's throwing a lot of hooks in the water, seeing if he can ride the shark. I almost, *almost* wish I'd just let him start with Lizzie.

I'm wondering if I should ply Bubba with details about my actual research, or if that is a direct route to self-destruction. My throat is dry. Desert dry. I work hard to refrain from clearing it again. *I can do this.* "Boca Chica is a great spot for launching," I squeak out. "It's so far south that it leverages the Earth's rotation to fling ships into orbit. That's why Musk picked it."

"That's a nice, science-y answer, but it doesn't fully address the *coincidence* or fear factor that has arisen since these nutty billionaires have snuck into remote areas of Texas to operate secret bases. I'm wondering if their interest here has something to do with the mystery lights in the desert outside of Marfa. We've been wondering what the hell those are for centuries. Aliens are here already, aren't they? Big Bend is the true Area 51. Come on, Dr. Bouchet, let's break the story right here, right now."

I lean back toward the mic, furious. "You can't just . . . say things. My research is a painstaking, often monotonous, effort to find unexplained light among the stars. I realize that doesn't have the same hype value for your show as clinking margarita glasses with aliens on the desert floor."

"Everything I do is dedicated to the unexplained," he barks back. "To saying the things no one else will. I take my cues from one of the most legendary journalists in Texas, God rest her misguided political soul. Molly Ivins lived and died by the slogan *Molly Ivins Can't Say That, Can She?* I'd say we're alike in trying to get to the truth any way we can."

I consider ripping off the headphones. Slamming the door. Exactly what he wants—a memorable visual on iPads and cell phones everywhere.

I lean back into the mic. "You can't equate yourself to Molly Ivins," I say coldly. "And you can't equate Elon Musk and Jeff Bezos when it comes to interplanetary travel. Whatever you think of Elon Musk, he has hired the world's best scientists and engineers. He's not afraid to fail to make progress, which he's proved by exploding things again and again. His SpaceX operation is planning trips destined for deep space, with the idea of colonizing it. Jeff Bezos right now provides short carnival rides up and down for tourists. Sort of like this show. A carnival ride."

I suck in a shaky breath. Brig had advised me on the phone before I left the house to stick to three things.

Sound like a scientist. Don't lose control of the interview. Keep him on the defensive.

One for three.

"Well, this has been fun so far," Bubba Guns reports. "Dr. Bouchet looks like she could use a commercial break, and I could use a beer. Back in two, folks, for what you've been waiting for: the mano a mano interview with this psychic looking to the stars to find the grave of Fort Worth's legendary lost girl, Lizzie Solomon. Is Dr. Vivian Bouchet the real deal? Or a bona fide astrological nut with a little murder in her own childhood? Light up Twitter with what you know, people."

My brain is aching, spinning with whiplash. Surely the same is true for his listeners. I wasn't nearly as prepared as I thought I was for his trademark schizophrenia. Maybe there was no way to be.

A commercial for an online class on trout tickling is suddenly blasting through my headphones. For only $19.99, I can learn how

to catch trout by rubbing their underbelly with my fingers and sending them into a trance.

Bubba Guns is already out of his chair, disappearing through the
door. No chitchat.

Two minutes. Two minutes for me to regroup.

22

Bubba Guns slips back into his chair while my head is still down on my list. He's sucking a Pepto Bismol–pink smoothie, not a beer.

Bubba Guns's index finger jabs the button. The crescent scar in the soft spot beside my thumb starts to throb, remembering that snakebite like it was ten minutes ago instead of fourteen years. So does the permanent white streak along my right calf, carved by the fender of the blue Mustang. Two scars that are tattoos for the people I love most. One for Brig. One for Mike.

"Round two, folks," he booms. "Great job on your tweets. I'm surprised so many of you had a hard-on for your middle school science teachers. Our star girl in studio right now is pretty easy on the eyes, too. The myth about stuffy scientists, busted. Before I get in trouble with our guest, who has a Supreme Court sexual harassment case look on her face right now, let's switch gears to the gingerbread girl, Lizzie Solomon, a child who needs justice. If you know something about the Lizzie Solomon case, or you think you *are* Lizzie Solomon, we've tweeted the number for a special tip line set up right after the show from seven to eight p.m. Dr. Bouchet, I'd like to start this segment with your lineage. Did your mother, a Fort Worth resident, use to call herself a psychic?"

"Yes. She had a number of clients. Regular, loyal ones." The last three words, unnecessary. Defensive. Already. I feel like I'm on the witness stand.

"But Asteria Bouchet, not her real name, right?"

"No, it wasn't. I'd prefer you didn't mention her real name. For privacy. She just . . . passed away." It's a sudden and ugly snapshot in my head—her body dug up and pecked to ribbons by the vultures of Bubba Guns. Her fresh grave is still piled high with red dirt, a highly visible target.

"My sincere condolences. But my team is looking at public record, so anyone out there can look it up. Out of respect, I won't say it on the air. Let's take a trip down memory lane. When you were a kid, you, your mom, and your sister—Brigid, is it?—lived in a rental house in the Blue Ridge Mountains where a woman's body, long missing, was found. It was your mom who claimed that her psychic intuition was responsible for the discovery. And, now, here you are, her progeny psychic, declaring you can do the same thing for our Lizzie Solomon."

"I'm not declaring anything. I don't call myself a psychic. It's one of the reasons I agreed to come on your show. To make that clear."

"Interesting. So why did the Fort Worth police come to you? And why did you agree to help? Let me rephrase all that because I don't want to use up any of my three allotted questions about the case. Have you ever predicted something that, say, saved a life? No need to hesitate. Again, public record."

"I was just a kid. I knocked a boy out of the way of a car. It made the papers."

"A blue Mustang, right? And you'd warned that boy ahead of time to watch out for a blue 'horse'? Clever. And that's the same boy who grew up to be Fort Worth cop Mike Romano, the cop who got you involved in solving the Lizzie Solomon case, the cop who is married to your sister, Brigid? To be clear, I'm *stating* all of this in question form, so I'm not cutting into my three questions about the case. Mike Romano certainly seems to believe in your powers. Is under your spell. Have you ever been prescribed medication for schizophrenia or bipolar disorder?"

A shot out of nowhere. "Have *you*?" I breathe out.

"Touché, Dr. Bouchet. Touché. I've been waiting thirty minutes to use that little rhyme, but you haven't given me the right moment. Did your mom set up the blue Mustang incident to get attention? For money? More clients? Did she use you, her own child? Never mind, I know the frustration of tangled relationships with dead moms. Here's my first official question: Have you slept with any of the cops on this case? Because there are rumors at the station."

"What?" It rushes out, panicked. That's all Brig needs to hear. "Of course not."

"Do you have a clue where Lizzie Solomon is? Progress you can share with our listeners?"

"Not. Yet." *Weigh. Every. Word.*

"Can you see dead people? Like Lizzie? Whoa, folks, you should see her face. I'm going to call that a yes."

Bubba Guns isn't even looking at my face. He's fiddling with something under his desk, eyes on a digital clock. "And last," he booms, "is this just a big publicity stunt on the part of a few cops because it's been more than ten years and they still can't find a body? Because they can't finish resolving the highest-profile missing kid case in the city's history? That fourth question is rhetorical. Or maybe it's the fifth question, but who's counting?"

"Would you like a reading from me?" The scars, at this point, shrieking.

"What?"

"I'm getting a lot off of you. For instance, are you being sued by four hundred and twenty-six companies and individuals? Wait, wait, I mean *five* hundred and twenty-six. Do the charges include defamation, harassment, bribery, and tax evasion? Is your defense in at least thirty of those cases 'temporary psychosis'? Has your pastor at First Baptist Holy Rock asked your family not to ever come back after you said aloud on your podcast that you thought it was OK 'for women to have a boner for Jesus'? Have the heads of the Republican Party and the Libertarian Party in Texas ceremonially voted to have you removed from their rolls? Oh, wait. I don't have to ask. *It's public record.* How did you get court clerks to use your initials only on these court cases? Why keep it a secret? Are you close to bankruptcy? Divorce? Have I used up my allotment of questions?"

Bubba Guns seems to have forgotten he's at the controls—that there's a button he can push to shut me up. It's like I rubbed his belly into a trance. He suddenly comes to, lurching violently forward at the mic.

"That's the kind of attack I'd expect from a Harvard grad who throws the mumbo jumbo of science at us like a Pedro Martínez changeup. Vivian Bouchet represents the greatest *problem* of all time: an elite underground community of people whose job it is to distract us from the truth, whether it's about Elon Musk's efforts to lure aliens and Californians here to take over our God-blessed Texas or about police who think they can distract us from their incompetence over the Lizzie Solomon case by conjuring up a psychic. Bubba Gunzers, I can't make this stuff up. Well, I could, but it wouldn't be this good. This is the question all y'all should sleep on tonight. Why is Vivvy Bouchet, with her ties to lying NASA and local cops, suddenly in our orbit? And do we want to do something about it?"

A swift recovery. A barreling fastball straight at my head. He's signing off, all grin. I can't make out most of his closing words over the adrenaline pounding in my ears.

I got to seven of my talking points, all of them courtesy of Brig, and a couple that I made up on the spot. Or intuited. Hard to know, my head is such a loud rush of water. How did I possibly think I could take down a tyrant, a liar, in his own bully pulpit? Are my sister and sweet nephew now even more in the line of fire?

Dead silence in my headphones. I remove them slowly.

For the first time, Bubba Guns is staring at me through the shield that divides us, no grin, like I'm suddenly a bunch of atoms that exists.

He rises and stretches lazily backward with both arms like he's waking up in a breakfast commercial. His T-shirt rises over the waist of his jeans. The snatch of belly, white like a rat snake.

I know exactly what he's doing. He's making sure I see the handle of his gun.

23

stick to my chair after Bubba Guns exits the studio. His silence absolute, and as powerful as his tirades.

I hope his plan is to hurtle straight down the elevator of this sixty-story architectural glass diamond, a façade for his house of lies. I crack open the door to the outer office, where Joie operates from a "welcome desk," just in time for the yelling. I push the door open another inch and listen. I can't see either of them.

"Where the hell have you been?" Bubba Guns, barely controlled.

"I was here for the whole show, I promise," Joie assures him nervously. "I just took a quick trip to the bathroom afterward."

"Well, thank *God* you were at the controls," Bubba Guns drawls sarcastically. "Who the hell gave us the tip on Bouchet and the Lizzie Solomon case?"

"It was an anonymous tip, sir. We use them all the time."

"Are you making excuses? You do realize this was a setup, don't you? That I tip you like a shot girl in Vegas to keep something like this from happening?"

"When I realized you weren't cutting her off, I went right to commercial," Joie rushes out. "Right after the . . . Jesus part. I was scrolling your Twitter while I was in the ladies' room down the hall. Nobody's that stirred up about what she said about you. Just a few tweets. It's running half about Lizzie Solomon. The other half is tweets about heaven, UFO sightings, fake science, personal psychic experiences, California bashing, catfish noodling—apparently, it's sort of like trout tickling but more dangerous. You are more likely to get bit or drown. There are a few talking about how smart people with autism are. You know, because Elon Musk is on the spectrum. Also, how Mark Zuckerberg is an alien. That one has been coming up a lot lately." Joie is talking rapidly, like she's reading off a mental list.

"Male or female?"

"Sir?"

"Was the person who called in the tip *male or female*?"

"Female. I took the tip myself."

"Well, do you have the number?"

"It's here somewhere in my phone. I keep a list."

"Find it. Don't bother coming in to work tomorrow if you don't. For all we know, Vivvy Bouchet is the one who made that call. I want you to leak her address and her mother's name. I want you to announce she's not just in the mile-high club with the local cops, she's in the three-hundred-and-sixty-three-mile-high club riding Elon Musk and Jeff Bezos like ponies in their spaceships. I want her grants canceled. By morning, I want her polished into a shiny symbol of everything my listeners hate. I want them to munch on her with their morning cereal. Elitism, fuzzy science, powerful secrets, a world that works to keep them nose down in their ant piles. Are you hearing me? A tweet about her every hour on the hour. Stay up all night."

"Who will man the tip line?" Joie's question stumbles out timidly. "Colton says he has the flu. And Elisa is at her sister's wedding. It's just me. I'm your team tonight."

Nothing from Bubba Guns.

"I'm talking about the tip line that you've asked me to set up for the Lizzie Solomon case," Joie whispers.

"I know what the hell tip line you are talking about. That's *your* problem now, isn't it?" A sharp slap echoes in the small space. Bubba's hand hitting the desk or Joie's face?

I have a gun, too. I shove open the door all the way just in time to see Bubba slam out the one to the hall. Joie's letting loose the loud, sloppy sob she'd been holding back. Her head is down on her desk, shoulders shaking. I'm two feet away when she shoots upright, like she has a built-in motion sensor.

"A little too well played in there," she says, sniffling. "I don't think you're going to like where it goes from here."

"Did he hurt you?"

"You mean physically?" She snorts and wipes a stretch of mucus across her upper lip. "Not his style. His words are plenty punchy. Really I'm . . . fine." Another brush of her finger under her nose. "In six months, I've been almost fired more times than I've had time to put on mascara. Which works out, because then I would walk around looking like he hit me."

I nod but don't move.

"Really, I don't need your protection." Joie, an irritated strain in her voice. "I appreciate it, but you can go. There's a good martini bar a block down. You look like you could use one." She looks pointedly at the door. *"Why aren't you going?"*

The red in Joie's eyes, already paling to pink. "What do you want from me?"

"I want to man your Lizzie Solomon tip line," I say, "while you destroy me on Twitter."

☽ ✧ ☾

It took Joie about thirty seconds to consider the benefits of the deal. I would be giving her the ammunition that kept her employed. She wouldn't have to man the tip line herself short-staffed. It would be a secret screw-you to a man who expects her to hold her pee indefinitely.

"Don't make the mistake of thinking he's dumb." Joie is shoving a stack of papers and six empty Starbucks cups aside on a second desk in the corner, setting me up. "He's a double major in political science and world history and a lifelong student of existential motives and why people believe in conspiracies. The need for the illusion of power and control over a world that we don't have control over. The natural human instinct to not trust anyone. It's why we weren't eaten by dinosaurs and lions and Stonehenge aliens. Bubba plays that to the max."

She slides one of her coworkers' laptops over to the edge of the desk with the coffee cups. The laptop lid is defaced with a slaughter of stickers: *Meghan Markle Is a Robot. The Earth Is Flatter Than My Sister's Chest. Vaccines Will Kill Me Before My Peloton Does.*

Joie is half watching my eyes as I read them. "Colton, my assistant, is a little overeager to prove his loyalty to Bubba Guns. He wears a daily barrage of T-shirts, too."

"My favorite conspiracy theory," I venture, "is that Stanley Kubrick was hired to fake the moon landing for television, but he was such a perfectionist, he insisted on shooting on location."

Joie rolls her eyes. "Hah. And I don't even know who Stanley Kubrick is. My favorite conspiracy theory is the one that says we're all going to be OK."

I watch her plug a multiline land phone on the desk into the wall and untangle the wire of what I think is an illegal recording device. "You want to really piss off Bubba Guns on his show? Call him Birtwhistle. When he calms down and sees the ratings, he'll be baiting you, up for another showdown."

"Burt what?"

"Bubba Guns–slash–Bob Smith is really William Marion Birtwhistle. His father was a professor of philosophy at Oxford. His mother is a ballet dancer born in the United States. His parents were barely married before she yanked Bubba back to L.A. He bounced between University of Southern California and Cambridge. He pays a few million a year to keep that from the top of Google searches. You'd think it couldn't be done. But it can."

I'm remembering Brig's notes. In a margin, she had scribbled *England* with a question mark.

"Don't look so surprised," Joie says. "I was hired for my hacking, not my pretty."

I'm not that surprised. Not that she knows this, or that Bubba has zero Texas blood. I did figure, at least *some* Southern DNA. I'm surprised she's taking me into her confidence. And she has the look of someone not finished.

"You want to know why he ran out of here?" she asks. "Not because he was done with me. Because he was late for his weekly night session with his Texas dialect coach. And when I say 'dialect' and 'session,' I mean his pretty little coach is also a Dallas Cowboys cheerleader. She works especially hard on getting him to say the 'aah' and 'ew' sounds. If you know what I mean."

"I figured his accent was . . . exaggerated. Just not completely fake."

"Molly Ivins's accent was just as fake," Joie retorts. "She was a California girl, too. She went to Smith and studied in Paris. How many Texas liberals know that? When you get to this level of political discourse, whatever side you're on, it's always about performance art. I figure a psychic cookie like you would know that. Ivins knew the way to get her voice heard above the good old boys was less about geography than it was about identity."

"You surprise me, Joie. With your deep insights into our pathological culture."

"I'm not sure if I should take offense at that. If you're psychic, I wouldn't think you'd need to up your insight by taking over our tip line. But whatever. Do me a favor and up your drawl. Our fans, especially rural ones, identify with a drawl. They'll spill more if they trust you. A lot of young people are now more drawly than the parents they popped out of. Bubba's all over that younger generation. As for my own *deep* insights, I went to Brown. I'm all-Ivy, baby. Like I said, it's a big, big mistake to think all conspiracy theorists are uneducated. That they're rednecks cart racing in Walmart or sitting in their attics with tinfoil cowboy hats. They're anxious people with a lot of anger about how their lives turned out. That covers a shitload of territory these days."

"I never believed all conspiracy theorists are dumb, just that a subset of them are lacking a curiosity to get at the truth. You said you majored in English lit?"

"Double major in lit and women's studies. Computer hacking to pay the bills."

"And you landed here."

"Yeah, go figure. My mom would die if she knew I worked for Bubba Guns. She thinks I'm finding myself after graduation by interning for the Texas Coalition to Abolish the Death Penalty." She pulls out the chair for me. "You're all set." She glances at her watch. "While you talk with a caller, there will be a maximum five calls on hold, listening to Bubba Guns singing "God Save Texas" followed by "I Walk the Line," the songs he focus-grouped to pump people up. After five callers are in the queue waiting, the others start spilling into voice mail. So be efficient. Voice mail is a mess for me to deal with because Bubba insists that we call everybody back who leaves a number."

She tugs her phone out of her pocket. "OK. Now, it's time for you to make good on *your* promise. What's my Deep Throat tweet about you that will assure I keep my job?"

24

Back at her desk, Joie pokes at her screen, stirring up my life on Twitter. I wonder how far she'll go with what I gave her and how much she'll just make up—if she has a conscience to flick on. I'm on caller number 7.

The tipster, a woman who has lived for thirty years two blocks from the Victorian where Lizzie disappeared, is worried about the ghost of Lizzie Solomon that floats in her backyard swimming pool.

According to her, Lizzie stares at the moon and whistles one note in a monotone that sets the cicadas quiet. Sometimes Lizzie's head transforms into a cat face *even though cats don't swim.* The woman's voice trembles.

I sense dozens of calls tumbling into voice mail while I silently debate why I think this woman is crazy for seeing the monotone-whistling spirit cat of Lizzie Solomon when I've personally spoken with far crazier apparitions. If nothing else, I'm getting an excellent sense of why people besides Bubba Guns wonder if I'm on medication.

"Before we hang up, what color cat face?" I want to be respectful. I feel sorry for her. I've already written down "black" but she surprises me with "orange tabby." I dutifully make a note of that, following Joie's wishes, so she can skip through the recorded messages later to listen to anything "significant" herself—significant being anything outrageous enough to tweet and boost ratings. I have no intention of giving Joie any genuine tips that could lead to Lizzie, and I doubt she'll plow back through every recording to double-check. So far, it doesn't matter.

Mike was right when he said that a missing person tip line is like opening every lonely motel room in hell.

I glance over to Joie while caller number 8 assures me that a current U.S. congresswoman successfully consulted Asteria Bouchet, which is why she was elected. I know that congresswoman, an Independent, now in her fourth term. She stopped by twice "for tea" when I was in high school, with a Yankees baseball cap pulled low and her mother's old Bible.

Caller number 21 is a surprise from the Blue Ridge Mountains. An unpleasant one. Mrs. Whiplock, my sister's former math teacher, a longtime verb in the Bouchet house. As in, *You have been Whiplocked.*

"Everybody thinks it was just Vivvy who was odd," she snipes. "But she was just shy. I always wondered if she got answers wrong on purpose so she'd look average. The other one was the trickiest. Brigid. I watched her finish a test in ten minutes. Scored one hundred plus the twenty bonus points. Nobody has done that now or since with one of my algebra tests. I gave her a zero for cheating. Once, I saw her whisper in a boy's ear after he complimented her ample chest, which she knew how to operate at age twelve. If you ask me, she was whispering a curse that went down to his toes. That boy didn't come back to school for a month and when he did, he limped. He was the town's early hope for quarterback and a run at the state championship. It never came to pass."

"Your hair will start falling out tomorrow," I hiss. "Thank you for calling the Bubba Guns tip line and have a God-blessed day."

Twenty more callers. Forty. I lose count.

Lizzie sightings of girls too young or too old to be her. Opinions about Bill Gates, Bill Maher, Amazon Prime, cops, me. I don't disagree with all of them. There's a self-proclaimed psychic who says she will reveal the killer and the spot Lizzie is buried in Colorado for $500 and twenty minutes on the air. A man who wonders if the cops pushed their fingers along every piece of trim in Lizzie's house looking for the secret room where he's sure they'll find her remains.

My eyes drift out the window, my mind to the turret. I feel like I'm at the top of one made of glass. The fountains far below are lit like tiny fires.

I glance at the large clock on the wall. JFK's face profile is sketched in black and white, his blue-blood nose pointing at the nine and a red bullet hole in his temple at the twelve. Only fifteen minutes left, and nothing to show for the last hour.

7:58. That's when the last call comes through. I let it ring three times.

The big hand moves to 7:59.

I almost don't answer.

☽ ✧ ☾

"Welcome to the Bubba Guns tip line." My voice is hoarse. Maybe skeptical.

"Hel . . . lo." Soft. Young. Maybe she's been crying.

"Thank you for calling," I reply, a little more gently.

"I think I might be . . . Lizzie."

She's the fourth caller today who's told me that, all more insistently than this one. But this is the first time my scars have begun to ping.

"What makes you believe you are Lizzie?"

"I don't look like anyone in my family," she says vaguely. "I have the same color hair as the girl who went missing. Her eyes. I saw pictures of her online."

It's 8:02. Joie is locking the glass door to the office, miming the get-off-the-phone-now sign. She's gesturing so dramatically that I wonder if Bubba Guns is on his way back.

"That's your only reason?" I turn my head away and lower my tone. "That you look like her?"

"No."

"You're going to have to hurry. The tip line has already closed." I glance up as Joie begins to switch off lights. "We could be . . . cut off." I've used every twitch of accent I could for the last hour so I didn't sound like me. Now my voice is genuine, and urgent.

"I found an envelope in my sister's closet. She'd copied stories off the internet. And something from a genealogy website."

I see the flash of a tabloid headline, like it spilled out of her envelope on the other end of the line and onto the desk in front of me. Is it just something I'm remembering, maybe from the file? And which tabloid? The *New York Daily News*? The *Daily Mail*? The *Mirror*? The UK papers were always dazzled by Lizzie's disappearance because the late architect of the Solomons' Victorian grew up in Maidenhead. His son was able to dig around in his father's old trunk and produce detailed renderings for the cops, a full double truck in the *Sun* and, in the *Sunday Times*, a more stately piece by the architecture critic.

"*Did Her Mother Take Forty Whacks to Lizzie?*" I breathe out the headline without thinking. Definitely not the *Times*.

Five seconds pass on my watch. Six.

Across the room, Joie's thumbs are texting or tweeting.

"You're freaking me out," the girl, now at a high-pitched whine. Definitely, on the young side of teenager, like Lizzie, who would be fourteen. "Are you the psychic who Bubba Guns just interviewed?" she asks. "You didn't sound like her but now you kind of do."

"Did you find anything else?" I push.

"This wasn't a good idea. I'm not sure why I called. Maybe I just wanted to say it out loud and see how it sounds. It doesn't sound good."

I glance at the phone readout. *Private Caller*. "What's your name? Are you living in Texas? Another state?" I ask.

"I'm not telling you any of that. I don't want my mother to go to jail. I mean, like in theory, then both of my mothers would be in jail."

"Have you asked your sister about this? About why she's keeping these clippings? About the DNA results?"

Another pause.

I shake my head at Joie, who is over-antsy to leave, trying to get my attention by manically shutting an overhead light on and off. "*Now*," she mouths.

I ignore her and focus on the caller. "Did you hear my question?" I press.

"I figure she has to be keeping it secret for a reason. She gets ticked off if I snoop in her things. And then Mom would find out. Dad would go nuts."

Something about her train of excuses, the hesitations, suddenly makes me worry *I'm* being set up, that there's an adult listening, typing out her script on a computer screen. Or an actress with a very, very good dialect coach.

Decide. Quickly. *Now.* "This number won't be working almost as soon as we hang up," I rush out. "Don't call any Bubba Guns tip line, ever again. I'm going to give you my number and the number of a cop I know. Mike Romano. Call either of us. We can help. Quietly."

I rattle off the numbers into silence. "Are you still there?" Nothing. I rip off the headset, hoping she'd hung in there.

Joie shuts off the last overhead light so abruptly I'm grasping for my backpack in the dark. When I reach the door, her demeanor has changed dramatically. No more chitchat.

She hurries us down the hall, pushing me into the elevator, punching the lobby button as manically and repeatedly as the light in the office. Right as the doors are closing, she squeezes out of them. She taps her Apple watch. "I think I'll take the steps down. Need to close the circle."

Her last words slip through a two-inch gap before the elevator doors click shut.

"I'm sorry," she says. "I didn't have a choice."

Whatever she's talking about, I'm guessing it's both a lie and the truth.

$$\text{☽ ✧ ☾}$$

I exit the lobby and reset my backpack over my shoulder. The Texas night is unbearably hot and close. I'm sweating after the first block.

Parking in a city lot seemed like a good idea earlier when the street was glaring with sun and crawling with people. I waste a few nervous minutes scanning the shadowy car rows for my Wrangler instead of the Jeep I drove here—a brand-new, shiny black loaner dropped off at my house today, courtesy of the body shop where it was towed.

A few clouds are flurrying across an iron-skillet sky, playing night tag. The budding moon means I'm off Blue Horse duty at Mike's tonight. In the Jeep, doors locked, windows down, I try to breathe in the intoxicating smell of these buttery leather seats and breathe out the toxins of Bubba Guns. I imagine them drifting out the window as a sickly cloud of pink and yellow that smells like pee and Pepto Bismol.

I fiddle with the high-tech array of buttons and lights on the dashboard. Any other time, I'd be enthralled. But my phone, propped up in one of the artful niches, is flashing like a slot machine.

I'm scared to look at Twitter and see what I've become. I'm worried about what waits for me on my doorstep—journalists, Bubba Gunzers, Jesse Sharp, a stalker with a bag of charms.

The highway between Dallas and Fort Worth is a sea of headlights and semitrucks with half-awake drivers. When I finally turn onto my block, I ride my foot on the brake and slink by Mom's house. A quiet little wasp's nest with seething dark holes.

I don't stop. Nobody's there, but I feel them coming.

$$\text{☽ ✧ ☾}$$

I could say I don't know why I ended up near the Solomon mansion at ten p.m., aiming a telescope up at its windows. But that's like saying I don't know why I aimed a telescope at the exoplanet that finally blinked at me. It's because I hope I will be lucky. It's because I hope I will see something. It's because something I will never be able to explain is calling me.

So far, I've seen the mottled fur of a calico cat under a streetlight and the cop in the car out front who flashed on the dome light for a minute, cigarette dangling out of his mouth, bored.

The Solomon mansion itself is an unlit abyss. Without a light source inside the mansion's windows, my telescope will detect nothing. It will only zoom me closer to darkness—something else will have to light it.

I mentally thank the anonymous person at the body shop who was kind enough to unload the contents of my Jeep into the back of the loaner, including this precious and powerful telescope that I carry around like high school baseball players lug around bat bags. It's an easy one to set up on a tripod whenever there's an unexpectedly perfect night. It's nothing like the mighty telescopes on the roof of my little refuge in the desert. But its eight-inch mirror can rove the rings of Saturn. It can see the rings on the fingers of a mother and little girl taking a walk a block away.

I was about that girl's age when my first primitive cardboard telescope arrived. I sat for hours, spying out the window through its Coke-bottle lens. Those blurry, close-up images were my first taste of power and control. Me reaching out, instead of visions reaching out to me.

I shift back to the Solomons' house. A light is flickering in a third-story window. Before I can zoom in, the glimmer is gone. Lizzie's room, if I'm counting across correctly.

I refocus the lens, aim it at the window, don't pull my eyes away, a patient pro at waiting for light.

When it rewards me, I make out a red cooler with a Coors can and a bright camping lantern on top. A card table chair.

I'm a block away. But close enough to see the folds in Marcus Solomon's chin.

☽ ✧ ☾

My phone breaks the silence of the neighborhood, the phone I thought was on Do Not Disturb. I almost drop the scope.

My sister.

"Hey, Brig."

"Why are you whispering, Vivvy? Where are you? I need you to take Will for a couple of hours, like right now." Brig, in familiar, full-on demand. "He woke up while Mike and I were . . . arguing. He won't go back to sleep. And Mike and I, we need to get to a stopping point. I figure you of all people should get that. Will's already in his pajamas. I'll pack his bag."

"Brig. Is this a good idea?"

"Make something simple for once. Just be here for me."

25

I takes an awkward fifteen minutes for Mike and me to leash Will's car seat into the back of this monster-sized loaner. The two of us speak only to curse or ask the other to pull a strap tighter.

Brig stands near the house, at the highest point on the lawn, watching Will race in circles in the moonlight. I can't help wondering if she already regrets setting this impulsive, late-night affair in motion—if she is teasing fate until it backfires.

"My poop came out blue yesterday," Will announces as soon as I pull away from the curb.

"Hmm. Did you eat a blue crayon?"

"No. My teacher says not to do that."

"Did you eat a piece of the sky that cracked off in the storm?"

He giggles. "No."

"Did you nibble on a blue whale?"

Silence. "That would be too scary."

"Did you fly up to planet Neptune and discover it was a blue cookie?"

"*Is* it a cookie? Can you take one of your rockets up there and get me some?"

"You'd be so old by the time I got back you'd forget me."

"I would never forget you in a million billion years. Here's what happened. I ate *Batman*."

"Did you use kryptonite to trap him? Was he crunchy or smooth?"

"Aunt Bibby! Kryptonite kills *Superman*. And the real Batman is in the TV."

"Just testing."

"It was a Batman *cookie*. I ate his ears first. Mommy said to ask *you* why black icing made my poop blue."

"If you mix equal parts of red, blue, and yellow frosting dye together, it creates black. We can experiment sometime at my house."

"Why didn't my poop come out like a rainbow?" he asks insistently. "It doesn't make sense. Black is black. It's not other colors."

I think about how much to explain. "In science, black is the absence of light."

"That's why I have a night-light. So the monsters don't come." He's satisfied. Matter of fact. Problem solved.

His trust is almost unbearable. I stop just short of visiting that dungeon of pain in my heart where I'd live if that Mickey Mouse night-light ever stopped doing its job.

"What is Batman's weakness, Aunt Bibby?" Will pipes up. "Is it another kind of 'nite?"

How should I answer? Will, more than anyone—one year short of kindergarten—makes me think hard about my answers.

"Well," I say slowly, "some people believe it's because he refuses to kill anyone. But I'm betting your daddy would say that is his greatest strength."

☽ ✧ ☾

I circle the block five times, looking for any sign of unwanted activity on my lawn. Will keeps pointing his chubby finger at the house as we drive by, yelling, "Stop!" On the third twirl, to distract him, I have him practice the word *bougie*. It's a thing we do, expanding his vocabulary. Last time, it was *equinox*.

"OK," I say, turning into the driveway. "I think you've got *bougie* down. Use it in a sentence."

"This new Jeep is is boooooooogie."

"Excellent. My work is done. Let's hop out. I think I have a choc-olate chip cookie from Earth with your name on it."

I walk up to the front door with Will in one arm, keys in the other hand. My backpack is slung over one shoulder and the ten-pound bag Brig handed off with all the things required to keep my nephew alive for two hours is slipping down on the other.

I'm still fumbling with the key to the front door when the hum-ming drifts from the corner of the porch. Monotone. Am I imagining it? My keys clunk to the mat in a flash of silver. Almost simultane-ously, Will's favorite stuffed pig tumbles out of the bag to the porch. He leans down to reach for it, pulling me off balance. I drop to my knees, place Will firmly on the ground, and whip around.

The silhouette of a young girl occupies one end of the swing, rocking back and forth in a steady rhythm, feet flat on the ground. She's humming a tune I don't know.

She sticks a flashlight under her chin and flicks it on, like my mother when telling ghost stories in the tent. I make out a very short cotton nightie. Lips painted bright pink. Hair sticking up like knotted barbed wire.

Will screams.

"Emme," I eke out, just barely. "Will, sweetie, it's OK. She's a friend. She lives next door."

"Is this like hide-and-seek?" Will asks tremulously. "I want to play."

"Hi, Miss Vivvy."

"Emme. You shouldn't be out here by yourself. It's past eleven. It's . . . not safe."

I glance behind me. Now I have *two* smaller humans to protect. The street is a deceptive still life of locked cars, drawn shades, plants sneakily closing their flowers. Shadows that might or might not de-cide to get up off their knees.

"I miss Miss Asteria," she says. "I got lonely. My mom is on a date."

I glance over at Emme's house, every window dark except for the one with the light over their kitchen sink, which stays on all night, every night. The white Volvo station wagon, missing from the driveway.

"You can hang here until your mom gets home. But we need to text her."

The exhaustion of the day is catching up—the combat round with Bubba Guns, the mystery Lizzie on the tip line, my intrusion on Marcus's agonizing vigil.

And now? Now I'm apparently operating a midnight day care. I lean over to retrieve my keys. "Flash your light over here on the mat, Emme." She obediently does, hopping off the swing.

Even after my fingers close over the keys, they continue to drag along the empty mat, under the edge. The crunchy shell of a cicada, a dirty worm of string, a bobby pin. No new charms.

"Aunt Bibby, I want my cookie." Will, insistent, tugging at me to get up.

"Why do you call her Aunt *Bibby*?" Emme asks Will as they trail me to the kitchen.

"Because that's her *name*."

They continue their debate while I close the blinds in the kitchen and check the lock on the door. I text Emme's mom. No immediate response. I find an opened package of Chips Ahoy, throw them in a communal bowl, pour three glasses of milk. The clock on the wall, always six minutes slow, says 11:22 p.m.

"Hey, how about we draw?" I insert false cheerfulness, tumbling a set of colored markers out of their box onto the table. My mother was a color-coding fiend with her astrological charts.

"I'm drawing Batman," Will says. "What are you drawing, Aunt Bibby?" I set a piece of blank paper in front of each of our places. Will grabs the black marker.

"I'll surprise you."

Emme has snatched three markers and is already head down, arm curved around her paper so we can't see. "I'm going to need the black marker, too," she mumbles. "Will will have to share."

"Will will," Will repeats, giggling.

I pick brown, figuring it will be an unpopular color. The pen drifts and so do I.

I'm inside the photograph I saw at the police station, lifting the charm bracelet from its bed of dirt and leaves and berries. The chain feels like cool water in my fingers. I'm twirling it around, watching the charms fly, the blur of a carnival ride. My eyes travel to the leaves at my feet. Crisp and exact, like gingerbread stabbed from cookie cutters. I drop the bracelet and pick up a leaf. It crumbles in my hand, an ancient scroll I shouldn't have touched.

"Aunt Bibby! Look at my Batman!"

I snap back. Will is waving his paper, a black blob with pointy ears.

"Wow," I say. "That's going on the fridge museum."

Will is examining my artwork, clearly disappointed. "Why are you drawing boring brown leaves? I thought you would draw a planet like the moon. With a face."

"The moon is not a planet," I say automatically.

"I love to draw leaves," Emme interjects. "I like the horse chestnut tree best. Its leaves are toothy on the edges with lots of veins. *Aesculus hippocastanum*. That's the Latin name. When the leaves fall off the branch, they leave a scar like a horseshoe on the bark."

"That probably hurts," Will says. "I feel sorry for the hippo *and* the horse."

I consider both Emme's earnest face and my drawing, with its exacting, academic quality—as if it fell out of a book and not a dream. "Where does the horse chestnut grow, Emme?"

She shrugs. "The Balkan Peninsula. Ohio. I found a really good tree chart on the internet. It shows you every leaf. It tells you where every tree lives."

"Will you send that link to me?" I tap the piece of paper. "I'd like to identify this leaf. I drew it . . . from memory."

"Sure," she says.

Will's eyes are beginning a slow, predictable blink. He stumbles over to Emme's drawing.

"Emme's picture is scary," he announces, holding it up.

Emme has drawn her tent in the backyard with skilled dimension. Flap open. The moon, pocked with craters, sits in a scratchy black sky. Beside the tent, a shadowy outline of a girl hangs as if suspended in time.

"Not scary," I assure Will. "It's just Emme and her tent."

Emme shakes her head. "Not me. Someone else. I saw her out my upstairs window."

☽ ✧ ☾

I'm going to need to tread carefully with Emme. Will's eyes blinked shut for good five minutes ago. Emme helped me tuck him in on the couch, carefully placing the pig under one arm.

"He's not so bad," she says.

"Emme, when did you see this?"

"The other night. I think she was a ghost."

"Do you see ghosts all the time?"

"No. Just this one. Just once. Do you like my lipstick?"

"I do. Could you see a face?"

"Nope. Miss Asteria said ghosts are misplaced energy. They come and go. They don't always tell you who they are. She said I was sensitive enough to see one." She puckers her lips. "My Aunt Miriam gave this lipstick to me for my birthday. She said smart Southern girls know that if they're looking a mess, all they need to do is put on earrings and a little lipstick. She says I look a mess a lot."

I laugh. "Too bad nobody ever gave me that tip."

"My aunt is a color psychologist," Emme says importantly. "She says blue lights keep people from killing themselves. A train station in Japan put them up so people don't jump on the tracks. Aunt Miriam says pink is for hope when you're sad and red is power when you need to be brave."

"Emme, is that why you're wearing pink lipstick? Are you sad tonight? Is it because of Miss Asteria?"

Silence.

"Things hurt," she says. "I think that the chestnut tree feels it when the leaves fall off just like Will said. Like when a boy yanked on my braids and pulled out a hair. I heard that tomato plants scream when you cut them. My mom says that's a conspiracy theory to keep kids from eating their vegetables." Her eyes are little brown caves, no entry. "I heard you talking about conspiracy theories tonight. What do you think?"

She listened to the Bubba Guns show. Ah.

I begin to stack the markers back in the box. "There is a study that says tomato plants emit ultrasonic distress sounds for an hour after they're clipped. Maybe a warning to other plants nearby."

"Do you believe it?"

"I keep an open mind."

"Then I'm not eating tomatoes anymore."

"Emme. Where does that end? You'll be lost in a world of silent screams." *In a world of obsessive compulsions and endless knocking on a bedroom wall.*

Her sweet face is working all over the place. She's struggling not to cry.

"You want to know why I'm really sad?" she whispers. "I'm sad because I was so excited about being like Elon Musk. I looked him up after the show and found out he's autistic like me. But then I read he thinks it's a one-billion-to-one shot humans are real. He thinks we're living in a video game. I don't want . . . to be nothing."

I wish Emme could still be a kid. But her switch was flipped a long time ago. Like mine. She is everything I was at twelve. Labeled. A girl with too many thoughts in her head and not even a pin to let them out.

"My boss, who is very, very smart, actually wrote a book about that theory. She discounts it completely."

"But what do *you* think? Miss Asteria said you were the second smartest woman on the planet." *The smartest*, I know, *being Brig*. If only she'd ever told Brig.

Now is clearly not the time to talk to Emme about ghosts. Or about what I think in my own black moments—that heaven *is* nothing.

That our souls don't exist after our brains shut off—that our bones are eaten by the earth or our ashes digested by the sea and that's that. Cynical thoughts and theories that would set Bubba Guns's Twitter aflame.

How my boss's book is full of flaws. I have stepped a toe in Elon Musk's mind and wondered why these enigma UFOs that pilots have described can behave in unfathomable ways. If they might, indeed, be objects outside a computer simulation we live in, able to visit inside the game, affect things, but not be subject to Newton's laws. If this could explain the things in the universe that don't behave according to physics as we know it. That a detached, uncaring hand has set the dial of the universe to *expand forever* so we can never find our way out to the truth.

How very little this earth, humanity, would mean if that were true. Lost girls like Lizzie, just a flick of a finger. Everything, pointless. This is not what I told Bubba Guns. Or what I'm going to tell Emme right now.

"Vivvy, am I not *real?*" Emme, impatient.

I stand up and let her dissolve in my arms. "You feel real to me. You know what I do when I'm not sure of things? I hug someone I love. I look at the sky. At the mountains, so mysterious and grand. Proof."

I release her and look directly into her eyes. "That's when I know that there is faith, intention. God. *Meaning.* That the puzzle has been designed for us to figure out and so what if it takes a billion years? Who wants to solve an easy puzzle? Certainly not *you.* There are right answers to every question we ask, even if we don't know the answer. And if there are right answers to all our questions, nothing is random."

"I'm still worried," Emme says. She's chewed her pink lipstick ragged. I see a tiny fleck of blood.

"That's going to be status quo for a big thinker like you. But eat your tomatoes, OK?"

I bend over to pick up a few cookie crumbs from the kitchen floor.

My mother's chain slips from under my shirt, the charm swinging back and forth like her pendulum that Brig and I used to make decisions. *Yes or no. Hers or mine.*

This bit of silver defies physics by feeling like it weighs both enough to sink me to the bottom of the sea and almost nothing at all.

When I stand up, Emme's eyes are glued to my neck. She's reaching into her shirt, pulling out her own chain. Dangling from it, a shiny silver star, just like mine. *Emme* scrawled like a beautiful, dying comet.

"Did Miss Asteria leave you one, too?"

It takes interminable seconds to get the words out. *"Emme, who gave you that?"*

Before she can answer, we are startled by a noise on the porch. A Bubba fan. A postman with charms. The monster that Will is certain exists in the absence of light.

I try to grab Emme as she runs past me to the door, but her thin cotton nightie is a whisper sliding out of my fingers.

26

A swath of musky perfume. Bright yellow silky polyester against polished black skin. A postcoital buzz.

Emme has thrown open the door to her mother.

"Emme Louisa Grubbs, you are supposed to be in bed with the door locked. We had a deal. You are also not supposed to open any door until you are sure who is on the other side!" She turns to me. "I'm sorry. I thought I'd just be gone an hour. My boss called me over for a quick consult."

Consult. Date. Who am I to argue? I want to remind her that Miss Asteria is dead and no longer her daily Plan B.

My mother and Emme's coexisted in a fragile peace like territorial cats, only because it worked best for the ecosystem. For Emme. They weren't pals, for reasons like this. Emme "ran away" because of her mother's procession of boyfriends and an endless stream of nannies not nearly as bright as their charge.

When I'm irritated with someone, you don't have to be psychic. Mary takes one skim of my judgmental face and hustles her daughter out the door.

Emme is already flying across the yard, halfway to her house. Three steps from the porch, one of Mary's three-inch red heels sticks in a soft patch of grass. She lands with a painful rip of polyester that

needed more room to breathe around the generous curve of her bottom. I jump down the porch steps to help her up. Instead, she tugs
me down into the grass with her, and not gently.

"We won't be bothering you again," she says under her breath.
"You have no idea what it's like to raise Emme. She's never *still*.
You're here now, but you'll be running away again before you know
it. And it will be just us again."

"I know that she's a gift," I say.

Mary has pulled off her other heel and is rubbing a bare foot.

"Preachy. Just like your mom. You think *I don't know* my own
daughter is a gift?"

"What are y'all talking about?" Emme yells from their front porch.
"I want to go to bed."

"Miss Asteria, sweetheart," Mary yells back. "How much we all
loved her."

I stand up, yanking Mary to her feet with me.

"Where did Emme get the charm she's wearing?" I ask under my
breath.

"She found it. A couple of days ago. In the tent. She thinks the
spirit of Miss Asteria left it there. Tells me it's good luck. It makes her
happy. Who's to say it's not true? Your mother was a nut in person.
She's probably a nut in her afterlife. No offense to your mother, of
course. She respected my daughter. Not everyone does."

"Will Emme be alone again tomorrow?" I ask.

"Not that it's your business, but she's with her father for the next
three days."

The oppressive heat and pure exhaustion are melting our masks. I
see a single, weary mom with a complex daughter she loves but can't
always understand. I'm not sure what she sees.

The warning on my lips about the charm slips away. I have a little
more time to figure things out without adding any weight to her
pile. I clear my throat. "I was just going to say, it's probably better if
she doesn't come to the tent for a while. For her safety. I'm not the
best person to be around right now."

"If I could keep her away from this house, don't you think I would? You think I want my daughter believing you can talk to dead people?"

I watch her limp barefoot across the yard, strappy red heels dripping from her fingers.

Inside the house, I kiss Will's forehead, stealing comfort, before I attach the ghost that Emme drew to my refrigerator door.

☽ ✧ ☾

Will is dead weight in my arms when I hand him over to Brig on her porch an hour later.

She'd texted that Mike was coming to get him. I saw that as a problem. I offered to bring Will back instead.

Neither of us wants to make a sound to wake him or to stir the turbulence between us. We enact a powerful silent movie, exchanging something we love.

☽ ✧ ☾

The lights are blaring at Mom's house just the way I left them. I drop onto the swing, spent. It's one of those rare July nights where the breeze feels almost cool. The honeysuckle is making mad love.

A déjà vu night. I feel like I'm sitting in a memory, in a mixture of the present and the past, dread and longing. I'm so tired, I ache with it.

I lay my head on the hard slats of the swing. *For just a second*, I tell myself.

I start awake, disoriented. Nudge myself upright.

He's watching the house from across the street, leaning against his car. His face is half illuminated by the streetlight, a match to every nerve in my body.

I shove off the swing. He sees the movement. That's all the invitation he needs.

☽ ✧ ☾

Mike's foot is already on the first step. Two, three, four, five, six. He won't stop coming. He's wearing a white T-shirt and old jeans, something he threw on without thinking. Morning stubble is breaking through his chin. My mind floods with all the Mikes I've loved. At eleven, thirteen, sixteen, twenty.

I'm trying not to imagine his powerful arms crushing me until I forget I'm hurting.

"I dropped off Will at your house two hours ago," I stammer.

"I'm aware."

"It's two thirty in the morning." I have no idea what time it is. "Have you been drinking?"

"One drink. I was going to turn the car around if your lights were out." He nods to the house, shining like the world's biggest nightlight. "Brig told me, Vivvy. What she said to you. That she could never be certain unless we were."

"So you came here for a little certainty."

"It's not like that. I just want to talk."

I don't believe him. I see the expression on his face, and it isn't platonic.

"What your wife wanted you to say to her tonight," I say unsteadily, "is *I will never sleep with your little sister*. For you to say she is the only one you will ever love, end of story."

"I do love her. I know we are a better match in ways you and I never could be. But I love you too, Vivvy. I knew it at our wedding when you handed her my ring at the altar. I know it now. I've known it since we were kids. I'm sorry. It's easier to reconcile when you aren't here. But I've never reconciled it. I've tried. I don't *want* to be in love with two women, two *sisters*. What kind of man is?"

The words, a straight, honest punch. He's finally said what I've been both wanting and fearing to know. It's not the catharsis I thought it would be. Speaking it out loud feels wrong. Like a bird is finally freed from its cage but realizes it can no longer fly. It would have been better to never know.

"*Don't*," I struggle out. "It isn't fair. For you to say that now. For you to say that *ever*." Their wedding, one of the worst days of my life.

I wore a pale blue dress my sister picked out that swished the ground like a waterfall and a smile I practiced in the mirror that was straight out of a toothpaste ad. It took a full year to recover enough to date a guy more than once. If I let Mike touch me now, I will be back at the beginning.

"If you were sorry, you would have never pulled me into any of your cases in the middle of my grief. If you're sorry now, and the husband and father I hope you are, you'll turn around and leave."

He takes a tentative step forward. I take one back. "I need to know," he says quietly. "If I'd asked . . . back then . . . would you have stayed?"

"Do you want me to release you?" I ask, disbelieving. "To confirm that I was an impossibility? Let me make it easy for you, Mike. You made the right choice."

Maybe there is no fate, I want to scream. Maybe there are no right and wrong choices, only choices. Beauty and pain, good people and bad, are born from all of them. We can't see far enough into history for a reason. If we could, we'd never make a choice at all.

"I want to stop hurting my wife." Mike, pleading. "To stop hurting *you*. Vivvy, you're shaking. I can't stand it."

And I can't control it. I'm a twenty-eight-year-old astrophysicist and a seventeen-year-old girl about to leave for college. I'm standing on this stifling porch and back in time on a rickety dock, the sun drying the bubbles of lake water off my body, Mike's rough hand untying the red bikini string around my neck. Both places, his arms are around me. Both places, I don't know who moved first. Both places, I'm kissing him back like I want to drown.

Where is the interventionist now, asking Mike to catch his rope? Breaking the spell?

The old man's boat had appeared out of nowhere, a disturbing ripple across a lake that had been flat as glass. The sunset was igniting the water with a torch. I stood humiliated, shivering, covering my breasts, small white triangles outlined against golden brown skin, the tattoos of a sated teenage summer. Except I wasn't sated—it was the first time the boy I always loved had made a purposeful move to love me back.

After helping tie up the man's boat, Mike drove me home in silence. When I jumped out of his car, he said he was *sorry* to my back. Sorry. Too much humiliation to bear. I left for college a week later. By Christmas Eve, my sister was the one untying a red string, on his gift to her. A necklace with a heart-shaped charm, speckled with diamonds. A year later, they were engaged. Right on course? Or a flaw in the operating system?

His fingers are roaming, burning prints on the bare skin under my shirt. Proof. Ridges that would emerge if my sister sprinkled fingerprint dust on them.

Is this what dying stars feel in their final, fiery dance?

Ecstasy that is a searing, shrieking pain?

If I don't do the right thing now, I won't be at the beginning.

I'll be at the end.

I rip my lips away and step back. His face, as stunned as I feel. We have staggered into a reckoning twenty yards from the sidewalk where we began.

Somewhere in the dark, a harsh chuckle cuts the air.

"I guess Bubba Guns doesn't always get it wrong."

Jesse Sharp's drawl is a lasso tossed around Mike's neck, yanking him away.

The interventionist, better late than never.

27

Mike and Sharp are arguing on the porch, two trained, tightly wound Texas cops. I make out a few words and phrases from the other side of the door I just slammed in their faces.

Jackass. Screwing the pooch.

I'm not sure if the last one was about me, or the Solomon case, or both. My neighbors must be irritated, awake, fumbling for their phones in the sheets, calling the police, not knowing the police are already here.

I'm too exhausted to intervene and too angry with myself. I can still feel the bruise of Mike's kiss on my mouth and the fiery humiliation of Jesse Sharp catching us. Why do I still have this sick feeling in my gut after seeing the disappointment in Sharp's eyes, like I was letting him down personally? I want to believe Mike is a good man just as much as I want to believe Sharp is a great cop, dedicated to the proven, the *knowable*. His worst flaw, that he has no interest in explaining himself to someone like me, who dances between worlds, a witch without a broom.

But there's the other voice, the one I want to bat away but can't. It's telling me to run to Mike because it's the only way I can save him. It's telling me Sharp's flaws could be much, much bigger.

The second I met Sharp, I knew he could tether me to the ground. I just didn't know if it would be with rope or logic. If he is on the side of the angels or cuts their wings and lets them fall.

I can't listen to their arguing anymore. I grab my phone from the kitchen table and shut myself in the bathroom, cranking on the shower for angry white noise. Go straight to Twitter for the first time since I walked in Bubba Guns's studio.

Sharp must also be fuming about my decision to do the show, probably why he turned up. Unlike what I told Bubba Guns, there was no agreement with law enforcement to answer only three questions about the case on his show. There was no agreement or permission *at all*. Who knows? Maybe they would have jumped at the shot if I'd puppet their words.

My thumb scrolls the feed, each tweet like the stab of a butter knife. I didn't think Joie would go this far.

On Bubba's behalf, she has posted a wide interpretation of my "postshow" interview. *Oh, yeah*, I think. *Sharp's mad about this tweet.* And this. And *this*. Bubba Guns, most certainly thrilled.

Is the #TexasJonBenet alive? Self-proclaimed #Harvard #NASA ghostbuster #VivvyBouchet says little #LizzieSolomon's bloody pink bow told her so. #Vivvyvoodoo #thebubbagunsshow

Psychic #VivvyBouchet admits to hallucinations and obsessive-compulsive disorder since she was five. #hauntedchild #childhunter

#VivvyBouchet has alien-hunting grants stuffed like hundred-dollar bills in her G-string theory. #yourtaxdollarsatwork #deepspace #deepstate #GodblessTexas

Did you listen to #thebubbagunsshow today? Science nut sky scoper #VivvyBouchet better be real careful someone doesn't push her off our #flatearth.

Run, run said #thegingerbreadgirl! You can't catch me!
#lostinspace #copsneedaclue #LizzySolomoncase

And on and on.

I blame myself for this vitriol and lunacy, even though I never imagined it aimed at me. Because I agreed to the show. I talked to Joie. And for what? To make a case for Mike? Science? As a trade, to briefly talk to a scared girl on a tip line who has slipped into the ether, maybe never to emerge again? So Joie could keep her job with the king of assholes? So I could stop being ashamed of things I don't want to be ashamed of anymore? To release a well of anger at being used?

All of those sound about right.

I rummage through my makeup bag on the bathroom counter until I find the bottle, which has less rattle and roll than I remembered. Only six pills left. I lower the lid of the toilet seat to sit. I toss back two of them, one more than I should.

I close my eyes again, waiting for the tablets to dissolve in my bloodstream like microscopic bits of sand. I try to conjure up any image of Lizzie at all. The charm girl. Both, ominously silent. But isn't that what I want, for the pills to poison them?

The old claw tub is filling with water, even though the drain is unplugged. When I twist off the shower, no more voices, inside or out.

I pull every shade and close every curtain, a callout to the shadows. This house will need at least three hyper kids and a slobbering dog to scare out the claustrophobia. That, or a single, well-placed match in a snake of kerosene.

At the kitchen table, I take out a marker and my engineering pad. Flip on the computer. I chart out the next few days like I'm charting the course of a planet spiraling in a wider and wider orbit. I hunt on the computer. Write down every thought I can think of about Lizzie Solomon and her entourage before the edges of my world go pleasantly fuzzy.

I stumble into the bedroom, fall into unmade sheets. The chain around my neck tightens like someone is giving it a cruel tug. One of the charm's sharp metal points, biting me. I fumble with the clasp, so impossibly tiny for someone without the long nails of my sister.

I give up. The charm drops flat and hot to my chest. It feels like it's heating up, waiting to brand me in my sleep.

☽ ✧ ☾

Nickie Solomon is my alarm clock, ringing at 9:04 a.m.

"What the hell? You think my daughter is alive? Shouldn't I be the first to know? Instead of learning it from the woman in a hairnet who slopped fake scrambled eggs on my tray this morning?"

"Nickie . . ." I'm mentally scrubbing at the sticky film on my brain, regretting the extra pill last night like I always do the morning after. I can't believe I slept this late, already both urgently behind my agenda for the day and swimming like a goldfish cracker in Nickie's furious soup.

"Don't 'Nickie' *me*. Don't make a single excuse. You fed this to that asshole on *Twitter*." Pause. "Is she really alive?" There's a catch in her voice. I can't tell if it's genuine.

"I don't have any physical proof of that, just my own . . . intuition." I'm waking up fast. I weigh whether to tell her about the mystery girl on the tip line. Decide against. "Jesse Sharp is still positive you were in on it with your boyfriend Looper. So there's a lot of momentum the other way. You must think Looper was involved too, or you wouldn't have written his name in braille and handed it over. That, or you are manipulating me."

"You don't have a clue the creative things we have to do to pass messages in here. As for Looper, half the time I think he is alive. That he crawled out of the lake and abandoned me. And, yes, that he took her. The other half, I think he's locked in a cage in hell and Lizzie is the angel who decides if he gets fed worms or roaches. The thing is, I'm not sure. I wanted you to figure it out, not get caught up in some twisted cop theories that put me in here."

"I understand Looper was an abjectly cruel man."

"I thought I was . . . in love. I think . . . now . . . he could have had something to do with it. I called him that day because he was late showing up to the house for a little quick stand-up action in the pantry. It was our Monday morning thing. I'd left the front door open for him."

"And Lizzie was in the kitchen."

"Well. No. I was in the kitchen, waiting in the pantry. Looper liked things kind of kinky. He liked me naked, *in place*. But he didn't show. I called him to see if our rendezvous was off. He didn't *actually* pick up when I called him that day. His mother did. She said he must have forgotten his phone, that she was there cleaning his apartment. I think maybe he didn't want people to know where he was. He always had a burner going and a little heroin action on the side. He provided to his rodeo friends. It's a hard life, all those weeks on the road." She talks about waiting for a sadist naked in a pantry with the pork and beans like it is nothing.

My head is busy with the lies Nickie told the police and has let sit for a decade. She's on a burner again. Once again, no caller ID. But there's a difference this time. She's holding nothing back. I'm guessing she's paid dearly for the use of a private corner, a shanking spot with DNA splattered on the wall. I have no doubt this phone will be crushed under her foot as soon as we hang up.

"*Where was Lizzie?*" My voice, at high-decibel pitch in the hollow ache of morning.

"*I don't know*, OK? She was *around*. The last time I saw her she was in the turret, playing with a doll. Or maybe she was in the backyard. The gate was locked, though."

"I don't believe you."

"Which part?"

"All of it." I seethe. "I don't care if you didn't kill her. You should be in a prison for bad mothers. For life."

"Oh, honey, I am. And you know what? I don't believe you, either. I think your mother was a scammer, and you've put on her robe."

Well, she's partly right. The daisy print robe is hanging off the bedpost, in my direct line of sight.

"Look, Viv." Nickie is wheedling. "Let's get back to the beginning. I want to know what that guard censored out of the letter your mother wrote me. You're cute. Smart. I bet you can wiggle your way into his brain. His name is Brando, remember? I don't think I told you his last name. Wilbert. Have a chat with Brando Wilbert, do a little digging on Looper, and I'll set you free. I won't ever call again. Come on. I know your type. If there's an answer out there, you aren't going to let it float down the river."

Another question is pressing, one that's been bugging me since our conversation at the prison. I'd never wanted to give Nickie Solomon any sense that she had something I needed. But, more than that, I don't want to ask Mike.

"You told me that Sharp got suspended for messing with a crime scene. What crime scene?"

"Aren't you the one with the back door to the cops? It was something to do with a missing girl's bracelet. Focus on my Lizzie."

☽ ✧ ☾

Nickie's words thud but barely make a dent. I already knew what she would say.

I take a steaming hot shower, tub water rising until it tickles my ankles. I think about answers floating down rivers with old tires and water hyacinths and dirty diapers and silver charms. Slipping through cracks to the ocean. That's where so many answers are, a thousand leagues under, in the belly of a shark.

I towel off and stare at my bare face in the mirror, a face that would be instantly carded. No disguises today. No lipstick, no liner. *I let God do my makeup this morning*—I can hear my mother saying it, blowing a movie-star kiss to me.

No more sundresses, either. Back in the bedroom, I rummage through my duffel in the corner. I throw on stretchy green hiking pants, a black T-shirt hanging loose over my holstered gun, good running shoes, and my backup glasses. I'm running out of contacts. I'm starting to run out of a lot of things.

Outside, I hear a *clank*. The chatter of voices. I raise the edge of the living room curtain.

A man with the hulking body of a former football player has set up a camp chair on the sidewalk. A *Bubba Knows Best* baseball cap.

A few yards down, a teenager with a face as pale as baby powder slouches on top of a bright red cooler, sipping a Diet Dr Pepper with one hand and videoing the house with his phone with the other. His legs are partially hiding the words spray-painted on his cooler. I can make out the word *Lizzie*.

Same species, different agendas.

A journalist, male or female, I can't tell, sits in a blue Prius parked across the street. I'd learned to recognize the body language of the pros as a child peering out of a Blue Ridge Mountains motel room.

Three isn't that many, right? I tamp down a snail of panic.

Back in the kitchen, I spoon stale Cheerios and milk into my mouth and scribble another question on my to-do list.

Who would know if Looper is alive?

And then I underline the very first question I wrote last night.

Why would Mom know anything about Lizzie Solomon? And where would she hide it?

Outside, more crows are gathering.

☽ ✧ ☾

If Lizzie is buried in my mother's computer, she's buried deep.

I'm staring at 221 puzzle pieces laid out on a field of red poppies. Folders, icons, documents, PDFs clutter her desktop. Nothing in a straight line. There are a hundred practical reasons to clean out this desktop before I go back to the desert. This is not one of them.

I take a breath. It would be hard enough to concentrate on this screen *without* the protesters collecting outside. I have expected them every day since Bubba Guns's first live tirade about me, and now I feel like my expectations have prodded them out of bed. Their racket is only slightly more muffled in my mother's tiny office at the back of the house, and I'm too unnerved to do what I usually would with a tedious job of confusing data—stick on my noise-canceling head-phones and shut out the world entirely.

Where are the cops? Who will protect me from the thirty-two humans now waving signs in front of my house, their faces scrunched with vitriol for *me*, the little girl with glasses who always just wanted to be normal? The one who *did* barely pass her elementary school science tests on purpose so she could fit in.

Part of me wants to stride right out there and find common ground. Explain that I'm a nerd whose wishes on shooting stars didn't come true, either. That Bubba Guns and the conspiracy-wielding freaks of social media are turning all of our pain to gold, building a new aristocracy.

But the rage on my lawn. The chants. It lights my PTSD, sweeps me back in time to a little girl in a Virginia hotel room, hoping mass hysteria wouldn't drown her.

The shouts outside are bullets through the walls.

Liz Is Not Your Biz!

Don't Musk with Texas!

Your Nobel Is Waiting in Hell!

Clumsy but effective. Clever, even. The odds are, one of the people out there will blow, today or tomorrow, or in twenty years, maybe when Taco Bell gets their order wrong, and they get a Diet Coke instead of a regular one. I don't want to be today's Diet Coke.

I'm nudging the cursor along, but Mom's computer is a dinosaur. It struggles to wake up from its coma every single time, and every single time I'm worried it will be its last. Since I've been home, I've only logged on to ferret out documents I need to execute her will.

Four days before Mom died, Brig said we should take a hammer to this "box of junk."

She considered Mom a digital hoarder, whereas I thought of her as a digital chipmunk, hiding nuts in a forest of paranoia, the kind of organization I can get behind. Outer space is ordered this way. Folders inside folders *inside folders*, most of them untitled.

I start with the four folders that sit in each corner of the screen. Corners were important to Mom. She didn't just place an X in the four corners of a piece of paper. In the four corners of every room, she nailed up a bit of sage like mistletoe.

Over the kitchen sink, she hung her favorite Bible passage, from Ezekiel, about the angels standing on the four corners of the Earth.

And in the four corners of this computer, she has titled a folder for each of the four corner stars in the constellation of Orion. *Rigel, Betelgeuse, Saiph, Bellatrix.*

In *Rigel*, I find questionable tax preparation, in *Betelgeuse*, pictures of my nephew, Will, in *Saiph*, astrological charts for clients dated from before we arrived in Texas.

Lizzie was an unfertilized egg, not even a probability at that point.

Disappointed, I drag everything in those folders to the trash except for my nephew's pictures. I replace the generic red poppies wallpaper with Will's face.

This way, every time I kill a file, I will uncover his mother's intelligent eyes or a childhood freckle from his father that will eventually wear off or the tiny scar in the middle of his forehead from an encounter with a sidewalk that a girl will kiss one day.

One trashed icon at a time, I will reveal the puzzle of Will's beautiful little face. It will be my reward for patience and my motivation for never opening the door to Mike again.

I move the cursor to the bottom corner, to *Bellatrix*. In Greek mythology, a female warrior.

My mother has stacked her computer into a fine baklava. The probabilities of success this early in my search, low.

I click, and the file sputters open.

In life, like in science, sometimes you're just lucky.

28

I almost forget the clamor outside. I'm looking at my mother's client call diary going back more than a year—the period of time it took for my mother's brain tumor to grow from a bean pod to a little monster with curious fingers.

Mom declared herself more prescient than ever as she started forgetting things, fainting, struggling with blurry vision. Maybe she was. Her clients certainly thought so. She claimed not one of them dropped her when she limited all her readings to telephone calls. FaceTime, Zoom, email, text—she refused to use any of them because *they distracted the spirits*. I think her cramping fingers and mind struggled to operate them.

On the screen in front of me, a record for almost every call during the last year and a half of her life. She was religious to the minute about writing down incoming and outgoing calls. Her income depended on it. She knew exactly how much time she spent with clients, even if she didn't charge the poor ones past one hour. The only problem with this list, not all of them are real names.

It was my mother's standard policy to invent nicknames for her most paranoid clients, an obsessive way to assure them confidentiality. I hurriedly skim. Some of the nicknames in the call log are long-time clients who'd shown up at the house since I was a teen.

Cup of Joe, for a barista named Joanna. *Virgin Mother*, for a school janitor and single mom named Mary. *Cher* for a stripper who uses an iron on her waist-length black hair. *Scout* for a civil rights attorney. The real names mostly match those on the voice mail messages I've been returning, pleas that have now slowed to a trickle.

A couple of names I don't recognize. They set off a little ping. The nickname *A Thing of Beauty*, along with the words *No charge*. I count seven calls between Mom and A Thing of Beauty, two in October of last year and then several more in the months before Mom got really sick.

The name *Hauptmann* keeps showing up once or twice a week and for long calls—sixty-nine minutes, forty-two minutes, ninety-five minutes. For months, he was her highest-revenue client. Then the calls abruptly stop.

Hauptmann might or might not be a real name. And it's odd—no phone number by any of his dozens of calls. A phone number *is* listed by A Thing of Beauty.

A text flashes on my phone while I'm stabbing ATOB into my contacts for later consideration. The message is from Joe's Body Shop and Repair, where Sharp had my car towed. My Jeep is ready, and the shop is closing early, in less than an hour.

I'm getting a shiny new windshield, a replacement driver's-side window that rolls up, new shocks and tires, a bonus oil change, and a wash and detail courtesy of Barbie's apologetic husband who is try- ing to prevent me from filing a civil suit. I'd ignored three voice mails from Joe's Body Shop about this turn of events. They were almost done with the work before I called back this morning.

The question is, *How am I going to get out of here?*

A cheer has gone up on the lawn, ending any hope that it will be through the front door. I slip back into the living room and lift the cur- tain. The entire tableau, in motion. At least sixty people, maybe more, are being physically negotiated off my yard by uniformed cops.

The brashness of it is stirring more anger than fear, but it isn't night yet. It seems semi-controlled. Two more policemen are setting up temporary barriers to keep people off my lawn. Another cop is gesturing toward my door, as if he's about to venture up my walk and make contact. Mike and Sharp, nowhere in sight.

A pickup has pulled into my driveway, an inch from the back of my loaner. The truck is set up like it's offering natural disaster relief, people crowding around an open tailgate groaning under the weight of bulk cases of water and dozens of paper-wrapped sandwiches. Even if I wanted to duck and run out the front door, the loaner is boxed in.

The shout—that was for their hero, now emerging out of the back seat of a black Mercedes that has pulled up out front. He's tossing his white cowboy hat to the crowd, which says to me that Joie orders them in bulk from Amazon. No kombucha in sight. He's being handed a bullhorn.

Joie wasn't wrong. She said Bubba Guns would pivot quickly. Well, I'm not giving him the satisfaction of smoking me out of my own home for a public confrontation. And I have very specific plans for the day.

I quickly strum through the notes I made last night at the kitchen table, grab one of the sheets, and tuck it in my backpack. I decide on the bathroom window, a large single-pane crank that Brig and I left open more than once so we could crawl back in after curfew. There is no true back door in this house, one of its oddities, only a side door in the kitchen.

I'm halfway across the yard when I stumble and fall. Vibration, everywhere. In the air. In every cell in my body. Bubba Guns, on his bullhorn, praying to our God Almighty loud enough to shake the whole block. My tailbone, stunned, shooting a pain to my head. Eyes, fogging with tears. It takes a second for me to realize I tripped over a tent stake.

I'm struck with the urgency to run and the futility of it. I expect protesters to start dropping over the fence like angry monkeys.

Every second counts. Mom's voice, the first time I've heard it since she died. *Get up.*

I do. Once again, I'm straddling a fence, this time with a long daylight view.

Sharp's pickup is already parked in the alley, motor running, pointed west. His arm curls lazily out the driver's side of the pickup, gesturing for me to get in.

It scares me to the root of my soul, his ability to read my mind.

I take off at a run, the other way.

☽ ✧ ☾

The rideshare driver picks me up eight blocks from my house in a blue Honda with a smashed fender.

Sharp is nowhere in sight when I climb in, breathing heavily. The driver has barely shoved the car in gear before he's jabbering something racist about his last customer.

I'm trying to decide whether to get into it with him or take the precious time to give him a terrible rating online, or both. I'm especially angry right now—at the brain power of my species, irrational love, excessive hate, killers, terrible mothers, the idea that I should have to expend any energy or thought at all on this racist stranger in exchange for a seven-minute ride to Joe's Body Shop.

While he turns his rage on the white cyclist veering in front of him, I think about the length of seven minutes.

In the seven minutes I'll be in this Honda, the Earth will have traveled 7,770 miles. It was a famous Seven Minutes of Terror for the rover to pass through the atmosphere of Mars and land safely on its own.

In seven minutes of streaming, Bubba Guns can convince a million people of a lie they will carry to their grave.

I tell the driver to shut the hell up and begin writing a scathing customer review in notes mode.

All the while, I'm looking for Sharp's tail behind me. The driver stops with a jerk in front of Joe's Body Shop, just to show me who's in charge.

My Jeep is parked near the door of the body shop, hardly recognizable without its silty desert coat.

Sharp, well, he's parked across the street.

☽ ✧ ☾

I retrieve the keys from the teenager in the office, hop in the Jeep, do a squeaky U-turn, and pull two inches behind the rear guard on Sharp's pickup.

I wait him out, all while thinking it's a bad idea. My hand is reaching down to shift in reverse when Sharp climbs in the passenger side and slams the door.

"Holy mother, what's that smell?"

"Watermelon Smile." I flick my finger at the air freshener hanging from the rearview mirror, watching it swing like a big pink grin with black teeth. "It was included with the detail."

I'd forgotten how enormous his hands are. Deep under his fingernails, black dirt that I don't remember. Two of his fingers halt the cardboard grin in mid-motion. He snaps it off the rearview mirror, rolls down the window, and flips it into the bed of his pickup.

"There's a little anger in that flip."

"Yeah, well, I'm a little angry."

"Congratulations. You took care of about two percent of the smell problem. According to the kid who handed me the keys, Barbie McClean picked out the fragrance and asked them to—and I quote—*spray it good*. He assured me he did."

Sharp points to his truck. His expression, stone-faced pleasant, if there is such a thing. "I'll take you wherever you want to go. If that's back home, I don't recommend it. Judging by the size of the growing mob in front of your house, this Jeep would be back in the shop tonight. Maybe totaled, although it seems about one pothole away from that anyway. My pickup is right there, *Vivian*. Its air freshener is called Smells So Much Better Than This. We could drive by your house. Pick up a few things. I could take you to a hotel where you could ride things out. I think I could get the department to cover it. Or maybe your sister's house?"

I try to ignore the way *Vivian* sounds in his mouth, and the jab about my sister because it *is* a jab.

"Here are the rules," I say icily. "You can ride along. But you do not intervene with my plans for the day. If I tell you to stay in the

Jeep, you do. You do not mention Bubba Guns, Twitter, or Mike. You do not call me Red. Agreed? Otherwise, get out."

He shrugs. "If I get out, I'll keep following you."

"I don't care." *But I do.* I made this move because I didn't want the added stress of trying to dodge him all day. This way, I can use *him.* Not just for Lizzie. For the girl whose face is clipped flat to Sharp's truck visor without a view. She felt as desperate as Lizzie—even more—when she lay down beside me in my mother's bed jangling her charms. This dead girl has all of eternity to shake her tuneless melody at someone but sees her moment, now, with me.

"Before we start . . ." I'm staring straight ahead, keeping emotion out of my voice with an effort. "I have never slept with Mike. I never will."

"And that is important for me to know because . . . ?"

I flip my head toward him, furious. "It's important for you not to tell anyone you . . . think otherwise. I love my sister. I want to clear the air."

"That didn't work so well on the show, did it? Your plan to clear the air."

"You're already breaking the rules." The reassurance I wanted, not on his lips.

"You're the one who brought up Mike. Can we stop at that Whataburger?" He points across the street. "I haven't had breakfast or lunch. I thought you'd be sneaking out of the house at dawn."

I reach behind me for my backpack. Pull out a folded sheet of paper and thrust it at him. "You're navigating."

He unfurls the paper carefully, like a piece of evidence. "Very distinctive handwriting," he observes. "Tiny. Like the self-loathing elf who writes the naughty list. Or Roy Norris. I might need a microscope. And a psychologist."

"Drafting lettering is a dying art for engineers and scientists," I retort, "because who needs it when you have five thousand fonts on a computer at your fingertips? But, for me, it's like using a paper map. Every stroke helps me think. And I have no idea who the hell Roy Norris is."

"Roy Norris was a diagnosed schizoid and one-half of the serial killing team of Lawrence Bittaker and Roy Norris, a.k.a. the Toolbox Killers. Their first victim together was a sixteen-year-old girl named Lucinda walking home from the Presbyterian church she attended in Redondo Beach. Her last wish, according to Norris, was for 'a second, to pray.' His handwriting has been described as frozen motion with compulsive punctuation."

My stomach is a knot tying a knot tying another knot. Why is he telling me this?

"Are you really comparing me to a serial killer?" A tight bubble lodges in my throat. "You think I could kill someone?"

Sharp's eyes are caught up in my list, focused on my first destination.

He slowly lifts his gaze. "I'm certain you could kill someone. But it has nothing to do with your handwriting or Roy Norris. Every one of us can. It's just a matter of stepping over one line. And then another. And another. Until the lines don't matter anymore."

☽ ✧ ☾

The smell of Whataburger onions is not taking the slightest bite out of the watermelon air freshener.

In maybe our first agreement ever, Sharp and I roll both our windows down in ninety-six-degree heat on I-30, the roar of semis sucking away any attempt at conversation. Sharp is gesturing for me to get off at the next exit, stuffing down the last of a BBQ Bacon Whataburger and onion rings.

"That watermelon shit could cover the stink of a corpse," he grumbles as I slide off the highway.

"Most air fresheners contain formaldehyde," I reply automatically. "It's linked to cancer of the throat. In general, air fresheners are loaded with toxic chemicals." Barbie Jean McClean, no dummy with a spray can.

"You should lay that one on Bubba Guns. The government, killing us by air freshener. Whoops, sorry, I said his name."

Sharp jumps out of the Jeep before I've pulled to a complete stop in front of the first address on my list. I'm a little slower opening the door. I instantly don't like this house, an innocuous low-slung ranch home in the pretty rolling Fort Worth neighborhood of Ridglea Hills.

Maybe it's because Sharp just threw out a serial killer story, but this house reminds me that evil hides inside the ordinary. *Silence of the Lambs* comes to mind. Wasn't the brick on Buffalo Bill's childhood house a neat canvas of red, like this one?

A similar color to the brick on John Wayne Gacy's house in Chicago, where he buried kids in his crawl space? On the home of Jakiw Palij, the Nazi war criminal, hiding out in Queens? Our rental house in the Blue Ridge Mountains, the purse of a murdered woman lodged in a vent?

Sharp has circled around the side of the Jeep and is looking at me strangely. "Are you getting out?"

I stand a little unsteadily. The street itself has settled into a quiet afternoon détente. But the eighteen-wheelers are starting up their engines again in my head. They're almost drowning out the voices that have rock climbed their way from the knots in my belly to my brain. Sweat has picked its spots, clinging between my thighs, soaking the hair resting on the back of my neck.

Red brick, red brick, red brick.

That's what the voices are saying.

This is a bad house.

It would be cruel to ask Sharp to stay in the Jeep, exposing him to air freshener cancer, shortening his life.

Halfway up the walk, I can't smell anything but vanilla.

29

I t takes about twenty of Sharp's fist pounds for a large woman in a flowing, stained pink kimono to open the front door, an oxygen tank in tow.

"Goddamn Sharp" are the first words out of her mouth.

I'd narrowed my list to two addresses for Looper's mother after a brief White Pages search last night. Sharp eliminated the first address, a house in the small town of Ponder near Looper's hunk of land. He'd directed me to the second address under her name, in the city. Now I know Sharp wasn't just making a lucky guess.

Of course, Sharp would have checked all the boxes. He would have interviewed every relative of Looper's, every friend, every coworker. Like me, he would have drawn concentric circles outward until all that was left was howling, empty space with nothing left to touch. He would have done this twice. Not just when Lizzie disappeared, but after Looper did. And maybe, I'm realizing, many more times after that.

"Good afternoon to you too, Helen," Sharp says dryly.

"What's your plan this time, Sharp? Take the oxygen tubes out of my nose while you question me?" She turns, her eyes traveling my body with the kind of hateful stare perfected by bitter Texas women. It can halt your digestion, take an inch off your height for the day,

pinch your heart with two sharp fingernails. Right now, it shuts up
the voices in my head like she slapped them.

"I don't know who the hell you are," she hisses at me, "but you're
my goddamn witness to this."

She leaves the door hanging open and waddles into the darkness,
dragging her tank. I can make out the shape of a couch, a coffee
table, and the blue flicker of the light from a television, which is running at an earsplitting volume.

Sharp holds open the screen door and nods for me to go in.

I'm immediately hit with another smell—of a woman who struggles to bathe herself. I know she didn't used to be this way because
hanging behind her head is a detailed, framed charcoal portrait of
her on a beautiful quarter horse. She once had thighs strong enough
to communicate with him.

A champion roper was formed from a clump of cells in her body.
A picture of a boy who must be Looper, smaller, lesser, is nailed right
below hers. He's swinging a lasso, in a red cowboy hat, about eight.

She plops in a large recliner, eyes back on a rerun of *Shark Tank*.

"I could have invented the goddamn Squatty Potty," she says.

Sharp walks over, picks up the remote from the arm of her chair,
and mutes the TV. Man taking control, and I'm suddenly too busy
with a flood of images to care.

A wooden spoon in a kitchen drawer. A baseball bat in the hall
closet. A leather belt buried shallow in backyard dirt. "Help" scrawled
backward with a waxy crayon on a bedroom window.

A rope looped and looped around a bedpost.

"Helen, this is Vivian," Sharp is saying. "She's a psychic. In fact,
I think she's having a moment right now."

"A goddamn psychic." She chuckles. I snap back in place, glaring
at Sharp for the introduction. It's a bitter look, but not nearly enough
to take an inch off his height or stop his Whataburger from running
its course in his gut.

"Well, well," Helen says, regarding me with new interest. "Are
you seeing my boy Looper on the bottom of the lake? Can you point

to the spot on a map? Take a boat out and raise him up like Jesus himself so I can finally have a proper funeral?"

"I'm very sorry about your son." The words are thick in my mouth, while the images—the rope and belt, the spoon and bat—tease me like haunted objects in a disturbing fairy tale.

I'm sorry he was born to you. That's what I'm sorry about. If he wasn't, I wouldn't be standing here breathing the rot.

"Sure, you're *sorry*. Let's get on with this. What do you want?"

"Could you go through exactly what Looper did the day Lizzie Solomon disappeared?" I ask. "And the day before? Maybe it could help me . . . clear his name."

"Helen and I have been over that." Sharp, abrupt. "I don't need you to do the police department's job."

"Well, this is fun." Helen grins, her eyes roving between us. "Watching you two lovebirds peck at each other is a way better show than mothers pitching their organic-baby-food crap to billionaires with nannies. Those women are trying to starve our kids is what they're doing. Looper grew up on SpaghettiOs and red Doritos, and there was more muscle and brain on that boy than Troy Aikman."

"Sharp and I aren't involved." It seems important to correct her. "It's a very short-term alliance to find Lizzie Solomon."

She nods her head at me, rolling her eyes. "Sure it is. All business. And you want to clear my boy's name, eh? Like I told your boyfriend here, I'm sorry about that little girl, but I'm done talking about my son, on the advice of my lawyer. I have a wrongful death case going right now against the Solomons. It ought to be for murder, but I can't prove that woman and her husband had him outright killed. My boy was a witness to what they did with their girl. He tried to stop it."

Proud, without any proof but her imagination.

Her eyes narrow. Something has dawned on her. "You're that Bubba Guns chick, aren't you? The science lady psychic on his live show yesterday? You called him on some of his horseshit." Her eyes, sizing me up. "I like a woman who stands up to a man. Have a seat, right here."

She pats the arm of the filthy couch next to her, suddenly friendly. I feel compelled to sit because she continues smiling and patting, but I'm just as inclined to keep my butt off a biohazard. She's swinging just a bit of the emotional whip that sliced her son's skin open every day. Looper's mother was the bull he could not beat.

She likes me, she likes me not. Sit or don't sit.

I don't sit. She stops patting.

"Honey, let me tell you about my Looper. His father had him running the hills of this neighborhood till he dropped when he was just twelve. He could swim across that lake by the time he was fifteen. Let's talk about the day before *my son* disappeared. The last time I saw him, eight years ago in May. My boy Looper kissed me on the cheek, said he was going fishing, and that he'd be back with my birthday cake from Costco the next day at eleven. My *birthday*. No son kills himself right before his mother's birthday. And no Texas lake could take him under. Maybe an ocean made by God. But not a lake made by men. Sharp, you gonna tell me again that no fifteen-year-old could swim across Texoma?"

"No, Helen."

She sniffs, satisfied she's won something. Her constant mood shifts are like watching an octopus unfurl.

"Until you prove my son is innocent and find his body, I got nothing else to say. Sharp, you and your girlfriend can find your way out. I bet the sex is real good tonight." She flips on the volume of the TV. A voice is pitching skinny mirrors for dressing rooms so women will feel better about themselves and buy more clothes.

"I'll be back if I can prove anything," I say, raising my voice over the TV. "And that anything might be about you." It takes no time for her to get the insinuation. She angrily tries to shove herself forward to physically come at me, using the rocker feature as momentum. Her weight is too much. She falls back into the chair, huffing a little with just the attempt.

I jam my hand into my pocket and press my thumb into the sharp edge of Lizzie's hair clip.

"What do you got in your pocket, girl? A knife? Mace? You think I can't take you? You're worse than Sharp." She's shrieking now, still struggling with the chair. "You think I killed my own goddamn son?"

"I don't think you held his head under. But I think you might as well have."

Sharp has had enough. He's pulling me across the room to the door. Helen is stabbing at the remote volume until the room is trembling.

Sharp pulls the door tight behind us, keeping a grip on my arm.

I yank away from him.

"That house is like reading a twenty-page suicide note," I spit out. "How could you say with such conviction that Looper didn't dive off that lake and happily sink right to the bottom? Never mind. Just tell me, why didn't Helen inherit her son's land? Why isn't she living like a queen?"

"Looper had a fully executed will that left everything to a local boys' club. He wanted to be sure his mother never got a cent."

"And I bet his lawyer was Nickie Solomon." I state it flatly. "His lover."

"That's right. Nickie drew up the will. It was how they met."

I stop just short of the Jeep.

"Who knows for sure if Looper's dead," I say flatly. "But his mother believes it. She's not hiding him, that's for sure. She's only a good liar to herself." I hesitate. "Something terrible happened in that house. A long time ago. I'm just not seeing it fully."

An admission drifts across his face. "What?" I demand. *"Tell me."*

Sharp is gazing past me, toward the house. "Looper had a little sister, June. She died in the backyard when she was eight months old. In one of those small plastic baby pools. Two inches of water. Looper was told to watch her while Helen took a phone call. He was five."

It punches the breath out of me. I drop to the curb.

Two inches, seven minutes—life just feels too fragile, too teasing. Like we're all just looking into one big skinny mirror, pretending.

I can no longer separate my emotions about Looper. The revulsion is being swallowed by the pity.

I finally lift my head. "Is that why you wonder if he took Lizzie?" I ask. "Out of twisted sorrow and regret? Or do you think he was a stone-cold psychopath who killed them both on purpose?"

"The second. But I'd lay money on either one. I'd also lay money that Looper isn't walking the Earth anymore."

"You're so sure of that."

"As sure as you are that the girl with the charm bracelet is dead."

I'm stunned. A crack. He's brought her up.

"I know you carry her picture in your truck," I say softly. "I know she is the same girl who belongs to the bracelet in the crime scene picture. You can tell me about her, or she eventually will. Your call."

"I knew you searched my truck within the first five seconds of getting back in it."

"Did you leave a charm on my doorstep?" I try to keep a nervous thread out of my voice. "Emme got one, too. Are you playing a game with me? Trying to figure out whether I'm a scam artist?"

"You're the game player, Vivvy. I'm just trying to keep up."

Sharp watches as I pull Lizzie's hair clip out of my pocket and jam my hair into a chaotic bun.

I gesture to the red brick mausoleum behind us. "If I take that bloody lasso out of the back of your truck to Looper's mom, will she say it was her son's?"

"From my experience, it will depend on her blood alcohol level. Sometimes a lasso is just a lasso, Vivvy. A little blood is just a little blood. Sometimes a man is missing, or a girl is dead, and it's better to leave it alone."

30

Those aren't the words of a cop, at least not the kind he pretends to be. I stumble up from the curb.

He opens the driver's side of the Jeep for me and slams it. While I'm turning on the ignition, he's still outside the Jeep, his back to me, taking or making a call. I consider pressing the gas and leaving him where he stands but I debate too long. He's back in the Jeep, draping a seat belt over his long torso. His face, back to a smooth rubber mask.

"Brando is not working at the Fort Worth jail today," he says.

"What?"

"Brandon, a.k.a. Brando Wilbert, part-time guard. Next person on your list."

Our tense back-and-forth on the curb, like it never happened.

"But I called the prison," I protest. "The man I finally got to was talky, a friend of his. He said Brando had a freelance gig at the downtown jail today, running the front desk."

"What Brando has is several unscheduled days off because he touched a prison matter that's a little hot. Not Solomon related. He's a pretty reliable police mole."

"You know him?" I say.

"I know him."

"His apartment address is right below the jail on my list. Punch it in."

"He's not there, either. I'm surprised you didn't . . . intuit this."

"Just take me to him, OK?" I don't tell him that all I can see is more red brick.

$$\text{☽ ✧ ☾}$$

We ride in silence.

Sharp has aimed the navigation at The Usual, a Fort Worth bar with a barely noticeable door, intricate craft cocktails, and the motto "All manner of slightly esoteric libation." And the front façade? Red brick.

The bar's motto is a mouthful for your slumming Texas beer hopper, which I've already stereotyped Brando to be. The Usual is the last place I'd expect a twenty-nine-year-old part-time prison guard who lives in a dying apartment complex on the south side of Fort Worth to hang out and spend his precious pennies.

It has taken fifteen minutes to get to Magnolia Avenue, an eclectic strip of bars, bistros, and BCycle stations. Fifteen minutes of powerful silence and watermelon air freshener.

Once again, Sharp's a gentleman. He opens the door to the cool, dark sanctuary of The Usual like I'm a date. It takes several seconds for my eyes to adjust from the searing sunlight. The last time I was here, on the barstool right there, a debutante bride had a few too many Fuzzy Ducks and Mamie Taylors and Silent Discos and flashed the bar crowd with one too many of her breasts.

Late afternoon, right at the tipping point of happy hour, the bar's still practically empty. Just a couple in a corner booth and a man behind the bar in a Megadeth T-shirt carving delicate lemon peel twists like he's Picasso. Sharp settles us on barstools at the other end. He seems at the top of his manipulation game, whereas I'm thinking, *If he just wants to get drunk and quiz me, I'll take the Jimador's Revenge.*

Sharp is nodding to Megadeth, but Megadeth is clearly pretending he doesn't see. His lemon curling has taken a turn since we walked in the door. He's sucking a little blood off his finger. He glances at us, then away, like he can't make up his mind. Finally, he mummy-wraps his whole fist in a bar towel and slinks over.

"Look, man, my boss here doesn't know I work at the prison," he whines to Sharp. "I told them I'm going to the CIA in the fall. You know, the culinary one. They think my vibe gives the bar . . . character."

"If you can just answer a few questions for her"—Sharp jabs his finger at me—"and serve me a Bloody Mary without the blood, we'll be on our way in fifteen minutes."

"Sure." He turns to me nervously. "What do you want to know?"

I'm not expecting such instant cooperation. "What did you censor out of the letter that a woman named Asteria Bouchet wrote to Nickie Solomon?"

"I censor a lot of letters," he says vaguely. "Hard to remember."

"That one's not going to work on her," Sharp says dryly. "She's psychic."

I shoot Sharp an angry glance. Again, not a revelation I wanted him to open with.

Except the words stick to Brando with powerful effect. He's more nervous. More eager. Leans in. I smell lemons.

"Is my sister going to die?" he asks.

"What?"

"My little sister, Shelby. She's in Cook Children's with leukemia. I'll pay you all my tips tonight if you can tell me anything." His eyes, a piteous and unremarkable brown, are bugging out of his round face.

Enough, enough, *enough*. Enough of somewhat vile men who have a backstory that tugs my heart apart like a wishbone.

"I honestly don't know, Brando," I say carefully. "I'm not getting anything on your sister. It might help if you had an object of hers, something she touched."

"I do." He's calling my bluff, literally rolling up his sleeve. "It's one of her hospital bands. I never take it off." Before I can stop him, he's slit it with his paring knife. "Here."

I rub the slick paper between my fingers. Read her name. Shelby Lynn Wilbert. Her birth date. She's only eleven.

I try. Really *try*. It could be the tag on an endangered sea turtle for all I'm getting. Sharp is watching this surprise turn with interest. He fully expects that I'll use Brando's vulnerability to my advantage. He's going to be disappointed.

"I'm sorry, Brando. Really sorry. I can't tell you anything. I'd love to, but I can't. But I do need to know. The other thing."

"Are you going to arrest me for what I tell her?" The question, directed at Sharp. "Tell my boss?"

"Which one?"

"Either one."

Their drawls are lengthening, one mimicking the other, a three-letter word becoming two syllables. *Wuh-un.*

"Come on, Brando," I beg. "It's a missing girl. What if it was your sister?"

"OK, OK. Don't beat on me, all right? A man called and said if I'd read him every piece of Nickie Solomon's correspondence, he'd leave three hundred dollars in my mom's mailbox on the tenth of every month. So that's what I've been doing. My sister's bills are bad."

Again with the backstory. Killing me.

"I'd read her letters to him over the phone," Brando continues, "and he'd tell me if there was anything I should scratch through. It's illegal for us to censor any official correspondence like from her lawyer so I just do it with her personal mail." He says this like it retains his dignity.

"I didn't know this was part of your job as a guard," Sharp interjects. "Handling mail."

Brando studies him, deciding how to answer. "It's not my *official* job or anything. Anyway, this man didn't like that this Bouchet lady said she knew who took Lizzie Solomon and wrote down a name and phone number. I told him prisoners got bullshit letters like this every day, but he insisted I black out the detail. I thought it might be *his* name. You know, the guy wanting me to do the censoring. He always called himself Mr. Anonymous when he called."

"You remember the name you censored out of the letter?" Sharp asks crisply. "You remember the number?"

"My teachers told me I didn't have a head for remembering names and numbers. Except I remember real good that he didn't leave me three hundred bucks last week like he was supposed to. I think he's done with me. That's all I know. You still want the Bloody Mary?"

"To go," Sharp says.

Brando turns to head off to the gleaming wall of liquor bottles on the other side of the bar.

"Wait." I hold out his sister's snipped hospital bracelet. "Don't forget this."

He pivots, hesitating. "Will you wear it? You know—just in case you can get something?"

I don't instantly say no, which Brando takes as a yes. He returns in five minutes with two Bloody Marys in tall plastic cups and a roll of Scotch tape.

On one of the cups, *Brando* and a phone number are written across the side in black marker. He hands that one to me, the other to Sharp.

Brando rips off a piece of tape.

I hold out my wrist.

'm wearing an alarming number of accessories. A trifecta of metal, paper, and pain.

The hospital bracelet on my wrist handcuffs me to the soul of Brando's little sister fighting to live. The charm left by a stranger on my doorstep is a silver noose around my neck, a reminder of Sharp's dead girl begging me to find her. The clip that I stole from Lizzie's bloody bow at the police station is like a broken fingernail hidden in my hair, clawing at my scalp.

Alive.

Three girls, tugging and tearing at me, pulling me apart.

"Are you all right?" Sharp asks. "You're pretty pale."

I nod, climbing in the Jeep, not about to explain that I can't bear to wear anything else.

I roll down all four windows before taking a single breath. I sip enough off the top of my drink so that it won't spill in the drink holder, Tabasco clawing at my throat.

Sharp, beside me, has already gulped down half of his, tossed back the blue cheese–stuffed olive and deep-fried jalapeño, and is gnawing the celery loud enough that I can hear it above a motorcycle jamming by.

I've had a touch of misophonia since I was a kid, the scientific label for a hatred of sounds. One more thing in my bag of extreme sensitivities. One more thing Sharp is using against me, whether he knows it or not.

Normal sounds, like someone breathing in bed beside me or chewing across a table, can shriek like a howler monkey under my skin. The tapping of a pencil on a desk. A fingernail on a dashboard.

It's not all the time, but it's often enough. My mother always told me I could hear a toenail growing or a star falling. Which one, she declared, depended on the romance of her mood.

Right now, Sharp might as well be crunching a child's bone in his teeth.

I slide my seat back, feeling cramped. "What did you think of Brando?" I ask.

Sharp snaps off another bite of celery. "About the same thing I thought before."

"The mystery guy who paid him to censor Nickie's letter—that doesn't intrigue you?"

"Like Brando said. Lots of crazies. Doesn't necessarily mean anything."

Sharp is lying.

He reaches a long arm down and picks up my list off the floor of the passenger seat where he dropped it. "That appears to be the end of today's tour. It's about five. Good time to check into a hotel. Not too early that your room's not ready, not too late that you can't switch rooms if you get one that stinks like feet. If the department won't pay, it's on me."

I switch on the ignition. "I'm dropping you back at your truck."

"You're really going to take the unnecessary risk of sleeping at home tonight."

"I've calculated risk assessment for rockets that launch astronauts into space. I think I can assess whether I should sleep in my own bed tonight."

"If I only believed that were true."

"Maybe you'll understand better if you think of it this way. For these commercial flights shooting tourists into space, the FAA is not focused as intently on whether the occupants will live or die as they are on calculating the safety risk for the humans on the ground. You know, if the rocket explodes and hot debris and body parts rain down on people while they are sunning themselves on a beach. We worry about innocents. We worry about the space tourists too, but they're like stuntmen taking a risk that has been accepted."

I want to draw the line for Sharp so that he'll understand. "That's how I've thought of myself since I was ten. As a stuntwoman. I want to survive—I will try *one hundred percent* to survive—but jumping into the unknown, being watchful, never letting my guard down, is routine for me." I'm not at all sure I've expressed myself well. I don't want to sound like a martyr. The DNA of me, the risk baked in at birth, just *is*.

He shakes his head. "Living this way—it's not sustainable. Are you talking about your relentless loyalty to the voices you hear? You aren't a millionaire going up on a birthday joyride. And you didn't ask for a conspiracy nut to entice his fanatics to your front lawn. There is real physical danger here, Vivvy."

It's the closest thing he's said to an apology, the most concern he's ever expressed for me, but I focus on the words that tick me off. *Not sustainable. Relentless loyalty.*

"You have no idea what's sustainable for someone like me," I say stiffly. "I'm OK with who I am. It's you and people like you who aren't."

Is that true? Am I OK? Better or worse than when I was ten, fifteen, twenty? My mind flits to a bottle with four pink pills left, and not for the first time today. Soon there will be three. Two. One. What will I do then? The same thing I've done for the last three years? Slink into a strange psychiatrist's office for a forty-five-minute conversation that doesn't scratch the dirt to get a ninety-day prescription?

Maybe I'm more like Sharp than I want to believe. *Stare into the abyss, and the abyss stares back.* Thank you, Nietzsche, who believed science killed God. I may search for light in the sky, but on Earth, I follow my darkest instincts like a string of muddy footprints.

Just like Sharp does.

My eyes fall to his boots, caked with dirt. I see a flash of a girl's lost grave. I just don't know which one.

☽ ✧ ☾

We ride in silence until I nudge the Jeep behind his pickup. Sharp isn't making an immediate move to get out. He reaches over and tucks a finger under the inside of the hospital band, his touch on my skin like the end of a live wire.

"It's got to be tough," he says.

I understand instantly. He isn't talking about Brando's sister, a little girl fighting a dragon in a hospital bed.

He is talking about me, adding her dragon to my fleet.

He traces his finger down the palm of my hand before pulling it away.

I hate myself for wanting it back.

He's out of the Jeep, slamming the door.

He leans his head through the open window.

"Don't ask about the girl or the charm bracelet again."

It's grime in his throat.

He's gone before I can respond.

☽ ✧ ☾

I park the Jeep in the alley. I'm becoming much more confident about vaulting my backyard fence like a teenager, much less confident about my ability to probe the darkness that is Jesse Sharp.

Don't ask about the girl again.

It's a worm in my head that won't stop repeating. It's so hard to balance the two Sharps—the one who empathizes with my dragons and the one who warns me not to push him too far.

I berate myself while I crawl across the yard on my knees, skirting tent stakes and tarantula holes.

I should have asked Sharp directly: *Did you kill Looper with his lasso and then keep it as a souvenir?*

I should have been more cinematic—pulled the charm out from under my shirt and demanded to know if he left it on my porch. In Emme's tent. Asked how he even knew how to spell Emme's name, short for her great-grandmother Emmeline. Nothing about him or the charms, making any sense.

My head is so cotton-stuffed with Sharp that I don't immediately register. There is no bullhorn activity drifting from out front. No sound of any kind except the distant grind of a grass trimmer.

When I throw my leg over the bathroom windowsill, the silence inside feels thick, muck I'm about to wade in. I turn up the air-conditioning on my way to the living room, desperate for the sense of something else alive in here, anything to crack the quiet.

The lock on the front door, intact. No broken glass. The only person I see out the window is a ponytailed multitasking jogger with a stroller and a German shepherd straining on the end of a leash. She tosses the house an uneasy eye on her way by.

I don't know why until I'm on the porch.

A stuffed dummy hangs by a rope from the chain of the swing. The T-shirt declares *The End Is Near.* The head is a globe of the Earth. Googly eyes, red yarn for hair, a mouth drawn like a scream-ing star. Me, I presume.

A kid's rocket ship is jammed into the chest, right where my heart would be.

☾ ✧ ☾

I cut down the dummy and drag it through the house to the garbage cans in the back alley. Only then do I venture into the front yard, which is littered like the aftermath of a demonic kid's birthday party. Broken lawn chairs, empty water bottles, sandwich wrappers, potato chip bags, signs poked in the lawn. An ugly amoeba-shaped oil stain from the pickup in the driveway. The loaner is gone, too, picked up as quickly as the body shop promised. Or stolen. I don't want to think about that.

I jump when my phone buzzes in my pocket.

A text from Brig.

> I saw Bubba Guns on TV in front of
> the house. Are you OK?

I finger back a reply, relieved she's reaching out. That kiss with Mike, a piece of lead in my heart that shifts every time I move.

> I just got home. The protesters
> have left. All's quiet.

I leave out that I've been hung in effigy.

The gray bubble is going on Brig's end, three dots romping their flat roller coaster.

> This is much worse than I thought it
> would be. I shouldn't have told you
> to go on the show.

I begin to respond, but there's already another bubble. Typing. Still typing. The bubble disappears. Now it's become an anxiety bubble. For me. *Was she erasing something about Mike? Did he tell her about last night?* One of my coworkers ended up in therapy over the emotional damage caused by these disappearing digital bubbles.

I continue to stare at the screen.

Nothing.

Brig has shut the door. I feel the firm click in my stomach, just like when I was a kid and she vanished into the blue cocoon of her bedroom. Everywhere we moved, she painted her room the same color. *Sanctum.*

No color chip from another brand would do, even if it *almost* matched, even if Mom had to scour eight stores on a Saturday to find it. The three of us would stay up all night to paint, a ritual Mom encouraged because Brig was manic, wouldn't sleep until the walls were covered in *Sanctum*.

The bedroom she sleeps in now with Mike is *Parmesan*. A two-hundred-dollar-an-hour interior designer insisted on doing it himself, the trim line so perfect it hurts to look at it.

I stare at the phone for five more minutes. No more bubbles. No more Brig.

☽ ✧ ☾

I drink two Modelos before retrieving a garbage bag from under the sink and heading back outside. I see the cruiser almost instantly, now parked two houses down. One cop. Aviator sunglasses like Sharp's shoved up on his bald head.

I've met him. He grows squash and peppers in his garden and hands out bags of them at the station like they're money. I'm sure he also knows how to use a gun. But I don't think they've sent their A game.

I glimpse a flash out of the corner of my eye. Someone is back in the yard. My hand drops to the holster under my T-shirt before my brain has time to process.

The flash is Emme's mom, Mary, in a neon pink sports bra, pulling up a sign jammed into the corner of the yard. She nods, walking toward me with the sign under her arm and three smashed cans in her hand.

"I don't wish this on anyone," Mary says. "Dumb people and rage. When I was a kid, my older brother got beat up for being Black. And let me tell you, on a daily basis. He'd come home crying, and my mother's wisdom was, 'Whatever the question, love is the answer.' Emme is sweet as soap, just like my mama. But I'm trying to wash a little of that out of her. Because my mama was wrong."

She drops the Coke cans in my garbage bag with one hand and gestures to the yard with the other. "These people don't understand real love. They never got it or gave it. They only understand lies that give them power over people who don't look or act like them. Black folks, we've got our own conspiracy theory problems. You ever heard of the King Alfred Plan?"

I shake my head.

"Look it up," she admonishes me. "Get some history. Tell me there's not *some* truth in it."

"I will," I say awkwardly. "And thank you. For picking up the sign. I'm sorry for all of this."

She nods toward the police car, hands on her hips. "I see some surveillance. That's what you get when you're white with a sister married to a cop."

I don't deny it because it's the truth.

"If it's not enough," I rush out, "I'm going to hire security for the block with the money my mother left me."

"Your mother never let anyone back her against a wall," she says. "You don't, either."

Surprising me. I can see so much in people, but not always the most important things. She stalks back across her yard, done picking up my trash.

Your enemies will become your friends, and your friends will become your enemies. Keep them both close.

That was *my* mother's wisdom.

For dinner, I eat cold leftover Whataburger french fries from my backpack with six Ritz crackers from the cabinet and some questionable string cheese.

While I sip sobering ice water, I type *King Alfred Plan* in my search bar. Not what I expected—a fictional plot in a 1967 novel about a top secret CIA plan to lock away Black people in concentration camps.

The author—critically acclaimed, with an early knack for viral marketing—stirred up hysteria by leaving flyers in the New York subway that excerpted his book but didn't mention it was fiction.

The novel is pretty much forgotten, but the King Alfred Plan is still woven into the fabric of Black America, prescient and terrifying.

Because there *was* J. Edgar Hoover and Martin Luther King Jr. and Malcolm X and the FBI.

Now there's Bubba Guns. His Elon Musk–bashing and gay catfish theories seem benign in comparison, but they are still a deep and terrifying hook.

I don't know if it makes me feel better or worse to be reminded that conspiracy theories aren't an invention of the terror-filled twenty-first century—that they've literally been on fire since Nero was accused of burning Rome to the ground in A.D. 64.

Did Nero really play his fiddle while his city turned to ashes?

No proof, but history records the accusation because there's a thread of reason. A fuse. Because Nero proceeded to rebuild the city in his image and executed hundreds of Christians along the way, accusing *them* of starting the fire.

A power-hungry dictator plus paranoia plus time. Was it possible he lit a match? How do I know? It doesn't seem *impossible*. And that's really all that matters.

I pick up my phone.

Brig has finished her bubble.

Maybe you should go.

32

've barely absorbed the gut punch of Brig's text when the phone begins to ring in my hand. I don't recognize the number.

"He wants you back on." Female. Highly charged. "The ratings were through the roof."

"Joie?"

"His first choice is tomorrow at three p.m. You'd need to be in the studio by two thirty-five."

"My first choice is never again. How did you get my cell number?"

"One of your neighbors gave it to Bubba this afternoon in return for an autographed stomach."

Not Mary. *Who?*

"I thought you might hesitate," she continues brightly, "but think about how pissed he was that you didn't come out your front door to participate in his event today. Then triple that. In absentia, he'll roast you like a pig. Plus, you don't come on the show, you'll look like you're afraid, have something to hide about your so-called psychic abilities and Lizzie Solomon. You'll look bad. The police will look bad. This way, you can throw some nice cool water on that. Keep up your fascinating scientific patter. Throw some more personal darts at Bubba's gut. Distract, distract, distract."

"Does this kind of intimidation usually work?"

"Yes." A pause. "The other good news is, this will be recorded for his podcast. Not live. That seems to ease most people's minds. You know, because of the panic pressure of *live*."

"Give me a break. That's not good news. It means you will be able to edit out whatever he doesn't like before the podcast drops."

Another short silence extends on the other end.

"Bubba Guns is willing to offer up something. He'll tell everyone to lay off your house."

"That's not going to stop the idiot who made the *Shiv Viv* sign that my neighbor yanked out of my lawn today. Or the one who wants to ram a toy rocket into my chest."

"Look, it will stop *most* of the idiots. Trust me, I've been through this a few times and no one's dead yet. And he'll throw in a bonus. He *won't* tell people to start hanging out at your sister and brother-in-law's house."

"How old are you again?"

"Twenty-three. Five years younger than you. We could be sisters. Can I schedule you for two thirty-five?"

"Whatever you're paid, it isn't enough. Didn't you say you told your mom you're working on behalf of the Texas coalition against the death penalty? You should consider making that true. They could use a bulldog like you."

I hang up.

Let Bubba Guns tap his toe.

I have another call to make.

☽ ✧ ☾

I debate briefly before deciding eight thirty p.m. is not too late for a phone to ring. The hard line in Texas, about nine. You might be in bed, glasses and iPad and *Yellowstone* on, dog settled at the foot, irritated for the disturbance, but not asleep.

I plugged ATOB into my phone's contact list just this morning, which feels like a very long time ago. *A Thing of Beauty*. The person on the end of so many of my mother's calls as she prepared to leave this realm.

A Thing of Beauty. Mom used to read that poem to me. She loved Keats, the idea that a beautiful object has the power to remove darkness even if its beauty is just part of your memory. I want to believe this reference isn't a coincidence, that it's a clue she left knowing that I'd be the one finishing up her unfinished life.

No one leaves a finished life. Yet another piece of Asteria Bouchet wisdom.

I hit send on the number. I know what I hope for—instant answers about Lizzie Solomon. I know what I expect—for it to be another random, lonely soul whom I will clumsily counsel. Or, more likely, for the number to be as dead as my mother.

One ring. A pickup. A quick intake of breath.

"Did you change your mind already?" she asks.

Joie.

Did I accidentally hit redial on the last call?

I did not.

A thing of beauty is a joy for ever.

A thing of beauty is a joy.

A thing of beauty is a *Joie.*

The French spelling.

My mother and Joie knew each other.

Not a coincidence, not by any scientific calculation of probability.

"How'd you get *my* cell phone number?" she asks suspiciously.

A question I won't answer. I have in front of me a list of tidy questions for A Thing of Beauty in that serial killer print of mine. I ask none of them.

"I did change my mind," I stutter. "Here's my offer. Only fifteen minutes. And the show has to be live."

I hang up, feeling the hot, moist breath of a little girl on the back of my neck.

☽ ✧ ☾

I slide out a piece of engineering paper on my mother's kitchen table. I draw a simple diagram of balloons, a solar system run amok.

Lizzie gets a balloon. So does Nickie, her mother. Marcus, her father. Looper, the lover. I add my mother. Joie. Bubba Guns. Anonymous Girl on Tip Line. I draw the lines that connect them and wish for the invisible ones I know exist. I still don't get it. My diagram, two-dimensional, no matter how long I stare at it.

My second conversation with Joie was short and abrupt. I didn't confront her. I don't know enough—whether she's friend or enemy or somewhere in the middle, if she's working with Bubba Guns or on her own. Were they extorting my mother because she knew something about the Lizzie Solomon case? If so, it apparently didn't work, and I was the putty that was left.

I know one thing: Joie may be young but she's nine years too old to be Lizzie Solomon. I slide my phone into my hand. On the Bubba Guns website, she's listed under staff as Joie Jones. A quick search leads me nowhere, not even to an article on a high school track meet or basketball game. No LinkedIn, Facebook, Twitter, TikTok, or Instagram accounts under that name, either.

She's hiding herself. To avoid fallout from Bubba Guns haters? Or something else? Bubba Guns would be the last person to care if she made up a stage name.

My pencil tip rests on Marcus Solomon's balloon. I picture the folds of his forlorn face in the snare of my telescope. Lizzie's father had been interviewed by the police and media more than any other single person at the heart of the case, including his convicted wife. Two of his interviews are transcribed in the file Sharp gave me, along with Marcus Solomon's bleak address in a Fort Worth mobile home park.

Marcus Solomon has been drained of blood by Sharp and countless others. Yet, that face. It tugs at me. Like a clue is buried somewhere in the folds, a lost crumb. He had an alibi, just like Nero when his city burned. He wasn't there. Marcus was keeping vigil two hundred miles away at his mother's bedside in the hospital. His father, sister, and a nurse confirmed it.

What's too late to knock on someone's door? In Texas, in a trailer park, those lines are very, very blurry.

☽ ✧ ☾

I know as soon as I drive up that Marcus Solomon has a female in residence.

A bright bulb in the porch light is defiant in the dark.

Neat pots of red geraniums in plastic pots sit on either side of the door, still alive in July because someone makes a tedious note in her head to treat them to a glass of water every day.

A scrolly metal *Live Love Laugh* sign hangs on white aluminum siding that is probably still roasting to the touch even with the sun long down.

The sign gives me a pang. Those three words are Brig's pet peeve. When we were on good terms, she sarcastically signed every text LLL, her inside joke. Except when she signed off with GBT. *God Bless Texas*. Or GBV. *God Bless Vivvy*. The last two sign-offs sincere, if conflicted.

I can't think too long about what's irreparable with Brig, or it will drown me. Certainly not now, in the gloom of a trailer park, where the stars are an occasional freckle above a string of anemic trees.

I pull the Jeep door closed as quietly as I can, hoping I don't attract attention.

I'm sure that both good people and bad people live in this transients' park off the highway, but they have one thing in common—the wariness they put on at night with their pajamas. The Big Three are always lurking—tornadoes, fire, and strangers. A gun will only shoot one of them, but it's still always on the table.

Lights are blazing around me like a Christmas village. TVs flickering on porches. The churn of window air conditioners. The fury of Tucker Carlson, still inexplicably alive. The gravelly voice of Warren Zevon, still inexplicably not. The piercing-to-the-bone wail of a baby.

Two trailers down, an ash from a cigarette is falling silently like a cinder from a star. Too dark to see the hand holding it.

I knock, feeling as tinny and vulnerable as the door.

I wonder if Sharp is out there.

Hoping he is. Hoping he isn't.

33

The first thing I think when the woman opens the door is that she is too old by at least fifteen years to be Lizzie Solomon. I didn't even realize I was holding a breath on the idea that Lizzie was hiding here, doing the watering.

The second thing I think is that she's pretty, even shiny with sweat. Even with the slightly crooked nose and the part already showing her pink scalp, a sign she probably began bleaching her hair when she was twelve, an acceptable Texas milestone.

She's been told not to let me in, but she's not the kind of person who does that by nature even though she is so slight that the roaches under the counter must wonder if they can take her while she sleeps.

She's the kind of person who allows stray handymen to use the bathroom, who invites Jehovah's Witnesses in with the hope that she can save them, who lets high school boys stuff a hand down the front of her tight jeans because she wanted to be liked.

She's the kind of woman willing to live "in sin" with a middle-aged man who has been accused of killing his daughter and boarding up her bones, still visits his convicted-killer wife once a week like it's church, and is sitting on the sale of a giant, decaying Victorian that would provide the nest egg for a house to keep her at a cool and steady seventy-six degrees.

She exudes eternal hope even though life has dealt some unfortunate cards.

I instantly like her.

I *want* her to live, love, laugh.

And it's not going to happen if I don't walk through her door.

I feel it. I *know* it.

"Is Marcus home?" I ask.

"No." It sounds like a question mark could be attached.

"I'm a psychic working with the police," I announce. "I think Lizzie Solomon is alive."

In less than a minute, I'm sitting in the taco valley of her brown velveteen couch.

☽ ✧ ☾

Marcus's girlfriend introduces herself as Beth and immediately begins apologizing for the broken air conditioner and her state of undress—a spaghetti-strap top sans bra and a ghostly thin pair of white cotton pajama shorts. The sweaty sheen on her tan arms is like a fresh coat of varnish.

An ex-Odessa girl, she says she ran like a jackrabbit from a life shaded by oil wells instead of trees. She's been living with Marcus Solomon for sixteen months—seven months after they met in a grocery store parking lot when he rear-ended her Volkswagen, a few Titos and lime to the wind. I'm not sure what drew her to Marcus Solomon, but some women are born to save.

Other than the worn couch, the living room is crammed with furniture that I expect has been hauled straight out of the Nickie Solomon antique collection. An imposing glass-fronted dining room cabinet is lodged tight to the ceiling, a train track of scrape marks leading from the door.

The air can't find a path to move.

Only one lamp lit.

The tiny kitchen that I could reach a hand into from the couch is dark except for the red blink of the digital clock on the microwave. I know from broken air conditioner experience that Beth doesn't want to produce another degree of heat.

I'm ready to strip to my bra already.

Beth, perched on the edge of a Victorian high back, is not shouting to the back of the trailer for Marcus, and he isn't popping out of one of the three doors visible down the tiny hallway that extends past the kitchen. I'm guessing the whole place tops out at nine hundred square feet, quite a fall from a three-story turret.

"I want to get on with our lives, you know?" Beth says wistfully. "My mama doesn't think so, but I *know* Marc is more likely to divorce his wife and stop drinking if she gets out of prison. You think you can convince the police?"

"I want to be clear: I have no physical proof that Lizzie is alive. Not yet. I'd love to ask Marcus a few questions."

"He's out," she responds, instantly nervous again. "You know he had nothing to do with this, right? You feel it?"

"I do." *I don't.* "Would you mind if I walked around your home a little? To get a vibe? Touch things? Is this furniture from the house?" If only Sharp were here to witness me acting out his stereotype.

"The stuff is creepy, isn't it? I think it hates me. I keep banging into it at night. Marc is finally letting me price it to sell online. Most of my stuff is still in storage." She pauses. "I had to threaten to leave to convince him. But I wouldn't have. Left."

I push myself out of the couch's crevice as if she's already said yes. I'm just like everyone else who has ever taken advantage of her sweet hesitation. I feel guilty but not enough to stop myself. "Can I start at the back?"

"I'd rather you get Marc's permission."

"I just saw him at the prison. He seemed to accept me as legit— that I'm only interested in finding Lizzie."

"He didn't say anything about that." She sounds more hurt than suspicious.

"Can you text him?" It's a risk.

"Not really," she replies reluctantly. "He's not much of a texter. At night, anyway."

So he's drunk. Or back in Lizzie's room, observable in a high window with a high-powered scope. Maybe both.

I don't know why I'm pushing this poor woman so hard. What I expect to find. Maybe it's the fever of this metal box, maybe it's Lizzie's mad determination under my skin.

"How about this—you follow right behind me," I encourage. "If you don't want me to touch something, I won't." I'm already on the move, dragged by an invisible magnet toward the hall.

"It has to be fast." Beth's eyes dart to the front door. "Like five minutes or less."

She's close behind, her sweetness airborne, a natural, intangible musk.

"Let's start here. Just a feeling." My hand rests on the knob of the door on the right.

"That's Marc's home office. He's doing a little freelance family law out of there for now. You can't touch anything. He'll know. Once I shifted some letters just an inch. He still gets ugly ones, you know. Parents, who were on the other side of the table, lost custody, who say he deserved what he got when he lost Lizzie. They blame him instead of blaming themselves for being shitty parents."

"Do the police know about this? The threats?"

"He turns every email and letter over as soon as he gets it. You know, in case one of them did it out of revenge. We have a system for the letters. Gloves and a Ziploc bag are right there in his office drawer."

The door doesn't budge when I turn the knob. Locked.

"Move," Beth says, pushing in front of me. "It swells in the heat." She bumps it with her hip, springing it open, flipping on a harsh fluorescent light. It's like she opened an oven preheated to five hundred degrees. Hot, trapped air knocks both of us back. Our lips almost touch as she squeezes by me. I see why she didn't enter the office ahead of me. There is about three feet of room available for standing.

A desk, sleek and modern and important, swallows almost the whole office. There's barely expanse for the massive leather swivel chair behind it that sits an inch from the back wall. A file cabinet lunges out of a corner, consuming the remaining space. It's a mystery how any of it was maneuvered in here.

It's a room of ones. One picture is centered on the top of the desk. One Bic pen protrudes from a crystal pen holder. One document rests in a wooden tray.

One diploma is framed and centered on the wall behind the desk. It draws me closer. It makes the balloons I drew on that piece of paper at the kitchen table begin to tumble and blow. I see a connection I didn't see before, but I'm not exactly sure what it means. Beth is already pulling on my arm—much wirier than she looks.

"I've changed my mind. Marc will kill me if he finds out I let you in. He could be here any second. He says I have got to stop trusting people. Jesus, you didn't even say your name."

"It's Joie," I lie, not sure why. "Joie Jones."

☽ ✧ ☾

Beth kicks me out. The rattle of the chain lock assures me she means it.

A minute later, she is a wraith in her bare feet, wispy, white pajama shorts, and thin yellow hair, rapping at my Jeep window until I roll it down. I wonder for a second if she is real. I've been leaning my face into the air conditioner vents, heart pounding in my skull.

"You know why I let you in?" she asks.

I shake my head.

"Two reasons. One, because of that hospital bracelet. You'd only wear it for one reason. You have a good heart. That girl Shelby, whoever she is, is the same age as my niece. I'll pray for Shelby tonight, not knowing if she's in heaven or on her way or if she gets a reprieve." Her drawl, lyrical in its sincerity. "The second reason is because if there's any possibility I can help set Nickie Solomon free, I want to try. Even if . . ." She gulps back a sob. "Even if he goes back to her."

I watch her straighten herself, align her thin skeleton, retain hope for the thousandth time. "Hold out your hand," she orders. Whatever she drops into my palm is so light I barely feel it. It's too dark to see.

"I don't care if Marc discovers it's missing. It was Lizzie's. She wore it every day. He found it in the grass in the front yard. He couldn't bear to part with it. Touch it all you want. Do your thing."

"Beth . . ."

"Don't say anything. If you're a hustler, I don't want to know. You think you're the first stranger who's shown up here with some tale about Lizzie? I let them *all* in. Because, you know what, at least I will have *tried*. Odds are, one of you is going to be special. I'm counting on it being you, *Vivvy Bouchet*."

She's also the kind of person who is smart.

I'm ashamed I missed that.

She's gone before I turn on the overhead light.

34

'm back in Bubba Guns's hot seat, trying to control my heart rate, fingering Lizzie Solomon's friendship bracelet that Beth dropped in my hand last night like a feathery wish.

I had expanded the braid of yellow-and-red threads with a white piece of string from the kitchen drawer so it would fit around my wrist. It now nestles beside Shelby Wilbert's hospital band. The bits of jewelry on my neck, at my wrist, in my hair are leaving red marks on my skin. They are rope and chain, growing rougher, rustier, heavier.

Bubba Guns is stretching his jaw up and down for preshow exercise. Summoning the kind of charismatic electricity that seems like it would elude a man in Teva sandals, but then barefoot cult leaders have managed it since the dawn of time.

He leans into the mic, and I feel a bolt shoot through me. I'd agreed to the recorded podcast, just a cozy conversation, but it feels like the world is watching me sweat. "Welcome, Bubba Gunzers. We have child hunter Vivvy Bouchet sitting in the electric chair. She can't stay away. Her price: She wants you folks off her lawn for good. But I think you'll agree, she's going to have to earn it. I'll start with a softball question before we get down to the business of Fort Worth's most famous missing person's case, the legendary Lizzie Solomon.

Dr. Bouchet, let's test your general psychic powers about famous killed kids, shall we?"

He lifts an eyebrow at me and holds it like a conductor's wand. "Here's a theory my assistant dug up. Katy Perry and JonBenét's eyebrows match, and eyebrows don't change from birth—ergo Katy Perry is JonBenét all grown up. You look confused, Dr. Bouchet. Jon-Benét performed in pageants, Katy Perry is a pop princess. You see where I'm going. JonBenét was never killed, found in her basement, the whole bit. What do you think? Or should I ask: What do you *feel?*"

I force myself to let him wait, counting to two, three, four. "I *think* you attended the University of Southern California at exactly the same time as Nickie and Marcus Solomon, Lizzie's parents. I recently saw Mr. Solomon's diploma with my own eyes. It took me all day to find your record with the help of a very nice person in the USC records office. You ask, what do I *feel?* I *feel* like this isn't a coincidence that you are harping on the Lizzie Solomon case. That you actually know a lot more than you're sharing with your listeners."

"Hey. Whoa. I wouldn't step my pinky toe in California, much less let it educate me."

"I just tweeted out your alumni record." I hold up my phone. "Proof. See? USC. You're Trojan all the way."

"Well, I won't sit here and deny my virility. But, honey, you know I can't see. You're thirty feet away behind my protective acrylic shield so none of your Wiccan spells get through." He chuckles. It's like I've barely wounded him. "I do know that whatever you just tweeted is a lie. A *falsified* record. Look for typos, people. Or maybe look for perfection. I've never read an official record without a careless mistake or a good lie. Besides, who cares *who* I know?"

He yanks off his headphones. Furious.

"To hell with you," he says. "I'm not airing this shit on my podcast. I just tweeted, too. Your tweet will be disappearing down the trail while people google *Katy Perry JonBenét eyebrows*. Your tweet is a baby bird dying in the womb."

I hear a bit of a chirp now—of an English accent. Fury, the great revealer.

"If you want me to stop exposing you, you'll tell your followers that I'm old news. You'll butt out of the Lizzie Solomon case."

"And why would I do that?"

"Because you've never encountered anyone like me."

"I think I have. My grandmother read fortunes from playing cards. She said I would be a brain surgeon or a Baptist preacher. How'd she do? I kind of like to think I'm the best of both without a degree for either."

"I'm not talking about that," I snap. "I'm a scientist. I regularly travel back *light-years* in time. I'll draw DNA charts on your family that go back a hundred years before your grandmother. If I was just a nobody scientist tweeting out your diploma, it wouldn't matter. But you're pissing me off *and* you're making me famous. I racked up fifty thousand followers in the last forty-eight hours. A reporter at *The New York Times* is following me." The last one, a lie, but I figure they'll eventually turn a snotty nose.

His fingers drum the desk. "Touché, Bouchet. I just love saying that. Look who's picked up a few things from listening to Bubba Guns. Threatening people is invigorating, isn't it? I'm curious. How'd you find out about my California background? Was it Joie? She blackmails me with it for a raise every three weeks. What else did she tell you? It doesn't matter how you answer, she's fired."

I don't answer, which is an answer. Conflicted about protecting her because Bubba Guns certainly doesn't indicate a bond, and Joie is not an innocent. Conflicted about when to confront her about her calls with my mother. I'd strolled into the studio much too late to do that, about two minutes before we were scheduled to start recording.

Joie had been at her desk in the outer office, a slew of papers and empty coffee cups in front of her, eyes veining red again. Bubba Guns was fuming in the studio as he got familiar with the possibility of being stood up.

"Tell me what you know about the Solomons," I demand. "How long *you've* known the Solomons."

"Did one of your police lovers dig that up? Oh, what the hell. I've got nothing serious to hide on that front. I know *one* of the Solomons. I never met their unfortunate child, Lizzie. I certainly didn't kidnap her. If you ever say I did, we're going to have some real problems."

I grip the handle of my backpack. "*Real* problems? Your followers are threatening my life. You've made unstable people believe I'm part of an elitist plot to overtake Texas. I'm asking you nicely, right now, to stop. If you even mention my sister's name on one of your shows again, I will come for you in ways even you can't imagine. And, for the record, the shape of your eyebrows doesn't stay the same from birth. They get pointier every decade. Like little mountains. Look in the mirror."

"Now, if that had been your answer a minute ago, we might still be going." Big joke, like the last minutes were a tea party.

I stand up. Shaky.

Bubba Guns has drawn on a grin that curdles my stomach.

"Look, honey," he purrs, "conflict is how humanity evolves. I make a lot of people with no power a little less afraid. I inject excitement and purpose into hot afternoons otherwise spent with a lawn mower. Nobody's off-limits in this life. Not from me. *Nobody.* Not the Solomon parents. Not Dr. Vivian Bouchet. Not Lizzie, God rest her little grave.

☽ ✧ ☾

I swallow a deep breath on the other side of the door.

Joie's desk is empty, completely cleared, the glass top shining.

Her workout duffel, weathered Kate Spade purse, and big pink bag of extraneous personal belongings are no longer bulging out from under the desk. The desk lamp is off, along with all but an overhead light by the door, just to be sure it's understood that her decision is permanent. A final and polite *Take that.*

I'm not surprised Joie's gone. It appears to be for good.

I don't think she ever planned to be here long.

I can't hear anything through the acoustic lock on the studio door. Bubba Guns might be off the phone, he might not. I keep my eye glued to the knob as I stumble toward the desk where I handled the tip line. Mold is growing on the surface of some of the black dregs left in the coffee cups.

I grasp the cords for the phone and the recording device and rip them out of the wall. No way am I leaving the fragile voice of an anonymous Lizzie Solomon for Bubba to discover.

I'm in the elevator, equipment in my arms, wires dripping past my knees, before I breathe again.

I've descended twenty-eight floors when I remember to turn off the recorder on my phone. It's evidence that he's threatening my life but I'm not sure evidence matters. Or at least it might not matter in time.

35

think of Joie racing down the stairs, closing the circle on her watch. The circle with Bubba Guns. She had a plan. She's an interventionist. I just don't understand the how and why yet.

I stumble through the bathroom window, dropping the phone equipment to the tile. I step over it. I pass my mother's room, the bed like inviting water because my sister smoothed out the wrinkles and plumped the pillows while she told me to sleep with her husband. I'm tugged to it. In my old bedroom, the fitted sheet has come off the corners. The top sheet is tangled, with a ripped hole that I stuck my foot through in the middle of the night.

I glance at my watch. Only 4:46. No sign of Sharp tailing me on the way here. Not a soul on the lawn. It feels more frightening to think of them as unseen soldiers waiting for a command.

I drop onto my mother's bed. Remove the holster. Place the gun within easy reach on the side table.

Just a quick nap.

According to my mother, dead people don't lie down beside you in the daylight.

☽ ✧ ☾

I'm dreaming again.

Above me, a clear, unpolluted universe. The moon, a clipped yellow toenail.

Mars and Venus, tiny diamonds in precise positions.

The number twelve.

The incessant *thump, thump, thump* of hooves in the distance.

The classic Blue Horse dream, the one that tells me I still have time to save Mike. In others, my hand is painted with blood from his trampled chest. In the latest, I saved Mike but not myself. The thump is louder, faster, so close. The future, still up for grabs. I struggle to pull the veil away, to return to the world where I can change it.

I startle myself awake, disoriented. Pitch-dark. *Thump, thump, thump.* My own fist, still at my side, not battering the wall.

A flashlight at the window, dancing on the covers. Someone pounding on the glass.

I cover my head with a pillow like I'm ten again, until the room falls silent. I creep over on my knees and place my palm on the windowpane, chilled from the air conditioner. Did I fall from one dream to another?

The shadows of the room are taking shape, drawn in charcoal pencil by an invisible hand. The bed, the dresser, the chair, the lamp, the knob on the closet door. I reach into a pocket and pinch myself with Lizzie's hair clip.

I stand still at the threshold of the door, listening. Expecting. I hear a creak and know what it is. The bathroom window. I'd left it unlocked.

36

Two of them. Whispering. Stumbling. Unfamiliar with the floor plan. Tripping over half-packed boxes. Another *thunk*. Something heavy rolling across the floor.

Not ghosts. Not a dream. My fingers, tight on the cool metal of my gun, tell me that.

I round the corner to the living room. Enough moonlight has leaked through a blind that I can make out a crystal ball on the floor near the front door. My mother's favorite, the one she'd never let anyone touch.

"Vivvy!" The cry behind me, pitched and shrill.

I jerk around, my gun pointed at two slight forms. Two faces, indiscernible in the dark.

I waver. Lizzie and the charm bracelet girl? Emme in double vision?

One of the shapes steps closer, into that small crack of light.

"Joie?" Her name leaves my mouth like the squeak of brakes.

"Oh, my God, put down that gun. Why didn't you just open the bedroom window? Didn't you hear me? I wondered if you were dead. If some Bubba nut actually got in and hurt you."

I keep the gun steady. "Why didn't you just knock on the front door?"

"I think Bubba Guns is having me followed."

My eyes are traveling over her companion.

Is she a vision? Does Joie know she's there?

"Meet my sister," Joie says.

"Alyssa," the girl says nervously.

I flip on the light.

The girl is staring out of Nickie Solomon's eyes.

☽ ✧ ☾

A blinding, excruciating headache almost drops me to my knees. The images come fast and furious, dark and light, sweet and disturbing. Melting ice cream, a tiny shaved head, a Christmas package, a dog's nose, a bloody bow, a turret with a broken lock.

Joie is talking, but I'm barely listening.

Lizzie is alive. A mythological creature, the lost princess in the forest, is sitting in my ordinary kitchen chair. Calling herself Alyssa. She's pouring Dr Pepper into my Wonder Woman glass, bubbles of CO_2 fizzing and rising like it's a celebration.

Who got the glasses out? When did we sit down at the table?

Why is this girl looking at me like I'm as much of a ghost as she is?

Where did she come from?

"Are you OK?" the girl asks, concerned.

With those words, she removes the knife from my head. Presses her cool voice on my brain to stop the bleeding.

The images stop. It's the here and now.

"Give me a minute," I breathe out. "You're the first girl who has come to me . . . alive."

☽ ✧ ☾

Joie is still babbling, pacing the tiny kitchen. The girl is tapping her nails nervously on her glass, every tap shooting a pain through my skull.

"Are you paying attention?" Joie, in full Joie mode, is looking like she'd like to slap me. "Your mother first called our house ten months ago. I thought she was a scammer. She asked if anyone who lived in the house was about fourteen. She said she'd had a vision about her. I hung up. I mean, who would say anything to a psychic named Asteria who rings up one night at nine?

"She called back the next night. Used my first name. Asked as soon as I said hello if I knew who Lizzie Solomon was. That stopped me. We live in Maine. Texas is the third world. But I remember seeing the case on *48 Hours*. I remember thinking Lizzie Solomon's eyes were just like my sister's. I hung up on her again, but I couldn't let it go."

The girl—Lizzie, Alyssa—sits up sharply, an angry posture. "My sister took my spit out of the sink. She sent it to an ancestry site. Without my permission. Without telling me the results."

"How many times have I told you to wipe your gross globs out of our bathroom sink?" Joie retorts. "And I did it *to protect you*." She swivels back to me. "I'm not *psychic*, but I knew something wasn't right. I mean, one day when I'm twelve, my new sister shows up. My parents had always been secretive about Alyssa's adoption. My mother never took her picture until she was five. When I called your mother back, I had DNA proof."

She stops. What is she waiting for?

"Tell her," the girl demands.

"Nickie Solomon is her mother," Joie says. "And Bubba Guns is her father."

$$\text{☽ ✧ ☾}$$

Bubba Guns?

Not once did I feel it. Can I accept the word of this clever woman in front of me, when I'm sure she's never given me her real name? This girl who still feels like a ghost? Why should I believe either of them?

"Nickie's DNA is in CODIS," Joie is saying, "and Bubba Guns uploaded his to an ancestry site." Alyssa is circling the rim of her glass with a finger. She's left-handed. Was Lizzie left-handed? I know there is a heart-shaped freckle on Lizzie's shoulder. Does Alyssa have a heart-shaped freckle? It was a fact not released to the media to eliminate the Anastasias, the impostor Lizzies, the trolls, the fame seekers.

My head, still a wreck.

I know one of them, Bubba Guns had told me about the Solomons. "You're sure," I say flatly to Joie. "Positive. *No doubt.*"

"Bubba Guns's DNA is a fifty percent total match to Alyssa's DNA, zero percent mitochondrial. That means he's the dad. I did have to hack around to find his real name. Everything was coming up Birtwhistle. It was tedious but not that hard if you know what you're doing. Nickie, also a certain match as her mom. Don't ask me how I got into CODIS." It's the first time I've heard Joie sound defensive. It makes her seem less than sure, no matter what is coming out of her mouth.

I have to ask. "Why would someone like Bubba Guns, with so much to hide, shoot off his spit to a lab?"

"I worked that into a conversation once, over a drink. You know, casual. He said he tried it out to prove his 'ethnicity.'"

This sounds . . . believable. "So you got the job to blackmail him? You think he's the one who took Liz—Alyssa. And then gave her away."

"Why would I blackmail him?" Again, impatient. "I'm not sure he even knows my sister *exists*. I've been waiting for him to break, prodding him along, bringing you on the show, trying to get *you* to break, and there wasn't even a sliver of a sign that either of you had a clue. I would have gotten in his face by now, but I've decided he should never be in my sister's life."

"I get to decide that," Alyssa snaps. She turns to me. "My sister has been keeping this a secret. My *whole family* has been keeping secrets. You pulled me here with your . . . mind, didn't you? So I could know who I am, who took me and why. So I could know my whole story." Her voice, a violin string, has so many complexities. Fragile on the tip line. Screeching when I touched that evidence bag, like a frantic bow drawn over and over.

"Alyssa insisted I bring her here," Joie mutters. "Hopped a plane and showed up at my apartment tonight. Made me tell her everything. Mom is going to kill us."

"You pulled yourself to *me*, Alyssa," I say. "You're very brave."

That's what I tell her, because I think it's true. I don't tell her that my scars are pulsing. That every instinct is warning me that a faceless, ruthless kidnapper is out there watching and not about to go down for a felony after eleven years of freedom.

My job is light-years past finding her in the ether. It's now pinch-your-arm-blood-and-flesh-Earth-bound real. To find out why she was taken.

To keep her alive.

☽ ✧ ☾

I double-check the lock on the front door while their sentences tumble over each other, two sisters at love and war. It's like watching a movie of Brig and me. I'm just not sure if I'm Joie or Alyssa.

I need to focus. I need *them* to focus. "Joie, you talked to my mother a number of times. It's in the diary of phone calls she kept. What else did she say?"

"Nothing. I begged her to tell me what she knew. By the time I called her back with the DNA results, she was shut down. Said she'd been threatened by the kidnapper and didn't want me or Lizzie in danger."

"She didn't give you any hints who the kidnapper was?"

"She said it wasn't Bubba Guns, but who knows? She kept calling the kidnapper Hop Man."

Why does that tickle something?

"I want to go to the Solomon house," Alyssa announces. "Like, *now*. I want to see what I remember."

"Absolutely not," Joie retorts. "It's dangerous. We don't even have a way in."

"You have me," I say.

37

W ait," I spit into the dark.

It's too late. Alyssa has already dropped from the tree. She's jiggling the lock to the back door of the Solomon mansion before Joie and I have touched the ground.

"Alyssa runs hurdles," Joie says. "Even with those short legs. She'll be the fastest freshman on the team." She can't keep the pride out of her voice.

A screen door slams next door. Joie and I freeze in the middle of the yard. The motion sensor light on the neighbor's garage flares on. A trash can lid clanks.

Alyssa continues to jiggle the outside lock like she's trapped in a room filling with water and it's up to her chin.

There's no chance she isn't being heard by whoever is on the other side of the fence. It's not loud enough to rattle the cops on Solomon duty in the patrol car out front. But the neighbor is certain to have a cell phone in her hand, ready to dial. It's not too late for us to turn around; I'm just wondering if Joie or I will say it first.

"Hey, you, over there!" The voice traveling through the slats, not a woman. A teenage boy, maybe. A kid taking out the garbage late because he forgot and now his mom is nagging him at midnight. Alyssa's fight with the door abruptly stops.

"Want me to give you the tour?" he shouts. "I know all the places Lizzie's ghost likes to hang. I charge twenty bucks. It's another ten if you want to climb the spiral staircase in the turret. I can bring my rock climbing harnesses."

Don't respond, don't respond, don't respond.

"No, thank you," Alyssa yells back. "I've got it. My boyfriend and I are just leaving. I forgot my phone here last night."

Silence, while Joie and I remain motionless. The boyfriend, the leaving—a nice touch. "We should go," Joie hisses. "This was a terrible idea."

"The door is locked." Alyssa, flushed and breathing hard, is suddenly on top of us in the yard. Her interaction with the boy next door, already dismissed. The teenage code of honor. My eyes and Joie's are still watching the top of the fence line between the houses for his head.

The garage light flicks out. The boy is being perfectly still, too.

"We'll be fast," I tell Joie with a confidence I don't feel. "There are plenty of places to hide in the house if we have to."

"With the bones?" she mutters. Part of me knows she still clings to a terrible hope that a little girl who never made it to fourteen is waiting behind the plaster—that the DNA results were a mistake or that Alyssa is not Lizzie but a random love child of Nickie and Bubba's put up for adoption. Anything is better than knowing her sister was stolen from someone else, that her own family has lived a lie so huge, it could bury them.

We move forward. On the porch, I quietly lift a large clay pot, flip it over, and place it under the kitchen window. I'd unlocked the window while Sharp was banging away on the dog door. I knew even then that I'd return.

Joie and Alyssa watch silently while I climb on top of the pot and begin to carefully work the edges of the screen with a pocketknife, then the frame of the deteriorating window. My shirt drifts up, exposing my gun. I'm certain their eyes are on it.

I shove open the window. In seconds, we're standing in the gutted kitchen.

"I want to go in the castle part." Alyssa's voice sounds like a small child's.

"I think there's a door to the bottom floor of the turret," I breathe. "This way."

In the butler's pantry, I flash the light on each of the four doors, all tightly closed. "Alyssa, do you know which one?"

The weight of expectation overwhelms the tiny space. She reaches for the handle directly in front of her. The padlock that was attached when I was here with Sharp is lying in the floor, cut off, shavings sprinkled at our feet like silver glitter. My hopeful guess is that a teen-age vandal severed it with his father's saw.

"I'm going first," I insist, but Alyssa is already ahead of me. Then Joie, who immediately trips over a running shoe someone left just past the threshold. Maybe while running. The two of them scatter to opposite sides of the room.

My light travels the slick glass faces of the thick-paned windows that line every side of the turret while I pray that the sweeping live oak out front is limiting the patrol car's view. No latches on any of these windows. Sealed with caulk and paint. It's a miracle they aren't smashed.

The circle of parquet floor is buried under a slew of disrespect—beer cans, candy wrappers, rodent droppings, a pair of men's athletic underwear, a half-deflated orange beach ball, a paperback with scattered pages ripped out.

My light tricks its way up. Way, way up. More windows. A spiral staircase rises with no landings at any of the three floors—just a dizzying ascent of thin metal. It's clear that this was added long after the birth of the house but it's not clear to what purpose. Since the Solomons moved out, teenagers had risked their lives at every level to lean over and graffiti the curved walls with the history of their fleeting love lives.

It was a dangerous playroom for a three-year-old girl determined to climb.

Alyssa has kicked trash out of the way to make a space. She is standing in the center of the room, staring up.

"I don't remember this." She chokes back a sob. "I don't remember this at all."

Joie is instantly clutching her. "This is all my fault," she whispers. "You're my sister. Nothing else matters."

The turret, a hollow façade. No romance, no heartbeat, no answers. The twisted spine of a staircase rising from its center. Even with my knowledge of physics, I'm not sure how that staircase stands. I slide closer to Joie and Alyssa, shivering against a sense of doom. I press my thumb into the sharp edge of Lizzie's hair clip in my pocket. I rub my fingers along the frayed threads of Lizzie's bracelet. I check for my gun.

The sky is shifting. The moon, yellow liquid running across the floor.

"Do you remember a mermaid carved into a staircase by the front door?" I ask.

She shakes her head.

"Maybe someone took you up to the widow's walk where there is an incredible view of the sky? Stars? July Fourth fireworks?"

"Don't do this to her," Joie says.

Alyssa is suddenly reaching for my arm. "What's that bracelet on your wrist?" A thread of hysteria. "Isn't it mine? Didn't Daddy make that for me at a birthday party? Didn't he say the red was . . . for luck? That I was a lucky ducky?"

"Our daddy?" Joie asks, shrill. "Yours and mine?"

"I don't know." Her voice falters. "I can't see a face."

☽ ✧ ☾

I almost ask to see the heart-shaped freckle on Alyssa's shoulder right then. But something holds me back. Maybe Joie's eyes—she isn't ready to know her sister is marked with physical proof. The crescent scar in the crook of my thumb is burning again, reminding me that I'm marked, too.

Outside, I'm careful to put the window screen back, gently hammering it in with the handle of the pocketknife. Joie and Alyssa are impatient, but I hear the chatter of a cop radio out front. I insist on preserving things like we were never here.

I'm the last to drop from the fence to a concrete patch in the alley.

"Who's that?" Alyssa points. A man, about a hundred yards away, stands in half-lit shadow. Moths, nocturnal followers of the moon, are dying in a frenzy in the streetlamp above his head, fooled by artificial light. In their ancient DNA and ours, an attraction to the glitter, to a false compass.

"I told you Bubba Guns was having me followed," Joie says under her breath. She keeps glancing behind us. The man makes no move, even as our walk turns into a run, even as we take the street corner at high speed and three more street corners after that.

I don't tell Joie that I had glimpsed his face.

I don't tell her that professional tails are invisible unless they want you to know.

And Sharp, he wants me to know.

☽ ✧ ☾

Alyssa has scooted up on the back seat of the Jeep, her arm lying faceup on the console. I'm at the wheel, half-turned, tying the faded bracelet on her wrist. She begged me to after I told her how it came into my possession and about the father—possibly hers—who saved it. I told her that Marcus Solomon kept a vigil in his daughter's empty room and refused to sell the mansion in case she ever found her way back.

Joie is face forward in the front passenger seat, not wanting to watch me tie the knot, as if this act acknowledges too much. I tell her to keep her eye on the rearview mirror even though I know we will never shake Sharp.

Joie punches her apartment address into my navigation, unfamiliar with how to get back there from this part of town. I tell her I'll pay for them to stay in a hotel so they can sleep without worrying. My house, maybe not a safer option.

"I rent a small place in a gated complex," she says. "The apartment is what I use all my Bubba money on, at least half my salary. To protect myself from his lunatic haters. His last assistant had to move three times."

Ten minutes later, I pull to a stop in front of one of the most exclusive old buildings in Fort Worth. I'm staring through a tall ornamental fence with copper finials. Venetian arches are nestled among live oaks. A nationally renowned TV chef and a jazz legend make this place their home. An ex-president rents the top floor for guests. A billionaire rancher is rumored to visit his ballerina mistress here.

Joie nods at the man in the guard booth. "Former Green Beret."

I shove the car in park, suddenly certain. "You have to go back," I say to Joie.

"You don't have to tell me twice."

"Not home. To Bubba Guns. To your job. Grovel, apologize, tell Bubba Guns you never told me a thing or tell him you did but that I tricked you. Tell him he is a mentor, a father, a god to you. Whatever it takes. Tell him you want to personally burn me at the stake on Twitter, on his show, IRL. I have a new plan to get at the truth about who kidnapped your sister." So far, ill-formed, but a plan.

"I have a plan, too," she says. "It involves booking two tickets to Portland."

"Joie, I need you to get me on his Sirius radio show."

"Are you kidding? He'll never let you back on, especially live. His random YouTubing is one thing, but he stacks the deck very carefully for that show. It's the jewel in his crown. You're too much of an antagonist. He's built you, now he's shoveling twenty feet of dirt on your grave."

"I don't have to be a guest. I'll call in. Tell Bubba you'll personally vet the callers ahead of time and load the show with fans," I persist. "That it will be his highest-rated show ever because of new information an anonymous source says she's willing to announce on the air about the Lizzie Solomon case."

"What new information? I don't see the point of this. How could you possibly accomplish what your mother couldn't, what *I* couldn't in six months of producing his shows and hacking around?"

"The point is that an innocent woman shouldn't be in prison for a crime she didn't do. The point is that the kidnapper should be held accountable. The point is that your sister should know exactly who she is. We're all marked, Joie."

Alyssa leans forward from the back seat. "Please listen to her. Our family will implode if I go home and pretend that none of this matters. You can't change who I am." She slides her hand onto Joie's shoulder. "Don't be freaked out, but I remembered that tent in Vivvy's backyard before I ever saw it. I think I've . . . been here."

It sounds ridiculous, it does. Yet I know Emme's picture by heart. The scratchy black sky, the pocked moon, the girl standing there, out of sequence with the rest.

I watch Joie's face work. What she believes—the stench of truth in her mother's silence, in the scrapbooks that don't show Alyssa's face, in DNA science that didn't lie about O. J. Simpson and isn't lying about Alyssa now. And what Joie *doesn't* believe—that I have a mystical connection to her sister.

"You don't know what you're asking," Joie says finally. "His abuse. What I've put up with. He makes me feel . . . filthy." In her hand, she rattles the key chain decorated with the rainbow flag. "I'm gay, for Christ's sake. I'm sure he'd have fired me on the spot if he knew that."

"I'm betting he doesn't care. You of all people should know he's a showman. Not someone who really believes anything."

She shoves open the passenger side door. Pauses.

"OK," she says.

"What?"

She whips her head around. "I said OK, all right? You can't reveal my sister's name on the air, or that she's Bubba and Nickie Solomon's kid. She stays out of it."

I nod, relieved. "Of course," I say. Joie—scholar, sister, chameleon—back to close the circle.

"Before you go, I have a question," I say hesitantly. "You said my mother called the kidnapper Hop Man."

"Right. I hacked all over for that reference. It never made sense."

"Could it have been Hauptmann?" I spell it out. "The tumor made her hard to understand sometimes."

Joie looks uncertain. "It might have been that. Why?"

I wave her off. "It doesn't matter."

Joie levels me with that bulldog stare of hers. Our agreement is too fragile for me to hold back.

"Hauptmann is a name listed in my mother's diary of calls," I explain. "A pseudonym. She made up nicknames for clients to protect their secrets and identities. It would make sense for my mother to use that specific nickname to reference a kidnapper. A man named Bruno *Hauptmann* was convicted of kidnapping and killing Charles Lindbergh's baby. It was the crime of the last century, an American hero brought to his knees, long before he was reviled as a fan of Hitler. She was always fascinated by the details of the Lindbergh case. The excessive number of ransom notes. The construction of the ladder reaching up to the window of the baby's room. The possibility that it wasn't Lindbergh's infant who was found dead in the woods four miles from his house, but another infant's body exchanged for his. She entertained the idea that the Lindbergh baby was still alive even though Bruno Hauptmann was electrocuted for it. It was one of the fairy tales she told me at night."

Now I'm the one who is babbling. I can tell by Joie's face that she's confused, still pushing for an explanation that I don't want to deliver.

"I don't think there is anything psychic about my mom calling you, Joie," I say reluctantly. "I don't think she had a dream or a vision. I think one of her clients confessed his secret to her and she didn't want to die keeping it."

38
---

park boldly in the driveway and wrestle with my sticky front door
for the first time in days. The police have apparently abandoned
their protective surveillance of me after twenty-four hours without incident. The neighborhood, asleep. The shadows in the yard,
paralyzed.

Back in my bed, my mind and body are neither of those things.
I don't trust Lizzie with anyone but myself. I feel with every part of
me, psychic and not, that if the police are involved, the kidnapper
will slip away. Things will go badly. That I am the interventionist, on
a fragile path of glass. What did my mother say? A psychic doesn't
always need to see the way, just know where to put her foot.

My phone vibrates. I glance down at the caller ID. It's as if Sharp
has a bug in my brain.

"What?" I answer rudely.

"Seriously? You're asking what? Who in the hell were those
young women with you at the Solomon house? I almost arrested
all of you."

"But you didn't, did you?" I shoot back. "This investigation was
going nowhere before I entered the picture. Your detective instincts
are telling you to let this play out a little longer."

I hold my breath in the silence.

"Stuntwomen die horrible deaths, Vivvy." His voice, like God himself.

"Goodbye, Sharp."

$$ ☽ ✧ ☾ $$

I forget about sleep.

I thumb through Bubba Guns's Twitter. The feed is wild and all over the place without Joie conducting. Eyebrow memes, Lizzie memes, alien memes, me memes. My tweet about Bubba's USC affiliation is already losing traction, just like Bubba said it would. He's still trolling me, but it's mostly about Lizzie's case. I know he has a move up his sleeve; I'm just hoping I'll be able to make mine first.

I wonder if Joie's on the phone with Bubba right now, begging for her job back, or if she'll wait until the morning. If she'll change her mind.

If I can trust her.

I lean back into my practical side. What proof did she give me? I only have her word that Alyssa shares DNA with Bubba Guns and Nickie, that the conversations with my mother were congenial. What if Joie and Alyssa are working together? With Bubba Guns? I didn't even push for Joie's real name.

But the friendship bracelet. Alyssa recognized it. I stare at the ceiling and redraw the balloon diagram I'd made of the Solomon case at the kitchen table, this time in my head.

Balloon one. Lizzie, now Alyssa from Maine. Balloon two. Nickie, her imprisoned mother. Then Bubba Guns, her biological father. Marcus, the long-suffering husband. Looper, the lover, possibly dead, possibly alive.

My mother, the interventionist, definitely dead, still playing her hand.

I stick Joie off to the side as a lone moon.

I squiggle the name *Hauptmann*, floating free, a string of dark energy. Is he an alias for someone already in my balloons? Or is he someone else my mother knew, someone anonymous? Someone in the case files everyone overlooked? I draw strands from one bubble to another until it becomes a web of crazed orbits.

I'm aching with frustration. When I can't make a scientific equation work, the problem is always a wrong assumption I've made, often at the very beginning. One that I was almost one hundred percent certain was correct but wasn't.

I roll out of bed and spend the next hour fluffing the pages of my mother's books, ransacking her drawers, fingering through her file cabinet again, wondering if I'd already tossed the one clue that would tell me who Hauptmann is.

I hit play on the answering machine, but the calls have slowed to a trickle of telemarketers worried about my dead mother's car warranty on a Buick she sold three years ago and a Mac virus on her Microsoft computer. I'd left a new message on the machine yesterday explaining my mother's death, and it seems to be working. Her clients are moving on.

It hits me at 3:43 a.m. while I'm fingering my way across the stars of Andromeda.

One of my assumptions, possibly shaky.

I get up.

I'm wondering again how late is too late. At what point too late becomes too early.

I'm shifting the Jeep in reverse when Emme's face appears in her kitchen window, the one that's always lit.

Back from her dad's early. Her mother's car, in the driveway.

Emme had found the purest part of my mother's heart. I'm glad someone did. Brig and I lived in her craters and shadows.

Her hand is a tiny, waving bird as I back into the dark street, my mother's gun on the passenger seat.

☽ ✧ ☾

Brando Wilbert lives in the *least* exclusive—and most dangerous— apartment complex in Fort Worth—a plain-Jane, four-story box of dirty white brick, sandwiched on either side by a hulking, jagged junkyard. In the daytime, it's a tragic American commentary on discarding people and things.

At night, it's an apocalyptic movie set that reminds me of George Lucas's vision of the universe—an outer space that is clanking, dirty, broken. Lucas had the insight to add entropy to his films, the scientific measure of disorder.

I'm surrendering to entropy now, climbing an unlit set of concrete steps strewn with marijuana joints and decorated in pee. The bullet casings in the corners are as ignored as the Shiner beer caps. The silence so eerie, I hear my breath.

I imagine protective mothers and fathers, faces melting into the inky space behind their windows, fingers playing with triggers. I pull my own gun out of my purse with no real expectation it would save me here and set off along the narrow balcony.

Crinkled aluminum foil is the window treatment of choice for every unit I pass except for an optimist with a Santa suncatcher. A perfect bullet hole hollows out the center of his cherry nose. Physics says it was a high-velocity weapon, or Santa would have shattered into a hundred-plus pieces.

I keep my gun pointed at the ground and slip into deeper shadows so dark that I'm counting my steps between doors. I stop at one unit to trace my fingers over the numbers. Three doors down, I knock.

Brando doesn't look that surprised to see me or my gun when he opens the door to number 212.

He reaches over and takes the pistol out of my hand like it's a plate of cookies, removes the magazine and the chambered round, sticks them in his pocket, returns the gun.

He shrugs. "Habit."

His eyes are stuck on the hospital bracelet on my wrist.

"Is my sister dying?" he asks.

☽ ✧ ☾

I don't answer. I let him shut the door behind me, already knowing this would not be a close or fair fight if things turn physical. Already certain he's had a hand in playing me.

I tell myself that he can take all my bullets he wants. I have extra ammunition. A little girl in a hospital bed.

I tuck the gun back in my purse while Brando watches with a practiced casualness that Southern boys start mimicking when they're five.

He's shirtless, jeans unsnapped at the top, feet bare. The tiny studio reeks sharply of a clogged sink disposal and beer, with a window air conditioner loudly blowing the stink around.

A double mattress swallows up a quarter of the space. Brando has reserved two corners for clothes, clean and dirty. Four handguns lie on a card table with a gun-cleaning kit, salt and pepper shakers, a stack of hole-punched playing cards from a Vegas gift shop, an open bag of tortilla chips, and a jar of Mrs. Renfro's Ghost Pepper Salsa. The tall kitchen garbage can is so full the lid won't compress. I'm torn about whether to be glad or not that the bathroom door is shut.

I say no to an offer of beer while he pops the top on a warm Shiner he pulled from one of four cases stacked next to the refrigerator. He swallows half of the can in one chug, maybe to impress me. He casually slides the edge of one hip onto the card table, swinging a bare foot. His toenails are like a tiny set of knives.

"I've got my eye on another place," he says. "This is temporary. And my sister?"

"As far as I know, there is no change. I'm here for another reason. To make a deal. I know you wrote down what you censored in that letter between my mother and Nickie. I know you write down everything you censor. You're that kind of guy. Much brighter than your teachers gave you credit for being."

He shoots me a grin. "You got that right. I was smart but couldn't ever prove it." He swigs down the rest of the beer, tapping the end for the last drop. "As far as a deal, you've got only one thing to offer."

"I can't save your sister's life. I won't promise that."

"You can visit her," he wheedles. "Touch her forehead with some fancy oil. Tell my mother there's a life after this. You believe that, right? And you can keep wearing that bracelet in case anything comes across from the beyond?"

"I do believe that. And I won't take off the bracelet."

"Can you see Shelby's face? In your visions?"

I hesitate before answering. There's a line I won't cross. I won't lie about Shelby. Brando's vulnerability is flooding this wretched room. It's more unsettling than before. Does Shelby take up ten percent of him? Fifty? Ninety? Is Shelby the only thing left that prevents hell from fully adopting him?

I can see Shelby's face. It popped up in my random search for her name—a picture used for a fundraiser for her hospital bills last month. It wasn't too late to donate, so I did. A lot.

"She looks like you," I say. "Only much, much more innocent."

"That's right," he says, face eager. "It's why I shaved my head. Not to intimidate felons like everybody thinks. So me and Shelby could look even more like twins. She loves me for real, you know. It's hard to do."

He walks over to the fridge and pops it open. It holds a stack of money, a shelf of gold chains, two more guns. He slides a plastic bag from under the cash and tugs out a notebook, which he brings to the card table. He flips through the pages before he begins scribbling, copying something onto the back of a junk mail envelope.

At the door, he hands me the envelope, folded in half, and my bullets.

I hand him three hundred-dollar bills even though he doesn't ask for it.

I was prepared to give him much more.

☽ ✧ ☾

I don't unfold the envelope until I'm four miles away. I've pulled over into a gas station with row after row of fluorescent lights shining on empty pumps. At five a.m., the sky is lighter but not nearly light enough to stop my heart from pounding.

I'm about to know the name of the person who kidnapped Lizzie Solomon. My mother, still speaking to me.

I smooth out the paper. Read it twice.

Brando has printed his sister Shelby's name, their mother's name, a room number at the hospital, a password to give the nurse, and a time. Eleven a.m. day after tomorrow.

Underneath that, Brando scribbled, "You didn't think I'd make this easy, did you?"

39

You're set."

"What?"

The phone had jolted me awake again. This time, it's Joie on the other end. I'm sprawled out in my mother's bed where I fell, exhausted, after the Brando excursion. I glance at my watch. Five hours ago.

"You're set for his weekly radio show," Joie is saying impatiently. "Bubba Guns wants to give Lizzie one last ride and you one last kick in your astronomical ass. That's a direct quote."

"What exactly did you tell him?"

"Just what you said. I told him an anonymous caller is going to reveal Lizzie's kidnapper on the air. I told him, the less he knew, the better."

"He bought that?"

"He did after I played him a little recording of a man making that claim on the tip line. I paid Arthur, a homeless man who hangs outside my coffee shop, to do it for me. Bubba Guns said he should have appreciated me more. Missed me. We're kind of in a domestic abuse–like situation."

"I should never have asked you to do this. What if he is having you followed? What if someone overheard you making the recording?"

What if he has figured out who you are? What if he thinks he has nothing to lose, which is what he always seems to think?

"Look, Joie," I stress. "I don't have the name of the kidnapper. My goal is to prod the kidnapper to make a mistake and reveal himself. You need to leave that office as soon as I start speaking."

"The show is at four p.m. My promo tweet already has 10,012 likes. 10,013. 10,014. It's rolling up as I speak. Dial in at three fifty. You'll be caller number one."

A disturbing thought keeps poking at me, one that Joie and Alyssa and I have been unwilling to voice. What if their parents orchestrated this kidnapping? What if Lizzie's circle ends right back at her own house?

This time, Joie hangs up on me.

☽ ✧ ☾

I can't push a call through to Nickie at the prison until two hours later. My fury and frustration with her are boiling by then.

Joie has tweeted thirty-two times, promising that *The Bubba Guns Show* is going to reveal the identity of Lizzie Solomon's kidnapper today. The retweets tallied at 60,482 the last time I looked. CNN and Fox have picked up on it. I feel like Twitter's suicidal ship captain steering into an iceberg.

I don't say hello when Nickie picks up the prison line because time is wasting, and Nickie has been wasting my time.

"Why didn't you tell me that your husband, Marcus, is not Lizzie's real father?" I demand.

"What the hell are you talking about?"

"Stop lying to me. *Just. Stop. It.*"

"You need to show me some respect. I spent my whole career trying to prove that prisoners are people, too."

I swallow a deep breath. I doubt that.

"OK. I respectfully ask, why the hell didn't you tell me that you screwed Bubba Guns and nine months later Lizzie popped out?"

"I made a big mistake ever involving myself with you. You're just like everyone else, thinking up more reasons why I should die in this pound."

It's hard to believe, but she seems genuinely offended.

"So as far as you know, Lizzie is Marcus's daughter? Your husband's." My tone, not much softer.

"Are you not getting the message?"

"You were never raped by Bubba Guns, he was never a sperm donor for an embryo, you never slept with him."

Silence.

"I didn't say all that."

"Which part didn't you say?"

"Look, we slept together once for old times' sake. Bob—I knew him as Bob—and I had done the occasional hookup in college and then we both ended up here, two outsiders. We were fated to run into each other, it seems. I was at the courthouse trying a case. He was there to testify in a nuisance suit. Some catfish restaurant chain was suing him because he turned things up a notch and indicated that if people ate gay catfish, they could turn gay, too. We had lunch, and the afternoon went on from there. I specifically remember that he wore a condom. He made a big deal about how he had to wear a Magnum size and how I could never tell anyone he went to USC." I hear the realization, the possibility, creeping in. Because it's a lot of very specific remembering.

"I called him a few months ago." It stumbles out of her mouth. "I asked him for old times' sake to take up my case and prove me innocent."

I'm not sure why I'm surprised. "How did that go?"

"Not good. He said he might get to it if he ever thought I was innocent. So I said I might get around to telling everyone he was a fraud when I could get to it. He said things . . . I don't want to repeat them. Let's just say he was gonna make me the number one baby killer in here to screw if I opened my mouth."

"And when he started up with Lizzie on his show?"

"I knew it wasn't on my behalf."

"What if I told you there is DNA proof that Bubba Guns is your daughter's father?" It occurs to me, one more time, that *I* haven't seen the proof.

Silence. A reckoning with herself, maybe. Or preparation for another lie.

"This is going to kill Marcus." Her wail slices the line. "He's been there for me. He refused to testify for the prosecution. He forgave me for bringing Looper into our lives. He visits me every Tuesday. Puts money in my commissary account so I can bribe every nasty bitch in here. He even taught me how to meditate. He *believes* I'm innocent. Like, truly believes it. And he loves . . . loved . . . Lizzie." Her voice is breaking over a man she cheated on multiple times. The type of man women should never cheat on, but the exact kind they do.

"So as far as you're concerned, Marcus doesn't know? Bubba Guns *doesn't know?*"

"How could they?" she sobs. "I didn't know until you told me. You've found her, haven't you? That's how you know about the DNA. You've found Lizzie's bones."

40

'm sitting upright at the kitchen table, headphones on, ready. I've shaken the paralyzing dread of the turret, washed away the stink of Brando, cut off Nickie Solomon's questions about her daughter to protect both of them.

I smell like Ivory soap and my mother's strawberry shampoo. For morbid luck, my hair is pulled in a high ponytail with Lizzie's hair clip. I've put on pale pink lip gloss and crescent moon earrings. The snug black dress I wore both leaning over my mother's casket and accepting the Annie Jump Cannon Award in Astronomy is creeping up my bare thighs.

All this effort to look nice, even though it's just going to be me at the kitchen table, alone, no video, with a reckless little plan.

Oddly, I had found myself with extra time. I polished my nails with a pale violet called Pigment of My Imagination that I found in the bathroom. I rifled through Mom's jewelry box, stuck on seven of her rings, and watched them flash and click across the keyboard like silver roaches.

Now I'm sitting in Bubba Guns's virtual waiting room, very little time to go.

My eyes are on my watch. My head and stomach, swimmy with fishes.

Four, three, two, *one*.

His voice, infecting my house again.

"Welcome back, Gunzers and Americans, to *The Bubba Guns Show* on Sirius. We are coming to you from the great state of Texas, busting some news in the tragic tale of Lizzie . . ."

He's suddenly cut off. "Is this caller number one?" Joie asks crisply in my ear.

"Yes," I stumble out.

"I'm having some technical difficulties. You can't listen in to the intro. Just wait for your cue in three minutes." She's immediately gone, abandoning me to a black void.

Humans weren't meant to sit in utter silence. I hear my breath, my heartbeat, the high-pitched hiss of my auditory nerve firing, the earworm of a Tom Petty song about prayers in Southern accents.

Three minutes turn to five. Six.

"Caller number one," Joie intones, no warning. "You're on."

"Miz Vega, welcome to the show," Bubba Guns booms. "An interesting name, Vega. Are you Mexican?"

Why does he think I'm somebody named Vega? Is this a mistake? More technical screwups?

"Senorita?" Bubba, polite and vaguely racist. "You there?"

I jerk to attention realizing I *am* Vega. Joie's made up an alias for me, the name of one of the most luminous stars in the sky. Such a precocious girl.

"No," I say hoarsely. "Not Hispanic."

"Are you a true-blue Texan?"

I think about this for a second. "I am." I've begun mimicking his drawl.

"Let me ask you this. It's a little off course for the day's business about Lizzie Solomon, but we have time, and I'd like to get it out there while we've got people across America hanging on our every word. How do you feel when Hollywood types compare Texas women to Afghanistan women?"

I missed the intro. I have no context. But I'm learning with Bubba Guns, there isn't any. And I know the answer to this one.

"Angry," I say, truthfully. "Women in Texas aren't wearing burkas, trampled on by men who are terrorist dictators. We are strong, and we are tough. Tough enough that we don't think our friends have to agree with us about everything. When our rights are trampled on, it's by men we allowed to take office, the C-average nerds who picked their noses at the back of our high school classes, who barely passed science, who became half-time Texas legislators because no one wants the job. Texas is an outsized stereotype because the extremes are better at vocalizing and organizing. Because people like you, and actresses picking up their Golden Globes, spouting politics, make the headlines. Not the fact that 145 languages are spoken in Houston or that Texas runs by far the most wind farms of any state or that we are at the forefront of peering into the cosmos."

What is wrong with me? Why didn't I just say Texas is a nice place to live despite some abhorrent policies? I lost the drawl somewhere around *picking their nose*. My voice, my own. I'm certain Bubba Guns recognizes it.

A few seconds of silence while he decides what to do with me.

"Sounds like it could be an acceptance speech for Best Actress to me. Folks, we have a gate-crasher here. Our first caller today is a V but not a Vega. It's Dr. Vivian Bouchet, the famous psychic–alien chaser feeling around the walls for the cold spot that holds Lizzie's bones. I'm just gonna put two hundred down right now and say that you are the anonymous source my producer assured me is going to reveal the name of Lizzie Solomon's kidnapper on the air today. To be real honest, I had a hunch it would be you calling in." His eagerness, now overriding any anger at being fooled.

"I'm not anonymous now," I point out. "And when were you ever *real* honest?"

"Oh, let's not squabble in front of the kids. Tell us what you got. Fox News and *The Washington Post* and the *Daily Mail* are all waiting. I'm guessing the kidnapper is out there waiting, too." No trademark schizophrenic turn this time. He's focused, sensing his moment as an icon seeking truth and justice for a little girl.

Now would be the time for me to change my mind about taunting a kidnapper with a massive and devoted audience listening in—to turn the Twitter ship into its vast, endless sea. To go back to the desert, where I feel safe. My mother always said that safe is just an illusion. That evil trips us with a slippery, invisible puddle when it isn't even raining.

"I found the kidnapper's name in my late mother's diary of clients," I announce. "Detailed notes on their conversations. She was his psychic. He used her like a therapist. He laid it all out, begging forgiveness. I hope he turns himself in to the police so he can find it."

Of course, there are no notes. No names but Hauptmann, which is maybe an allusion to Lizzie's kidnapping or maybe to some nice old Jewish man sitting in a chair, missing his dead wife, who died of natural causes.

"And Lizzie?" Bubba interjects. "Bones or breathing?"

I hesitate.

"I can't say. But I'd like to say to your million listeners that you are an abomination." I'd also like to say, *You are her father, you son of a bitch*.

"We're up to two million listeners these days, honey. The name of the kidnapper, though—you'll say that, right? You don't want to reveal yourself as the ultimate scammer."

"I think that's you. The ultimate scammer. And I have a little recording of our last conversation as proof. I think your fans would love to hear it."

I toss my headphones across the room. Let Bubba Guns dangle from his own rope for the next thirty minutes of his show.

Of course, I had trussed up a couple of other ropes, too.

One for a kidnapper.

One for me.

☽ ✧ ☾

My phone, exploding on the kitchen table. Mike, Brig, Sharp, my boss, colleagues, reporters, haters. I speed through texts and tweets. Joie telling me she and Alyssa are *outta here*. Mike berating me for nailing a target to my back. Brig questioning my sanity and how much I love her, telling me to *go, go, go*.

All I know is that the force compelling me to ferret out the truth about who stole Lizzie Solomon is the same one that always orders me to wait outside Mike's house at ridiculous hours, staring at a wafer moon, hoofbeats in my ear.

I step onto my mother's front porch, immediately shifting my body behind a large column to hide myself from the street. They're already gathering. Right after I hung up, Bubba Guns announced a camo-and-candle vigil for Lizzie Solomon "at Vivvy's house," seven p.m.

A group of Bubba acolytes are setting up camp for a front-row seat, in head-to-toe digital camouflage. I wonder if a single one of them understands the scientific concept of disruptive coloration, that what they are wearing is an idea stolen from nature's brilliance. The zebras with their stripes, so bold and memorable, that are dizzying when they run in packs, confusing their predators. The tigers' bright orange and white stripes that make them disappear to color-blind prey.

That's what I've turned myself into. Prey. An *elitist* prey who judges whether her predators understand anything about the hard-and-fast rules of science.

Traffic is already jamming a street that usually sees about seven cars an hour. SUVs and pickups are maneuvering into what tight street parking is left. Houses across the street have already shut their blinds and tucked their cars into crowded garages.

I feel exposed. I imagine the bead of someone else's scope counting my freckles and scars.

I slowly nudge myself back toward the door. I'm almost inside when my eye catches a large white envelope on the swing. No name on the front. Another threat? Something else? Something important? Is it worth dodging into view to retrieve?

I make a split-second decision.

A primal call goes out from the crowd when they see a glimpse of me, the star girl they're hunting.

☽ ✧ ☾

I slam the door behind me and wait for my hands to stop shaking so I can slit the flap. Not what I was expecting. A printout of a bush with a clump of round black berries. I shake the envelope and a note falls out.

> Dear Miss Vivvy,
>
> You didn't ask, but this is my guess for your leaves. I think they came from a chokeberry bush. Aunt Miriam says chokeberries make good jam. Although I wouldn't want to eat jam that chokes me. Hah! I hope this helps!
>
> I love my charm! I will never take it off until I die!
>
> Emme
> P. S. This bush is native to Minnesota.

I add the internet's rendering of a chokeberry bush to the refrigerator with my own alongside Emme's rendering of a ghost and Will's rendering of a black blob of a hero with pointy ears.

My mom told Emme she was an interventionist, and maybe she is.

I pull over my laptop and search for *missing girl Minnesota*, even though I'm sure the chokeberry bush grows many places. Nothing, at least not in a hurried search of the first three pages. I try *missing girl Minnesota charms* and find a story about a four-year-old who ate a decorative charm on an athletic shoe and died of lead poisoning.

I recall the picture of the charm bracelet in my mind. I breathe in deeply, summoning the richest earth, the blackest night.

No smell. The picture is static, inflexible, locked.

That's when Brando texts, while I'm fighting physics and reality to see just outside the frame.

Almost simultaneously, a fist pounds the front door.

☽ ✧ ☾

"Vivvy. Make this easy. Let me in." Low. Insistent.

Jesse Sharp, like Bubba Guns, even fiercer when holding the anger in his gut, not yelling. I feel certain that in a few short minutes he will kick the door in if I don't open it.

My eyes are glued to Brando's text. I read it again, trying to translate the misspellings.

"Vivvy." Sharp, louder. Another pound.

I unlock the door, and he's inside, almost on top of me. His eyes immediately fall to the star charm that dips into the deep V of my black dress.

"Where's Mike?" I ask in a snide tone. "And eyes up."

"Mike's off your case." His eyes are now rudely plowing their way through mine.

"I'm a case? Lizzie is *the case*."

"Do you really have a damn diary with her kidnapper's name in it?"

"No."

He shakes his head.

"Funny how you become the case if you start to interfere with an investigation and are a repeat offender at breaking and entering a crime scene. My boss has been talked into one more night of protection. You hear those snickering rats on your lawn? They're keeping you safer from Lizzie Solomon's kidnapper than the three cruisers assigned to you tonight. But at some point, those rats will find new food. They always do. You'll be on your own. Do you get this, Vivvy? Tonight, we need to finish . . . some things. You need to tell me everything you know. Everything." There it is. *On your own.*

"I absolutely do understand," I say. "Thank you for showing up for me. Would you like a Dr Pepper?"

My congeniality seems to knock him off balance. That, and the thin nylon of my dress, hugging me like a glaze of hot icing, as I turn toward the kitchen.

"You look nice," he says tightly. "Were you . . . going somewhere?"

"Just felt the need of a little female power. Would you like whiskey with your Dr Pepper?"

"Dr Pepper is fine. I'll get it."

He follows me, stopping short at the refrigerator. A little prod, courtesy of Emme, interventionist. He rips off the drawing of the chokeberry bush.

"Why do you have this on your refrigerator? Why did you draw it? *Why are you researching it?*"

"Why do you care?" I shoot back. "Why are you so afraid of what I might know? What I might see?"

I want him to say something, anything, to make me trust him—to assure me he is a dark crusader but one I can accept. Something that will convince me to trust him so completely that I will tell him right now that *Lizzie is alive.* I'll ask for his help. *I will help him.*

He abruptly turns, opens the refrigerator, and pops the top on a can. When our eyes meet again, his are black stone.

"I need a quick shower," I say casually. "I'd like to wash off Bubba Guns. But make yourself at home. Maybe you can figure out if there's a pizza delivery guy willing to brave the mob? And then, I agree. It's time for us to finish some things."

In the bathroom, I switch on the shower.

I slip into my all-black—yoga pants, T-shirt, running shoes. I drop my duffel out the window and sling my backpack over my shoulder.

I'm an astrophysicist who has choreographed human bailouts from a rocket ship. It's a mistake to not think I will have an exit plan.

The Jeep is waiting in the alley where I parked it after Bubba Guns's postshow rallying cry.

I'm hoping my clogged tub will be at least halfway full by the time Sharp finds that I'm gone.

41

B rando's text was equal parts urgent and illiterate.

Lissened to show. I know you lyed.
In danger. Redy to tell. No Sharp.
1 our. My place.

Not clear if it's me or him in danger. A ridiculously short deadline to get there in rush-hour traffic. The order of *no Sharp*, no cops, like we are actors on a bad TV crime show.

But all I care about right now is *redy to tell*.

That's why I tailed three semis and am now slipping into a parking place between two white vans beaten up by a life of questionable pickups and deliveries. By my watch, I'm ten minutes late when I knock on the door of number 212.

No one answers. I wonder if Brando is lying on the other side in a pool of blood, shooting the finger at fate by having met death before his sweet sister Shelby. I bang one last time, and the door jerks wide.

Brando's eyes are bloodshot from alcohol or tears, maybe both. He pulls me in by the elbow and throws the dead bolt.

Flashes. Shelby swallowed in a hospital bed, hooked up to an IV. Jesse Sharp, face frantic, my tub running over the edge like a waterfall. My mother, shaking her head over a crystal ball. Nothing good. I yank my phone out of my backpack, fumbling with the screen.

"Really? You're gonna let someone follow you here?" Brando grabs the phone, powers it down, and tosses it in the sink. The bathroom door bangs open.

I fight to keep my expression blank. I remind myself again that I was born with a weapon more powerful than all the guns in the room.

$$\text{☽ ✧ ☾}$$

Brando's companion who bursts from the toilet is a man, medium height, with the slope of a middle-aged potbelly. He's dressed from the neck down in a striped collared shirt, khakis, expensive but worn loafers. A professional.

Lizzie's kidnapper. I know it with every scrap of intuition.

From the neck up, he's wearing an orange ski mask, one of the eye holes askew. Brando has pulled all the cheap blinds so it's hard to see much detail. A small lamp casts a weak triangle of light in one corner. Just below the pump of my adrenaline is a vague gratefulness that this man doesn't want me to see his face. That maybe his goal is not violent.

He whips one of the guns off Brando's card table, scattering the playing cards onto the floor. He points it at the center of my chest. My heart immediately begins to rocket.

What is the purpose of panic? A therapist once asked a twelve-year-old me that question like he was chatting with Sartre.

"What the hell, man?" Brando yells. "I said you couldn't use my guns."

"Sorry for your loss," he says to me. "I need your mother's diary."

If that therapist were here now, I'd ask if he'd ever had a gun pointed at him. If he'd ever listened to a ghost girl cry for her mother all night like she was next to you at a slumber party, and then see her tossed by a faceless stranger into a hole that was ten years and a thousand miles away. I'd say panic is chaos, and fear is adrenaline, and neither will save you. I'd say, *Get the fuck out of my head.*

"There is no diary," I say. "I made it up."

"Brando? Can you help her remember where she put the diary?" His voice, muffled under the mask.

"I told you, I'm not your guy for that," Brando says. "I told you, she was just bluffing on the show. I brought her here so you could see for yourself that she's a nice lady like her mom. Can we let her go now? Can I have my money? It's going to pay for three chemo rounds."

The last part, said especially for me. An excuse I'd buy. Cheer, even.

The man is fighting the mask to breathe in the swelter of the room, tugging at the mouth hole. If he yanks off the whole thing, it's going to be a completely different game.

I have to hurry. "Why did you kidnap Lizzie?" I ask. "Is she still alive?" I need to know if he's going to lie.

"Don't provoke him, all right?" Brando, uneasy. "Maybe give him a free reading? Look, man, she can tell your future. I'll bet she's even better than her mom."

"I'll give you a reading," I say cooperatively. "You need to put down the gun so I can hold your hand, though."

"Right," he snarls.

"That's the way it works," Brando coaxes him. "She touches something. Then she tells you something." *Not always true.*

"How about this?" the man growls. "I hold the gun, and we *still* hold hands. Send her over, Brando."

Brando hesitates before poking me forward. The man catches my arm, twisting me around, pressing my back against his chest, the gun at my neck. His breath is warm and rotten with coffee.

I'm facing Brando now. He wears an expression of regret.

"Give me your best shot, Vivvy Bouchet," the man orders. "Before I give you mine."

"I can't . . . channel . . . with a gun at my throat." Also, not true. The images are flashing by so fast it's hard to sort them. Not one of them is a glimpse behind this man's mask.

"Try," the man urges.

"You drank four cups of coffee today," I rush out. "You are afraid to fly. You hated your mother."

The man slams me into a chair. Gun now pointed at my head.

"Tell him something—you know, *positive*—about himself," Brando begs.

"You kidnapped Lizzie and put her in a gray car," I spit at him. "You rented it at a place that starts with *A*."

"Avis, Alamo, what are the odds? I hate my mother. What are the odds? I don't want to die in a nosedive? *What are the fucking odds?*"

"You told Lizzie when you put her in the back seat that you were taking her for a hot fudge sundae."

Silence.

"Extra hot fudge," I breathe out. "Cake batter ice cream. Sprinkles. No cherry."

"How can you expect me to remember that?"

"I think you remember every second of that day."

"Asteria must have written down every fucking word I told her in that diary."

"There is no diary."

"I didn't *kidnap* Lizzie. I just rearranged her life. I had a right to."

And there it is.

"Give. Me. The. Diary." A rising panic in his voice.

Brando hears it, too. Time hissing and escaping.

I figure out Brando's move to save us before he even makes it. So does the man. His gun jerks to Brando.

Shelby's face flashes in my head, a fragile pearl nestled against a hospital pillow.

I don't think. I throw myself in the way.

☽ ✧ ☾

A bullet slices by like a hot knife. My head snaps back against a wall. Brando is at the card table, fumbling for a gun. A second shot. A third. The man in the mask crumples, his gun skittering like a turtle on its back.

I'm eye to eye with Lizzie's kidnapper, our cheeks planted on filthy linoleum. One of his eyelids is twitching like it can't make up its mind about whether to concede and die. Blood is staining the space between us. An ugly dark spot is spreading on his orange nylon mask. My blood? Or his?

Brando is turning me over, half sobbing. Behind us, the apartment door slams open. Sharp's voice. He's shoving Brando away, gripping him by the neck.

"Hey, man," Brando says. "The guy on the floor is who you want, not me."

"I don't give a shit. Hand me the gun. Drop and plant your face."

Sharp's on his knees beside me, barking into his radio, begging me to stay awake. He's pulling my hair back, pink sweat dripping from my head to his shirt.

"Did you turn off the tub?" I babble.

"Don't talk," he orders. Another shadow blocks the light from the open door. Mike's panicked face is suddenly inches from mine. "Vivvy. *Vivvy.*" My name in his mouth, like cut glass. I want to assure both of them I'm fine. My lips won't move.

"I've got her," Sharp growls at Mike. "You deal with them." The masked man is disturbingly still. Brando is sucking in huge, gulping sobs.

Mike flips the man over and cuffs him. Rips off his mask. The face underneath, a blur. Mike reaches into the man's back pocket for his wallet, tugging out a driver's license.

All the while, I'm aware that Sharp is cradling me. I just can't feel his arms.

"Son of a bitch," Mike utters.

"You know him?" Sharp.

"Oh, I know him. You do, too."

"Where's the damn ambulance?" Sharp asks. "Never mind."

Sharp lifts me up. It's the last thing I remember.

42

The charm bracelet girl is decorating my Cheerios with little black berries, assuring me they will help me sleep. I'm falling through a green computer matrix, stepping through tweets in the Twitter jungle, crawling around in the walls of the Solomon mansion, picking up phones that don't work and guns that don't shoot.

I wake up to Brig's face and an IV plugged into the crook of my arm.

"Welcome back, Vivvy."

I reach up to her cheek. "Are you real?"

Brig smiles. "It doesn't matter if I'm real. Even if you are the only conscious being in the universe, even if life ends and begins with Vivian Rose Bouchet and we are all just part of your beautiful, complicated dream. Because you, Vivvy, are pretty great. You are enough."

Word for word, it's the same answer she gave me when I was eight, long before a dark space tore open between us.

"I miss you, Brig."

"I miss you, too. You have no idea how much."

My hand reaches up again, this time to feel a wad of bandages on my head. She pulls it away. "Leave it alone. I have to tell you something."

"Did the bullet hit my brain?" I whisper.

She shakes her head. "You were very lucky. It grazed your temple. You have a slight skull fracture and a serious concussion from when your head hit the wall."

I can read the *but* in Brig's face. "How am I *not* lucky?"

"When they did the MRI, they found a . . . surprise. A tiny shadow on your brain. The size of a blueberry."

"A tumor. Like mom's." I state it flatly.

"*Not* like mom's, Viv. Probably benign. Maybe there . . . for years."

"And?"

"The neurologist says that as long as it remains stable, it is unlikely she would want to remove it. She says that if it doesn't change or grow, it likely isn't fatal. It's mysterious. Like you. A tiny hidden moon. But she wants to watch you for several days. Do a few more tests."

She hesitates again. "When you were unconscious—on morphine—you said a lot of things. You were so tortured, Vivvy. I think . . . you need to let the Blue Horse thing go. Please don't take this the wrong way. Mike and I think we're all going to be OK, you know?" She hesitates. "In every way."

It's strange because in my drug-induced dreams, I don't remember any hoofbeats. And that, more than anything, sets off a rattle of dread.

Just because I don't remember doesn't mean the Blue Horse has gone away. It might mean something worse.

Maybe the Blue Horse is finally so close, has traveled so many miles, he doesn't have to gallop. Maybe he's just waiting for the moon to turn thin one last time.

I grip Brig's hand and force a smile. My head, suddenly swimming.

"How did Sharp find me?" The words feel like a thick soup.

She holds up her phone. "My location app. I think you are getting tired. Maybe the morphine IV is kicking in."

"Who is . . . the man . . . behind the mask?" I slur.

I'm drifting away before she can answer.

☽ ✧ ☾

The next time my eyes open, Mike is pulled up in a chair beside my hospital bed. It feels familiar. For a fraction of a second, I wonder if I'm eleven. If it has been only hours since I knocked Mike out of the way of a car and the rest has been part of a spectacular coma. Our future love story, still there for me to shape.

Except my foot is not hiked in the air. The Mike back then never had these haunted eyes, a homeless stubble, coffee in his hand that looks like tobacco juice.

"Does Brig know you're here?" I ask weakly.

"Yes. I'm giving her a break. She's at home, taking a well-deserved nap with your nephew."

"How long have I been in the hospital?"

He glances at his watch. "About eighteen hours. Brig didn't want you to be alone and didn't think you'd sleep without an update on the arrest." It was generous of her, to trust us.

"Truth or Conspiracy," Mike says softly. A twist on our old game.

"Truth."

"Lizzie is alive."

"Truth," I admit softly.

"You should have told me, Vivvy. Lizzie a.k.a. Alyssa McBride is sitting at the police station right now. She and her sister showed up at the station after they saw the news of your shooting on an airport TV. Their parents are flying in. We're doing our own DNA tests. But Alyssa *is* Lizzie. The freckle on her shoulder is a match to a picture her mother took more than ten years ago."

"I'm sorry. I felt that I couldn't—that it would have all gone differently if I had—"

He holds up a hand. "I know. You've blathered on about it to me since I was fourteen—we're all strings of random music, disturbing molecules in the air, changing fate, don't mess up the tune, blah blah. Marcus Solomon almost *killed* you, Vivvy."

I think I misheard. "What?"

"Lizzie's kidnapper. Marcus Solomon. He slipped into his own house that day and drove her away in a rental car."

Surely, conspiracy. "That can't be." *I would have felt it, wouldn't I?*

"Now that he's caught, he won't shut up. He's a lawyer, hand-cuffed to a hospital bed, refusing a lawyer. Marcus found out that Lizzie wasn't his biological daughter several months after he and Nickie closed on the mansion. He went in for an issue with his flat feet and a doctor discovered he had a congenital chromosome deficiency—that he was sterile. He chose not to tell Nickie."

My muddied mind, still processing. "He visits Nickie every Tuesday in prison," I say. "He's always stood by her. One of the few."

"And enjoyed the control, the first time he'd had it. Nickie cheated endlessly. She'd regularly hinted at divorce and a fight for full custody since Lizzie was born. As a family lawyer, Marcus knew he'd never get custody if he wasn't the biological father. So he chose revenge. He used an under-the-table adoption attorney, a law school friend in Oklahoma, who showed him pictures of a family ready to take Lizzie without any questions."

I shake my head. "He kept a vigil in that house, waiting for Lizzie. But he knew she'd never come back. So why?"

"For theater? As penance? We've found your mother's number in his phone. He used her like a priest when he drank too much and says he told her everything. Including exactly where Lizzie was, down to the street she lived on. Marcus tracked Lizzie for years. He even attended one of her middle school shows."

"She was Audrey. *Little Shop of Horrors.*" I can hear her belting out "Suddenly, Seymour."

"What?"

"Never mind." Such a small, useless thing to know. *One more* A *in my head.* "Marcus had an alibi," I persist. "I read it in the file."

"Truth," Mike says. "We screwed up. The detectives on the case checked Marcus Solomon's alibi three ways. Both his father and sister confirmed he was with them at his dying mother's side. So did a nurse. The father is now dead. The nurse has a long history of gambling. The sister isn't talking to us."

He stands abruptly. "You didn't ask about Brando. I want you to press charges. He set you up."

"No," I correct him. "I set myself up."

I glance down for Shelby's hospital bracelet. Someone had removed it. Replaced it with my own. I see my first genuine flash of Shelby's future. She's silver-haired, pushing her granddaughter on a swing.

"I want you to think about it when your eyes aren't half-shut in pain." He picks up the chair and navigates it neatly into a corner. "I'm taking off. A policeman is posted at the door. The media on this is wild. Someone leaked that Bubba Guns is the father. You just can't make this shit up."

Mike pulls an envelope from his back pocket. "Sharp wanted me to give you this." He drops it on the table by a foil-topped cup of orange juice.

"I don't know what's going on with you two," he says, "and I'm not sure I want to. Please be careful. He's a great cop. But he's got a malignant spot. Brig once called him 'bottled thunder.' Perfect description. Women seem to be attracted to it. I hope one of them isn't you."

Jealousy? Or warning? If you have something to say, just say it. If you want to save me, then *save me*.

Shouldn't I take that same advice? Shouldn't I admit that the Blue Horse was never a sports car? That it's an animal far more calculated, persistent, destructive than a hunk of metal? That he shouldn't let his guard down?

Mike is almost at the door. My head feels so loaded with cement, I'm barely able to turn it. Even when I do, the words won't come. The how, the why, the what, the when—a cop's automatic, probing questions about a killer Blue Horse—if he asks, I wouldn't be able to answer any of them.

I lie back as the door clicks shut. I reach over for Sharp's envelope and slit it open.

A Hallmark greeting card. On the front, Snoopy is embracing Charlie Brown.

Inside, the message orders me to *Get Well Soon!*
Sharp has scribbled underneath.
We're not finished.
Below that, he's drawn a careless loop around his name.
I can't tell if it's a heart or a noose.

43

sleep and wake. Sleep and wake. The berry-sized tumor in my brain is analyzed by neurologists and machines like it is a glittering sapphire. They are attentive to—but slightly less captivated by—the concussion and crack in my skull. A few days in the hospital roll into almost a week. I'm an "interesting case."

I don't hear anything more from Mike. Sharp. The Blue Horse.

The charm bracelet girl, though, is in full swing when my eyes shut, jangling her bracelet, demanding that it's her turn.

Brig shows up every morning in big sister mode, reading to me alternately from *Beautiful Ruins*, her book club's selection this month, and *A Confederacy of Dunces*, because it always makes me laugh. She brought me a new phone, but for calls only. She keeps my eyes away from Twitter and television network news; fends off media requests; fields and rejects any offers from random people and legitimate businesses requesting psychic consultations with the woman who broke the Lizzie Solomon case.

But how much did the hunt for Lizzie really spin out of my intuition? How much of it was just drawing a line from star to star until we had the whole constellation?

The observatory sent an enormous bouquet of star-shaped dahlias and lilies that sits on the windowsill blocking any view I have of the night sky. My boss has texted saying not to worry about a thing. It's hard not to. The universe isn't patiently waiting for me. The light of an ancient civilization is beginning to slip past my grasp. I feel it. I might have to wait five years, ten years, twenty years—maybe never—for it to wink at me again.

My eyes drift to a side table stacked with love letters from hundreds of Lizzie followers who credit me with saving her.

I want to tell them I didn't "save" Lizzie, I only helped find the truth. And the word *truth* is like *closure*—a misnomer that is every shade of gray on the spectrum.

It isn't until the third day that Alyssa convinces the police officer at the door to let her slip through.

She sits down gently on the edge of the bed, appraising me.

"You don't look as bad as the media says you do. I'm here to thank you for not talking to them. And for risking your life for me. The detective told me what you did. The one with those great boots."

"You don't have to thank me, Alyssa. How are things going?"

Alyssa smooths out a few wrinkles in my blanket, hands busy. Reminding me of Brig. "Well, my mother and sister are not speaking. My father has hired a five-hundred-dollar-an-hour lawyer for the custody battle that is already gearing up between my parents and Nickie Solomon. Bubba Guns is denying that I'm his kid, calling it voodoo DNA, saying my family is after his money, and everyone should be thanking God he hyped the case so it could be solved. My sister—by the way, her name is Joyce not Joie—secretly set up a call for me with Nickie in prison. I want to feel bad for her, like a daughter, but she seems like a piece of work. I'm worried she'll call me ten times a day when the legal red tape is over and she's out. That she'll claim some right to me."

Her fingers travel from the blanket to her wrist, feeling for a threadbare bracelet that isn't there anymore. I hope Marcus's bracelet is at the bottom of a hotel trash can. "And who wants to be the so-called daughter of kidnapper Marcus Solomon? I keep thinking of *King* Solomon in the Bible. How he tested those two women fighting over a baby by suggesting he cut the child in two with a sword. Well, that's what Marcus Solomon did. He cut me in two."

She's trying to hold back tears.

"One good thing," she whispers. "I've met my grandmother. Nickie's mother. She says she wasn't a great mother herself. But she's a pretty great grandmother so far. Made me cookies and brought them to the hotel. Wants to teach me how to knit. She told me I was beautiful the second she saw me, and I believed it in a way I never have. She said Nickie wouldn't let her visit her in prison, so she prayed for both of us every week at my grave at the cemetery. That's so odd to say. *My grave*."

I buried a strand of my hair there. And a metal moon.

"I saw your grandmother at the cemetery on your birthday," I confirm. "This might not be the kind of platitude you want to hear right now, but my own mother always said that every bad thing does not happen for a reason, but that every bad thing brings meaning. I'd like to think that's true."

Alyssa stares at the steady peaks and valleys on my heart monitor. "I hope I can get there. But *my* mother, the one who adopted me, who I thought would *never* tell me a lie, is making excuses. Justifying it all. She and my dad said that it was a bit—*a bit*—of a questionable adoption but that it felt God-sent because Mom had endured six miscarriages in a row, and they were told my parents were abusive. For example, when they got me, my head was shaved bald. Now I know it was just so people wouldn't recognize me. The lawyers are trying for some kind of plea deal with my parents, so they don't go to jail for taking a kid through suspicious channels. I think it's true that they didn't know I was—*am*—Lizzie. So there's that."

She wipes a string of snot off her nose. Her expression, a tortured mix of child and woman. "Why do I feel so guilty?" she pleads with me. "Why do I feel like I need to reassure *everybody else*? Sorry to dump all this. It's just that we have . . . a connection. When I met you at your house that night, it was like I recognized you. Not your face or anything, just you. Is that crazy?"

"I don't think so."

"I've always felt different. Like I didn't quite belong to my family. It got worse every year. It might have destroyed me. Maybe *knowing* who I am will, too. I will always be the gingerbread girl whose bones were supposed to be trapped inside the walls of a creepy old mansion. What would people say if they knew I stood in that mansion and could not remember where it all began? The conspiracy theories, they've already started up on social media."

"Memories are not well-behaved ghosts," I answer carefully. "Neither are my . . . visions. Half the time, memories are drunk and partying with the imagination. Almost half of us have a first memory of childhood that is one hundred percent false. You are not alone, not by a long shot. The age of three is a cutoff for remembering, even without trauma. You need to give yourself a break."

"So *you* don't remember anything from when you were little."

"It's different for me. I remember too much."

"What am I going to do?" she whispers. "Can you . . . see . . . anything for me?"

"Not right now. Not that way. If I ask, it often doesn't come. It's like trying to conjure a dove, but instead I call up a sparrow or a dragonfly. The dove shows up when *it* decides to. But I can tell you what I think is going to happen. You're going to figure out this new tangle of relationships. You're going to get some therapy that probably won't help you as much as time—a lot of time—to heal. *You're* going to be the strong one, Alyssa. I'm certain that where you lead, the people who love you will follow."

"Thanks," she says. "For listening to me vent. For seeing *me*." She sits back in the chair, suddenly composed. "I hear you are getting out of here soon. What are you going to do?"

I gaze past her pretty face to the star flowers on the sill, dripping and wilting, ready to fall.

"I'm going to try to find a lost girl who wasn't as lucky as you," I say.

☽ ✧ ☾

I'm free. At least from the confinement of hospital rails.

My head still feels like an egg that was viciously cracked. I open the door to Mom's house and am met with the light, lemony scent of an essential oil mister that Brigid calls "air candy." It seems to have worked like wasp spray on the ghosts that usually greet me.

Brig had sent over her beloved, trusted, and utterly practical housekeeper while I was in the hospital. No more crystal balls scattered across the kitchen table, no half-dripped candles and outdated tea leaves, no random newspapers and half-packed boxes to trip over—all of it somewhere else, unemotionally disposed of. Every surface shines. Every curtain is pulled back to let in light.

Brig personally stocked the fridge with a pile of comfort food dinners, fruit, sparkling waters, fresh-squeezed juices, cheeses from six countries.

She removed the torn sheets from my bed and replaced them with a luxurious high-thread-count set from one of her favorite boutique stores and bought special pillows to keep my head elevated. She filled my prescriptions and lined them up on the bedside table.

We both knew that recuperating at her house was a nonstarter. Mike and I—not fully resolved. His second visit to the hospital, with Brig, full of stops and starts. It feels certain that the kiss on the porch was our last, and equally certain that we are going to live in dry, awkward territory for a very long time.

My neurologist ordered me to stay in town for at least a month in case I had any unexpected side effects from the concussion. She delivered a sharp *no* to any immediate return to the desert and my job, reminding me that Big Bend's single regional hospital serves twelve thousand square miles.

On the tumor, she is still circumspect. No surgery right now, maybe ever. *We'll watch it.*

I worked up the courage to ask her one more time. "You're sure this tumor wouldn't cause auditory and visual hallucinations? Voices?"

"Unlikely," she told me. And then, "You still have the psychiatrist's number I gave you?"

"I do."

For the next four weeks, I play by the rules and count the days. I nurture my relationship with my sister. I play Legos with my nephew, Will, and chess with Emme. I promise the charm bracelet girl that she's next, before I block her out every night with a pill. I fight the occasional blinding headache and nausea.

I watch with great satisfaction as Bubba Guns and his pulpit are blown to bits online. Alyssa goes public with a statement, with Joie and her parents at her side, and she is pitch-perfect. Sweet, lost, believable.

Bubba Guns's favorite weapons are turned on him, his life torn apart, by the truth from a fourteen-year-old girl.

He's now the turbulent center of dozens of crazy conspiracy theories. That he always knew he was Lizzie's father and used her kidnapping as bait for higher ratings. That he has tried to escape to England, where his father lives, but the Queen banned him for life. That he has tried to escape to Elon Musk's secret colony on Mars, but *aliens* banned him for life. That he ate a gay catfish and is now having an affair with Ted Cruz.

All of this, even though I really don't believe he ever knew Lizzie was his.

At the house, while Twitter feasts, the police still keep an eye on me. The vegetable garden cop does a random daily drive-by, handing me a bag of peppers or okra and a weather report if I stroll over. Mike slides by in a squad car in the afternoons, baseball cap low, like I won't recognize him. Sharp picks the middle of the night, accompanied by the low macho rumble of his pickup, knowing that I will.

I fade in public memory like a pastel dream. The biggest problem on my lawn is a new contagion of moles. Neighbors wave from their mailboxes and bring taco soup and jalapeño cornbread, squares of foil-covered Texas sheet cake on paper plates, brisket from Heim's. Texas loves a white hat.

I focus on recovering.

I imagine the thin crevice in my skull closing like a zipper and the blueberry in my brain shriveling like a raisin.

Sharp—he tugs at me.

Every day, I think what it felt like when his finger trickled inside my wrist, and he sympathized about my dragons. How he came for me at Brando's long before the tub ran over. How his shirt looked when it was spattered with my blood.

Every night, I replay all my worrisome questions about him. A lost girl he can't let go of. The lasso in his pickup and the man named Looper who disappeared. Mike's warning about bottled thunder. Nickie's insistence that he's a dangerous snake charmer. And charms, littered like dying stars, one caught around my neck.

On the thirtieth day, I get up early, pack my stuff, and load the Jeep.

I punch an address in my navigation at seven a.m. Twenty-nine minutes away.

I think, *What a long way and a short distance it can be to finish things.*

44

It was Brig who told me about Sharp's house on the outskirts of the city. It's set where unscathed land begins to stretch away, the Fort Worth skyline poking up in the distance. Sharp's apartment, she says, is just a box where he holes up during his shifts.

The 1930s Spanish-style house, stucco with a terra-cotta roof, is up a dirt road. A metal barn of undetermined age sits out back. Sharp's pickup is swung near a closed gate that says *Amber's Way* and leads into ragged pasture. No neighbor in sight. Brig said Sharp owns at least a hundred acres, fifty cattle, a couple of horses. She'd been out to a cop barbecue bash here once with Mike. *Pretty view*, she said. *I wonder what he does out there.*

Ride, mend, breed.

Dig, bury, chop.

Hunt, slaughter, rope.

Sharp's hair is wet from the shower when he opens the door. Eyes unreadable as always. A muscle working in his jaw. All my dread and uncertainty, all the words I'd practiced in my head, swept away.

Sharp pulls me inside without a word. Kicks the door closed.

He picks me up, his lips buried in my neck. I have the vague feeling of floating down a dark, cool hall, the sound of bare feet on tile, a framed red squiggle of modern art, feeling both safer than I ever have and scared out of my mind.

He delivers me to the middle of his bed, placing my head carefully on a pillow. After that, nothing is gentle. He's shoving up my shirt, nuzzling between my breasts, reaching under me to unsnap my bra.

For the first time in a month, maybe my life, every inch of my body aches more than my brain. I could die this way or be the happiest I've ever been.

"Are we going to talk?" My breath, coming in gasps. His hands are already yanking down my jeans. "Are we finishing things?"

"No," he says. "We're beginning them."

☽ ✧ ☾

Usually, it takes weeks for a guy to discover my scars, but Sharp has found them all. He has traced his fingers on them, his lips. I feel like he has consumed every inch of me before he turns away and falls asleep—his back like a mountain dividing us again.

I slip naked out of bed and into the bathroom, pulling its sliding barn door behind me. A black-tiled shower, big enough for four. Distressed concrete floor. Oversized gray towels. The morning light fighting its way through a row of glass bricks that border the ceiling.

I flip on the light over the sink and stare at myself in the mirror—slaked eyes, a cheek burned red from his stubble, the new scar at my temple, the charm at my throat. It was in his mouth at one point.

I'd worn jeans and a plain white T-shirt to his door. Now I'm not exactly sure where they are. I trace my finger along the wings of three butterflies embedded in the countertop, trapped by transparent epoxy, the most feminine thing in here.

It bothers me a little, this specimen case. Realistically I know that most butterflies live for only days. But a part of me hopes he didn't steal any of those days away, that he found these butterflies wherever butterflies go to die. That he didn't catch them in a net, tuck them in an envelope, shut them in the freezer for fifteen minutes to slowly die. That's what a scientist might do.

I start the shower on a whim. The water drills into my skin, setting every nerve alive again. I'm not surprised when the shower door slides open and he slips behind me.

☽ ✧ ☾

His phone buzzes while we're drying off.

He says, *There's an emergency at work.*

I say, *I'll let myself out.*

He holds my head as if it is suspended on the neck of a bird. He kisses me goodbye like he means it.

I think, *Maybe this is real.* I hear the door slam as I pull my T-shirt over my head. The pickup roars as I discover my underwear stuck between the mattress and the rough pine of the headboard. His absence leaves an unnerving, devouring silence.

I can't find a comb in my backpack, so I rummage through one of his bathroom drawers. I pull the teeth through the tangles in my hair, each tug sending a shiver to the crack in my skull.

My eyes fall on the butterflies on the counter.

This time I see past the beautiful wings.

I see their bodies.

And the body of every one of them is a lead bullet.

☽ ✧ ☾

They snap me to, those butterfly bullets.

Tell me where to look.

She's silent.

It isn't a large house to search, but it is also not the cab of a pickup truck.

I assure myself I have plenty of time, which I don't. A metal barn and at least a hundred acres wait outside.

His bathroom takes minutes to explore. It's shaving cream and razor, toothpaste and shampoo, deodorant and floss picks, a generous box of condoms, and old Tylenol. No mousse, no cologne, no cancerous air freshener.

A simple man.

I'd only seen the bedroom as a blur. Now I snap up the shades and sweep my eyes around. King-sized bed with a raw, hand-carved pine headboard. White sheets. No art. A big-screen TV on the wall facing the bed. Red Spanish mission tile on the floor. Under the bed, a gauzy layer of dust.

His closet and dresser, not much more complicated. Two high-end suits and four starched collared shirts, three ties, four pairs of boots, running shoes, a cowboy hat and a Cowboys cap, jeans, workout shorts, underwear, socks, and a drawer of T-shirts that demonstrate a love affair with Austin, the Turnpike Troubadours, Willie, the Smashing Pumpkins.

No bedside clock, no personal pictures. One charging station.

Spare, not suspicious. A bit of contrition, the memory of his tongue, begin to lick at me. But I don't stop. I travel down a hall, past the framed red squiggle of modern art, to a small bedroom and then a smaller one. More tile that's cold and Texas ranch gritty to my feet. White stucco walls, iron headboards, old quilts, an empty antique dresser, a bathroom that needed to be updated twenty years ago.

In the living room, the shades are drawn on two large windows at the back side of the house, holding out the sun. When I lift them, the barren beauty of the land, its infinity, almost topples me. This, we have in common, and I'm filled with both guilt and hope.

The sunlight brings the melting reds and blues of a beautiful old Mexican rug to life. I step around a weathered brown leather couch. Two chairs upholstered in bright gold sit on either side of a stone fireplace. Above it, an enormous graphite drawing of a vintage saddle, a stunning Marshall Harris piece. The intricate detail is both loving and obsessive, the story of a long-dead cowboy's most important possession.

I turn away, determined to find Sharp's.

No computer. Maybe in his truck. Maybe in his apartment.

The kitchen is last. A plastic sheet covers the window. Tile has been ripped off the backsplash, the floor half–pulled up, one wall down to the studs. A hammer sits carelessly on the counter.

No stove, just exposed piping for gas. On the Formica counter, an old microwave and a well-used Nespresso machine. Cabinets hold two misshapen hand-thrown pottery mugs, a set of black dinner plates and bowls. I open the refrigerator. Beer, assorted condiments, a thawing, bloody steak.

I hold my breath when I open the freezer.

No butterflies.

What am I missing?

$$ \text{☽ ✧ ☾} $$

I sit on the edge of Sharp's bed and think about fingerprints. His on me. Mine, everywhere. In the drawers, on the headboard, invisible in the threads of his suits. The way I tossed his drawers in a panic, not caring that it would look like I did.

I force myself to retrace my steps, to arrange everything as closely as possible to the way I remember it. I draw the shades in the living room and bedroom and turn the house back into a cave.

I make the bed, pulling the corners tight, plumping the pillows, until it looks like it belongs in a hotel.

But something is wrong. This perfectly made bed where I made almost perfect love to him *is wrong*.

I tear it up in a frenzy. Throw the pillows on the floor, rip off the sheets and blanket.

I stare at the bare mattress, out of breath. I remember my first meeting with Sharp. The pictures he laid out for me in the very beginning, the solved case he used to test me. The killer, Sharp had told me, kept the senior portrait of the girl he killed under his mattress until her picture screamed so loudly that he couldn't sleep. He seemed to love telling me these terrible stories. *Why?*

The mattress is like tugging at an elephant. I get it a third of the way onto the floor when I uncover the portfolio. Heavy. Stamped as intricately as the saddle on the wall but with just two initials. *A.S.*

There's a little rattle inside when I lift it.

A zipper on three sides that rips into the silence.

I open the portfolio flat.

Sharp's most important possession.

45

The portfolio is stuffed with the intimate insides of the charm bracelet girl.

She was an artist, a talented one. Every painting and drawing in this book signed with a tiny *A*, just like her bloody little squiggle framed in the hall. I wonder why Sharp picked that one to hang.

I flip pages of abstract storms and surreal six-dimensional moons, fantastical unicorns, and self-portraits of her every mood—pretty smiles and crazy eyes and screaming mouths.

She was a selfie girl with a brush. I instantly recognize the girl she saw in the mirror as the same one in the picture under the visor in Sharp's pickup. It helps that she labels her self-portraits, *Me*.

Her black-and-white sketch of Sharp is the most detailed, the most realistic. She captures the darkness in his eyes with the flat side of her pencil. He explodes out of the page like he's entered the room.

I find a plain white envelope taped inside the back. Slide it back and forth, listening to the rattle. I'm having trouble opening envelopes these days. It takes my fingernail three tries to break the flap.

Her charm bracelet spills into my hand, light as rain. The A, the unicorn, the butterfly.

I leave the mattress where it is. The portfolio on the floor. Everything on the bed, torn up.

The desire in me to run, now pounding.

PART THREE

―――――――――

In all this vastness, there is no hint that help will come from somewhere else to save us from ourselves.

—Carl Sagan, "Pale Blue Dot" speech, 1990

―――――――――

What the light reveals is danger, and what it demands is faith.

—James Baldwin

―――――――――

46

I want it all behind me: Sharp and his obsessions, lost girls and their cries for help, Bubba Guns and his manic conspiracies, Mike and the still ominously quiet Blue Horse, the berry in my brain that is making me question everything about myself.

I'm seven hours into my nine-hour drive to the desert before I text Brig. I beg her not to give any directions to Sharp or to mention to Mike that I've left town. I tell her I'll call her "from the top." She told me to go, and I have obeyed. Then I power down my phone.

My hideaway in the desert mountains is not a dot on Google Maps or in a crease on Sharp's paper ones. After Alpine, I'm off the grid. I keep one eye on the mileage counter and the other on scenery that reminds me I'm just a speck on the universe's time line, a period at the end of a sentence in a very rough draft.

The directions after Alpine are crazy geometry—left 2.7 miles after you cross the railroad track, right 22.6 miles later at a sharp fork, left 1.7 miles past a broken yield sign, right 3.2 miles at a dirt mountain road so unnoticeable even I still accidentally pass it.

I tell rare visitors they need four-wheel drive and good tires, to not turn around three-fourths of the way up the mountain when it devolves into more of an avalanche of rocks than a road. That it's only ten more minutes for the tip of my roof to jut into view against enormous clouds.

I can be found another way, but it takes extreme effort: digging for
a deed with my name, finding the plumber who fixed my sink or the
men who barely cleared a road, my insurance company, lucky drone
hunters, the 911 operators who need a GPS location to find you.
This is how Sharp will try to do it—through the cops. But they're
closemouthed out here and make their own rules.

That's because most people don't settle in Big Bend alone, soli-
tary, unless they are running from something bad. The Unabomber's
brother stowed away out here when the press wouldn't leave him
alone. Criminals and innocents in witness protection, spouses being
stalked by exes, mini drug lords with a price on their heads—as many
awful stories float out here as there are kinds of birds, and there
are more species of those than anywhere in the continental United
States.

Big Bend is an excellent place to hide but a hot, rugged, lonely
place to stay, so most people don't. They live in tents and makeshift
carports on unclaimed land, squatters on unforgiving desert, under
brutal sun, until being found seems like the better option.

Those are the transients. I'm a long-hauler who wants to be as
close to the universe and as far from the voices as possible. Out here,
my ghosts have more room to roam, less occasion to visit. I make
peace among the snakes and javelinas and bobcats.

But as my Jeep takes a shuddering breath to finish climbing the
mountain, the sun almost down, I don't feel peace at all.

For five hundred miles, it's been a steady drum.

Sharp is going to want the charm bracelet back.

☽ ✧ ☾

I jump out of the Jeep and twirl slowly, soaking in my favorite view, a
360 spectacle of mesa, mountain, and sky. A few stars already popping out. My house stands in utter isolation just as I left it, modern,
rustic architecture against primitive landscape. Big glass windows,
tongue-and-groove cedar, sheets of a special steel siding with a rusty

patina that never rusts through, a hybrid of solar panels and telescope domes on the roof.

The former owner, a man on the run, had drilled the pilings of
this four-room house into the dolomite rock himself, hammered the
boards and steel together like a wacky puzzle. He filled it with high-
end appliances, granite countertops, sanded floors, glorious windows
that let in the surround sound howl of the desert wind.

He didn't care about the hair-raising, intestine-juggling road.
No electricity. That his modern cave had to be propane- and solar-
powered and the water gathered from rain runoff, which sometimes
meant two-minute showers.

He didn't care about much of anything until he had to run again,
a persistent man on his tail.

He sold it to me fairly cheap, all cash. I justified the outrageous
purchase all kinds of ways. I was only an hour from the observatory.
I could make improvements.

And I did. I threw my wad of savings at it. I reinvested every
dollar from every grant, every speaking tour, every consultation,
every lecture. I transformed it from a bird's nest to a sophisticated
computational center to woo the space gods.

Only after signing the contract on the house did I learn that
it would cost $33 a foot to take electrical up to my mountaintop
home. I'd need the permission of every single landowner whose
property the power lines would cross. Most of those people are
scattered across the United States, clueless that they own anything
out here—the ancestors of pioneers who couldn't get approval for
roads, who gave up on the land more than a hundred years ago, the
deeds long lost.

My refuge did come with one very important and lucky link to
civilization—a cell tower that sits on the other side of the mountain.
My service is perfect. I hesitate, then flip on the phone. I keep it on
only long enough to text Brig that I made it to the top. After that, I
drag a chair off the deck and sit at the edge of a drop-off that peers
down on the strip of road far below.

For a very long time, I make sure there aren't any headlights that seek out my turn.

$$) \diamond ($$

I've been home for an uneasy forty-eight hours, only turning on my phone once a day for less than a minute. No word from Sharp. Brig. Mike.

In the daytime, I continue to prowl the internet for anything in the last two decades about a missing girl with a charm bracelet. No luck. Either she wasn't a high-profile "Lizzie," or the charm bracelet was a detail the cops held back from the media.

At night, I question my impulsive decision to sleep with Sharp. To swipe the bracelet. I beg the owner, a pretty ghost, to tell me what to do with it, but she doesn't answer. I stay awake until my eyes are like the lead in the gun on the floor beside my bed.

For the first time in my life, I dread night. I don't want to look up. Not with my eyes, not with my telescopes, not even after the news that the foundation has granted me two extra months and permission to share the satellite just a little bit longer. It means I still have a chance.

I stare out my big naked windows into utter blackness and feel a shiver.

Night will find you.

That's what one of my favorite professors used to say.

He taught poetry, not physics. It doesn't matter. Both feel like doom right now.

Tomorrow, my star and planet will align again. I will *have* to look up and bury this debilitating sense of panic if I want to move forward with a career that seems more promising than ever. How ironic that I've become a poster child for how the truth and the fantastical can coexist. My boss declared me "a symbol of unity for our times" in an interview with *The Washington Post*.

At midnight, I force myself into a remedial test run. I throw down one of my mother's quilts on the hard ground like the little girl in

Virginia who snuck out of bed to be alone with the sky. I had un-
knowingly laid my body almost directly on top of Lisa Marie Pressly's,
the young woman buried in the ground in the backyard of our rental
house.

Her grave is the spot where I learned that the night sky is an Im-
pressionist painting in progress. That it requires attentive patience.
You can't glance up and immediately see it all. You have to wait.

Every ten minutes, my paltry human eyes adjust as more and
more stars reveal themselves. I settle in. It will take two hours for me
to witness the full, heart-stopping emergence of the Milky Way, the
layers upon layers upon layers of stars and dust.

A metaphor, a tonic, for so many things.

Sharp's boot is the first part of him I see, inches from my head. It's
planted even with the new crack in my skull. I jump up.

He must have parked at the blind curve and walked up the rest of
the way so I wouldn't hear.

47

Sharp and I are standing on one of the darkest spots on Earth. I can't see his face, but I know that boot. The lights in my house are out for stargazing and preserving solar power.

No way could he have made out my flat shadow on the ground unless he'd been letting his eyes adjust for a while. Maybe he hid at dusk and waited.

Maybe he'd watched me through my bare windows all day. Or for two days, in desert camo, a snake crawling the landscape.

He steps closer.

The charm bracelet on my wrist jingles like a cat bell as I run toward the house.

☽ ✧ ☾

He grabs me at the door. I aim a few fierce kicks at his shin.

However strong I thought he was, he is stronger.

I think about all the lost places in the two hundred thousand square miles of Chihuahuan Desert he might bury me and his secret, whatever it is. The coyotes could eat me for lunch and scatter my bones so Brig can never bury them. I see a bird peck at my tiny tumor, fly away with it.

He pushes my arms up over my head and grips my wrists, shoving my back tight and flat against the door.

☽ ✧ ☾

"*I didn't kill her*," Sharp growls. "If that's what you think."

He lets my hands drop. Backs away. I rub my skin where one of the charms bit my wrist as he held me against the house. Think about my gun under the bed. Or about how, if I could just get past him, I know a path where the cactus will trap him for me.

"The charm bracelet belongs to my sister." He lets it sit for a second. "Belonged," he corrects himself.

My brain is filled with a vision of a head, slipping under, into black. This time, I can't tell if it's a grave of sand or water. I stumble a step back. I don't know what to believe.

"I wasn't trying to sneak up on you. I got a flat tire halfway up and hiked the rest. Mike gave me directions. He said he and Brig had been out here a couple of times to help set you up. He said the road was a son of a bitch. He was giving that road too much credit. Mike told me . . . to tell you everything. Will you please listen?"

I nod, barely.

"My sister disappeared twelve years ago, when she was a sophomore at the University of Texas. She was walking back alone from a club to her dorm. It was two in the morning. A street camera showed she took a shortcut through some construction. She was never seen again. She just vanished."

"Except . . . the bracelet."

"I'm getting to that. Four years later—a thousand miles away— two Minneapolis cops stopped to help a biker with flat tires on a popular scenic road. One of them walked over to relieve himself by a chokeberry bush and found her charm bracelet. A few yards from that, he found her college ID. He did his due diligence, plugging her name into the system. When my sister popped as a missing person in Texas, the FBI organized a search."

"Her name. It starts with *A*, too."

"Yes. It does." His eyes glimmer with the possibility that he's getting through to me. "Amber. For the color of her eyes since birth. She'd been collecting charms since she was little. Only a few were left on the bracelet. The rest were found scattered along a ten-mile stretch of the same road. CSI used metal detectors. I think of her, tossing those charms out the window like bread crumbs, counting on me to find them. They found bits of her blood and skin on them. They think she pried them off with her fingernails." He turns his head away, toward the desert. "Talking about her to you, to anyone, is like admitting she'll never come home. I want to find her. I am *committed* to finding her. But I'm not sure I can handle the details of knowing . . . everything. It's not that I didn't believe you could see it, it's that I was afraid you could."

I know as soon as he finishes that it's the jagged pain of truth.

"I'm sorry for ever thinking that you were a fraud," he says. "You were right that it is routine for me—sneaking the charm bracelet photo into random interviews in cases with crimes against women. It's my way of keeping Amber's case alive when my bosses have told me to butt out of it, that I'm too close to her. That photo is my secret way of not giving up. Hoping I will see recognition in an eye, a tic that shouldn't be there. When you picked out that photo, it was the first time anyone had. I was sure Mike hinted to you in advance, so I'd believe you had powers to find Lizzie Solomon. So we'd bond."

"Mike knows about your sister," I say softly.

"One of the few. He made a pilgrimage to the chokeberry bush with me once. He always thought it was my story to tell or not. He knows I stole her bracelet out of evidence. I was out of my mind when I did it. The property officer took pity and erased my name from the log. I almost lost my job."

I wonder if he's ever talked this much—this honestly—in his life.

"It's OK," I say roughly. "I believe you."

Still neither of us moves. Sharp clears his throat. "This is some kind of spaceship you live in. How'd you pay for it?"

"Half of it was guilt money from a father I've never met. He's a corporate VP in Virginia, with a nice, legitimate family. He turned out to be the anonymous donor who set up a trust for me right after the car accident with Mike. Through high school, I thought the trust was a gift from Mike's family. That's what my mother had me believe. At eighteen, I got a letter that told me differently."

"Have you met him?"

"A condition of the trust is that I don't. Although, I won't confirm or deny that I've aimed a telescope through his living room window. What can I say? I seem haunted by men with dark energy. Like someone who would use bullets for the bodies of beautiful butterflies."

His face shows surprise. "I didn't make those butterflies. Amber did. As a birthday present for me. "Bullet with Butterfly Wings" is one of my favorite Smashing Pumpkins songs. I wanted to incorporate her spirit into the house. She was the kind of weird and wonderful person who would look at an old broken lawn mower on the side of the road and say, 'Let's pick this up and turn it into a fireplace.' You would have liked her. Everybody did."

I cross the six feet between us. I unhook the charm bracelet and slip it into his hand.

"I want to be honest," I say. "If you're expecting answers about Amber, you made a long trip for nothing. I've rubbed your sister's bracelet like a rosary every night I've been here. She's mute. Even if I leave my quiet place here, go off my pills, visit the chokeberry bush . . . I don't know if I'll ever be able to help you. The only thing I know for sure . . ."

". . . is that she's dead," Sharp finishes. "You've told me. The cop part of me knows that's true. The brother part, not one hundred percent sure." He hesitates. "I almost didn't come find you. I opened the map just to see Mike's route on paper. And there was your fingerprint."

"What fingerprint?"

"A smudge of paint from when you opened up my map at the gas station. After your Jeep was cursed by Barbie's spray paint. Your print on the map was right about here." He spreads his arms wide to encompass my spot in the desert. "It seemed like an invitation. Or I wanted it to be."

He places a hand along my cheek. "I'm not here for Amber. I'm here for you. You want to know when I changed my mind—when I fell into your beautiful mind and couldn't get out? The second you told that asshole that your idea of heaven is traveling up atoms of water molecules to an orchid petal. Now, *that* was a butterfly bullet, right to his gut. Truth and beauty and justice—they fly on delicate wings. Everything worth protecting does."

NINE MONTHS LATER

EPILOGUE

THE BLUE HORSE

My shoulders are broiling, my feet bright pink, my gritty hair slapping me like rope.

It feels great. Mike is at the wheel of the boat, grinning, cutting the lake into white, fluffy ribbons.

Brig is convincing an unhappy Will that wearing an oppressively hot life jacket vest is the only way he'll get to continue riding in the boat. I reach up to feel the charm around my neck again, wishing I'd remembered to slip it off, hoping I don't lose it.

Everything is knowable, even if we never know it. I know a lot more now. Mary held the answer to the charms left for Emme and me. They were a gift from my mother. One for Brig too, still undelivered because Mary hadn't dug up her address yet. Mom had asked Mary to drop them off anonymously after she died, wanting us to feel a little magic and mystery from beyond.

This says a lot about how much my mother trusted that she'd have that kind of postmortem power herself. It's both weirdly coincidental and not—she finally gave Brig and me the charms we begged for as kids. And Emme, well, she was her third kid, the one who looked up at the stars without all our baggage and saw truth in the leaves.

Nickie has hauled her baggage to the Solomon mansion, where she's camping out while the legal system deliberates her pardon and visitation rights with Alyssa. Marcus pleaded to kidnapping charges and attempted murder and was quoted as saying that "inside Huntsville is a safer bet than outside with my ex-wife."

His other ex, Beth, is living and laughing with a nice guy in the trailer over, a double-wide. I refused to make any accusations against Brando. His sister, Shelby, is in miraculous remission that I know will last until old age. When I finally got to visit, I whispered it in her ear.

Bubba Guns, well, he has hired four attorneys as sleazy and famous as he is.

And Jesse Sharp, he's mine. A lot of back-and-forth weekend lovemaking has been going on in our two dusty worlds.

I scan the dock, about two hundred yards away. I don't see him yet. He's joining us for a picnic after his shift.

Will has managed to sneakily unsnap part of his life jacket without his mother noticing. I reach over to snap it back.

My sister, staring the other way, shrieks. Simultaneously, the boat feels like a bomb is ripping it apart. I'm vaguely aware of a teenager at the wheel of a small motorboat, of us being nipped at full speed, of bodies flying in slow motion.

I'm in the water, choking on it, tasting blood in my mouth. Both boats are spinning away, not sinking. The teenage driver is already swimming with a strong crawl to the dock.

The only head left in our boat is Will's. I make it over, the water fighting every kick. I grab the side of the boat, cooing to him. Will's stunned, crying, but appears OK. "Sweetie, stay here. *Do not move.* I need to find your mom and dad."

My own life jacket is half ripped, hindering my swimming. I make the spontaneous decision to strip it off the rest of the way. I hope I still have the legs that once upon a time could tread water for two hours.

I swim fifty feet away from the boat, scanning the water in a panic. The horizon tilts and swirls. The crack in my head feels like it is being drilled with an ice pick. I can't see Mike or Brig. And then I do. Mike is swimming Brig to the dock. She's dead weight.

Mike must have seen my head in the water and Will's in the boat. He's counting on me, I know it.

"Aunt Bibby!"

Will's cry is full of terror. I whip my eyes back to the boat. It's listing. Will's head is gone. I scream his name, swallowing more water. Mike is at the dock, pumping Brig's chest, too far away and too occupied and panicked himself to hear. No other boat around. My arms feel like rubber snakes as I work my way back to the boat, praying Will is lying down out of sight.

The boat, empty.

I'm unable to see on the other side of it, not strong enough to fight the waves and pull myself up. I swim around, frantically searching for his orange vest. It's bouncing on a wave several feet away. I can't tell if Will's little body is under it.

When I reach the jacket, it's half off, Will's face buried in the water. I grab his head, and he comes up coughing water. The waves, sloshing both of us, trying to drag us down to Looper. It takes every ounce of will and strength to hold his face out of the water and swim him back to shore.

Brig is lying faceup on the dock but conscious. Mike reaches down to yank Will up out of the water from my arms into his. The second our eyes meet, in that single exchange, we are resolved. Two heads in the water—mine and Brig's. He made the right choice. He chose Brig.

Because of it, we are all alive. Mike turns to work on Will, who is still sputtering.

I slide back into the lake, spent. The adrenaline, gone. My arms, not working at all. The water has crept over my nose. My eyes.

The last thing I see before I slip under are the blue seahorses stamped along the bottom of Will's life jacket.

☽ ✧ ☾

The day of the boat accident, the stars were in place, just invisible to my eye.

The moon, a clipped yellow toenail. Mars and Venus, tiny diamonds in precise positions.

The number twelve—for noon, not midnight.

The blue seahorses on my nephew's life jacket, confirmation that this was the moment. I was looking from the wrong perspective all along. At a black sky, instead of a blue one.

I wasn't meant to save Mike the way I thought. I was meant to save his son, not even born when we first met. A scientist might say that I'm extrapolating from coincidences. But *I'm* a scientist, and truth isn't held down by gravity.

I can't explain why I believe a Conductor is at work. Not just in the sky, giving second-by-second commands to the heavenly bodies. Down here.

The same hand that pulled my head out of the lake two weeks ago is around my waist right now. I didn't even hear Jesse walk in the room. I felt less space, less air, less me the first time he did. Now I feel more.

"Have a good night," Jesse says, his lips in my ear.

He shuts the bedroom door behind him, and I go to work.

☽ ✧ ☾

It's almost like fainting. Everything around me has gone black except for the circle in front of my eyes, the size of a quarter. I'm staring through a tunnel into the past, hoping for the future.

Heavenly bodies are in motion. Tweak the telescope's azimuth, adjust an aperture, change an optical filter, switch a COM frequency. Second-by-second commands in real time. Computers blink as a satellite downlink dumps data.

In this vast space, there is no room to think about anything else. Not lies and conspiracies. Not killers or regrets. Not the fractures in mankind.

There is only this dance led by the universe.

A spark of light to find.

ACKNOWLEDGMENTS

All my thrillers are set underneath a big Texas sky. In *Night Will Find You*, Vivvy Bouchet, a young, emotionally complicated astrophysicist, busts through that blue sky to the rest of the universe. Vivvy taught me a healthy respect for conspiracy theories, government lies, science, faith, psychic phenomena, stars, and the big fat wad of everything we don't know.

I would have been unable to imagine Vivvy without the brilliance, endless humor, imagination, and long email strings from Sean Stapf, a rocket scientist and surfer who also happens to be my cousin. He freely offered up his beautiful mind for more than a year. (His scientist wife, Mandy Koons-Stapf, told me she fell in love with Sean while she watched him teach flight safety physics, which says it all.) His résumé includes calculations for the Mars Science Lander, Apache helicopters, explosive ordnance disposal anti-terrorism cannons, NASA's space shuttle, and SpaceX's *Falcon 9*, and that barely covers it. He's worked on projects for NASA, the U.S. Air Force, Space Force, the U.S. Navy, and the Federal Aviation Administration. Also important: He partnered with me as a kid on beach treasure hunts and has told me the safest place to sit on a plane.

Sean pulled his friend and astrophysicist Tom Ricketson, with a star-studded résumé of his own, into my fictional reality. Both allowed me to see much farther into space and myself than I ever imagined. Vivvy's career—her search for unexplained light and some of her very thoughts—is a direct result of their philosophical musings about God and extraterrestrial life and what-ifs. Like most geniuses I've met, they didn't mind my hopelessly stupid questions. In case this isn't perfectly clear: Any scientific mistakes in this book are mine alone.

As for other research fodder—a sincere thanks to Neil deGrasse Tyson for making joyful noise about science and for his book *Astrophysics for People in a Hurry*, and to Claudia Hammond, the author of *Time Warped: Unlocking the Secrets of Time Perception*, and the BBC piece *What We Get Wrong About Time*.

I'm also grateful to:

Sherry Jacobson, a journalist friend who told me I should include a conspiracy theorist podcaster in my next thriller and sent me endless fodder about why. Bubba Guns is for you, Sherry.

Ross Orren, who provided the inspiration for Vivvy's solar-powered roost on the top of a mountain in the Big Bend area. Vivvy's place is a fictional replica of a glass-and-steel vacation rental Ross built with his own hands to showcase a stunning 360-degree view of the West Texas desert and a Van Gogh night sky. I've never met any civilian as in love with one of the darkest places on Earth (except, of course, Vivvy). Those butterfly bullets in this book lie under his bathroom counter in real life because his wife told him he needed to add a feminine touch in his castle to the sky gods. In the book, Vivvy, of course, added some rooftop telescopes.

J. R. Labbe, an open-minded and intellectual representative of tough Texas women, for always being there with her gunshot advice in more ways than one.

On the editing and publishing front lines:

Everyone at Flatiron for making such a great home for me: my lovely editor, Christine Kopprasch, for being so creative, patient, and inspiring; publishers Megan Lynch and Bob Miller, for believing in my work; superwoman editorial assistant Maxine Charles; managing editor Emily Walters; production editor Frances Sayers; production manager Jason Reigal; associate production editor Morgan Mitchell; Jen Edwards for the interior design; marketing experts Nancy Trypuc, Maris Tasaka, and Erin Gordon; publicity guru Marlena Bittner; audiobook producer Steve Wagner; jacket designer Lisa Amoroso; and copy editor Jeanette Cohen.

On the UK side: publisher extraordinaire Maxine Hitchcock, editor Emma Plater, publicist Gaby Young, and many more.

On the agenting side: Kim Witherspoon at Inkwell Management, editor, adviser, and magician, who must have carpal tunnel from waving her wand so much for me in the last couple of years, and guardian angel Maria Whelan, always working tirelessly on my behalf, including offering sharp-eyed literary advice on early drafts.

On the always-in-my-heart side: Anne Speyer and Jesse Shuman (who also came up with this book's title).

On the friends, family, and readers front line:

My thank-God-down-to-earth soul mate, Steve Kaskovich, who continues to decipher everything from royalty statements to first drafts to my writerly moods. My son, Sam Kaskovich, and *his* soul mate, Risa Brudney—ER docs who face life's terrible repercussions every day and still wear smiles that remind me not to stop writing redemptive endings.

Stephanie Heppenstall for her constant support of me, my writing, and our animals. Laura DiCaro for dragging me away from the computer screen into the joy of real life. Lynn Ferebee for a cool and supportive place to write when my own house was full of noise.

My great-niece, Vivvy Kaskovich, and great-nephew, Will Kaskovich, for allowing me to steal their names, and to their parents—Paul, Katie, Rob, and Chelsea—for letting me place their namesakes in harrowing if recoverable experiences. And to Katie and Laura Heaberlin, my other two nieces, and my brother, Doug, who remind me all the time that we're in this together even if their sky watches over Vermont and mine is in Texas.

The generous Bookstagrammers and readers who shined a bright light on my previous book, *We Are All the Same in the Dark*, when it entered the world in the horrific days of early Covid. It was hard to spend two years on a novel and suddenly realize maybe no one would read it—all while knowing that was an utterly selfish and shallow thought.

The legendary forensic scientist Rhonda Roby, to whom this book is dedicated, for *being* so dedicated—to science, to truth, and to the families of crime victims. She holds bones in her hands and sees a life. Her expertise in mitochondrial DNA has helped identify victims of 9/11, serial killers, plane crashes, and soldiers. I'm forever grateful for everything she has taught me about life and forensic science and for deeply affecting my writing.

My dad, for all those swings and talks on the front porch.

My mom, for her love of the night sky. She slipped to the next realm while I was in the Texas desert researching this book. I'm not sure I've ever heard anything more beautiful than the music of the desert wind whistling through the open windows at night. Sometimes, I think it was her.

ABOUT THE AUTHOR

Julia Heaberlin is the internationally bestselling author of six thrillers, including *We Are All the Same in the Dark*, *Paper Ghosts*, and *Black-Eyed Susans*. Her books have sold in more than twenty countries and have been optioned for film. *We Are All the Same in the Dark* won the 2020 Writers' League of Texas award for fiction, and *Paper Ghosts* was a finalist for best hardcover novel at the International Thriller Awards. Before writing novels, Heaberlin was a journalist for the *Fort Worth Star-Telegram*, *The Dallas Morning News*, and *The Detroit News*, which fed her interest in true crime and the forgotten stories of victims, a theme she carries into her fiction. She currently lives in the Dallas–Fort Worth area with her family, where she's working on her next psychological thriller.